A
Southern Place

A
Southern Place

Elaine Drennon Little

WiDō Publishing • Salt Lake City

WiDō Publishing
Salt Lake City, Utah
www.widopublishing.com

Cover Design by Steven Novak
Book design by Marny K. Parkin

ISBN: 978-1-937178-39-0
Library of Congress Control Number: 2013941334

Printed in the United States of America

Chapter 1
1989

THE ICU OF PHOEBE PUTNEY HOSPITAL WAS THE LARGest in South Georgia, contained within the ultra-modern complex and attached to the near-century old institution.

It was not a first visit for Wally Purvis, sheriff of nearby Dumas County, yet few of his experiences here had yielded positive outcomes. The strange buzzing and pinging of complicated machines and the smell of disinfectants and rubbing alcohol made his sinuses ache and his stomach churn, yet his concern for the lady in Bed 07-A outweighed his clamoring urge to leave. He reached into his pocket for another stick of Doublemint, wondering for the umpteenth time if giving up his two-pack-a-day Camel habit was worth it.

Purvis had been camped out in the ICU waiting area for hours. Shift change brought a little more life to the place with one set of white coats and dresses leaving, a new set coming in. He watched the goings on with half-interest, the diversion at least helped keep him awake. Just as the breakfast cart meandered through the hallway, a tall, thin male stepped out from a closed door into the waiting area.

"Sheriff Purvis?" he asked. Both men stood.

"Wally Purvis," the sheriff answered in a raspy drawl, offering his hand.

"Ian Finch, Internal Medicine Specialist." The doctor extended his own hand. "Mrs. Hatcher is conscious. Her condition is very serious but no longer considered critical. They've moved her to a private room just off the ICU ward."

"That's good," Purvis mumbled, nodding.

"Did you know Mrs. Hatcher—before this unfortunate incident?" the doctor asked.

"Her whole life. Knew her mama, her grandparents, too, family's been in Dumas County for generations."

"I know you need to talk with her, but it's my job to take care of her the best I can. This poor woman has been through a lot. Let me check with the nurses to see if her relocation is complete," the doctor said.

Checking in at the nurse's station, the doctor came back with the news that they could proceed in ten to fifteen minutes.

"Thanks for being patient, Sheriff," he said. "Can we talk a minute first?" Dr. Finch sat down on the leather-like loveseat beside Purvis and spoke.

"Mary Jane Hatcher is a fighter. After a concussion, a detached retina, a broken jaw, a broken nose, multiple contusions and internal bruising, several earlier unattended breaks and a seriously damaged esophagus, she is now off the critical list and slowly recovering. None of these injuries, however, are the most astounding; almost three months pregnant, Ms. Hatcher must have given up every other part of her body to protect her abdomen. The fetus is intact and still relatively healthy."

"Praise God." Purvis slowly shook his head. "Poor child. No daddy, but better off without the one he had."

"The question I wonder about is how Ms. Hatcher will feel about that," the doctor said. "She hasn't been told—"

"You mean she don't know about—?" Purvis asked.

"She doesn't know about the death of her husband or Mr. Foster. She doesn't remember how she got here or much of anything about why she's in the shape she's in; or at least she hasn't said anything to hospital workers." Dr. Finch took off his wire-rimmed glasses, holding them against his leg. "She did ask if her husband had been here, and the nurse said she seemed to be a little relieved when they told her no. I was hoping there'd be family here, to help with catching her up on what's happened. We don't know how she'll react, and trust me, a big emotional blow could really set her back."

"Little Mojo—Mary Jane—don't have no more family. Her only uncle died before she finished high school, and then her mama a few months later," said Purvis.

"There's no one we can call?" Dr. Finch wrinkled his brow, replacing his glasses. "No aunts, uncles, cousins, girl friends? What about her father?"

"I've known the Mullinax family my whole life, and Mojo is the last of 'em. S'far as I know, she ain't never known of her daddy. The Treadways, that run the grocery store, Mojo's worked for them since she was fourteen or fifteen. I guess they might be close to her. She worked as a waitress in the bars for a few years, that's how she met that lowlife she married. But she's pretty much a loner. Her mama was, too. Quiet-like, but good folks, you know?"

Dr. Finch eased to the edge of his chair. "Sheriff Purvis, if you've known her so long, and it's obvious you care about her, maybe you should tell her. Could you?"

The sheriff stood, shuffling to the window that overlooked a parking lot. He shook his head, finally saying, "I reckon it's my job, but I sure don't want to. I speak plain; thirty-eight years in law enforcement and you call a spade a spade. I'd hate to hurt the little girl any worse than she's already been hurt."

Dr. Finch rose, walking toward the sheriff. "I guess I'm the one trained in bedside manner," he said. "You'll be the one she's known the longest. We'll get through it together." He gestured to Purvis.

Entering the room and seeing the victim made the sheriff's current reality even worse.

Her hair was drawn back or perhaps even cut off, due to her injuries. The very front, near her temples, still showed spots of dried blood, as were also evident on her arms, hands, and around her lips. One eye was blackened and swollen shut, the other half open and reddened, both a greenish eggplant underneath. Her nose was covered in adhesive tape, a strip of aluminum showing through in the center and her nostrils stuffed with hardened, bloody gauze. One cheek and its corresponding lip were three times the size of the other, while errant bloody stitches held the balloon-like face together in a Frankensteinian fashion. Her skin was transparently thin, every vein exposed and ready to split apart. The most frightening feature was her neck; pencil-thin, it seemed impossible for holding her swollen, lopsided head, yet a perfect impression of ten fingers shined purple against the translucent corpse-white of her throat.

When she opened her mouth to speak, a cracked and fragile soprano resonated against the sterile silence. "Sheriff Purvis?" she asked.

"Yes ma'am, Miss Mary Jane," the sheriff said, walking to her side. "You've had a rough go of it, but you've stood strong and it's all gonna be all right now."

"Mrs. Hatcher," Dr. Finch said, "the sheriff needs to talk with you about all that has happened, but I'm only allowing him to stay as long as you feel up to it. Do you think you can talk a little?"

She nodded, the pain of such a simple task showing in her half-opened eye.

"Honey," said the sheriff, "what's the last thing you remember before coming here?"

She closed her eyes for a moment, then stared back at Purvis.

"Did Mr. Foster bring me here?" she asked.

"Yes, I believe he did. Do you know how you got hurt?"

She closed her eyes, longer this time, a single tear trailing her cheek.

The men sat quietly, looking to each other for cues on what to do or say next. Before either ventured to speak, the patient grimaced and seemed to choke, both eyes opening wildly and then rolling backwards in her head. She violently shook as alarms, beepers, and flashing lights joined in the chaos.

"Code blue," cried a voice through the intercom system. In a matter of seconds, the room filled with medical personnel, ushering out the sheriff.

Wally Purvis returned to his previous seat in the waiting area. He leaned forward, closing his tired eyes and letting his head fall and rest in his hands. To passersby, he might look to be a relative—a husband, father, brother, or uncle waiting for news on a loved one.

In a sense, perhaps he was, offering prayers for a lost soul with no one left to care.

Chapter 2
1989

Mojo

LOOKING BACK ON MY HOMETOWN, IT SEEMS THAT THE time in Nolan was not measured by days or weeks but by the number of eighteen-wheelers that drove through town.

Mojo is what they called me back then; I guess most folks had forgotten my real name was Mary Jane. A fifth generation Mullinax of Dumas County, Georgia, pronounced "Doom Us" to most Georgians. Nolan is the county seat: a triangle of abandoned buildings, junked cars, and kudzu. Barely deserves a dot on the map. They say it's some of the richest farmland in the world, but I never knew much about the farming. I lived in town, or what was left of it.

Nolan was once a real community, with a red brick courthouse outlined in azaleas, a town square with seven stores, and a real artesian fountain in the center. After the war there were baby boomer houses bought with FHA loans, and soon there were three full time churches. Then came the Flood of '65.

I was barely five years old, and our whole town was drowned in dirty brown water. The government declared it a natural disaster, but I called it a big adventure. The Flint River, usually just a muddy stream, flooded its banks and filled the streets. Inches of smelly sludge covered the floors of our two-room rental house, and the radio claimed it was rising over an inch an hour. I grabbed the radio and a pillowcase filled with my clothes. Mama put her stuff and the few groceries we had in a cardboard box, and we headed for Uncle Cal's.

Mama's brother Calvin was a young man then, in his late twenties and full of life. He had his own house, a sky-blue two-bedroom ranch house that sat on stilts, near the Flint Bridge on the banks of the river. Uncle Calvin had only one arm, but where his other arm *would* have been was a heavy steel hook that could open doors, unclog drains, light cigarettes, roast marshmallows and wind his rod and reel. He'd lost his arm, clear past his elbow, in a peanut picker when he worked the fields for Oakland Plantation. They *paid* for him to get the hook-arm, then gave him money to buy a boat, a new truck, and build his cool house. He didn't work much now.

Mama and I walked from our house behind the water tower to the Phillips 66 at the edge of town. There was a makeshift ramp where people docked their boats. We waited, holding everything we owned and looking like hobos. Grownups passed around bottles in brown bags, some kind of liquor, I guess. The sun was low in the sky, and a slight breeze stirred a sour, wet smell, like the whole world had mildewed. A loud outboard motor roared up the dock, parting the water like brown foam. It was Uncle Cal.

"Mojo," he shouted, "get your little Cajun butt in this boat, girl." Uncle Calvin always called me his little Cajun, even though we had no Cajun blood and were miles from any bayous. I didn't even know what a Cajun looked like, but I liked the sound of it. His special name for me.

"Calvin, I told you a thousand times." Mama stepped from the ramp into the boat, cardboard box on her hip like a baby. "That girl ain't no Cajun. And what took you so damned long?" Mama didn't like much of anything that Uncle Calvin did.

"Shee-it fire, Sis," he said. "You're in the middle of the New Nolan Resort, and you're about to be put up in the king's castle." He set down the brown bag he'd been holding, put out his good hand and helped me into the boat, anchoring himself with the hook against the dash.

"Besides, it's party time, Sister. Get the stick outta your ass!" He laughed, pretending to pinch her arm with his metal claw.

Mama smiled and reached for the bottle in his hand. She took a hard swig and rolled her eyes, her shoulders dropping as an easy smile settled onto her face. "Have you got any food at your house?" she asked. "Your little 'Mojo' can't live off Jim Beam and Coke. And did you make it fit for a kid to walk around in?"

Uncle Calvin laughed a loud belly laugh. "Shit, Delores, you live in a shingle house the colored folks abandoned, with holes in the floor so you see the red clay underneath, and you're worried about taking Mojo into *my* house. I swear, you beat all—"

"You *know* what I'm talkin' 'bout, Cal. My house may not be much, but it's good enough for me and the kid. She ain't used to seein' drunks passed out all over the place. We wash our dishes when we finish eatin', and we sleep in the damned *bed*. And we don't have no animals, or whores either, that think our house is theirs, too."

"Seriously, Sis, Mojo loves Hank and Jerry Lee," he continued. "And Kawliga's made rats and snakes a done deal for me. And my house *is* clean. Lighten up, won't you?"

I squinted out at the thick, muddy water, and over at the line of stores on my left.

No stores were open, but there was so much to see all around me. Random objects floated by: empty tin cans, a large, misshapen cardboard box, a single Converse shoe, a naked plastic doll with no head…

"Mojo loves any animal that'll pay attention to her skinny ass, and Hank and Jerry Lee are fine dogs, kept outside. I can't believe you can get those dogs up that long staircase, or back down either. And why they keep going back is beyond me." Mama was shaking her head and letting her dark blonde curls free to wave in the breeze.

"Those ol' boys love the house, just like they love to hunt. It's a man's house, and they know it. You won't never feel no safer than you do twelve feet above the ground," my uncle told her.

We rode down Main Street in a boat, but the conversation with Mama and Uncle Cal stayed the same as always. Only when we passed other boats would they stop, and Uncle Cal would grin and salute with his hook. Sometimes I'd wave, but Mama mostly looked the other way.

There were boards nailed over the windows of the bank and the drugstore, but the grocery store windows were broken. A man in a small boat pulled up to the broken glass. He fished out what he could with a long stick. If Mama had been watching, she'd have called him a thief. If Uncle Cal had seen him, he'd have been mad that he didn't think of it first. I figured they'd both be right.

"Damned foolishness, that's what that house of yours is," Mama said. "And a waste of good money you won't see again. You're young and spry now, but you won't always be able to scamper up and down those stairs. And when you finally come to your senses and decide to sell it, who the hell is gonna buy that house? You'll be stuck there forever. Unable to come down, we'll have to bring up your food. You'll just stay shut up, and eat and drink yourself to death. And when you die, the fire department'll have to get you out. And they'll tell everybody in town how you was livin', too."

Mama had a way of imagining things in the future like they was really gonna happen. Uncle Calvin looked out at the water, rubbing his good arm with his hook and seeming far away and fidgety at the same time. Like he wanted to be somewhere else, maybe even *be* somebody else, but would never want me or mama to know what he was thinking. I tried to help the best I knew how.

"There was a man in a newspaper Mama brought home that was like that," I added, "'cept he didn't live in no nice house like you, I don't think. Anyway, that man, he was really fat, and he couldn't walk, not even to the bathroom, and one day somebody called a ambulance cause they thought he was havin' a heart attack—"

"Mojo, that ain't got a damned thing to do with this, and I done told you I don't want you looking at them papers," Mama said.

"You ought not be bringin' them papers home, no way," Uncle Calvin told her. "Talk about *me* wastin' money—" I could see a thin line of sweat forming over his lip, the back of his hair peeking out from his Coker Seed cap and blowing in the breeze.

"I don't pay nothin' for 'em, they throw 'em away when the new ones come in. And I take 'em home to cover cracks in the walls—"

"Good God, Delores, Mojo deserves better than this, you two livin' with cracks in the walls and holes in the floor—"

The sun lowered, a perfect sunset melting away into the clouds on the water. The world around us was winding down, while the voices of Mama and Uncle Cal rose in volume. I wondered if people in other boats could hear us, or if they all were busy living out their own little dramas, just like we were. I tried again to quiet them, to maybe get them on a happier subject.

"And the man, the fat man!" I said. "They couldn't get him off the couch, cause he was stuck to it. He had laid there—"

"*That's* enough, Mary Jane, right now," Mama scolded, standing up for no reason and bracing herself on the boat's dash. When she used my real name, I knew it was time to give it up.

"Give her a break, Sis, she's just trying to help us all get along." He reached his hook toward her shoulder, gently easing her back down. "Ain't that right, Cajun girl?" He smiled. I only nodded.

"How long is this damned water gonna be here, anyway?" Mama sighed.

"Another week, maybe longer, they say." Uncle Calvin steered around a fallen tree, its branches decorated with rusty cans, unrecognizable bits of garbage, and a large unmistakable pair of ladies' underwear.

"And are you *sure* that crazy house is safe? I know it's above the water, but what if the water rots those poles? Will the house fall over or just come crashing down? Oh, God, Cal, we can't stay in that house—"

"Delores Virginia Mullinax, how can you be so damned smart and so damned ignorant at the same time? I swear, if Mama coulda sent you to college, you could've—"

"I know that, Cal, I'm not a damned fool—"

"You got a lousy job at the panty factory and then got yourself knocked up by the great unknown, for all I know. And you stay in that same house you've been in like some stupid—"

"That's not how it happened," Mama shouted, fighting tears. "At least it didn't happen in that order. And I'm *not* stupid!" Tears rushed down her cheeks—Mama was mad. She lowered her head so I couldn't see her face.

"Now, Delores, I didn't mean nothing by that. I'm sorry, really, don't cry." Uncle Calvin backed off, like he always did when any woman cried. It was part of what made him so sweet, and how nobody could stay mad at him for long.

He put his good arm around Mama, though she turned the other way when he touched her. I stared out at the water, still listening to them but trying to look uninterested.

"You *know* I don't think you're stupid. Hell, you're the smartest person I know."

Mama turned and searched his face. She put one hand on his shoulder, then the other on my knee. Uncle Cal smiled, then opened his mouth and sang. Mama joined in and soon I was singing, too. We all loved Hank Williams' songs.

"You cold?" she asked me. "You could get something to put over you, another shirt or something, outta your bag. It's gettin' cold out over this water."

"I'm okay," I said. "Besides, we're almost there." I looked out at another boat, filled with what looked like the insides of someone's house, coming toward us. The driver waved with both hands. Uncle Cal shut down his motor. When the other boat was even with ours, the other driver switched off his engine as well.

"Calvin!" he said. "I's a hopin' to run into you. Movin out my mama's stuff—she's gone to her sister's, the water's over a foot deep in her house already. I got ever thang I could, but it'll take three or four more trips using just this here boat. Reckon you could hep me out?"

Uncle Cal fingered his chin with the hook, then grinned.

"Arrrrrr—" he said, lapsing into his Captain Hook impersonation. It was funny; Uncle Cal's hook was a silver-ish metal contraption that could open and close. It looked more like some sort of a mechanical claw or carpentry implement than the big black hook I pictured a pirate having, however, a hook was what folks called it, and Uncle Cal took full advantage of the idea. "A freebooter to boot? Gotta get me sister and the little landlubber to the house. Meetcha at your mama's in an hour?"

"Sure," the man said, smiling and showing crooked teeth in need of cleaning.

"See you then, old man," said Uncle Cal. He cranked his motor and pushed forward, making new brown waves in the runaway stream. "To pillage, plunder, and hornswaggle, arrrrrr!" he cried out to the world, using his hook to point out our now visible destination.

We were still singing when we reached Uncle Cal's house. We emptied the boat and went inside, his two big dogs greeting us and vying for our attention. To Mama's surprise, the house was clean and the refrigerator full. We put our things in Uncle Cal's bedroom, where the double bed was made up and ready for us. The bedspread was printed with mallard ducks and hunting dogs, and his calico cat slept in a circle like a throw pillow in a catalog ad. The bookcase headboard was filled with cowboy stories, colorful paperbacks of Louis L'Amour and Zane Grey. Burying myself in the soft covers, I closed my eyes as Mama and Uncle Cal sang more Hank Williams' songs in the next room. In no time I was fast asleep, dreaming of dogs and cowboys and a pirate king, singing happy songs in a castle on stilts.

Despite Mama's worrying, Uncle Calvin's house held up fine, and for the next two weeks my world was a cross between normal living and a family vacation on some crazy TV show. Uncle Cal worked a lot; the phone rang constantly with people wanting a delivery service, moving van, or whisky runner. He checked in with us at least once a day, always bringing something he thought we might want, like snacks or the newspaper or just news from the outside. Then the phone would ring and he'd be gone. Mama started calling him "The Water Taxi," but it seemed like she was really proud of him. For that sweet section of time, it seemed the whole world knew Uncle Calvin was a good guy.

When the water receded, our little house behind the water tower was nowhere to be found, my uncle told us. Mama said he was pulling her leg, and grabbed that cardboard box and started throwing things inside.

"Delores, listen to me, babe," he said, grabbing her shoulder with his good hand. "Let me take you over there, first, before you start clearing out of your big brother's crawfish trap."

"Your ol' crawfish trap ain't so bad," she said. "I won't never forget how you took us in and looked after us. Mojo's had the time of her life, thinks she's been at some high adventure summer camp, or something like that. Hell, even the animals have been pretty good, for animals that live in a house." She twisted her hair with one hand, a kind of girly gesture I'd never seen her take on before.

"And just *being* here," she said. "It—well, it's good sometimes to remember you've got family. There's lots of folks that ain't got what we do."

Uncle Cal hugged Mama, looking like he might cry. While still holding her, he pretended to pinch at her behind with his hook. She jumped. Uncle Cal did this kind of thing to everybody—he didn't mean anything by it, it was just his way, and most folks seemed to be used to it. It was like making fun of his own problems, having a mechanical tool instead of an arm-and-hand like everybody else, and it made Uncle Cal more *funny* and less *different*.

"Dammit, Cal, just when I'm thinking you might not be a total waste of breath, bones, and britches, then you have to go and act like the sorry piece-a shit you really are."

"For shame, Delores, stop cussin' in front of the child," he said in a Baptist preacher kind of voice.

"Me stop cussin'?" she cried. "You can't say two sentences without—"

"Yeah, yeah, yeah," he laughed. "And besides, I was just exercising the pinchers. Have to, every day, to keep um in shape and not rustin' up on me."

"You have to exercise your pinchers?" I blurted out. This was news to me.

"Don't listen to a word he says," Mama said.

"Twice a day, every day, more if possible. If I was to go three days without grabbing a fanny, the damn thing might just close up on me. Couldn't have that, now, could we?"

I laughed. Mama did too, though she tried not to.

"Well, are ya'll ready to hit the road, in a *road* vehicle, this time, to tour the sights of Nolan?"

Mama grabbed her purse and keys, and we all piled into Uncle Cal's truck.

The outside smelled different—not wet like before, but still kind of musky and sour, with a whiff of nastiness like outside the boys' restroom at school. Brick and cinder block buildings in the town square were dirty, coated in a brown film from street level to three feet upward. Even the grass yards seemed soiled, rinsed in a filthiness that was now part of the landscape.

And everywhere—even in the street—were random pieces of garbage and refuse. Rusty cans, an old tire, Sunbeam bread wrappers, dirty plastic flower arrangements once anchored in a cemetery. And lots of torn green garbage bags with little to nothing spilling out, like a trash truck had left them, one or two per address.

No one said much as we rode through our sad little town.

Turning at the water tower, Mama cried when we saw the bare patch of wet red clay that used to hold our house. A rusty piece of chain link fence and a mangled lawn chair sat in the corner of the lot. We'd never seen either before. There were bits and pieces of trash scattered about the small yard, but the space where the house had been was oddly vacant and clear of debris.

"I'da thought there'd be—there's not even a hint of the foundation. It's like it was never here," Mama said.

"The foundation, as you call it, was a few concrete blocks on each end. The house didn't sit on the ground, you knew that from the holes in the floor. This may be the best thing that ever happened to this poor little lot," Uncle Cal said.

"But it was our home, Calvin," Mama said as her chin quivered.

Uncle Cal put his arm around me, wrapping the hook arm around Mama. He nuzzled her ponytail and shook his head.

"Come on, Sis, use the sense God gave you. What's there to miss? Walls covered in newspapers and plumbing that works maybe half the time? I say good riddance to this dump. The Lord knew what he was doing on this one."

"Easy for you to say, Cal. What about us? What'll we do?"

"Exactly what you've been doing—stay with me. Save your money and maybe with any luck, you can move from this rat hole town, get Mojo to a better place. Get both of you a better life—things can only move up from here."

"Uncle Cal," I said from underneath his shoulder, still caught in his bear hug of me and Mama. "Maybe the Lord *did* know what he was doing—"

"Mojo, don't get involved in this," Mama said. She was particular about what I said about God and was full of advice on how to live holy, although we seldom went to church.

"I'm not, Mama," I explained. "I was just gonna say that the Lord destroyed the earth by water, but he kept the good people in Noah's Ark, to start over again. Uncle Calvin was our Noah, and his funny house was our ark."

They both laughed, and we went back to the house on stilts.

Me and Mama stayed on for over a year. She put up with the animals and even seemed to like them when she thought no one was looking. Uncle Cal's card playing friends came a couple of times a week, just like my uncle was gone a couple nights a week as well. We kept the house clean, and Mama did the cooking, but she always said our living there was "temporary."

The grocery store, and then the panty factory, reopened and Mama went back to both her jobs. Saying we'd be moving soon, she took a third one on weekends, being a waitress at a bar. It was the closest I ever had to a normal family; me and Mama cooking supper together before she left for the bar, listening to music or watching The Three Bs (*Branded, Bonanza,* and *Bat Masterson*) with my uncle until bedtime.

Then Uncle Cal was drinking more, a *lot* more, I realize in looking back.

My uncle hadn't had a full time job in my lifetime, but he'd worked odd jobs around town and on farms so much it seemed full time to me. I'd never known him without the hook, and as far as I could tell it never held him back. It was just part of him, like red hair or a big nose or needing glasses, the kind of things that make folks different from each other. Looking back, I remember how he used to laugh and make fun of himself, especially when his buddies would hassle him about not having a wife or a girlfriend. There were other things he'd shy away from—swimming, water-skiing, stuff like that. I remember he got really mad one time when his friend told him he was lucky, that he'd never have to worry about the draft or getting sent to Viet Nam—that was the shortest card-playing night he ever had, threw 'em all out.

I guess it all started going downhill at the same time, though I can't for sure remember it that way. The odd jobs got fewer, and Uncle Cal spent more time at home. He started to drink more. Then he was always sad, moody-like. If Mama tried to talk to him about it, he slammed doors and then left for days at a time. He took to bringing folks home with him, some loud and some quiet, but all dwelling in the same, sadly passive world where he lived.

Mama finally gave up on him, and we moved out.

Our new home was a single-wide trailer behind a fire-condemned gas station. It was smaller and nastier than our first house, but Mama said it was the best she could do. I missed the dogs and Uncle Cal and looking out over the river at night.

Uncle Cal came by to visit a few times, trying to laugh and joke and be the guy he used to be, but he wasn't much of an actor. I could tell something was wrong, so I knew Mama had to know it, too, but we acted like everything was fine. When my uncle was there, Mama never stopped talking about how she was doing better, saving up to move us to a better place, find me a better school, maybe even prepare me for a college scholarship. Uncle Cal would smile that fake smile with the sad eyes, hug us, and leave.

His visits became further apart until we rarely saw him at all, even though he lived just a couple of miles away. By the time I turned twelve I'd learned to sneak over on my bike after school a few times, finding my uncle alone and barely awake in a stale-smelling house in need of a good picking up and cleaning. The dogs were usually outside and starved for attention, greeting me with powerful, sloppy kisses and following me up the stairs and inside. His truck was always in the driveway, and if knocking did no good, the key was under the mat.

Whether Uncle Cal laid on the couch, in his recliner, or in bed, two things were always the same: the television was on, and Kawliga lay on his chest, softly purring. From the shows flickering on the screen (soap operas or game shows) I figured my uncle simply never turned it off; when we lived there, he only watched the weather, old westerns, and *Hee Haw*. I'd try to make conversation with Uncle Cal, but he was different—reluctant; it was almost like he was ashamed to talk to me, like I'd walked in on him in the bathroom or something. Only one time can I remember a visit being less than awkward.

It was a late fall afternoon, overcast when I started out but already beginning to sprinkle when I first saw the house on stilts. Uncle Cal opened the door before I was halfway up the stairs.

"Cajun girl!" he cried. "Get your little butt in here before all that sugar starts to melt." He grabbed me in a hug as the dogs, already wet and smelling, slid by us and settled themselves on the couch. "Does your mama know you're out gallivantin' in the rain?"

"It wasn't raining when I left," I told him, leaving out the fact that Mama didn't know I was out at all.

"Well, take a load off, girl," he said, motioning towards the couch. "Tell me 'bout how life's treatin' you these days." He sat in the recliner, and I nudged between the two dogs. An old shoebox, big enough for a man's work boots, lay open on the coffee table. A faded green lid with a Thom Mcann logo lay on the floor beside it. From my seat I could see yellowed papers, something bound in black leather, the corner of a framed photograph, and a plastic baby toy.

"What's all this?" I asked, nodding toward the box.

"This," he said as he reached for it, "is our family, condensed down to a shoebox."

I didn't say anything at first. It was like Uncle Cal drifted into another time and place, and maybe if I just let him, he'd take me there, too. He took out what I thought were two books, their bindings identical and old, but not really used. The black covers were brittle and dusty, but the spines bore neither cracks nor lettering.

"You know what these are?" he asked. "You'll have one, too, one day—maybe more than one, your mama hopes."

I had no idea. "Books?" I offered.

"Close but no cigar," he laughed. "These are our high school diplomas, mine and your mama's." He opened the first one. The spine made a crisp crackle followed by the soft wisp of the thin tissue he removed from inside.

"Delores Virginia Mullinax," he read, handing it over to me.

I stared at the off-white paper glued inside the book-like covering. It smelled old, like clean linens left too long in an unopened drawer. "Dumas County High School" was printed in fancy old English lettering across the top with "1957" centered below. My mama's name was underneath the date, and a paragraph in the same style, but smaller, in the middle. At the bottom were three names, signed in blue ink, then typed in black underneath. There was a blue seal reading "FHA" in the left hand margin, and a yellow one reading "Beta Club" in the right. It was the fanciest piece of paper I'd ever held in my hands, and knowing what it was made me feel proud but funny inside. Uncle Cal opened his own, and we both stared at the diplomas like they were crystal balls with special instructions inside.

I broke the silence. "What does FHA on this ribbon mean?" I asked.

"Y'all don't have FFA and FHA anymore?" he asked, turning the paper around in his hand and looking at the backside.

"I don't think so," I said. The couch was minus its springs, and it felt silly sitting with my knees near my chin, but I didn't care. I was learning about my family. "I mean, I don't really know. We don't have many clubs at school, now."

"That's a shame. Probably went to the wayside with desegregation, when they put the two public schools together and so many folks left." Uncle Cal looked at his shoes and shook his head. "Don't know what they were thinking, pulling out nearly all the white children and sending them to those little private schools. Drove the numbers down so low I guess there just ain't enough funding for things anymore, or maybe it's just no one cares. It's a damn shame, though. FFA is for Future Farmers of America," he said, taking a drink off a beer bottle on the crate he used for an end table. "And FHA is for Future Homemakers of America. Back when we were in school, there was a pretty darn good chance we'd end up being one or the other."

"I guess so," I said, not really understanding. The rain pounded harder on the roof and I watched it slant sideways against Uncle Cal's front window. "Don't most people go somewhere else when they graduate, to get jobs? "

"Nowadays sure, Cajun girl. Small farms are becoming a thing of the past, and on them big plantations, they've replaced man with machine." He reached down and scratched Jerry Lee behind the ears. The dog grunted and licked his chops. "But years ago, they hired labor, lots of it. Callin' a boy a Future Farmer of America was an honor." He paused for a moment, his scratching dropping dander on the rug. I could smell dog more than ever now. "And a hell of a lot of fun," he said. "I learned more about life in FFA than in any readin' and writin' class."

"What's a homemaker?" I asked. "A construction worker?"

"No, sugar." He laughed and ran his finger around the empty beer bottle. "Homemakers, women who worked at home. FHA taught girls to sew, to cook and can, freeze, pickle, all that stuff."

"So that's why we have to grow all those tomatoes every summer, and buy that stuff from roadside stands to put up and eat in winter?" I thought about Mama's raw red hands when she hulled and peeled things to can. "Thank God they *don't* make us learn that in school anymore—when I'm grown, I'm gonna buy my food at the store. I hate putting up all those vegetables."

Uncle Cal chuckled. "Store-bought won't taste half as good."

"Sure," I said, rolling my eyes.

"You'll be like my daddy, and that story about the first light bread," he said, peering out the window at the gray rain on the river as though it showed him a film clip from long ago. "Your mama ain't never told you?"

I shook my head. Jerry Lee raised his snout to look for Uncle Cal's hand; he brought it down on the dog's stomach and commenced rubbing again. "Our Daddy was raised on the family farm, probably never left Dumas County a dozen times in his first twenty years."

"Wow."

He nodded. His beard had grown into a gray stubble and he touched it while he talked. "They didn't have a lotta money, but they ate good—killed a hog every winter, cured it themselves, kept chickens for eatin' and eggs, and enough spring and summer vegetables to eat all year long."

Uncle Cal's green eyes lit up from behind while he talked. It was as if he spoke to the rain and the dogs, in a faraway voice I remembered from when he used to tell me stories as a kid, sitting on his lap on the porch of the house on stilts, watching the fireflies light and go black. "This was back in the Depression," he said. "And most everybody was poor as Job's turkey, so it's not like they were the only ones. Daddy was seventeen or so, been up to Arlington to trade some hogs. He stopped at a general store to maybe get a cold drink. The man behind the counter had a loaf of light bread, fresh off the truck. Told Daddy it was the latest thing, everybody'd be buyin' it 'fore long."

"He'd never *seen* any light bread?" The idea was crazy.

Uncle Cal looked over at me and shook his head. "Never in his life," Cal said. "He had biscuits and cornbread, maybe even some homemade loaf bread once in a while, but never any store bought bread. Ever." The dog was breathing regular between us, his black nose moist. "The feller behind the counter gave him a piece, hoping to sell a loaf. Daddy ate the whole thing and then told the feller thank you, but he'd pass. Said to him it was what paper would taste like if you tried to eat it."

I laughed. The rain slowed down, sounding gentle on the roof.

"The funniest thing was what he told his family when he got home, 'It'll never catch on,'" Uncle Cal said. "Folks'll never pay good money for something like that." Uncle Cal pulled out a small gold pin in a clear plastic square of a box. "Your Mama won that," he said, passing it to me.

A tiny emblem of a needle and thread and the word "4-H" were embossed on a green four-leaf clover, stamped in the center.

"Mama got this for sewing?"

"There's more medals in here and probably as many more gone to the wayside. Your mama got awards for sewing, cooking, planting trees, and growing a garden. She took to sewing most."

"She did? She never told me." My stomach grumbled and I hoped Mama wouldn't wonder where I'd got to, but I loved being at Uncle Cal's house. It was like a present to me with the rain pattering outside and the box between us.

"Your mama loved to sew, nothing made her happier than a purty piece a material and a new pattern." It was like he described someone else, a younger, happier woman. It made me feel strange, thinking of Mama in a life without the panty factory, or bills to pay, or me.

"I know she don't have time to do a lot of it these days, but your mama's made you some pretty dresses you could never of afforded from the store. You don't wanna learn to sew?"

"Sort of," I admitted. "Mama helped me make a skirt one time, and she was gonna show me how to put in a zipper so I could make a dress, but I guess we forgot or got too busy. And her sewing machine don't work too good anymore. That's how Mama learned to sew?"

"Yes ma'am. You tell her bring that machine by here—no sense taking it somewhere that'll charge you an arm and a leg—" He stopped, looking at his hook.

My eyes stung, and I knew crying would make him feel worse, so I did the only thing I knew to do: I gave it right back to him. "No use lettin' somebody charge an arm and a leg when you already gave up an arm, Captain Hook. Arrrrr!"

My uncle laughed and shook his head. Reaching underneath the papers, he pulled out the picture frame. "This here's your Mama and me, right 'fore she graduated. She made that dress for the Junior-Senior Prom, got mad at the boy she was supposed to go with, and took me instead. Now ain't I a sight for sore eyes?"

The frame had been metallic gold once but had rusted with age. The color picture was faded, but the two familiar faces were brighter than I'd ever seen them. Uncle Cal wore a white coat, white shirt, black bow tie and black pants with pinstripes. Even his shiny shoes were black and white, and there was a yellow flower in the pocket of his jacket. His curly brown hair was combed back, and he was grinning, his arm around Mama. He had *two* good arms, then.

Mama looked like a princess in a floor length, off-the-shoulder dress of baby blue dotted-swiss. It was perfectly fitted through the bust and her tiny waist, which was belted with a long white ribbon and a corsage of daisies in its center. The skirt flared out in big, perfect ripples like waves of whipped cream around a layer cake. Her hair was curled and put up tall, weird by the standards I was used to, but perfectly elegant with the dress in the picture. Her lips were painted pink and smiling—bigger than I could ever remember her smiling. Her basic features still looked the same, but not really. The excitement in my mother's face made her a different person altogether.

"Why does she look so—so happy?" I asked.

"She was a fine-looking girl, in a new dress she made herself, going to the biggest event she'd ever been to. Her life was just starting to get to the good parts—graduation was a few days away. She was happy to be alive, I guess."

"But she graduated, and then she went to work at the panty factory. She was looking forward to that?"

My uncle's face clouded over, his eyebrows pulling tight against his skull as he sucked in air. "She wasn't planning to go the factory, not at first," he said, bothering about for his cigarettes. "She got a little scholarship, not much, but enough to send her to the vocational school if she worked part-time and watched her spending." He tried striking a match but the pack must have been wet, and he threw them on the floor. "She was real good at typing and shorthand, wanted to take some more courses, and some bookkeeping."

"Why didn't she?" This was more information than I'd ever gotten about Mama's life before me.

"We had some hard luck, Delores and me. Mama died." Cal leaned over and grabbed another pack of matches from the windowsill. "And the little house we lived in wasn't really ours, it was mortgaged to the hilt." He stuck a bent Lucky in his mouth. "We thought if we both worked like crazy we could hold on." He opened the book of matches. There was only one match left. "I was working fulltime for Oakland, and Delores worked two jobs that summer, then for the next year, too, thinking she'd be able to drop one of 'em and go to school the next fall."

He sighed and struck the match. The flame burst out and caught the end of his cigarette. Exhaling, he watched the smoke rise to the ceiling. "Then I lost my arm, you know that old story," he said, looking far away from the room where we sat. "That put us behind even more. Delores was gonna start school the *next* year. Then—" Uncle Cal was silent. He smoked.

After a minute or more of deep thought he said, "Things don't always work out the way you think they will. That's all. But she's been a good mama to you, Cajun girl. Don't you forget it." Reaching over, he patted my knee, then grasped the box lid on the floor with his hook and with that, signaled an end to my family history lesson.

"Wait!" I cried, grabbing inside the box before he could restore the lid. "What about this?" I took out a red plastic cube about the size of a jack-in-the-box. There were holes in four sides, holes in the shape of circles, ovals, rectangles, squares, and stars. Flipping open the top, I found little plastic pieces in all of those shapes. "Whose was this?"

Uncle Cal stood up, rubbed out his cigarette in a little tin ashtray, and looked out the window again. He took the box from my hands.

"It's quit raining, you better be getting back home before it starts again. Your mama'll have my hide if I send you home in the rain," he said. The plastic cube, the picture frame, and everything else went back beneath the Thom Mcann logo. He closed the lid and put the box under his arm.

Mama'll have my hide if she finds out I came here, I thought, but I didn't dare say it. Uncle Cal rose and walked to the door. Why was he trying to get rid of me? How could a plastic box, a baby toy, make him so—so whatever he was? I wasn't ready to go home: I wanted answers. I sat on the couch with my knees practically in my ears and said, "That little box didn't look so old. I've seen ones like it at Woolworth's in Albany. They're for little kids to learn shapes. Whose was it?" I asked.

He smiled, his hook on his hip, pretending to be put out with me. "Well, okay, Miss Smarty Pants, *you* played with it when you were a little critter. Had to give you something to keep you outta my dog food." He turned and opened the door to usher me out. I hiked myself off the couch and the two dogs looked at me, Hank never lifting his head.

"Tell your Mama to bring me that sewing machine," Cal said. "Put me to work, make an honest man out of me." He gave me a quick hug and stood watching as I walked down the stairs. He waved as I climbed onto my bike, then he went back inside, closing the door.

Back at home, Mama was standing in the doorway, wearing the same expression Uncle Cal had worn when I left. When she asked where I'd been, I told the truth; she always knew when I was lying anyway.

She grounded me for a month.

"It ain't Cal I don't trust, Mary Jane, it's those houses you pass between our house and his, and then the riff raff he's likely to have inside."

I wanted to tell Mama about the things I'd seen: the diplomas, and awards, and how pretty she was in that picture. But she seemed about as closed to new information as Uncle Cal was at giving out the old kind. I left well enough alone, thinking I'd find a better opening later.

Chapter 3
July 1958

Delores

DELORES MULLINAX WAS UNASSUMING, UNSOPHISTI-cated, and unexcited about life in general. Born smart and willful, her girlhood was cut short when she was forced into a quick transition from high school to factory life, strapping her in the monotonous struggle of the tired and weary working class of the south.

She was outside under the smoking tree, on break from her job at the Nolan Manufacturing Company, a sweatshop that produced ladies' panties from size 4 to size 44. One pattern. All cotton. In white, pastels, and various florals some big-wig found for next-to-nothing at going-out-of-business warehouses.

Just panties. That's all they made. Her mama had worked there years before, and she'd tried to find those panties in a department store, on the few and far between treks she'd made to real cities—Tallahassee, Albany, Columbus. She never saw a single pair on any rack—bargain or otherwise—which made her wonder. Where did those panties go? Whose bare buttocks slid into those 4s and 14s and 44s? Delores never found out.

She'd worn a few. The plant manager had a heart: he let them take out the rejects, the ones with flaws too big to sell to outlets. They weren't much to speak of—a big flaw might be a pair that had no leg holes or no elastic in the waist. But Mary Pearl Mullinax taught her daughter not to waste a thing, and Delores made some of those blunders into almost perfect underwear for herself. She felt good wearing them—she could count on one hand the times she'd had anything *new*, and to her it seemed a shame she couldn't wear them on the outside, where people could see.

Maybe it was some kind of sign. If she *had* worn them on the outside, the way she'd laughed about doing, he might have noticed her, but he would *never* have tried to talk to her. Not that he tried, then. No, Delores knew she was responsible for that fiasco. The one she'd remember the rest of her days.

She'd been with Bertha June, the thirty-eight-year-old wife of a Pentecostal preacher. Bertha had spent six months in the state asylum at Milledgeville after what doctors called a "mandatory hysterectomy" following the birth of her fourteenth child. She'd returned to work the week after her release, but co-workers agreed she'd never been quite the same.

"The doctors are still trying to get my medication right," Bertha had told them, admitting to a definite problem she couldn't explain. It seemed that her days fell in two categories: depressed older woman or horny teenager.

Delores sucked in her last drag as a car drove up to the front door. Not just a car, *the* car: a 1958 Corvette, brilliant white with red interior. The radio was on; she heard the end of "Maybelline" and then the Johnny Reb Radio jingle before he shut off the engine.

He looked in his rearview mirror, ran his fingers through his sleek black duck-tail, and climbed out. He didn't lock his car; he didn't put up the top. He seemed oblivious to the fact that he drove the American dream. He was tall, but not gangly, just lanky enough to be damned near perfect. There was only a scant breeze in the air, yet it found its way to his collar, his un-tucked dress shirt, his shining hair. He didn't walk, he *floated* across the dirt brown grass and onto the concrete landing in front of the entrance.

Nolan Manufacturing Company had a somewhat impressive entrance, though no one used it but the owner, Mr. Foster, and his secretary. According to the workers, some "business people" who had dealings with Mr. Foster used it, too, but such people were never viewed from the smoking tree. The entrance had a forest green awning, two plastic trees that set in gold pots, and a door with the company's name on it. Blue carpet could be seen through the glass. Factory workers, maintenance people, custodians, and the like used the "service entrances."

The handsome guy in the gorgeous car strode across the landing to the entrance door. It was at that point that he had a bit of a problem. He pushed against the aluminum crossbar. Nothing happened. He pushed again, with the same result.

He coughed, or made some kind of vocal noise, and looked as if he were summoning some special strength provided by the gods-of-the-unbelievably-good-looking in such circumstances, then pushed again. Nothing happened.

"Must be a joke," Delores mumbled. "Showing off, giving us hicks on break something to laugh at. Cocky bastard." Bertha smiled, then burst into girlish giggles uncharacteristic of her matronly size.

He looked in their direction, smiling back at them like a movie star giving autographs to schoolgirls.

"Look," Bertha said, pointing. "Ain't he just be-yoo-ti-ful?" Her eyes lit up, her chubby face looking cherub-like as she stared in awe.

"A beautiful idiot," Delores muttered, looking away, then back. He was still battling the front door.

"You needin' some help?" Bertha beckoned in a voice an octave higher than normal.

"He's fine, Bertha, leave him alone," Delores said.

The self-assured Adonis walked toward them. "I guess the door's locked," he said, looking a little confused. "But he *said* he was here this morning. Is there a way in from the back?"

"There's three ways into the back, them's the way we always come in," Bertha explained.

"But if you really want to use the main entrance, it's not locked," Delores said. "It's always open from eight to twelve and from one to four."

"Weekdays, that is," Bertha added.

His face showed a faint line of perspiration and his breathing became more auditory. The pretty boy was pissed. "Okay, I give up. It's Friday. It's ten-thirty. It's not a national holiday that I know of. And the damned door is locked. Can you show me the back entrance, or do you just enjoy being a bitch?" he asked, looking directly to Delores.

She returned his stare as she answered.

"There's a service entrance on all three sides, but the south end is most likely to be unlocked. The front entrance is unlocked, too, but it does require the ability to read. Above the handlebar you'll see the word 'pull.' And I don't enjoy being a bitch, but it does come pretty natural when someone else is being an ass." Delores turned and pretended to drag on the smoke she'd stubbed out minutes before.

When she looked up, he was gone.

She didn't see him again for weeks. Never even knew his name. Didn't care.

Sundown Liquors had a tiny lounge in the back, not much to speak of and only open on weekends: A haven for local drunks who didn't want to leave town and neighboring dry county folks hiding from their wives. Just a bar, six tables, and a jukebox. A couple of gals from the factory were going there, after work on payday. Delores decided to splurge and join them. She rarely went out, and hadn't been anywhere since she and Cal had closed their parents' house and moved to Oakland.

The place was full. Her brother was there, sitting at the bar. He shooed away the loser he was talking to and gave her a seat. It turned out the owner was looking for a weekend barmaid, eighteen being the legal age in Georgia liquor establishments. When Delores came in the next day, the owner showed her around, and she went to work that night. Pay wasn't great, but it was cash plus tips.

A month or so later, the handsome jerk from that long ago day at the factory showed up at the Sundown. He wore seersucker shorts and a shirt that screamed country club/golf course and probably looked great against the car he drove all day. He sat down at the bar like he owned the place.

"A shot of Glenlivet, over ice," he said.

This was a brand Delores had not heard before, one she didn't think she'd seen on the shelf. "Glenn What?" she asked.

"Glenlivet. Single Malt Scotch," he said.

Delores turned quickly and examined the section containing Scotch. There was no Glenlivet.

"I'm sorry, sir, we don't have that brand," she said. "Could I get you something else?" He appeared not to hear her, staring intently into the plastic sphere of a clock that sat on the bar. His eyes traced the tiny Clydesdale horses and their continuous circular path around the inside of the globe. "Sir?" she said again.

As though the one word broke his trance, he looked back into her eyes again.

"We don't have any Glenlivet," she said. "Would you like something else?"

He smiled. "Any Haig & Haig, then? Dewar's White Label? Just a good single malt."

Delores glanced back at the names she'd just read. She was pretty sure he wouldn't like her answer.

"We have Johnny Walker Red and River Train. We don't get a lot of Scotch drinkers, I guess."

"River Train?" he laughed. "Never heard of it. I'll bet it's a rot-gut brand they age six months or less. Give me the Johnny Walker— I guess when in Rome—" He didn't finish his statement, and she made no comment.

He'd gone over to the jukebox when she left his drink on a napkin. It was a slow night, and Delores went back to straightening things that weren't messed up. He picked his quarter's worth and sat down.

Taking a long pull on his drink, he swallowed slowly and nodded in her direction. Then his attention shifted back to his liquor.

Nat King Cole crooned over *Mona Lisa*. Delores figured that was the voice God would have, if He was really there, and if He sang. Delores smiled as she wiped ashtrays and listened. She always enjoyed *really* listening to Nat. It was like right then, in that moment, she wasn't Delores, she wasn't poor, she wasn't in Nolan, and all the possibilities she'd dreamed about as a kid could still come true. Just for that minute, she floated on a cloud, someplace that none of the shit of the real world could come through, not then. Just for a minute, such a beautiful, delicious minute she wished could last forever.

"You've got a nice smile, too," he said.

Delores looked in every direction possible, then realized he was talking to her. "Thanks," she said, meeting his gaze, then darting her eyes away.

"And maybe I could grow to like the working man's Scotch," he added. "Could I get another?" He handed her his empty glass.

She took it, turned away, poured another. She wondered, not for the first time, why the phrase "working man" seemed a term of endearment when some folks said it, yet with others, like this guy, it referred to the low end of their caste system. A part of her wanted to rise up and take offense, like he was making fun of her heritage, but—Delores looked back at him, and could see no signs of hatefulness in his demeanor. He was even going out of his way to make conversation, though he wasn't all that good at it.

I guess he can't help where he came from, no more than any of us can. She turned back to face him with his new drink; the cool sweat on the glass made it slippery in her hands, and she wondered why she'd never had to work at holding on to a glass before.

She set it on a fresh napkin. He finished in one gulp, then left. The jukebox still played, this time with Johnny Ray's "Cry."

It was only at closing that she noticed the tip. The empty pickle jar on the bar, the one that collected nickels and dimes at best, sported *real* money. She tucked the $5 bill in her pocket as she closed up for home, where she dreamed of stars, music, cool-clear-water—and seersucker.

←

As the summer wore on, Phil Foster showed up every other weekend. Like clockwork. He always drank Scotch. And he had the best taste in music of anyone that darkened the doors of The Sundown.

"Delores!" He smiled as he seated himself at the bar. "How's it going?"

"How's it that you know my name?" she answered back, but nicely. He'd never used it before.

"Doesn't everybody know the name of Nolan's most beautiful barmaid?" he teased.

"Nolan's *only* barmaid," she reminded him. He laughed. He was flirting, the kind of thing she usually ignored, but it was nice to be noticed, to be something besides Cal's little sister or the gal that brings the beer.

"Could I get some change?" He offered her a dollar.

"Sure," she said as she handed back four quarters.

"For the jukebox," he said. "Any requests? Surely the lady has a particular favorite," he added.

Delores liked that—asking her opinion, like she was somebody.

"I . . . I like Nat King Cole," she admitted. "And I like Hank, but not the ones on that jukebox."

"Your wish is my command." He bowed and left.

She heard the opening of "Too Young," the big introduction where the swirling violins answered the call of the vocals. It was Delores's favorite Nat song, though she'd never told anyone. It was syrupy and romantic, the kind of song fit for the climax of a fairy tale. To admit her love for such songs would be a sign of weakness. Just because it was her favorite was no reason to share that truth.

The bar was full that night. Delores was grateful to keep busy. He sat at the end, staring at the Clydesdales, then off into space again while stirring his drink in slow a circle. He was working on maybe his third one when he looked up and asked, "Why in the hell do you stay here?"

Delores was startled. It was like the blurred voices and laughter, even the jukebox music seemed to fade, his voice being the only real sound in the room. She suddenly felt the cool of the wet rag in her hand, yet the scent she took in was not smoke or liquor or the suds in the sink, but only his faint cologne, a smell like new leather and leaves.

"Whadda you mean, stay here?" she asked. "I don't *live* here, I just work here, and only weekends. I have a real job, this is just extra. And I'm going to school in the fall."

Of course, he wouldn't understand about extra jobs, he'd probably never had a job in his life.

"No, silly, I know you don't live here," he laughed. "I mean why do you stay here, in Nolan, why don't you move?"

Delores said nothing.

"You're gorgeous: There are bars, lounges, restaurants, supper clubs, resorts, *real* night clubs—you could get a job anywhere. Why the hell do you stay here in this shit-hole town?"

She stared back at him like he was crazy. Sure, she thought about things like that. How could any girl read a book or watch a movie and not imagine herself in that place, being someone else, somewhere else? But she'd never say such things out loud.

Her mama had taught her to be practical: to make the most of everything she learned, to be frugal in everyday living in hopes of saving up for the frivolous little extras life might present later. Both her parents had placed a high priority on a good marriage, reminding their children that life's burdens could be cut in half when a man and a woman chose to share their lives with each other. After Daddy died, Delores and her mother had spent many evenings talking about the difference in romantic love and everlasting love, and she was determined to hold out for the relationship that would have met her parents' approval.

But Delores was tired—tired of waiting on something she believed in but couldn't see, while watching easy couplings of the other kind happen night after night with none of the consequences her Mama had warned about. So Delores had allowed herself to dream, but to only dream, and to keep it to herself, hoping her Mama couldn't read her mind from the afterlife with some sort of heavenly x-ray vision she wasn't privy to. Besides, she was going to school in the fall. She'd have a better job than being a bar maid or working in a factory. And that would be enough.

But *he* had said it, and he didn't care who heard him. He thought she could find work anywhere, at any of those fancy places. In a real town. With apartment houses and city buses, where all the women weren't married. Where people lived, not just existed.

"I might, one day," she answered, surprising herself. "I'm going to, later on. After I finish school, I'm savin' up til I can move, and go work in—" She wondered what she'd say next. She'd never considered actually leaving Nolan. "In Savannah," she decided.

Delores didn't know a thing about Savannah that she hadn't read in *Gone with the Wind*, and she was pretty sure it might have changed since then.

"Savannah," he said with a smile. "Beautiful town. The squares, the architecture, the food, River Street! Yes ma'am, I can see you behind a bar in a little bistro, dressed like the St. Pauli girl, drawing beer. A beautiful picture."

Delores didn't know what the hell he was talking about, but it sounded so wonderful that she couldn't let it stop. Busying her hands to look hard at work, she doled out questions to keep him talking.

"Where would I live?" she asked him.

"Oh, there are great places to live, reasonably priced, in the historic district."

"The historic district?" she asked, staring straight ahead as she wiped down the immaculate bar. She liked the way he said "reasonably priced," like he was sensitive to her finances without calling attention to the difference in their economic situations.

"Let's see, I think you'd like a little flat, maybe one on Bay Street, the floor over the day businesses, the banks, and offices, quaint little shops."

"Sounds nice," she said, working hard to keep her interest and excitement in check. As Phil talked, she saw the city of Savannah sweep by in Technicolor, a sneak preview of a coming-soon feature where she was the star.

"Or if you'd rather, there are plenty of apartment complexes with all the amenities, even a swimming pool if you like."

"That's okay," she said, practically drooling as she surveyed the classy brick duplexes, shingled chalets, and mock-stucco flats panning by in that reel running inside her head. It was hard to concentrate on the things he said, there was too much footage to view before he moved on to the next sentence.

"But I still see you as more of a loner, not the typical party girl. I think you belong on the waterfront..."

"The waterfront?" she repeated. Delores had never thought about water having a front or a back. It was just water. The movie changed for a minute. She saw the Flint River running through Dumas County, but it wasn't much more than a narrow stream. How did he know that she was more of a loner? She thought of the first day she saw him, when he'd called her a bitch. She'd been making fun of him; she actually was being a bitch. He'd never put two and two together, figuring out that she and that girl were the same, or maybe he'd forgotten that day altogether. But here, where she was no more than a barmaid, he still treated her with a kindness and respect she considered untypical of those from his class. Delores smiled as she folded the damp rag into a perfect square, savoring the moment as she listened to him talk.

"The historic district, which Sherman spared from fire because of its magnificent southern charm, backs up to the Savannah River, the largest shipping port east of the Mississippi," Phil continued. He sounded different as he talked about these places, like a radio announcer or a politician. Delores wondered how liquor made other people sound worse, even stupid sometimes, yet this guy's voice came alive with a few drinks.

"It sounds beautiful," she said, "but how do you know all this stuff?"

He laughed, the smile in his eyes warm and kind. To Delores, he sounded apologetic, like he was proud of being complimented but had no idea how to react to such gestures. He was silent for a moment, as though gathering his words, and then he spoke again.

"My mom was a history buff, and I've been to Savannah with my dad—sometimes—he picks up a lot of his biggest shipments there."

His biggest shipments, Delores thought. What could she say as a comeback to that? The only time she'd ever even thought about that word 'shipment,' was as a kid, back in better times when they could afford store-bought cereal. Captain Crunch was Cal's favorite, so it was what her mama bought, when she could. "Contents may settle during shipping," she'd read on the side of the box, imagining a whole ship full of Captain Crunch boxes, crossing some unknown ocean for a couple of kids in Nolan.

Delores and Phil continued to talk, off and on, for the rest of the night. One of the last two customers, the handsome storyteller stayed until the bar closed. He offered Delores a ride home, and she accepted. They ended up at the river, sharing a bottle of Crown Royal he kept in his car.

They sat on the riverbank, passing back and forth the blue felt bag as he talked of Savannah and Atlanta and Charleston. She saw antebellum houses, cobblestone streets with rows of awning-clad storefronts, out-of-work musicians with open instrument cases claiming their posts along the river. The Flint, shallow in the current drought, lay quiet and stagnant before them, yet Delores caught a whiff of salt in the air, the cry of a far away owl sounding strangely like a gull or other sea bird.

Later, as he spoke of Boston, she crossed her arms and hugged herself, spreading her fingers and rubbing the tops of her arms to warm them. Her panoramic view grew less detailed geographically, then the camera zoomed in on smiling children with big teeth and windblown hair, running after frisky, two-toned little bulldogs, then laughing and eating pies of the same rich colors. By the time Phil reached Denver, Delores was chilled to the bone despite the ninety-degree weather. She listened and drank and basked in the sheer pleasure of hearing someone create beautiful pictures in words, just for her.

Delores woke up as the sun peeked through clouds and the moon was still visible. She was wrapped in his arms and lying on the red woolen UGA blanket he'd taken from the trunk of his car. Her head hurt and her mouth tasted horrible, and the romantic movie she'd envisioned the night before came back as an over-told story in a cheap, dime store romance magazine. Pulling the blanket to cover herself, she noted the dried orange clay on the white Bulldog insignia, then shuddered to imagine what other nastiness clung to the bright rectangle of fabric. Who carried a wool blanket in the South Georgia summer? Rich boys out for easy women, the kind you'd never take to where you lived. And in this case, who could blame him? A girl who stayed out all night with a boy she barely knew—outside, in a public place, where anyone could appear at anytime—was a tramp, pure and simple.

Delores had known some fast girls in high school, but she couldn't imagine any of them sinking this low. She still wore her clothes and didn't actually remember any unseemly behavior, but how could she be sure? This was reserved for actual prostitutes, the ones who literally worked the streets and were paid for it. And even they, she imagined, would finish quickly and put their clothes back on. It was what they had to do, in order to survive, Delores thought, remembering disjointed scenes from *Les Miserables* and a Hank Williams's song she always associated with it, the one about the bad girl that lived down the street.

Some women had no choice, and the God of Delores saw these women differently, and judged them from within, not from the worldly acts life had forced them into. This was one of the few topics she'd never been able to discuss with her mother, and—Delores felt a cold shock of severe nausea with the mere thought of her mother's face. She stood, jerked the silly blanket from the ground and wrapped it around her as she ran towards the water's edge, where she quietly vomited the fiery brown liquid of the night before.

Feeling better after her purge, Delores splashed a little of the lukewarm river water on her face. She had made a horrible mistake for which she had no excuse, and for the first time in her life she almost hoped there was no afterlife, no way that her parents could see how far she'd strayed from their teachings.

Shaking out the blanket and folding it into a square, Delores walked back to where Phil lay sleeping. He was out cold, breathing sour breath through his perfectly rounded mouth.

"Hey," she whispered, " it's mornin'. We gotta get up." She spoke softly and hoped he wouldn't hear. He was so nice the night before, but what would he think of her now? Delores didn't want to find out, she only wanted to leave.

Thankfully, he didn't even budge.

She used her fingers as a comb for her matted curls. Remembering that the day was Saturday, she felt relieved that her brother Cal was most likely at the all-night poker game. Good, she thought, half-smiling for the first time in her new, fallen-woman life. She knew she was changed forever, but perhaps no one else would have to know the details.

She grabbed a stick and made for home. Folks had seen her out fishing before sunrise since before she could read; they didn't need to know that, this time, the fish in question happened to be a smooth-talking Phil.

Chapter 4
July 1958

Phil

WHEN TWENTY-YEAR-OLD PHIL FIRST SAW THE CHEAP postcard-like community of Nolan, he thought the sad little town and the whole lot of Dumas County should have been dynamited and left for good.

Phil's father, however, was not of the same belief. Mr. Foster had been born with money—old money—but to his credit, he turned it into much more. Nolan Manufacturing was closed in 1945 when WWII took the men away, and the supply and demand for flannel shirts wasn't worth the bother. When the war was over, Phil's dad bought the boarded up building, traded some machinery, and set up shop with a staff of over a hundred poor, southern, uneducated women as his employees. He paid them almost nothing, and they were grateful for any wages at all. Nolan Manufacturing was the largest employer of women in the red clay of southwest Georgia.

Every Christmas he brought home candies, jellies, cakes, and pies made from homegrown gardens, government commodities and a few cents stolen from the mouths of their own children. His family did not eat them, but the servants at their house in Albany enjoyed them. The Fosters never let anything go to waste.

"Other than the boy," Foster sometimes said. Philip IV, a misfit in his youth, spent his teen years wasted as much as possible. Neighbors, teachers, and local acquaintances summarized Phil as simply "another spoiled rich kid," but a few close family members and long-time house servants saw the boy in a different light.

Phil was the last of three children and the only male. Truth known, if one of the sisters had been a boy, the Foster clan might've ended there. A male child was a must-have, the little prince, the heir to the family businesses.

As far back as Phil could remember, he knew he was a special boy. Though his father never actually vocalized "Your sisters are just girls, Phil, and *you* are what this family was waiting for," he emphasized his point, just the same. Before entering school, Phil took riding lessons at the Pinebloom Stables, swimming lessons at the Elks, golf and tennis at Radium Springs. On his fifth birthday, Phil was presented with his own dog: an AKC registered Brittany Spaniel sired by a former national champion.

"He's beautiful," the boy cried upon seeing him, kneeling and wrapping his arms around the half-grown pup. Phil rubbed his face against the dog's speckled coat, oblivious to his other gifts and the friends who brought them.

"Let's put him in his kennel while you open the rest of your gifts," his mother chided, releasing the boy's embrace of the dog and taking the dog elsewhere.

After hours of more games, gifts, and food, Phil was almost happy to see his party end, knowing then he was free to play with his new friend. *Mom took it through the kitchen,* he thought, *so he's probably there, maybe Thelma's giving him something to eat.*

But the dog was not in the kitchen or the family room or the garage. Phil raced upstairs to his room, imagining that the dog was sleepy and already knew by instinct the location of his little master's bed. But the dog was not in Phil's room.

"Mom-meee," he called, running back down the stairs. "Where did you put my puppy?"

Mr. and Mrs. Foster were in the family room, watching the news. The room smelled of Phil's father's pipe and his mother's faint perfume.

"Is he in here with you?" Phil asked.

"Hush, son, can't you see we're checking the Dow-Jones?" Mr. Foster said.

"Shhh," his mother said, then whispered, "is *who* in here with us?" She smiled at Phil, but her quick look at Mr. Foster, then back at Phil, told him they needed to be quiet.

Phil didn't want to cry, especially in front of his dad, but thought he might if he stayed in the room a minute longer. He looked quickly into his mother's eyes, feeling runny mucous sliding down his nose, and he ran out of the room.

"Don't run in the house," he heard his father say.

Phil went back into the kitchen, out into the garage, and back into the kitchen again, rampantly banging doors and opening cabinets.

"Phil, honey, what on earth are you doing?" his mother asked as she tiptoed in to join him. She closed each pastel door he'd opened, gently touching the wallpaper as if to straighten the posture of the little Dutch people in the design. "You don't want to disappoint your daddy, do you, especially after that nice birthday party?"

"Where is he?" Phil sobbed. "I've looked everywhere, and I can't find him. What if he ran away? He hasn't been here that long, he won't know how to come home. Where is he? I need to take care of him—"

"Are you talking about that little dog?"

Phil nodded, wiping his tears on his shirtsleeve.

Mrs. Foster picked him up and hugged hard, like she'd done when he was only two or three, then set him down again.

"The dog's fine, and you haven't done anything wrong. Bless your heart, you thought you'd lost him? The puppy's gone back to the farm, where your daddy's been keeping him, with his trainer." She pushed an errant hair behind her ear.

"But I thought he was mine!"

"He is yours, silly." She reached up high to some papers lying on the top of the new light blue refrigerator. "See here," she said. "There's his name, 'Sir Ogden Nemestrius,' and here it says 'Owner—Phillip

Twitty Foster IV.' That's you, sweetheart." Phil's mom was trying to teach him the alphabet, but he couldn't read yet.

"Sir Og what?" Phil sniffled.

"The first part is for his father, Sir Ogden. He won a lot of awards in dog shows. Your father picked 'Nemestrious' because it means 'god of forests and woods.' He's a hunting dog, a very valuable hunting dog. That's why it's important for him to stay with his trainer."

"I don't even get to name him?" Phil asked.

His mother smiled, replacing the papers and straightening the trivets hung on the wall. "I think your daddy had to supply a name when he got him, to fill out the papers correctly. But I'll bet he'll let you call him whatever you want. I doubt anyone would want to call him Sir Ogden, do you?"

Phil wrapped his arms around his mother's thin waist, hugging her with all his might. Just as she started to ruffle his hair, he stepped back, looking up at her.

"But I wanted to sleep with him tonight. And play with him everyday, and feed him and take care of him and teach him tricks and—"

"Do I hear a five-year-old boy bellyaching to his mother?" Phil's dad walked into the kitchen with an empty glass. "Refill?" he said as Mrs. Foster took his glass and walked to the refrigerator. "And what's going on with my boy—we didn't score enough presents for you?"

Phil sniffed hard, hoping there were no tears or snot on his face. "I got lots of good stuff, but the best part was my dog."

"Indeed, son, indeed," Phil's father said. "Not just a mere dog but a champion, like his father. I doubt there are many five-year-old boys on this earth who own such hearty stock."

Phil smiled, not knowing or caring what "hearty stock" might be. "But, Daddy," he said, "after they get through training him, could he come stay here some time, with me? I wanted to sleep with him, like the girls do with Gigi." Gigi was a miniature poodle of similar pedigree that belonged to his sisters. Gigi had painted toenails, regular visits to a beauty parlor, and an unexplained revulsion to little boys.

"Of course not, son, Sir Ogden is bred for hunting quail. He needs intensive training and a disciplined environment in order to reach his maximum potential. Besides, sleeping with dogs is a girly thing to do. But if all goes well, we'll be able to take him quail hunting in the fall."

"But Daddy, I've never been hunting," Phil said.

"And that reminds me," his father said, " I think you have one more gift in the family room. Why don't you go get ready for bed, then come down and open your last gift?"

Mrs. Foster handed her husband a fresh drink, a napkin wrapped around the bottom. "I'll go run your bath water," she told her son as she exited.

"Sure, Daddy," Phil cried, bounding out of the kitchen and up the stairs.

Phil grabbed some pajamas out of a drawer, stripping off his clothes as he went into the bathroom. He climbed in as the tub filled with bubbles, high enough to tickle his nose. He scooped them up with two hands and fashioned himself a beard.

"Ho ho ho, Meehhhhrry Birthday," he said in his deepest voice.

His mother laughed and shook her head. "Try not to make too big a mess, okay?" she said as she picked up his discarded clothes and left.

Phil wondered what his other present might be, but he had a feeling he already knew. They were teasing him, making him wait until bedtime to find out that his dog was really there. Maybe they *did* send him to the farm, and now they were calling someone to bring him back. But his parents weren't teasing him to be mean, they were just playing. Phil dunked under the bathwater, holding his breath as long as he could, then coming up for air. He made up a game, seeing how many dog names he could think of while underwater.

Rover, King, Sparky, he thought. *Fido, Sam, Duke, Davy Crockett, Hercules.* Phil sat up quickly and breathed deep. His eyes stung a little as he went down again. *Lassie*—no, that was a girl dog—*Laddie,*

Smokey, Lefty, Joe—that's what he'd wanted to call his own dog. Like *Beautiful Joe*, an old-timey book his mother had read to him at night, before his father said that bedtime stories were for babies and girls. Phil squinted his eyes tighter and shook his head. *Batman, Captain America*—that was a good one. *Captain America*. But it didn't sound anything close to Sir Ogden Nimstree—

Phil's last big breath made him shiver. He didn't know why, but figured it was enough of a reason to pull out the plug, reach for a towel, and dry off. He jumped into his cowboy pajamas, then looked in the mirror and combed his inch-long hair. Brushing his teeth, he thought his toothpaste tasted somewhat like the icing on his birthday cake, but he remembered not to swallow. After a few manly spits, he scampered back down the stairs.

Mr. Foster rested in his chair, wearing glasses and reading a magazine.

Seeing the long rectangular box across his lap, Phil's mouth became dry and cottony. "Daddy," he said.

His father laid down the book, took off his glasses, and took a long sip of the drink beside him. "Ready for the big one?" He smiled at his son, handing him the gift.

The box was heavy. Phil laid it on the coffee table and unwrapped it, but with none of the excitement and fury of the gifts at his party. Lifting off the box top, he saw a dark-wooden, shiny hunting rifle.

"It's a .410 Winchester, special edition. A bit of overkill for a rookie, but a good choice for the master of a pedigreed hunting dog. Perhaps this weekend we'll take it out to driving range, get you started with skeet shooting."

"Yes, sir," Phil said, biting his lip.

"Well, what do you say, son? Good birthday?"

"Yes, sir," he said again.

"Unwrapped it already?" his mother asked as she entered the room.

"Yes, ma'am," he said.

"Excited?" she asked.

"Yes, ma'am."

"Decided what you're gonna call the little dog yet?"

Phil's dad interrupted. "What do you mean? The dog has a perfectly good name already. What'll it be, Phil? Sir Ogden? Maybe Little Og? Or do we go with the classy moniker, the Greek name of Nemestrious?'

Phil gritted his teeth, but his face remained emotionless. "Could we just call him 'Sir'?"

Mr. Foster considered the idea. "Excellent choice, son. Simple, not pretentious, but commanding respect. I like it. Take the rifle up to your room, son. We'll see about loading it later."

Phil closed the box top and took the heavy package up the stairs.

"Goodnight, son," his parents called to him. "Happy birthday!"

"Goodnight," he answered back.

Phil laid the box on his dresser, pulled down his covers, and crawled into bed. He turned off the lamp, then doubled his down-filled pillow, pretending it was his own dog. Phil lay on his side, hugging it in front of him.

When sleep finally came, his pillow was wet, his birthday tears absorbed by the puppy who wasn't there.

To the outside world, Phil lived one perfect life. Then he started school, and the facade of the Foster's little prince began to show serious cracks in its veneer.

For his first day of kindergarten, Phil's mother made his favorite breakfast, helped him into his new clothes, and delivered him to the door of his classroom. It was decorated in primary colors and smelled clean and new. He joined a low rectangular table with two other boys and two girls, and they sat with military posture while listening to a litany of rules, consequences, and expectations. They worked at tracing the letter "A" on thin paper with dotted lines, then colored mimeographed pictures of apples and falling leaves.

There was a time called "recess," the part that Phil liked best. They could swing or slide or hang from the monkey bars, or they could just run and play and make all the noise they wanted. When recess was over, they stood in a straight line waiting for a drink of bitingly cold water from a metal fountain. Back in the classroom, they each received a stack of papers to be filled out and returned the next day. Stapled on top was a bright yellow paper star, showing the letters P-H-I-L and a smiling circle drawn with a red pen. At the front of the building where parents waited, his teacher helped him into the Foster's blue Chrysler.

"Phil is a wonderful boy," the teacher said. His mother beamed.

But the next day was not so wonderful.

"Phil's visual discrimination skills are less than age appropriate," his teacher said as she opened the car door. "And he's the only child in the class who hasn't mastered the alphabet. Could you come in for a conference next week?"

Phil's mother brushed imaginary lint from her collar and adjusted the pearls at her throat. "Of course I can," she said. "When?"

"Monday at two. In the meantime, could you try to work with him at home?"

"Sure," she answered as the teacher closed the door.

On Monday, Thelma, the Foster's maid, drove the station wagon to collect Phil from school. His mother returned home later, her eyes red. She went straight to her bedroom, slamming the door. Thelma fed Phil early and put him to bed. He heard his parents arguing, his mother crying as he fell asleep.

The next day, Thelma drove him to and from school, as she continued to do for the next three years. Phil's kindergarten teacher was smiling and kind, but Phil wondered why she'd stopped looking into his eyes when she spoke to him. She moved Phil to a smaller table at the back of the room, where he and the other boy and girl there were always given the same dull assignments and worksheets every day, the same ones the rest of the class had mastered in the first days.

"Mommy," he asked one night after dinner. "Why does my teacher keep giving me the same work to do?"

With his sister upstairs and his father away from home, Phil's mother seemed different than usual. Phil had wondered why she never played with him anymore, why she went places with Laura and Fran, but was never around for him the way she used to be. But today she talked to him, patted his head, listened as he talked to her—yet it was still different than before. Almost as though she were someone else's mother—like one of the mothers of his friends, a kind lady who acted as though she cared, but not the way she would care for her *own* little boy. It was nice, but just not the same.

"She's trying to help you," she explained with a smile. "But it's gonna be okay. The teacher said she wanted to hold you back a year, but your Daddy put his foot down, and now he's gotten you the help you'll need. Your Daddy's a special man; he takes care of things."

"What kind of help?" Phil asked. The idea of his father's brand of help made his stomach hurt. Daddy's help with tennis, swimming or golf usually involved belittling and criticism.

"Your father's hired a tutor," she said. Phil didn't know what a 'tooter' was, but the sound of the word made him giggle. His mother didn't notice.

"Mrs. Ramsey is a teacher from a special needs school working on her doctorate in something called 'educational intervention studies.' She's going to come and work with you everyday, so they won't have to hold you back a year. Isn't that wonderful?" Phil's mother made it sound like a party or a trip to the zoo. Anything his mommy thought was so wonderful couldn't be all bad, could it?

And it wasn't. Mrs. Ramsey was tall and raven-haired with a radiant smile and a serious face free of makeup. She always brought a briefcase of books and papers and a tote bag of brightly colored games and tiny objects to count. In her purse were special treats like granola, trail mix, sugarless gum, even M&M's she doled out as rewards.

Phil learned enough of the alphabet to show some promise at literacy, and he could work numerical problems with decent speed, given oral directions and allowed to use the colorful chips, sticks, and teddy bears. Learning the names of the numbers and reading actual words still escaped Phil's grasp, but he loved Mrs. Ramsey and worked diligently at the tasks she presented.

Phil's favorite game was the set of flashcards she'd made just for him. The first in the stack was the numerical word one. Mrs. Ramsey had cut out brown felt in the shape of a gun that fit around the letters. Two had zoo animals, a tiger and a zebra cut from colorful fabric, their heads sticking out around the shapes of the letters. Three was a bending knee with a real band-aid applied to it There was a card for all numbers one through twelve. Phil's favorite was nine, the stick part painted to look like bark and a tiny pinecone glued inside the circle. He liked to look at the cards, feel their textures, recite the words in his head.

Phil didn't see things the way other people did. Years later, he'd learn the term dyslexia and find that many successful people shared the same problem, but no one thought to explain this to a little boy. Mrs. Ramsey encouraged him to touch things, imagine shapes, memorize words that rhyme or other "little helpers" as she called them, and her wise words helped Phil to compensate for the rest of his academic career. Other tutors would come and go, but it was only Mrs. Ramsey who helped.

Phil's parents discussed his problem, but only with one another and usually late at night.

"Poor stock, your family," his father would say. "Should have recognized it before I married you. A blind uncle, that cousin with the hair lip, and the women—a bunch of beautiful idiots who turn into brood sows after a child or two."

"I'm so sorry," his mother would cry.

Though Phil was two walls away, he'd know his mother was crossing her arms over her midriff, an attempt to hide what she called the "fat" that accumulated after three children. Phil's mother was no bigger than his teenaged sisters, but she wore oversized clothes and had been on a diet as long as he could remember. Phil thought his mother was more frightened of becoming fat than of snakes or frogs or any of the things other girls and women feared.

"But Mrs. Ramsey says he's getting better—" she said.

"Mrs. Ramsey will keep saying he's getting better as long as she's getting a paycheck. She needs to be teaching the boy to work, not playing games with him. You'd think the head of a college education department could recommend better, especially with what we're willing to pay."

How could he say those things about Mrs. Ramsey? She was such a nice lady.

"She seems to understand a lot about his problems, and he absolutely loves her," Phil's mother said. "She does ask a lot of questions, though. Why do you suppose she wanted to know how old I was when he was born?"

Phil's father sighed. "Good God, Vivian, don't you know anything? She's saying you were too old to be having another child. It's a wonder he's not a Mongoloid. Then again, I guess he might as well be." Phil heard his mother sob. Maybe the thought of getting old frightened her as much as getting fat.

The fights went on for three years, his mother saying less and crying more as time progressed. Then they stopped. Just weeks before the end of his second grade year, Phil's parents presented him with a huge surprise.

"Hurry and get dressed for dinner, " his mother had said. "Thelma's made all your favorites, and your father and I have something really important to tell you."

Phil wondered what it could be. Was he getting a new brother or sister? No, that news would be for everyone, not just him. Was he going to another summer camp? He hoped not, the one last summer had been awful. No hiking, no horses, nothing fun, but special reading and math activities for eight hours per day. *What else could it be? Was Mrs. Ramsey coming back?* Phil hated Mr. Lord, the stuffy tutor who'd replaced Mrs. Ramsey last fall. Mr. Lord smelled like mothballs and constantly blew his nose into yellowed handkerchiefs.

"Well, son, how do you like your special feast?" his father asked at the dinner table. His adam's apple protruded like an extra elbow peeking out from his starched collar and loosened tie.

Phil glanced down at his meatloaf, mashed potatoes, and green beans, then about the table at his family. His father's plate could have been a picture in a restaurant menu: steaming, perfect proportions in a colorful array. His sisters had small helpings of meat and bread with nothing else. His mother's plate had a spoonful or less of meat and beans, filling less than a third of her plate. Phil's plate looked like a mini-version of his father's, but he wasn't hungry and the thought of having to eat it all made his stomach churn.

Who thought this was his favorite meal? He liked meatloaf and potatoes, but only in the kitchen when it was just him and Thelma, who gave him butter from the refrigerator and let him keep the ketchup bottle to use as much as he wanted. He'd never liked green beans. And why did he need a special meal, anyway?

"Phillip?" his father asked. "I asked you a question."

Phil swallowed. "It's good, I guess. I mean, thank you, sir." He hoped that was what his father wanted.

"And I guess you're wondering what special occasion this precedes?" he asked.

"Yes, sir," Phil answered.

Phil's sisters grinned at each other and giggled. This was nothing new. If they noticed him at all, they were laughing or complaining, usually at Phil's expense.

"What?" Phil asked, wondering if they could let him get in on the joke.

"They're shipping you off," Laura said matter-of-factly. She rolled her eyes and mimicked the word "finally." Her sister responded with the flip of a pigtail and a thumbs-up sign.

"For the rest of your life," Fran said, raising her eyebrow and smiling.

"That'll be enough, girls," their mother said. She twisted a strand of hair and looked at her husband.

"Your sisters are jealous, son," said Phil's father, giving the girls a stern look. "You're about to embark on a wonderful journey, the chance of a lifetime. You see, son, you've just been accepted at The King's Academy."

The King's Academy? What was the King's Academy? Phil imagined the sound of royal trumpets, a regal entrance with flags and a red carpet, knights on horses outside the gate. But he knew such places only existed in movies and storybooks. And even if they did exist, why would they want him? Phil's insides did flippy-things, like just before a dentist visit or riding a roller coaster.

"The King's Academy is an exclusive educational facility in the mountains of Tennessee. They have a strong curriculum and students from all over the world. Imagine the friends you'll make, the fun you'll have—what a lucky boy you are!" his father said, cutting a large morsel of meat, forking it, then holding it up as if to inspect it.

"But if it's in Tennessee, how long will it take to get there every day?" Phil asked. His sisters snickered, making retarded faces and pretending to drool. When their father cleared his throat, they immediately stopped and sat up straight.

"You won't be going there every day, son. The school is four hundred miles away—that's a good six/seven hour drive. You'll be living there. It's a boarding school. You'll live in a dormitory, like college boys do. Your sisters are green with envy. Older than you, but they still having to live at home with their parents, while you're a man on your own, hours away. You are one lucky, lucky, boy!"

Phil looked at his sisters: They didn't look green to him, and they didn't seem jealous. They did, however, seem to think the whole situation was funny. Laura was pretending to pick her nose, and Fran was doing the kid-version sign language for "crazy." Suddenly Phil wanted more than anything to simply play with his sisters.

"But what about—" Phil knew he didn't want to go to any King's Academy. He wanted to stay home but knew better than to say such a thing outright. His father thought this King stuff was like some great gift, and Phil didn't want to seem ungrateful. He needed a—what did they call it in golf? A strategy. Phil stifled a smile as he launched his amazing plan. "What about my riding lessons and golf and tennis and swimming in the summer, and what about—"

"You'll have all those opportunities and more," his father said. "The school's been established since the 1800's, nestled in the heart of the Smoky Mountains." Phil thought his father sounded like a museum guide, like it was someplace *his dad* wanted to go. "You'll have riding classes, then rafting and hiking as well. In the winter there's ice skating, something you'd never learn here, and the school has a strong athletic program, too."

"The campus is amazing," Phil's mother offered. "Some of the buildings are like the castles in movies." Phil had a sudden image of his beautiful mother dressed as a queen. Then he wondered when she had seen these "castles," and why everyone seemed to know about this King's place but him.

"We'll go shopping this weekend, get you some new clothes, and some things for your dorm room," his mother said. She sounded excited.

"No fair," said Laura. Now his sister did sound jealous. "*We* haven't been shopping in ages," she said. "And I need new swimsuits and shorts for the summer."

"Me, too," said Fran. Then her voice went all whiny. "And don't say I can have Laura's old ones. It's not fair. I never get as many new clothes as Laura, and no one even cares."

"Enough, girls," said their father. "Phillip will be leaving soon, his needs must come first. And if you can't rejoice with your brother's good news, you two young ladies can be excused for the night. Upstairs with both of you."

"Why am I leaving soon? School doesn't start until September. Take Laura and Fran shopping first, I don't care," said Phil.

"School begins in September, but you're leaving in two weeks for Kamp Kingspiration, a summer long program held on campus," his father said. "You can explore all the activities they have to offer, then decide what you like best for the fall. There'll be tutors available, to help you catch up in any area where you're behind. Before school starts. It's an amazing opportunity."

A lump of mashed potatoes sat in Phil's throat like a huge ball of wet cotton. He couldn't swallow it down or bring it up. Trying to wash it down with a swallow of milk, Phil choked, coughing rampantly, discharging milk from his nose and lumps of potato from his mouth.

Phil's mother rushed to his side.

"Careful, honey," she said, wiping his mouth with her napkin and patting his back. "You'll need to learn not to eat so fast. Things like this can be really embarrassing around people who aren't your family."

"My God, get him out of here," exclaimed Phil's father. He threw his linen napkin into his plate and stood up. "Never mind, I've lost my appetite anyway. Maybe they can make him grow up, without you to mollycoddle him all day long. And teach him some damned table manners." Phil's father stormed into the family room. Phil heard ice clinking into a glass. His mother gave him a slight hug.

"You'll love your new school, and the people there will love you," she said. She smelled like the flowery lotion she kept on her dresser. "Time for bed now," she dismissed him with a peck on his head.

Surprisingly, Phil loved The King's Academy from his first day onward. The campus was beautiful and his mother was right, it did look like King Arthur could be around any corner. The teachers were strict about no bullying, and there was no academic stuff during the summer. All students attended chapel every day: There were lots of memory verses to learn, but it was done by rote and Phil had no problems. The Fosters had not been big church-goers. Phil's mother was Methodist but practiced at being a twice-a-year Presbyterian with Mr. Foster. Phil became enthralled by the simple parables and soothing songs he learned in chapel.

"Even when we are bad, God loves us and is waiting for us to ask His forgiveness and come home," Brother Ron said. "Let's pray."

A room full of ten-year-old heads bowed, most of them closing their eyes. Phil loved chapel. The kind lilt of Brother Ron's voice made him feel warm and safe. At the sound of "Amen," the little heads popped up, all eyes on Brother Ron.

"Have you ever been a bad boy or girl? How did you know when you were being bad? Did your parents punish you?" Heads nodded, some smiled at each other. Punishment was fun to think about, as long as you weren't the one being punished.

"Jesus told a parable of a bad boy. It's recorded in the Bible in the book of Luke. Do any of you know that story?" A few kids nodded as if they did, but no one raised a hand.

"A man had two sons. The younger son wanted his father to give him his share of the inheritance."

Phil's father only had one son, Phil. Phil had two sisters, but it seemed that sons were more important, and because Phil wasn't a very good son, it caused Phil's father a lot of worry. He used that word "inheritance" sometimes when he complained about Phil to his mother.

Phil had stopped listening, lost in his own thoughts. He willed himself to focus again.

"...he journeyed to a far country and wasted his money," Brother Ron said. That's what Phil's father had said! That the tutors, special schools, and extra help for Phil was just wasting money. And though King's Academy wasn't in a far country, it was in another state.

"About the time he had spent all his money, none of the crops would grow in the land as a result of a mighty famine. The younger son had nothing to eat, so he went to work as a hired servant. He had a very lowly job, feeding pigs."

Phil had never had a job, but he would get one if his family needed it. Feeding pigs didn't sound like such a bad job. Wouldn't the pigs *like* the person who fed them? It might be fun having a lot of big, muddy pets.

"He barely made enough money to eat," Brother Ron said. "He made up his mind that he would return home and beg the forgiveness of his father, hoping to be taken back as only a hired servant. But as he returned, his father ran out to meet him and hugged him."

Phil pictured it all in his head. He'd run to his dad, everything in slow motion, his father's voice pleading like the kid who cried, "Come back, Shane" in Phil's favorite movie.

"And the son said unto him," explained Brother Ron. "Father, I have sinned and am no more worthy to be called thy son."

Phil's eyes burned as he blinked back tears. Phil couldn't read and write like other people, and that's why he was a bad son. He would never be able to help with his father's work: His father needed a smart son.

"But his father," Brother Ron said, "upon hearing these words, restored his son to his estate. He gave him the best robe, a ring signifying his authority as a son, and new shoes on his feet. Then they prepared a feast and had a big party."

Phil didn't need a robe or a ring or any new shoes. He didn't care about the feast or the party. He just wanted to be smart, smart enough for his father to—

"For this my son was dead, and is alive again, he was lost and is found!" Brother Ron used a different voice, deeper and wiser, to show the voice of the father. He stopped for a minute, giving them time to think about what he'd said.

Finally, he spoke. "This story is called the Prodigal Son. I think a better title would be "Our Loving Father" because the outcome of everything in the story depends on how the father reacts to his wayward son. The father could have refused to even see his son again after he squandered his living. Upon his return, the father could have hired him back as a servant for the rest of his life to teach him a lesson. Instead, we see a loving father that waits for his son to come to his senses, realize his mistake, and return home. We have all sinned, or been disobedient to God, but our God is a forgiving God. If you have faith as a mustard seed, nothing will be impossible to you. Let us pray again."

This time a few kids kept their heads up, and a few more were asleep. But Phillip Twitty Foster IV prayed with hope and fervor the young boy had never known. He had faith. He believed. God would fix him. He would learn to read and write. He'd have to work harder, but he could do it, nothing was impossible because he had faith. He'd become smarter and his dad would forgive him and want him to come home.

Phil walked out of chapel a different boy. He stood taller, had a quicker smile, and met the eyes of those who walked by him. He went into the classroom eager to learn, and though he still struggled, his new self-image allowed him to relax and use the coping skills he'd been taught. Phil began to learn, and he gave God all the credit.

Phil remained at The King's Academy for six years, going home only for Christmas and winning colorful ribbons in horseback riding, rafting, and ice-skating while at school. He became a Junior Counselor for Kamp Kingspiration his last two years, his most rewarding and fulfilling experience. Phil wondered if this was God's way of showing him a vocation, and had dreams of becoming some sort of youth counselor or minister when he grew up.

Many King's Academy families attended special activities throughout the year, some religious occasions, others simply labeled as "parent weekends." Phil's father dropped him off in September as necessary, and no other family member saw him until the next Christmas. Concerned about Phil's family life, his religious studies teacher sent a special invitation for the Easter Pageant.

Dear Mr. and Mrs. Foster,

Your son, Phillip, has been a joy to the King's family for six years. Although his academic achievements are not up to national standards, his work ethic, dedication to improving, and willingness to help others make him a fine example of the Savior's command to "let your light shine." Recently admitting that he is considering a career in the clergy, we felt moved to share this wonderful news with you.

Phillip has been chosen to portray the role of Christ in our upcoming Passion Play, held each night during Easter Week. We would be honored for you and your family to share this blessed occasion with us.

In Christ,
Rev. Ronald Edwards

Phil's family did not share the blessed occasion; in fact, Phil was not allowed to participate in the play. Phil's father found a "more academic" school for him in north Georgia, and Phil transferred the last week of March, before Easter.

The Darlington School, established in 1905, was bigger than King's and housed rich kids from six continents and forty-seven countries. There were crystal-looking springs and brooks running between hundred-year-old oaks, with the Blue Ridge mountains to the east and the quaint little city of Rome, Georgia to the west. The dorms resembled castles, but the classroom buildings were new and state-of-the-art. The school cafeteria was divided into three sections; a burger grill that also featured steaks and chicken, an Italian eatery, and an ethnic restaurant, offering the foods of a different country each night of the week. Students wore uniforms to class and expensive designer clothing the rest of the time. They were the most hateful, spoiled, and intimidating young teens Phil could ever imagine.

Phil did not enjoy his time at Darlington, and when his self-esteem disappeared, so did the academic progress he'd accomplished. He'd failed his father again, and he still wanted to redeem himself, but the prospect seemed like climbing Mount Everest. Still, Phil thought he could handle it. It would only be a few years. He'd figure things out and adjust. He always did.

The new school year had barely begun when Phil received a surprise visit from his father. Meeting him at the admissions office, Mr. Foster greeted him with a handshake.

"Good to see you, son," he said, lightly patting his back. "Could we go for a walk?"

"Sure," Phil answered.

They walked past the science building, the cafeteria, between the first sets of dorms. Leaves began to fall, and the air was crisp and cool. Phil's father motioned to a picnic table, and the two sat down.

"Son, your mother is the reason I came here today. There is something I have to tell you," he began.

"Is she here too? Can I see her?" Phil was excited. This could actually be a *good* surprise. His father said nothing.

"Are we going on a trip, like a vacation? When can I—" Phil continued.

"No, son, she isn't here and we aren't going anywhere. I came here to tell you—" his father stalled. "Phillip, your mother died this week."

Phil was quiet for a moment, staring blankly while digesting what he had heard. "She died? No, wait, she wasn't even sick," he said. "She didn't die, you would have sent for me if something was wrong, she would have needed me." Saying the words, Phil realized how silly he sounded. His mother wouldn't have needed him. She hadn't needed him for the last eight years.

"No, son, she wasn't sick. She had a heart attack. It was sudden and final. She didn't suffer."

"When?"

"Late last Sunday."

"But today is Friday. Why—"

"I had my hands full with your sisters, your mother's people, the funeral arrangements. I didn't want you to receive the news from strangers, so I waited until I could come here to tell you."

"But—she's been dead, all week, and I didn't know? You couldn't call me? Laura and Fran, why didn't they call me? You let me stay here all week, at this dumb school, going to my stupid classes, going to chapel in the morning and the tutor every afternoon, while I don't even know that I don't have a mother any more?" Phil screamed, jumping up from the table.

"Keep your voice down," his father reprimanded, pushing him back onto the bench. "Control yourself, you don't want to cause a scene, nor do you want other boys seeing you cry. You could make it very hard for yourself later."

"My mother is dead. I don't care who hears me, I don't care!"

Mr. Foster stood in front of his son, blocking him from any onlookers. He took a handkerchief from his pocket and roughly wiped Phil's face. "Be a man, son, it's time to be a man. Your mother's greatest hope was that you would get your reading straightened out and come back to school in Albany. You can still do that, but you'll have to work. Think about that, son, think about what your mother would've wanted. Can you do it for her?"

"Then why didn't I come back to Albany before instead of to this crappy school? Why am I still here?"

"We didn't think you were ready—yet."

Phil choked on his snot and nodded, agreeing just for show. Phil never wanted to see Albany, Georgia again.

"Get your grades up, study hard, and maybe we can get you home for Christmas."

Phil nodded, thinking *why now?* Christmas was a dead word. A fairy tale. Like Bible stories.

Mr. Foster grabbed Phil in a quick and awkward embrace and shook his hand. Then he brushed off his suit, as if touching his son had been contaminating.

"Time to go back to class, Phillip. I've got an important meeting in Atlanta tomorrow, I need to get on the road."

Phil walked back towards his classroom building, only to round the corner and disappear into the nearby woods as soon as his father was out of sight. That was the last time they spoke of his mother.

Phil stayed at Darlington throughout high school. With special classes and mandatory tutoring, he put in enough effort to earn a high school diploma, but Phil knew it was a farce. The classes helped him memorize things, and the tutors did a lot of the outside work for him. That's what his parents had paid for. Phil could still read only the simplest books without stopping and regrouping the words. He'd learned compensatory skills to deal with his disability, but the tools were lengthy to execute. He forgot most material before he finished reading it, and he'd lost the will to even care.

On graduation day, only his sisters attended. When he asked about their father, they seemed offended. "Good God, Phil. He bought a new *building* here so they'd let you graduate. What more do you expect?" asked Laura.

Phil shuffled along the path towards his dorm. Darlington was beautiful, and it looked more like Shakespeare's England than like a carpet mill town in the South. But Phil wouldn't miss the place. He wondered what he was supposed to do for the rest of the summer. No one seemed to expect him at home, but he was officially out of high school. Could he stay here? *Maybe since my dad bought that building*, Phil thought.

Phil had been accepted at the University of Georgia for the fall semester. He wondered if his father bought a building there, too.

College life at the University of Georgia had been strictly party time for Phil. He joined his father's fraternity, Sigma Nu, an on-campus social club filled with other spoiled, rich kids, and every day was a blast. He attended a few classes in his first quarter, but by the end of the year he seldom showed up at all. It seemed that he'd finally found a venue where his clothes, car, and spending money were enough, and life was good.

Phil and his fraternity brothers had plenty of female companion-ship, usually girls who'd hang out in the frat house for the free beer or ones they'd meet up with on the tracks, a section of railroad adjacent to the stadium, popular with the heavy drinkers on game nights. But in May of '58, a great many of the Sigma keg kings found themselves escorting gorgeous sisters of Alpha Omicron Pi to the UGA Spring Mixer, a formal affair requiring tuxedos and corsages.

The Sigmas weren't big on official college functions, but this was a master plan. In exchange for their duties as escorts, these stacked but somewhat conservative beauties would accompany their dates to the fraternity's Wild Water Weekend, a nonstop beach party held on St. Simons Island. The Alphas had their own hotel rooms, paid for by the fraternity, of course.

Phil and his buddies washed and waxed their cars, shook the mothballs from their spiffy formalwear, and made sure they knew the exact shades of their ladies' dresses. They sipped real liquor from discreet flasks and kept their buzz to a minimum, far less than a typi-cal school night. The Monarchs, a six-piece combo from Memphis, played, and the Sigmas showed their dates a relentless time on the dance floor.

"Mind your manners, Phil, my boy," said Kent, Sigma Nu presi-dent and resident ladies' man. "Watch the knockers bounce when she jitterbugs, lean into those bare shoulders and smell her perfume. If your hand brushes her ass when you slow dance, make sure she doesn't know it was on purpose. Cha cha with her like a faggot on cruise ship, but nothing more than a nice kiss when you take her back to the house. Perfect gentlemen, we are."

"Okay," Phil said.

"Then the next two nights we'll fuck their eyes out!" Kent laughed, slapped Phil on the back, then squeezed him in a brotherly hug.

Phil and the rest of the guys followed Kent's instructions perfectly.

Sunday morning was a bad dream. Only asleep for a few hours, the Sigmas awakened to police bullhorns outside, telling them all to come out, other officers pounding on individual doors. A girl screamed, a boy passed out, and several of the crew had to be shaken before waking up. The fifty reserved rooms were emptied, forty-six of which held one or more male-female unmarried couples. Several remaining gallons of liquor were confiscated, and an estimated $1,400 in damages were owed to the renowned King and Prince Hotel.

The girls left crying and hiding their faces, running to the arms of irate parents. Several were bruised but more ashamed and embarrassed than hurt. Two young ladies were taken to the ER to have their stomachs pumped, and one was treated on site for hyperventilation. Forty-three Sigma Nu brothers were escorted to the Glynn County Jail. After parents posted bail on Monday, a motley group returned to the Sig house late that afternoon. Awaiting their entrance were the Dean of Student Affairs, Chancellor of the Greek Council, and the President of the College.

Through the years, Phil tried his best to forget that painful alliance and the consequences it brought, but it still came back, decades later when he saw a showing of *Animal House* on late night television. Seeing practically the same experience happen to John Belushi, Phil threw up again then, too, wondering how the average American could view this flick as a comedy.

Phil and the rest of his new friends were sent packing. For once, Phil's father didn't seem that disappointed; it was like he'd expected it all along. He had a speech and a life planned for Phil, and it was mapped out and ready for execution the morning Delores first saw Phil at the factory entrance.

"Well, son, you've had your vacation," his father said. "I knew you didn't have enough sense to last, so I hope you enjoyed yourself. It's time to go to work."

"Whatever. Where am I working, Dad?" They sat in the office, door closed and piped-in music just barely loud enough to be audible. Phil breathed in the lemony scent of furniture polish, feeling both confined and out of place. His father had businesses all over the state, but Phil couldn't imagine a job he was qualified to do.

"About the only thing you're fit for, son. You like to drive don't you?"

"Yes, sir."

"Starting today, you will be delivering the payroll checks to all six of our businesses. Because it's the smallest and quietest place, I print them here at Nolan Manufacturing. In Dumas County are the factory and the farm, then we have the mills in Forsyth and Columbus, with two more in Albany."

"I just ride around and take people their checks?" It seemed easy enough.

"No, son, there's more to it than that. You take them in, follow the ledger you'll keep with you. Mark off every check you issue, and the manager in each office will verify the same in their own ledgers. If anything comes up missing, you will cover it or be fired."

"But I don't have any money. How can I cover people's mistakes if—"

"That's the point, son, don't make any mistakes. This is serious business."

"Yes, sir."

"This afternoon, we'll go over the routes. Payroll goes out every two weeks. You'll collect here on Monday and go to Columbus. Back here on Tuesday, then to Forsyth. Wednesday you come here, then the Albany mills. Thursdays you'll come here, then go out to the farm."

"But you said every other week. What'll I do on Friday, and then the rest of the next week?"

"The second week you'll stay at the farm."

"But, why—"

"Because I said so, son. Hard work will do you good."

"And Fridays?" Phil didn't like the sound of this.

"Every other Friday and the following weekend you'll spend at the farm, where I have a number of projects for you."

Every other weekend!

"And you may spend one weekend per month doing what you want to do, within reason."

Phil was speechless. The last nine months had been fun, the happiest he'd felt since the early days of King's Academy.

"Your first farm weekend starts today," his father said. "Shall we adjourn to the farm?" It was more a command than a question. He stood, took his coat from the back of his chair, and ushered his son outside. The tour of Phil's new prison was about to begin.

The farm was just a damned farm, so it seemed to Phil. There were fields of cotton. Fields of corn. Fields of peanuts, and fields of something else he didn't recognize. There were barns where equipment was stored, and a few old colored men plus a few young, dirty white men that drove tractors and "did stuff" to the various crops.

Whatever they do to crops. What the hell is my part in this? What a waste of time. Then the picture became crystal clear.

"Since driving is the thing you do best, and you definitely need to learn some kind of a skill you can use, I figure this is the best place for you," his father said. "During the week, you will drive your car, the one that was supposed to last through college, and deliver payroll. But every other week you will work here, learning farm labor. You can sleep in our lodge at night, but every other waking minute you work for these men. Whatever they say, you do."

Phil knew he'd pay for his sins, but this was beyond belief.

"These men, you mean, these white trash and old colored men? I work for them? Are you insane? You wouldn't tell Laura or Fran to work for Thelma, cleaning toilets and mopping floors! I can't work for these men. They're, they're countrified, and stupid, and uneducated. I can't do this, it's disgusting."

"These men wear the dirt with the sweat of their brows," Phil's father said, running a liver-spotted hand over his own brow, his voice becoming gentle. Phil heard an air of respectfulness in his father's tone that he'd never used when speaking of the factory workers.

"There is nothing disgusting about an honest day's work. You can't judge a man's intellect on his outward appearance. These men might surprise you."

The whole lecture was making him retch. Then his father laid a hand on his shoulder; his tired, steely-gray eyes looked directly into Phil's. "And unfortunately, son, as far as being uneducated, so are you."

That was about it for explanations. He introduced Phil to the workers; Phil couldn't believe his father knew all their names. Walking out to the barn with Calvin, the most vocal of the filthy men, Phil listened as he explained the difference in insecticides and herbicides and some other "'cides." Phil figured the guy was wasting his breath; there was simply no way he would be doing this stuff.

Phil looked up, and his father's car was pulling out of the driveway, then back on the main road. *He's left me!* Out in the middle of nowhere, with Calvin, Buford, Ezekial, and some other geezer Bible name.

"Okay, it's time to get back to the fields," Calvin said. "I'm on the Allis-Chalmers, but you can follow me on the little Oliver."

Phil's face must have given away his incoherence, so Calvin added, "They're tractors. Two different brands of farming tractors. You know, like a Ford and a Chevy, or in your case, a Lincoln and a Cadillac. Get it?"

Phil managed to crank the damned tractor, and he pretty much did whatever Calvin did the rest of the day. It seemed that once Phil caught on, Calvin left him alone. They worked until it was dark. Phil had never been as tired, or as dirty. The men left for wherever they went. Phil stayed in the lodge. Alone. Stranded.

What a hell of a bad day. The bitchy women at the factory entrance. His new job. Now this. He took a shower, fell across the couch, and beat its weathered surface with his fists. As soon as he closed his eyes, it was morning.

Time to do it all over again.

Chapter 5
1953

Calvin

FROM HIS PERCH ON THE TRACTOR, CAL SAW MR. DANner's car pull into the driveway. Being at the far end of the plowing row, he knew it would be twenty minutes before he reached the other end, nearest the house, and he hoped the county extension agent would hang around long enough for him to reach there.

When he climbed off the tractor, the sun was beginning to soften with the faintest hint of a mid-afternoon breeze. The rich smell of green peanut plants in the freshly turned soil filled his lungs and gave him hope of a good harvest. He stopped at the backyard spigot and cupped his hands for a quick drink and to splash some of the grime off. The cool water mixed with earth and sweat. He ducked to wipe his face against his shirtsleeve, shook his head and ambled around the side of the house.

In an ancient rocker on the wide, sagging porch of the Mullinax farmhouse sat Cal's mother. She shelled butterbeans and threw the hulls in a paper sack.

"Good to see ya, son." The ancient chain of the porch swing groaned as T.W. Danner stood to shake Cal's hand. He wore his standard "uniform," a short-sleeved plaid shirt and khaki pants. Cal shook his mentor's hand, glad his own lack of hygiene wouldn't be considered offensive, just a sign of a farmer's livelihood.

Mr. Danner patted Cal on the back and returned to his seat. Cal sat in the other rocker, seldom used in the two years since his father had passed. "Almost halfway through," Cal said. "The Hortons are supposed to finish up with their crop Saturday, and they're bringing their picker soon as they're done."

"Just hope the rain holds out til then." His mother wiped her hands on the faded apron covering her thin floral housedress.

"The reports say the atmospheric conditions are on our side," Mr. Danner said. "But we all know how far we can trust the weatherman." They laughed at the lifelong joke. "Nonetheless," continued Mr. Danner, "Cal looks to be doing an excellent job with your crop this year. Your daddy would be mighty proud, son."

"Thank the Lord, if he keeps up like he's been doing, we just might be able to hold onto these eighty acres, after all," his mother said. "He's done right good for a boy that ain't even got a driver's license yet."

"Three more months, and I will." Cal grinned. "December 1st comes on a Tuesday, and it's first Tuesdays that the state patrol comes to give driving tests. I can go up to the courthouse right after school."

"Better be studyin' up, I reckon," his mother said with a smile.

Mr. Danner chuckled. "That's right. Driving a car down Main Street in Nolan may be a little different from operating tractors, combines, threshers and peanut pickers."

"And how 'bout that Grand Champion pig Cal turned out this year?" Mr. Danner asked. "The finest in three counties. Makes me kinda glad I only raise cattle, don't know if I could handle the competition here."

"I was real proud of him," his mother said. "Even if I did get tired a that pig rootin' out of his pen ever chance he got. And the money, from the contest and from sellin' the hog, couldn't a come at a better time. Got the tractor fixed in time to harvest, without having to borry any more. And Cal got to go to camp, after all."

"Where he won even more awards," Mr. Danner said. "You need to keep up with your 4-H, Cal. Ag colleges are quite fond of boys who excel in 4-H and FFA."

Cal beamed. His mother stared blankly into the bag of hulls. "Delores likes the 4-H, too," she said, "and swears next year she'll be going to Rock Eagle with y'all."

"I hope so," said Mr. Danner. "She's a precious little girl, or should I say young lady? They grow up so fast, these days."

"Don't I know it," she said. "Having to let her hems out every few months, it seems."

"I better get back to the field." Cal stood. "It won't plow itself."

Mr. Danner stood with him. "I'd like to step out and take a look at what you've plowed up. Check out the competition, so to speak."

Mr. Danner had a peanut allotment of a hundred acres or more, with cotton and corn as well. "Sure, Mr. Danner. Come on out," Cal said.

"It was good talking to you, Mr. Danner," Cal's mother called. "Come back to see us."

"And likewise to you, ma'am," he said as he followed Cal around the corner.

Seeing Mr. Danner was always a treat for Cal. In many ways, the man was nothing like Cal's father, a working class, uneducated dirt farmer simply keeping up the small family farm the same as his own father and grandfather before him, yet each visit from the local extension agent made Cal feel a little closer to the man he missed so much. *Guess it's their love of the land,* Cal thought, *or how they both understood the simple pleasure of watching things grow and feeling like you're a part of what made it happen.* Whatever the reason, Cal looked forward to Mr. Danner's visits, and a compliment from him was like a loving pat on the shoulder from his daddy, or the closest he'd have to that, from now on.

Working the farm was Cal's greatest joy, but becoming its sole caretaker, manager, and laborer had been a huge and frightening undertaking. His father's sudden death had happened in early harvesting season, just days after he'd overheard the only serious parental argument he'd ever known of. Even years later, just remembering those harsh tones and cruel accusations made his face flush as he ground his teeth.

"You mortgaged the *house,* too? For now on twenty years I've lived through this borryin' from Peter to pay Paul ever spring, seeing you sign over seventy-nine acres that you've more or less just give away if there comes a bad drought, a flood, a plague of some new crop-eatin' varmit or some other act of God. But heaven forbid, come fall, it all works out, though some years better than others. You pay it back in the fall, and in good years, there's a little something for the rest of us, too. And though I grew up in a family that always said if you need to borry to get it, then you don't *need* it—"

"Now, baby, I done told you, every *year* I tell you, that's how farming operates, been that way my whole life and my daddy's before me and—"

"I know, I know, and through the years, I've got where I accept it. Don't like it, but just know that's the way it's gotta be. You're a good man, Hershel, and a good provider for me and the younguns—"

"Mary Pearl, I told you from the start it was a hard life, but you've always had food on the table and a roof over your head. And—"

"That's what the hell I'm talking about!" she screamed. Calvin had never heard his mother curse, or scream at his father. He'd heard both profanity and yelling in plenty of other places, but this was an evil, foreign sound in the little wooden farmhouse he knew as home. Standing silently in the hallway outside his parents' door, Cal felt a cramp in his stomach and wondered if he should go to the bathroom, but he couldn't. His feet were cemented to the floor, forcing him to remain statue-still and find out the origin of this unwanted intruder filling the atmosphere.

"Why the damned house, Hershel, why?" his mother continued. "For nineteen years the farm has been enough. I've always worried about losing the farm, but I got to where I could live with it. After all, if we lost the farm, you could just get a job—a normal job, with a steady paycheck and benefits. Like other people. Start to put some money back, so maybe the children could go on to school, do better than what they came from. We could—"

"What the hell do you mean, woman, 'do better than what they come from'?" Cal's daddy was raising his voice as well. And the way he'd said "woman" sounded worse than cursing. For no reason he could understand, Cal fought back an urge to cry.

"So that's how you really feel, do you?" his father asked. "So all along you've been hoping we'd lose the farm, so I could get a real job, with no dirt on my hands, like the one your mama wanted you to marry? Fine time to tell me. So—you done anything else to help it along—putting poison in my fertilizer or pouring out insecticide and putting in water? What else, Mary Pearl? What else have you done to make sure I go down in flames?"

They weren't making any sense. Cal knew his mother would never do anything to sabotage the farm, and he knew his dad knew it, too. But he could imagine how hurt Daddy was, just hearing her say that she'd thought about losing the farm without being upset about it. It hurt him, too. The farm was their life, the farm was like another member of the family, a big, all-encompassing one who held them all together, from the great-grandparents he'd never known to the children and grandchildren he and Delores would bring there someday. A family that lasted, like history, continuing chapters of the never-ending book that was the farm. How could she not know that? Calvin had always assumed that they all felt that way, and to even think that it might not be so was way more than frightening.

"I haven't done anything like that, Hershel, and you know it," his mother said. "I have loved this farm since the first day you brought me here to meet your folks. I've loved it more each year, because you love it so, and because it's where our children were born and grew up, and it's where *we* came to be *us*. I've tried to help out in any way I could, whether it be canning vegetables or keeping you fed at daybreak or scrimping and saving through spring and summer or keeping the kids out of the way so you could work. I know you didn't want me to go to work at the factory, but having that little steady money between planting and harvesting has been good to keep us going without having to worry so much. We've made a good life here, Hershel, and I do love this farm."

"We take out a mortgage every year, Mary Pearl."

"I know. But never before with the house included as collateral. The possibility of taking away my babies' home is different from taking the farm. I know it's a slim possibility, but what would we do if they took the house? What would it do to our family? I'd sell myself as a damned whore if I had to, if it meant I could take care of my children."

They were quiet for a moment. The pain eased in Calvin's gut.

"I know that, baby," Cal's father said. "And I love you and the young'uns more than the farm, too, but it's a different kind of love. Loving y'all is like something I do for me—y'all are the best thing that ever happened to me, and I thank God every day for the blessing you are."

"So do I, Hershel, so do I," his mother said, sniffling in a loud, wet sound that reaffirmed Cal's knowledge of her tears. He heard the bedsprings squeak and pictured them sitting down on the edge of the bed, his father's arms wrapped around her as she lay her face against his white, sleeveless undershirt.

"To take care of my family is my responsibility, and one I do with joy. But times is hard—seed, fertilizer, herbicides—they's all went up since last year, and I had to have more money just to get by. They wouldn't go over my last year's loan limit without more collateral, and adding on the house was all I could do. It's just words, baby. Words on a piece of paper. They ain't never tried to take the farm, and they won't be taking the house, either. It's just words, legal stuff."

"I know," Cal's mother agreed, "but it scares me. What if they did take it?"

"They won't. And if it come to that, we'd sell a piece of the farm to keep the house. My granddaddy had to back in the Depression, and if it comes to that, I'll do the same. A man does what he has to do to take care of his family. You know I love you, Mary Pearl."

Calvin heard a murmur, but couldn't make out his mother's answer. His father spoke again.

"You know, in all these years, I've never quite got used to the fact that all this is mine—you and Cal and Delores. I don't know what I ever done to deserve anything so perfect. If anybody'd a-told me when I was Cal's age I'd have a family like ours, I'd a said they was making fun. Telling something out of a book or something. I never believed I'd ever have anything like this."

Despite being alone, Calvin was a little embarrassed. He could move his feet now, and knew he should go back to his room, but this was too good to miss. He'd endured the bad part, didn't he deserve a little reward for being scared out of his drawers just moments ago?

"But Hershel, you always knew you'd be here, running the farm, living on the home place. And a farmer needs a wife. And the act of having a wife usually brings on children. What's such a surprise about it?"

"I wasn't much of a lady killer as a boy—too busy working to learn much of the social graces, I guess. I figured if I did get me a wife, she'd be one of those stringy, hard women that plow a mule good as a man, but even the mule might look better than her in a nice dress."

His mother giggled. Cal heard the covers rustling as they both lay down.

"And I never dreamed I'd have a boy that could work as hard as me, topped off by a little girl as smart and pretty as her mama," his daddy said.

"Hershel," his mother's voice grew serious. "Do you ever think about—him?" Cal knew they were talking about their first child, a boy who came early and lived only a few hours.

"Now, baby," he said softly. "Of course I do, but I don't dwell on it. It was a long time ago, we were young, and it just wasn't meant to be. We don't question the Lord—and look what come two years later—there won't never be no better son than Calvin. I reckon the Lord didn't want little Hershel to feel threatened, so he took him on up to be with Him, and my folks, and yours, too. And we'll all be together again, one day. Watchin' ol Cal carry on the work we all had a little hand in."

The bedsprings were slowly squeaking again, and Cal moved lightly and quickly back to his room. He was sure he didn't want to be around for whatever came next. Strange that this was the only argument he could ever remember. And knowing the feeling it gave him to realize the farm was not viewed unanimously, he seldom revisited the memory.

On a hot September Tuesday, Cal stepped off the school bus, swallowed down some sweet tea and cornbread, and ran out to the field to relieve his dad on the tractor. Standing at the gate, he heard the faint churn of the old diesel engine, their Allis Chalmers WD, a good little machine who had seen better days. Calvin trotted forward squinting into the full sun and following his ears. In only a few seconds he saw the tractor, in the top of the row and sitting still in the far north corner. He picked up speed into a quick jog; Daddy was probably adjusting the row widths for the PTO and plow, and could use some help.

Hershel Mullinax was known for using every square inch possible for cultivation. Cal knew the north corner, planted in peanuts this year, was the field's most difficult point to navigate. The rows were shorter, barely long enough to allow the tractor to turn around. Since the less-than-two-acre plot would call for slower, special attention anyway, Hershel decided to make the task more profitable by changing these short rows to be closer together, allowing more plants from a smaller area. Before working this section, Hershel would have to stop, reset the power shift rear wheels closer to the tractor, then adjust the row width of the plow.

The tractor's 30 horsepower allowed it to pull three plows, but only one could make it through the narrow plot, so the other two used in the larger part of the field had to be removed and set aside. The power shift worked by engaging spiral rails on the axel and was wonderful in its first decade, but time had taken its toll, and Hershel had "Hawkins-rigged" it in every way possible just to keep it going another season. The north corner was usually saved until the last part of the day to work, since it generally wore a man out.

A few hundred yards away, Cal could not see his father, but was not overly concerned. His daddy could be on the other side of the tractor or too low to the ground, working with the PTO, to be seen from a distance. He could be standing behind a bush relieving himself. To a farmer, there was no bathroom like the great outdoors.

Arriving at the tractor, Calvin did see his father, stretched across the ground, completely still. His eyes were closed, making him look peaceful and asleep, but Cal knew this could never be. Hershel Mullinax would never have taken a nap and left the tractor running.

Calvin stood frozen in the blazing sun, looking down on the man he loved with all his being. Health and safety rules he'd learned at home and school sent him mixed signals. He knew not to move anyone who might have a broken neck, or suffered a concussion or other serious injury. But getting immediate care was of the utmost importance if the injured person hoped to survive. Somehow, Calvin understood that none of those things really mattered for his dad. He was also aware that as long as he stood there, looking down on his sleeping father, he could hold onto the day he woke up to that morning, and still be just a farm boy with two loving parents. When he reached down to touch the man, that boy's life would be over.

Calvin continued to stand as tears formed, fell, and dripped on the dry ground below. Then he kneeled and took his father's hand in his. The skin was warmed by the sun and slightly damp with the remnants of earlier sweat, but stiff and lifeless. Cal scooped up his father and cradled him in his arms, being careful to support his head, like that of a newborn. His tears fell freely as he rocked the lifeless form, already only a symbol of the man he mourned.

"I'll do it, Daddy, always," Cal cried. "I'll take care of the farm, as good as I know how, always. Like you did, and your daddy, and his did. I'll take care of Mama and Delores and one day there'll be another Little Hershel, my boy, or Delores's if she gets there first, maybe. I'll take care of our farm, you just watch me, you, and my brother, and all the folks before me. I'll do it 'til there's another boy to carry on, and we can watch him together." Cal's chest heaved as he let loose in rasping sobs, holding his father's face to his, bathing him with tears.

As the sun faded, Cal's mother came out to the field to check on them. Seeing them both on the ground, she ran full speed to meet them.

"What on earth, son, is he hurt—"

"He's gone, Mama. I don't think he felt any pain, but he was gone when I got out here." Lulled into numbness, seeing his mother brought it all back, and Calvin began crying again.

"His heart," she said. "His Papa went the same way. Just a few years older, I think." She sat, holding Cal as he held his father.

"You'll need to call—the ambulance? Or the coroner—I don't know, but I think some medical person has to—" Touching her husband's cheek, she sniffled and gasped. "I guess we should call the hospital and ask—"

"Go call 'em, Mama," Cal said. "I'll stay with Daddy."

"Cal, you've got to come inside. Why don't you go call and I'll stay—"

"No, Mama. I found him, I'm staying 'til they take him away. I ain't moving."

"But, son."

"No, Mama. You make the calls. You tell Delores. I'll stay here; there's no place we'd rather be together than out here."

She left him for their last day of harvesting together. They remained entwined until the coroner came.

Even before his father's death, Calvin Mullinax could have been a poster boy for a title such as "young working man of the south." Born poor but proud, he embraced his family and never shied away from long hours and hard work. He was driving the tractor on the family's small farm before he started school, excelling at hunting, fishing, and all things outdoors. Winning district, then state honors in 4-H and FFA, he seemed destined to make something of himself.

Calvin mourned his father's passing by throwing himself into farm work. The day after the funeral, he returned to the peanut field to finish what his father had started. As is the custom in the farming community, many neighboring farmers pitched in to help at no cost, expecting only future help from Cal in their own peak times of need. Calvin finished harvesting the crops, and his mother proclaimed he'd brought in their largest profit margin in several years. In addition to working the family farm, Cal also hired himself out as a seasoned farm laborer whenever possible. With his mother's encouragement, he had both his own bank account and vehicle before finishing high school.

Just a week after Delores' graduation, the bad cold Mary Pearl had nursed for months was diagnosed as lung cancer, and she died in the hospital before the end of July. Calvin was not only an orphan, but the sole provider for both the farm and his younger sister. Unbeknownst to her family, Mary Pearl Mullinax had used her husband's life insurance to hold onto the farm, still heavily mortgaged. With no insurance of any kind on herself, she left young Calvin with abundant bills and little collateral. Within six months of his mother's death, Cal watched as the South Georgia Farmers' Credit Union foreclosed on his fourth generation family farm.

Cal had just turned twenty-one, his sister barely eighteen. With no influx of renters for their ramshackle home, the bank allowed the two to remain there for several months. By then Cal worked three plus jobs; Tuesdays at the Camilla Livestock Auction, Saturdays at Shiver's Garage, and every other waking moment as an employee and sharecropper on Oakland Plantation.

Calvin once had bigger dreams. With Mr. Danner's help, he landed a scholarship at Abraham Baldwin Agricultural College in Tifton, but Cal's plans seemed to readjust with each downward spiral that life sent. At first he imagined graduating, coming home to the family farm, raising it to new heights and adding more land as finances permitted. Then college took a back burner to the closer reality of providing for the family and saving the farm. When this option died, fantasies of reclaiming it fueled his non-stop work ethic. By the time Cal and his sister were installed in an Oakland tenant house, his goal was still to make a living from the land, but residing in the same county seemed to be the only connection with his farming ancestry. Still, he persisted; Calvin Mullinax was an optimist.

"It ain't ours, but it's still good farmland," he told his sister. "It's the same kind of soil our daddy farmed, and his before him. And Oakland takes care of its own. We'll have a place to live, equipment and supplies, a steady paycheck, plus a percentage of the yield I make happen. It's not a bad life, no sir, it ain't."

Delores's eyes looked sadly disillusioned, and she continued to point out the fallacies in this new life he'd committed them to. "But Calvin, our farm is gone. This won't never be ours. Wouldn't you be happier just leaving, going to a bigger place with other jobs, factories and, I don't know, railroads, trucking companies, stores, businesses where you always know what you'll make, and might not have to get dirty?" Delores asked.

"Why in the hell would I wanna do that? I've wanted to grow things from the earth since the first time Daddy let me ride on the tractor with 'im."

"But what'll happen when there's another drought? Or a flood? Or when the government decides the peanut farmer don't need any more help?"

"You worry so much, Sis. You're just like Mama was," he said. "Farming is a way of life, a good life for a man who keeps up with the times and ain't afraid of a hard day's work. Look at Mr. Danner."

"Mr. Danner went to college. Mr. Danner has a real job, a government job he gets paid to do whether the farmers around here make a blessed dime or not. I know he farms, too, but he farms on the side. He has a real job with benefits and security. The kind of job you could've had if you'd gone to college."

"Mr. Danner paid for his college by working on farms and saving his money. He owns farmland because he buys small acreage, a piece at the time, making a little more profit each year. He's been makin' more money on his farming operation than at his real job, as you call it, for several years now. And a lot of what he learned at college, I know already, just from working with him."

"But it's the college degree that got him the real job. And the real job has paid the bills while his farming operation came to be. You ain't got that, and you never will, sharecropping on somebody else's farm."

"But if sharecropping is my real job, along with all the other odds and ends I do, I can save up and start buying acreage too, some day. Hell, we might even own our Granddaddy's place again, stranger things have happened," Cal said.

"You'll do all this work, back-breaking work, day in and day out, just to save enough money to put yourself right back where we started from? Where spring to fall is a gamble every year? Where you pray for rain 'til your knees are scraped, then turn around and promise God the rest of your life if he'll hold back the clouds 'til harvest is through?"

"Wouldn't want it any other way, Sis."

"God help us," said Delores.

And in his sister's voice, Cal heard the voice of their mother.

Chapter 6
Summer 1958

Phil

I N A CHARMED, COLLEGIATE LIFE, PHIL'S SUMMERS HAD been linked to tennis and pool parties and weekend getaways at the beach. The heat was deadly, but a wonderful excuse for pitchers of margaritas and lazy afternoons. With Phil's first summer on the farm, the face of south Georgia heat became a monster of villainous proportion, enslaving those who dared stand up to him and making them fight for every shallow breath drawn from the humid, sun-parched atmosphere. The work itself was grueling but not impossible: Phil's prep school athletic training made him far more fit than those gangly or pot-bellied farm workers, but operating in three digit temperatures really changed things.

What the hell is wrong with me, Phil wondered, trying to disguise his near-dizziness and shortness of breath with resentment. He looked at the other men, spent but not panting, sweating but not pale. They performed their tasks as if by rote, appearing unaffected by the stifling succubus of the sweltering climate. Phil ran a hand through his sweat-drenched hair and blew upward, irritating the colony of gnats sticking to his eyelids just enough to fly a few inches away and return. *Strange,* he thought as he cautiously looked for the same insects around the eyes of the other men. *Why are the damned things only sticking to me?* He leaned over and spat on the cement floor of the barn, almost submitting to the gag reflex as he saw a half dozen of the tiny insects in his saliva.

"Damn, Mr. Phil," Will said. The thin black man looked somewhere between the ages of thirty-five and ninety. "You have you a gnat samwidge for dinner today?"

Phillip sniffled hard, fighting the urge to vomit. Did he swallow the little creatures or breathe them in? Were they going through his eyeballs and down his throat? Were they poisonous? Did they carry diseases? Why the hell wasn't anyone else worried? Hoping for some hint of a breeze, Phil turned quickly in the opposite direction and headed outside, away from the desensitized farming mutants and their knowing sneers.

But the quick turn, thrusting Phil into the zenith of the two o'clock sun, ended his tug-of-war with regurgitation, and his gullet won. Expelling the contents of his stomach on the dry, brown grass, he sank to his knees, hanging his head and willing the others to stay in the barn for just a few more minutes. He dry heaved and spit into the grass, trying to purge the vile taste from his throat, his teeth, his tongue. Then he felt a warm hand brush the top of his shoulder.

"Well, now. You've just officially guaranteed yourself a heatstroke, maybe worse. And you seem a nice enough guy, but I ain't wild on the idea of giving you mouth-to-mouth," Calvin said, helping Phil to his feet.

"I don't know what happened," Phil said. He looked to the side of Cal's face, avoiding his eyes. "Must be a virus or something." Phil thought of how pathetic he must look to the seasoned workers, like he was weak, powerless, ineffectual. And why wouldn't they think so? To them he was a spoiled kid; pampered, spoon-fed, never having to do a real day's work, and on that point they were right.

Calvin handed Phil a ratty bandana, faded to near-pink but folded in a perfect square. Phil wiped his face and neck, finding the fabric soft and incredibly cool against his hot, sticky skin.

"Thanks," he muttered. Tears stung the backsides of his eyes. Cal's small gesture of kindness seemed foreign in this frightening new world of heat and sweat and perpetual drudgery, a hands-on world he knew he could survive if only his stomach would let him. But Cal probably thought he was faking, and Phil was too embarrassed to try and explain or ask for advice, looking toward the ground and hoping to appear simply preoccupied.

"No problem, man," Cal said. "There's a lot more to farm work than most folks think, and we've all seen new-to-the-farm guys who hold up about like you have so far, to begin with."

"What happens to them? I mean, does it get better for them?"

"For most of them, sure. Course I've seen a few that got their first paycheck and never came back, usually city guys that'd never stepped foot on a farm before. Farming ain't for everybody, and a lot a folks think if ol' redneck white boys can do it, anybody can." Cal grinned as though making fun of himself.

Phil moved his head, somewhere between a nod for yes and a shake for no. Calvin was being nice to him, and he didn't want to say the wrong thing. But hell, he'd thought the same thing about farm workers. If they could do it, couldn't anyone? Phil looked up into the sunlight and felt his stomach lurch again. He gasped and covered his mouth.

"You still heavin'? Damn, boy, spit it on out. It'll feel better on the outside than it does still in. But you need to go on back to the house, cool off, lay down, drink something; a co-cola, ginger ale, something like that to begin with. When that stays down, drink water, a lot of it."

"Nah, I'm okay, musta been something I ate," Phil said.

"All you ate was a store-bought sandwich, and whatever you had for breakfast. I doubt that'd be enough to have you on your knees like you are," Cal said. "Put your head between your knees. Let your neck drop, loose-like. Now breathe deep." He placed his hand on Phil's shoulder and Phil did as instructed. After a few minutes, Phil rose, slowly.

"I don't eat breakfast," he admitted.

"And there's your first problem," Cal said. "There ain't been a farmer on the planet that didn't get up in time to eat a big breakfast before hitting the fields."

"I don't get it, how could not eating make me so sick?"

"Dehydration, pure and simple," Cal said. "You'll see it in the cows, every now and then, when we move the herd from one pasture to another. There'll be one or two that hadn't grazed much, or taken any water, the morning we start moving 'em. Now we herd them up and push them together, have them going at a pretty fast clip for cows. The one or two that haven't eaten, and are caught up in the big mass of them, and have to wait longer to get to the watering trough in their new pasture, sometimes they just can't handle it. The hotter it is, the worse it is, usually. But it's easier to lose your cookies when ya got some cookies to lose. Just the way the body works."

Two other men had joined Phil and Cal, and neither seemed as judgmental as Phil had imagined. An older man patted his ample belly and spoke. "Yeah, I tell my ol' Velma that's the only reason I keep her around, her biscuits n' gravy in the morning stick to the ribs and hold me together 'til dinnertime."

Phil had noticed they all referred to the noonday meal as "dinner." He tried to smile.

"Stick to your ribs, hell," said Shorty, a sickly-thin figure of over six feet. "Sticks to that donut you been carrying over your belt for ten years."

Will joined them, carrying his worn, green Coleman Cooler of water. "You feelin' any better, Mr. Phil?" His tired eyes were impossible to read, like his age.

"I think I'm okay, now," Phil said. "'Bout time to get back to work?"

All the men laughed. Phil cringed. *The minute I let my guard down, they laugh at me. Assholes.*

As if reading his thoughts, Cal spoke. "We're not laughing at you, we're laughing with you. Everyone of us has been where you are, one time or another, and most of us worked the fields before we started to school."

"I learned to drive on a tractor," said Shorty. "Took me forever to get used to automatic transmission."

"I remember skipping breakfast on a scorcher of a day, right after me and Cindy got married," said Jimmy.

"Early morning nookie," said Shorty. "The demise of many a man." There were catcalls and guffaws.

"Had to stop my tractor in the middle of a row," Jimmy said. "Got down and spewed soured beer and chili dogs from the night before all over those damned peanut rows. Burned like holy hell, and I swear it was comin' outta my nose."

Phil smiled. They were trying to make him feel better, to feel like one of them. There was no way he'd slink home in disgrace. "I'm okay, guess we'd better get back to work."

"No, buddy," Cal said. "We'll get back to work, but you need to pack it in for the day. Don't worry, there'll be plenty left for you to do tomorrow, and we ain't the kind to let you forget it, but the upchuckin' won't be ending 'til your body gets back up to snuff. You go on home and get some rest. Drink as much as you can stand, and eat some when you think it'll stay down."

"Make sure you eat a good breakfast tomorrow," offered Shorty.

"And bring something for lunch that'll set good on your stomach," said Jimmy. "Sometimes them store sandwiches have so much extra stuff in 'em, to keep 'em from going bad, that can make you sick to your stomach on a hot day."

"I don't think it's that," said Clifford, who'd been silent until then. "Remember ol' Jim Bob Simms, who lived in that old school bus out by the creek? Used to do seasonal work at the cotton gin?"

"Yeah. Used to say he was taking a leave of absence from the junk business. That old man was a piece of work," said Shorty.

"He never ate anything that didn't come out of a can. Honest to God. Like you and me, even in a bad month, we still have things out of the garden, and can fry a chicken, grill a hamburger patty, something like that. Jim Bob couldn't eat anything fresh. Said it made him sick, the way too many preservatives do us. Said he was raised on canned food, and anything else sent him running to the commode, using a tree worth of toilet paper."

"That's crazy. Ain't nobody ever got sick from eating fresh food. And can't nobody live offa just canned food, neither. That man lies like a dog," Shorty said.

"I swear it's the truth," said Clifford. "My daddy got in a poker game with him, and they got a little wasted and dared him to eat some homemade chili and cornbread. Kept offering him money, everybody put in a dollar, then two, you know how it goes. When it got where he'd make near fifty dollars for just eatin' a meal, Jim Bob obliged. But they said the stink was terrible, him on the toilet and the rest of them goin' out to puke from just the smell. Said he—"

"Dear Jesus, Clifford, can't you see this man's doing good not to spew on his own shoes, and here you're telling this damned—" Cal looked at Phil with apology.

"Oh shit, man, I'm sorry," said Clifford, looking to Phil. "But I swear it's the truth. Eat whatever you're used to, just be sure you eat something. And drink plenty of water. You'll be fine tomorrow."

"I'm gonna run Phil to the lodge," Cal said. "The rest of you head back out to Circle 5, we should be able to get it all sprayed before dark, maybe with a half hour to spare if we hustle."

"Damn any hustling," said Shorty. "I don't wanna end up like him." He gestured towards Phil.

"I can walk, I'm not that sick," said Phil. If he had to go home, he wanted to keep a little dignity.

"It's a good half mile back to the lodge," Cal said, but caught a glimpse of what Phil meant. "Okay, but only if you drink something first." He reached into the chest in the back of his pickup and pulled out a ten-ounce Coca-Cola, floating in cold water and a few tiny chips of ice. "Funny, ain't it, this is the best chest I've had, but they can only help so much. This was just drink bottles and ice at eight o'clock this morning." He opened the drink with a metal opener attached to his keys.

Phil took the cold bottle into his hands and drew it to his lips, fighting the urge to rub its watery sides against his blistered face. The drink had a bite—it startled him, brought tears to his eyes and a quick freeze to his teeth that was almost painful, but sinfully wonderful. He felt the coldness of the bubbly liquid through each passage—his mouth, his throat, his esophagus, down through his chest and into his sore, empty belly—a rush like none he'd had before.

"Slow down, easy," Cal said. "You drink it too fast and it'll come right back up, and it won't feel near as good on the way up as on the way down."

Phil's stomach clenched just as he processed the words, but not too late. He slowed down, breathed deeply, and waited a few seconds before trying another, smaller sip. This one was not as intense, but equally medicinal.

"Stay here 'til you finish that one, and take your time," Cal said. He pulled another bottle from the chest. "Here's one for the road."

"Thanks," Phil said. "For everything."

"Like I said, be sure to eat breakfast tomorrow, and I'll bring plenty of lunch and drinks for the day. Then you can get your own cooler, stock up on necessities and such, over the weekend. Sound okay?"

"Yeah," Phil said. "Thanks."

"Another thing," Cal added. "Not meaning to get in your business, but what you drink at night, especially when it's this hot outside, has a hell of a lot to do with how well your stomach can handle the next day. I've been known to out-drink all of Dumas County, but in the summer, I do my drinking on weekends. Just a word of advice."

"Taken. And thanks," Phil said again.

"And one more thing," Cal added with a smile, his eyes twinkling.

"Yeah?"

"About those gnats. They probably don't hurt anything, all of us breathe in a few in our sleep, but they are pesky little bastards, can bother the hell out of you. The reason they cling to you and no one else is easy: OFF."

"What?"

"OFF. O-F-F. You can buy it in the grocery store, the drugstore, Bill Tom's, probably anywhere around here."

"OFF?"

"Yeah. It's insect repellent you spray on yourself. Don't smell much like Chanel No.5, but gnats hate it, and that's all that matters. I'd have let you use mine if I'da known you didn't have any. Sorry."

"No problem, and—thanks." He said it again, like a zombie, as Cal got in his truck and pulled away.

Phil stood still, watching, then headed across the barnyard for the dirt road to the lodge. He was going home, cooling his face with the bottle as soon as he got out of sight.

Chapter 7
September 1958

Calvin

THAT SEPTEMBER WAS THE HOTTEST SOUTH GEORGIA had ever experienced. For over a week temperatures reached 107 or higher by midday, still hovering in three digits by the light of the moon each night. The mental time clock for peanut farmers ticked loudly against fate. Plants were mature and ready for harvesting, yet the hard, dry soil in which they grew was not ideal for reclaiming them from the earth. After much deliberation between the owner, overseer, and extension agent, Oakland Plantation began the process of harvesting their substantial allotment of peanuts.

When their morning began on that humid Thursday, four workers drove tractors into the rows of plants, pulling diggers which broke into the crusty soil, loosened the plants and cut the tap roots. Just behind the blade, shakers lifted the plants from the soil, gently coaxing dirt from the peanuts, then rotating the plants and placing them back down in a windrow, peanuts up and leaves down. When dug, the peanuts could contain 25 to 50% moisture and were usually left in the windrows to dry for two or more days. However, in this severest of weather, no one could agree as to the exact drying time needed for maximum production.

Thirty-six hours later, when the tractors had covered approximately one third of the rows, two more tractors were dispensed to begin retrieving the plants. Upon filling a wagon with plants, the drivers of these tractors pulled their wagons to the stack pole stationary picker set up in the corner of the field. With brute force and pitchforks, they hoisted the plants from the wagons into the pickers, then set out again for another wagonload.

Work in the Oakland peanut fields continued day and night for nearly four days. Five salaried workers, two sharecroppers, two neighboring farmers, and an overseer worked twelve to sixteen hour shifts in the unbearable heat. Jobs were rotated, but one seemed as difficult as the next in the rigorous uphill climb towards harvest.

Calvin Mullinax was one of the younger workers and definitely the strongest and most adept. Turning over the last plants in his second double shift of three days, he jumped off his machine and helped unload the next wagon.

"The end is in sight," he yelled, heaving a forkful into the picker.

"Damn, Cal, where do you get the energy? I'm about to pass out," said the usually quiet Will, an older, black worker who had lived through decades of too-slowly-processed social change.

"I was the same way, til I saw the end of the row. They're all outta the ground now. Just knowin' it gave me second wind, I guess."

Will said, "And not a minute too soon. You probably couldn't hear on the tractor, but there's been a little thunder over to the east. If we don't get em off the ground soon, they could be in for some serious bathwater."

Will's words sent Cal's movements into double time. "I've worked too damned hard on this crop to lose half the profits to moisture and rot. These suckers will not be rained on!" With ribbons of sweat pouring from each shake of his head, Cal finished unloading the wagon, then hopped on an empty tractor to retrieve more.

Cal and the other men worked non-stop for the next four hours with no other threat of rain. Four of the ten workers left for food, water and a few hours of sleep. Rejuvenated by adrenaline, Cal stayed on. Nearing noon on Sunday, he pulled one of the last wagons to the picker, unloading alone with one other tractor in the field.

The sun was a perfect circle of blazing orange, but the sky seemed grayer than blue. Though Cal had still not heard the rumble of thunder, his farmer's radar told him that the drought was coming to an end. His bone-tired weariness was forgotten with the thought of rain, and each cup of water he chugged from the barrel-shaped cooler was like nectar from the gods. Exhausted, dehydrated, but giddy with a sense of accomplishment, he grabbed his pitchfork and began feeding the picker once more.

Years later, Cal would remember the soreness in his shoulders as he raised the fork for another thrust. Sometimes he thought he remembered the sound of thunder, but of that he was never sure. Retracing those moments, he could feel the slick sweat on his hands, helping the fork slide a little further than he'd intended. He'd recall thinking he should slow down, and that skimpier forkfuls might make for better timing anyway. The one thing he chose not to remember, but would feel in his dreams for the rest of his life, was the great undertow. The violent pull of the machine against the tines of his fork.

Yes, he felt the pull, but for some unknown reason he did not let go. The fork handle became an extension of his own arm, and with one heave of the fork, both the handle and his arm catapulted into the picker, leaving the rest of Calvin dangling over the side.

It hurt—dear Jesus, it hurt; he saw lightning and stars and felt white-hot fire burning within him as it tore muscle, tendon, vein and bone. From this point forward, his later memories of the event were no more than pictures he'd pieced together from the stories he was told.

When Will saw him, halfway across the hot field, he shut off his own tractor and then heard the blood-curdling scream of a wounded animal.

"I ran to you," Will later explained, "but by then yo' screaming had stopped. You was breathing, but lifeless and bloody—hanging like a rag doll trapped in a monster's jaw. I touched you, but you's didn't know it. You couldn't see or hear a thang, but your eyes was wide-open when I jumped down and ran like lightning to the main road."

As the story went, Will was screaming at full volume when he approached the nearest residence, a hunting lodge occupied by the son of Oakland's owner, employed as a recalcitrant farm worker. Phil had already called for emergency help. The two ran back to the gruesome scene at the picker. Other workers had gathered, but no one knew what to do or how to do it. Tears streamed down many of the weathered faces. One man vomited. The sound of sirens told them of the arrival of the fire truck and local sheriff, but these figures of authority seemed as lost as the farm workers on how to handle the nightmare.

Arriving with Mr. Foster, the plantation owner, Ginny Palmer, the county's recently acquired public health nurse stepped out of Foster's car and assessed the situation. While her petite form in glaring all-white seemed absurdly out of place, a rush of respectful quiet filled the air as she walked directly into the scene and stared. As silent tears ran down her perfectly powdered face, Ginny gave orders with the precision of a seasoned military official. She took two hypodermic needles from her bag and filled them from large vials of clear liquid. She spoke quietly to the firemen and other men. Then, boosted up by the rough, brown hands of two sheriff's deputies, she climbed the edge of the wagon to where Calvin hung. She pressed her upper teeth over her rose-red lips as she inserted the needle into Cal's free arm, her shaking visible to all as she repeated the procedure in the other dangling appendage.

When she finished, she gently touched his shoulder, squinting her eyes and whispering some phrase known only to God, then turned and reached for the arms that steadied her somber climb back down. Rouge and mascara streaked her whitened face, yet her pristine uniform remained spotless: a cloud of hope in a dismal desert of despair. Stepping onto the ground, she nodded her command, and the frightened and untrained group of workers began the slow and tedious task of extracting Calvin from his captor.

Nearly an hour later, an ambulance from Phoebe Putney, the big hospital in Albany, took Cal from the open peanut fields of Oakland Plantation straight to Crawford Long Hospital in Atlanta, where he remained for the next seven weeks.

⨍

"I'm going to get you some more ice," Delores said. "You need any-thing else?" She held the plastic pitcher and peered about the hospi-tal room, trying to look busy.

Cal stared straight ahead and said nothing.

"Really, Cal. I can't help you if you don't tell me what you need," she said.

"I don't need a damn thing you can get me," he said in a dull voice void of emotion.

His sister left the room with tears streaking her face.

A young doctor, who seemed close to the same age as Cal, entered with a clipboard. A heavyset nurse followed him with a tray of sup-plies. He silently opened the large bandage covering Cal's stump. An inflamed flap of skin oozed drainage into an attached receptacle. The doctor fingered the area lightly, watching Cal for any reaction. There was none.

"How's your pain, on a scale of one to ten?" he asked.

Cal rolled his eyes and said nothing.

The doctor stood straight and stepped back, thinking before he spoke. "Look, sir. I won't lie to you. What happened to you is a hor-rible thing. It isn't fair, you did nothing to deserve this kind of pun-ishment, I would guess. But there are lots of things in life that aren't fair—cancer, famine, poverty, war—to name a few. There are folks a lot worse off than you. Your employer has made sure you get the best care, treatment, and rehabilitation measures possible. But we can't really help those who don't want to help themselves."

Cal stared intently into the doctor's eyes, still silent.

"Okay. Once more," the doctor said. "On a scale of one to ten, how's your pain?" He pulled up a metal stool and sat beside the bed.

Cal waited, then spoke. "My life hurts like a ten, but my arm is gone, so I guess it's a zero. The little piece that's still hanging on is a five or six, I guess." This was the longest speech he'd given in weeks.

"Well," the doctor said. "You're alert enough to have an attitude, and you're not bellyaching for more drugs, so I'd say we got your meds about right." He spoke to the nurse. "Give him another shot, wait a few minutes and change his dressing." He stood and walked out, turning back inside the doorframe. "You really need to heal a few more months before starting rehab. Wanna go home in a couple of days?"

"Sure," said Cal. "Might as well."

Cal's arrival at Oakland was calm but impressive. Someone had cleaned and shined their tenant house, tied yellow ribbons to the oak in the front yard, put food in the refrigerator and flowers in every room. On Sunday, a group of Delores's friends from the panty factory brought magazines, more food, and local gossip; Cal stayed locked in his bedroom until they left.

Word spread quickly that Calvin was not keen on visitors. However, when Delores went back to work, he found himself lonely and bored. On his fourth day at home, he dressed and was at the main barn by eight, when he knew the workers would be starting their day. Phil, Will, and another worker he'd never seen before stood by the tractors drinking their morning coffee. Calvin stood in the doorway with the sun beating on his back, smelling the hay, gasoline and livestock and wondering if he should enter. For the first time in his life, he felt like he didn't belong there. Will quit talking when he saw him.

"Calvin, what the hell are you doing here?" He shaded his eyes to obtain a better look at him. "Shouldn't you be in bed, taking care of yourself? Surely the boss man don't expect you back at work already?"

Cal walked forward. "Just tired of doin' nothing," he said. They made their little circle wider so he could join them. Sunlight sifted through the barn walls. He tried not to look at the tractor. "Besides, a man don't get paid to sit on his ass." He gave them a half smile.

"But you are getting paid." Phil pulled at the bill of his cap to make it straighter. "Same as usual. Didn't anyone tell you? Dad talked to a personal injury lawyer. You'll keep getting paid 'til your settlement's final."

"Damn, Mr. Cal." Will reached out and slapped him on the back. "Sounds like you got it made in the shade. I know I wouldn't be hanging around this buncha hard leg farm hands if I was getting the same pay to stay home."

"Yeah," said the other worker. He was young and had a space between his teeth big enough to set a nickel in. "I'd be layin' on the couch, having a cold one and watchin' TV. To hell with this shit."

"Impressive, Herman, impressive," Phil called to the new guy.

"But if you want to hang out after work—" Phil looked to Calvin. "Come on over to the lodge." He searched Cal's face as though looking for something that was missing. "Bet you do get pretty bored with nobody to talk to. If you're feelin' up to it, maybe we could do some hunting this weekend. Show me how to use that arsenal my dad keeps locked in the basement."

"Huntin'?" The young guy squinted at Phil. "How the hell's he gonna do any hunting with one arm. Even if he's left handed, how's he gonna prop his—"

Phillip coughed loudly. Cal could feel his neck redden. "My fault." Phil nodded to him. "You'll need to take care of that arm, get it healed up. But I'll bet there's all kinds of—" he faltered. "All kinds of—stuff they'll fix you up with at the rehab place. You'll probably out-hunt and out-fish us all." The others nodded awkwardly.

"Well, buddy, guess we better get out to the fields." Will threw his hat over his white-sprinkled head. "We're harrowing in the cotton fields now."

"Y'all think there's something I could do around here?" Cal asked.

They looked around the barn. Cal saw tires that needed plugging, a stack of fence posts beside posthole diggers, barbed wire ready to be strung. No jobs a one-armed man could complete.

"Harvest time's over." Will shrugged. "Pretty slow this time of year."

The young guy frowned. "Don't seem slow to me," he said.

"That's cause you're a damned idiot," Phil said, hitting him upside the head so his hat flew to the barn floor. "Come on, guys, let's do it." To Calvin, he said, "You go get some rest, take care of that arm. Enjoy the vacation."

Cal stood at the barn door and watched the men move out into the field. He turned and headed for home.

Days turned to weeks, and Cal's phantom pains lessened, but his dreams were nightmares and his outlook bleak. In his first month home, he spent one night with Phil at the lodge, returning drunk and resentful but refusing to talk to his sister about it. Phil came by often and brought books. Cal accepted them, but he always had an excuse to send away the giver.

Driving was impossible, since his truck had manual transmission. He spent his days reading; he could hold a book in his left hand with no trouble, and page turning had gotten easier with practice. He tried to imagine what kind of a life he could expect from now on, and most nights ended early in a narcotic haze.

In the evenings when his eyes were tired, Cal found himself missing the damnedest things. The two hands needed to hold a burger all-the-way. Rapping his knuckles as he peered into the refrigerator. Would ribs be worth eating if someone else pulled the meat from the bone? He had learned to light a cigarette by himself, but he wouldn't want anyone watching the sight. He daydreamed of grabbing his dog in a real embrace. Tying his shoes. Holding his own hand. Applauding. He guessed that was what the painkillers were for. That's where the real pain was.

Chapter 8
November 1958

Phil

THE FARM STUFF WAS THE HARDEST THING PHIL HAD ever done, but it turned out that he wasn't too bad at it. It made sense to him, and he didn't have to read a book for the instructions. He rigged an adapter for a broken corn auger, and the farm guys carried on like he'd found a cure for cancer. That's when they started treating him normal, not like the boss's son they had to baby-sit. And though he hated to admit it, Phil was beginning to like the farm more than the driving. And then there was living at the lodge.

The lodge had been the home of the previous plantation owner, but Phil's dad had furnished it in "man" stuff—animal heads, leather couches, prints of foxhunts and the like. But what the older Foster didn't know was that Phil had discovered his secret treasure, which was in his opinion, worth more than the whole kit and caboodle of the factories. He'd found his father's toys.

Kicking at a dip in the carpet, Phil detected a somewhat sophisticated trap door set in the floor. A tiny but sturdy lock held it in place, but a quick search of the nearby desk provided the key. He pulled back the door to see a stairwell with a single light bulb begging him to pull its string. He did.

He passed an assortment of wines, hundreds of bottles, but that seemed to be only an afterthought. Below his father's study was an arsenal of firearms. Purdy shotguns. Colt single action revolvers. Winchester rifles. Hundreds more he couldn't name.

It would be Calvin, the one-armed man, who taught Phil the names of the rest of them.

Phil knew Cal liked hunting. He'd talked about it constantly, back when he had two arms and was the most viable of the farm workers. Now Cal stayed inside, wandering out to the barn on occasion, making them all feel sad and uncomfortable. Phil had a true liking for the man and wanted more than anything to bring a smile to his face, to do something that for even a moment restored him to the Cal he used to know. Finding the gun collection seemed an answer to his unvoiced prayer.

Phil had noticed how Cal walked the fence lines just before dusk; and the next day, he joined him at his quiet constitutional. "How's it going, buddy?" Phil asked, sidling up to his friend.

"Well as can be expected," said Cal without expression.

"You still in a lot of pain?" The question seemed horrible, but he had to keep talking, just to make sense of his staying in step with him.

"Arm's gone, nothing there to hurt," he said. "Stump's still sore, but it'll heal with time, they tell me."

"Hell of a bad break for you, man," said Phil.

"Hell of a bad break for anybody," he said without remorse. "But at least I lived. If you can call this livin'."

Phil shook his head. He had no idea what to say in a situation like this one. He opted for changing the subject. "Well, hell," he said. "I'm glad I caught up with you. I've been by your house a few times, but you won't answer the door, and you got your sister trained to keep out the riff-raff."

Calvin said nothing and continued to walk.

"There's a basement in the lodge," Phil explained, his voice coming out all breathy as he near-trotted to keep up with Cal. "And there's a wine cellar. And I've lived there damned near a year and didn't know it."

Calvin's mouth turned up at the corners and his eyes crinkled, but he still looked straight ahead, walking at the same clipping pace.

"Guess I never thanked you for showing me the ropes about farming and drinking," Phil said. "Didn't believe you at first, but you were right. Weekends are fair game, but the weeknights are a bad idea." He pushed his hair, damp with perspiration, back off his forehead. "Especially when you know the next day'll be a scorcher."

"Guess that's something we all learn in time," Cal said, still walking but at least slowing down.

"You got that right. So how's about coming over and sampling some wine?" asked Phil, grasping for anything that would keep Calvin interested.

"Ain't much of a wine drinker, myself, but if it's free, I'll try it."

That night, Phil took him through the study, then opened the little door. But Calvin didn't look surprised at all.

"Wanna come down and see? My dad's got a few nice guns, too."

Cal cackled. "A few nice guns? What ails you, boy? Your papa's got one of the finest vintage collections in the state, maybe even the country!"

Cal spoke with an air of respect towards Mr. Foster's guns, but it still pissed Phil off. How did Cal know about these guns, yet *he* never did? Reverting back to a childhood memory, Phil wondered if Cal had known his birthday puppy, too. After the big show of presenting him with the champion dog, "Sir" had gone back to the farm to be trained by professionals. Once again, had his father deemed him too simple to understand?

Calvin walked down the staircase like he'd been doing it all his life. He caressed random guns, telling stories about each one. His crude illiterate manner gone, he could have been a curator at the Smithsonian.

"This one's a .36 caliber Remington Navy revolver. Copies of the Remington were the closest thing to a standard sidearm in the Confederate Army. Also an 1860 Colt Army, .44 caliber, the standard sidearm of the Union Army." Cal stroked the gun and moved on. "This one's a real beauty; refinished this one himself, just last year. A World War I issue Colt 1911A1 .45 auto." He continued down the wall.

"This one's a Thompson Sub-machine Gun, also called a Tommy Gun and chambered in .45 acp. This could be an FBI or a gangster gun used during Prohibition, a WWII issue gun, or a gun owned by security guards fighting labor unions in the 1920s." There were Hawking rifles, a Brown Bess musket, Kentucky long rifles. "This one's my favorite: It's a Mannlicher-Schönauer 6.5 mm mountain rifle. You could kill a grizzly bear with this baby."

How did Calvin *know* these guns?

"But your daddy's favorites are these two: The Webley Mark IV and Mark 5. These here was officers' guns in World War I that his daddy brought back from the war, hidden in a box of silverware."

Later, Phil couldn't remember when Cal had left, and he knew he must have drunk three bottles by himself. That night he dreamed of bears and wars and guns, and fathers who treasure beautiful old things.

Not their sons.

Chapter 9
December 1958

Calvin

CALVIN WENT BACK TO SEE HIS FRIENDS AT THE BARN A few times, but the awkwardness never lessened. There was nothing visible he could do, and the workers seemed to resent his helplessness as much as he envied their labor. He stopped dropping by at all, keeping to himself and staying safely inside until he knew the workers had gone home. Then, establishing his own private ritual, he'd walk the fence lines until near sundown, taking in the daily changes of crops and pasture no longer a part of his life.

One evening, Cal cut his walk short when he saw his old truck parked under the tree out back. *Delores is home early.* He recognized Mr. Foster's Lincoln Town Car in the front. *What the hell,* he thought as he crossed behind the pumphouse, heading for the backdoor.

Cal didn't wipe his boots on the rubber-treaded mat but stood silently to the side, peering through one of the three descending rectangular panes in the hollow door. Inside, he could see Mr. Foster, his sister, and a man he didn't know at the green formica table: Delores fidgeted with her hair and the stranger, who wore a bow tie and looked like Howdy Doody, was taking papers from a briefcase. Mr. Foster was talking in rapid sentences, and Cal could only make out some of the words.

"Medical bills," Cal heard him say, "and rehabilitation." There were sentences between that he seemed to mumble. Cal's stomach lurched, and he wondered if he needed another pill.

"Settlement," was the next decipherable word, with Mr. Bow Tie chiming in something else.

Delores nodded her head like a plastic dog in the back of a car window. Cal felt a wave of nausea and a sharp pain in what used to be his arm. He couldn't be sure if he was sick or just pissed, but either way, he wanted to puke or hit something.

Foster's voice grew louder. Cal heard, "Farming's no place for—" and then "fair to everyone."

"But he wants to work," Dolores said. "Getting that hook—"

"You agreed, Delores," said Foster. He mumbled some more, putting his hand on Delores's shoulder. "It's what's best for Calvin," he said. The two were looking face to face.

Cal couldn't hear the next words, but he'd heard enough. He gritted his teeth and swallowed bile, then shoved open the door with his single, still-strong arm.

"How 'bout it, Sis?" he growled, sucking in air and feeling his veins bulge. "What the hell is best for me now?"

The two conspirators looked up in shock, Mr. Foster recovering much quicker than Cal's sister, who remained frozen. "Have a seat, son." Foster stood, making a grand sweeping gesture towards Cal's knobby green couch. Cal continued to stand.

"A little present for you." Mr. Foster set out a hundred dollar bottle of Scotch—Cal could see the price tag. He ignored Foster's suggestion and joined them, standing behind the fourth chair at the table. "Sit down with us," Foster said, pulling the chair out. "We've done the research and spent a lot of time thinking about you, son," he said.

Howdy Doody spread papers on the table. "Of course," Mr. Foster continued. "We'll still take care of your medical bills up through your rehabilitation." Cal thought how out of place the man looked there, his silver hair parted perfectly, and his gold cufflinks glinting in the light. "But I know you're probably tired of hanging around here and having nothing to do." He spoke quickly as though beating someone to the punch line. Next to him, Howdy Doody ruffled through the briefcase. "And there's no reason you should have to. So if you agree to this settlement, we can get things squared away and you can be on your own in no time."

Howdy Doody passed Cal a pile of papers. Cal took the papers and looked at Mr. Foster. "I'm losing my job?" he asked. "I mean, I know I can't do what I used to do, but the doctors say after I get the hook I'll be able to earn an honest wage." He could hear a slight panic rising in his voice, and he tried to fight it back. "If it's about you still paying me now, you don't have to, I don't see why you still do. Delores makes enough to pay our light and telephone bills, buy a few groceries. If you could just let us stay on here 'til I get the hook and go back to work—"

Mr. Foster spoke quietly, calmly. "No one expects you to go back to work. And your sister will not have to take care of you, either. The settlement is, we believe, fair to everyone."

"But I've gotta get back to work sometime, and as soon as they fit me for that hook—"

"Working on a farm is no longer a wise choice for you," said Howdy Doody. He glanced nervously at Mr. Foster, who was nodding in agreement.

"Definitely not a wise choice," Mr. Foster said. "And Robert here has read up on the many reasons for this. Tell him, Robert."

"Certainly." Robert began a lengthy speech that sounded rehearsed or read off cue cards on the ceiling. He spoke through his nose in a twang that made Cal want to beat him.

"Research shows that farm environment is not a safe place for workers with prosthetic devices, which can become entangled with crops, livestock and equipment at an alarming rate. Amputees must deal with a loss of balance, additional stress on remaining limbs, the possibility of using the non-affected limb to break a fall or perform a task. Many workers forget their impairments in the heat of the moment, causing hazardous conditions to themselves and those around them. And remember, farm work is not without hazard to even healthy workers."

Robert smoothed his lapels and folded his hands on his lap as though he'd just been given a gold star in class.

"Frostbite—tell him about the frostbite," Mr. Foster said.

"Yes," Robert continued, licking his lips. "A very unfortunate circumstance for amputees is the delicacy of the remaining tissue near the amputation site. Scar tissue changes the surface area as well as severed parts within the site. And areas with nerve damage are extremely susceptible to frostbite."

The word "frostbite" hung in midair like a sudden cold front. Cal wondered how many south Georgians had ever suffered from frostbite.

"So you see, Cal, it's with your best interests at heart that we want to get this settlement in place. To take care of you, and let you get on with your life," Foster said.

Cal could feel the heat in his face as his pulse rose and his stomach turned to butter. "So I'm getting fired." His jaw was tight, he was trying to talk around it. "But you're calling it a settlement, and you say you have my best interests at heart. And what is this life I'm supposed to get on with? I don't have an arm, and now I won't have a job or a place to stay. This is my new *life*?"

Foster leaned forward. "No, son, a settlement is a lump sum of money given to compensate for your lost wages and lost quality of life. Our lawyers, insurance adjusters and rehabilitation experts have put together a plan that should keep you comfortable, even set you up in a new career, and help you in the coming years. At no expense to you or your family."

Cal reached for the Percodan bottle on the table and shook two out. They watched him. The lawyer cleared his throat. Calvin stuck the pills in his mouth and swallowed them without water.

"Mr. Foster's been out of his mind worrying about you, wondering what he could do to help. That's when I realized I had the answer you both needed," the lawyer said.

Cal stared at him, waiting for some logic to enter the picture.

"My father was a victim in the polio outbreak, but was rehabilitated through our nation's most state-of-the-art treatment program."

He reached into his shirt pocket and brought out a pair of wire-rimmed reading glasses.

I don't have polio, Cal wanted to tell him. *So what in hell does this have to do with me?* "Do you mind if I get up and get something to drink?" he asked Foster.

"I was waiting to toast signing the settlement, but would you like a little preview taste of this?" Foster asked, lifting up the bottle of Glenlivet.

"Sure," nodded Cal. Foster stood up. In his peripheral vision, Cal saw him go to the kitchen and take a jelly glass from the cupboard.

"The Warm Springs Institute was founded in the twenties by President Franklin Roosevelt," the lawyer read. "Our mission," he put the glasses on and read from a shiny pamphlet, "is to empower individuals with disabilities to achieve personal independence." He grinned. "Sounds good, doesn't it, Mr. Mullinax?"

Calvin stared at him. The old man cleared his throat and unfolded his treatise.

"With five decades as a comprehensive rehabilitation center dedicated to service," he read, "the institute offers technological advancement, program diversity, research opportunities, continuing education and future development on behalf of persons with disabilities."

Mr. Foster came back and stood by the table with the jelly jar in one hand and the Glenlivet in the other, smiling like Calvin had won the lottery. Or gotten his arm back.

The old man read on, as though milking his moment in the spotlight. "The history of the Roosevelt Warm Springs Institute for Rehabilitation predates FDR, to the Native Americans who first utilized the healing properties of the warm springs, to the pre–Civil War and later Victorian resort era of the late 1800s." His pace exhilarated, with radio announcer-like emphasis on "Native American" and "healing."

Calvin opened the pill bottle and swallowed another Percodan. The old man glanced up and then continued to read.

"However," he said with a lilt of legalese. "It was FDR who clearly made the greatest impact. He made forty-one visits here, and was the driving force for polio research and rehabilitation in general; and it was during that time FDR initiated The March of Dimes."

The March of Dimes, thought Cal. *So now I'm on considered equal with birth defective babies.* He listened as the geriatric speaker finished.

"Since his passing in 1945, the Roosevelt Warm Springs Institute for Rehabilitation has continued his living legacy, and is now a National Historic Landmark." He took off his glasses and crossed his arms. His sagging eye sockets were red, and he appeared short of breath.

"Do you understand the impact of this, son?" Foster squatted beside him and passed him the jelly jar of Glenlivet. "This is an amazing opportunity, right here in our state. And they'll take you for three months, six months, up to two years. Long enough to teach you a trade and make you fully independent."

Until that moment, Cal had believed he *was* independent. Now they were saying he'd be able to go to school—not agricultural college, not real college, but a place for defectives. He could learn a trade and become independent. And they thought he should be excited about it.

"So I have to leave here?" Cal asked. "What about my sister? You're kicking her out, I guess. She's gotta find a place to live."

"No one's kicking anyone out, son." Foster stood, flicked his arm, looked at his watch and then back at Cal. "You two can stay here as long as you need to, though I'm sure you'll want to find a nicer place. With the resources from the settlement, you might buy a place of your own. No sense having to live as tenants. There'll be plenty of means for taking care of your sister while you're away."

Cal drained his jelly glass in one swift swallow. "Okay," he said as he set the glass down. He wanted to refill it but decided he'd wait until they were gone. "Tell me about the goddamn settlement." He lifted his remaining hand to indicate quotation marks, then dropped it quickly in confusion and embarrassment.

The attorney took over the conversation, appearing perfunctory, business-like and efficient. "The settlement my client offers is one of great forethought and generosity." He smiled at Foster, who nodded. "In addition to the substantial medical bills not covered by insurance and worker's compensation which have already been paid, Mr. Foster's settlement will pay all costs for the fitting and care of your first prosthetic device, including but not limited to doctor's visits, orthopedic rehabilitation, and a complete evaluation, career assessment, and daily independent living skills inventory at an accredited institute for the disabled."

Cal remained silent while bewildered, overwhelmed, and more chemically altered with each breath.

"Upon signing and acceptance of this agreement, you will also be compensated by the one-time lump sum of $25,000," the lawyer finished.

Cal started to stand, then sat down again, dizzy. No one in the Mullinax family had ever seen $25,000 at one time. The bank had sold their eighty acre farm for less than that. He could buy his own place, a decent place for him and Delores. He could buy a truck he was capable of driving, put the rest back for when he could really work again.

He could work once he was fitted with the hook. He'd seen other men work. It wasn't like his life was over. Even without sharecropping, he could follow his dream, own a little piece of land for himself. To hell with Oakland. If they didn't want him working there, so be it, but they'd have to buy him off. And this was a pretty good offer. Mr. Foster was a fool.

"Sound like something you'd be interested in?" asked Cal's former boss.

"Reckon so," he answered, slurring slightly but trying to sound nonchalant.

"Sign here," said the lawyer, laying out groups of papers in pristine stacks.

Foster lifted up the Glenlivet.

It was the first time Cal had signed with his left hand.

He was fitted with a steel hook prosthesis the following week. A leather strap wound around the shoulder of his good arm, somewhat like a policeman's shoulder holster. The stiff leather chapped his skin like a pair of new shoes, but he soon grew accustomed to the annoyance. Prosthetic specialists at the Easter Seal Center gave him a booklet of simple instructions on how to wiggle his shoulders for operating the hook, then made him an appointment for therapy. The Warm Springs Institute expected him to be proficient with his appliance before entering for evaluation and training. Cal figured out the hook at home and never returned for his designated appointment.

Delores and Cal moved into Nolan's ancient and singular apartment house. At Christmas, he presented his sister with a book of samples—paint colors, linoleum, options for bathroom tile and such from the Jim Walter Home Corporation. Cal had paid, in cash, for an acre lot on the Flint River and had contracted for his house to be built there. He had chosen a popular two-bedroom bungalow on stilts, a wide deck to overlook the river. Delores was not wild about living twelve feet above the earth, but she seemed to soften up when given the chance to decorate. Like Calvin, Delores had never really had anything new, and the experience was exhilarating. At the start of the new year, Cal would leave for the Institute, and she would stay, continue to work at the factory, and supervise the details of Cal's new house. If all went well, it would be finished and waiting for him when he came home.

Cal drove himself to the Institute on January 8th, Delores riding shotgun to take his new truck back home. Personal vehicles were not allowed on campus. He climbed out of the truck with his single suitcase at the scenic Little White House where Roosevelt had stayed, now a historical museum. When his sister started to follow, he held up his hand in protest.

"No, Sis," he said. "I need to do this alone."

"It's a museum, Cal. What's wrong with me going inside?"

"I don't want you thinking about me here, and the best way for that is not to go inside. You can see the museum when I leave, when you come to get me for good."

He stood with his suitcase in his good hand, watching the truck wind down the blacktop drive.

Chapter 10
January 1959

Delores

DELORES PUT THE TRUCK IN GEAR AND PULLED FOR-ward, blinking back the tears as she followed the winding driveway back to the highway in the direction of home. It had broken her heart to leave him that way, to just drive away without even seeing the people and the place who took her brother, the only family she had left in the world. But no one argued with Cal when his mind was made up.

"With all the hell he's been through," Delores mumbled to herself, squinting to see the highway while she bit her lip until she tasted blood. "Who am I to deny his one simple request?"

So she'd let him go, watching him meander forward, a single suitcase in his remaining hand, into that house-turned-museum that promised to give him a new life.

Poor Cal, she thought, one of the few creatures on God's earth actually happy with the shitty cards he'd been dealt, and what happens? In the blink of an eye he had gone from dirt-poor sharecropper, working his ass off and thanking the Almighty for every minute of it, to a one-armed charity case, given a compensation check and a luxury vacation in a secret spa that may have been famous years ago.

And yet he took it, smiling that scared, sad smile, showing the world he still believed that honesty, hard work and a belief in the American Dream could still work for him, buy him that little piece of agricultural nirvana he'd been salivating over since Mom died.

Delores slowed down and yielded for a four-way stop. Pulling forward, she noticed a lone teenager on an old bicycle, parked beside an ancient live oak and starring upward into its jungle of lush, green branches. He seemed to be the little town's only inhabitant on this cloudless afternoon.

Her mama had told her how men were different, how the mere idea of what could come from the soil they thought they owned was more real to them than the concrete objects a woman could hold in her hand. "And it's not like they live in a dream world," Mary Pearl had explained. "We see the truth. It's bigger than that. They're smarter than we are, they can see the whole picture, generations beyond us. That's why the Lord put them in charge."

Delores had listened, and believed, as much as possible. Yet she heard the doubt in her mother's voice, the unspoken words that were sometimes louder than the parables spoken. "They're not making any more land," her mother had said, her vocal inflections exactly as the late husband she repeated. "Be thrifty, live frugally, pay off your debts," she said. "And—" she faltered for a minute, rubbing her iced tea glass with a dingy dishrag, "serve the Lord. Give joyfully to the Lord what is His."

Delores smiled, remembering when Cal, trying so hard to understand the mystic rules and regulations of that world he wanted to make his own, had tried to reason with Mama about just what she meant. Delores turned down the barely audible radio, as though clearing the air would make it easier for the scenes rerunning in her head.

"But Mama," Cal had said. "We *are* serving the Lord, by serving His land. We rotate the crops, and take regular soil samples, and then put back the nutrients we've taken out. We leave the grazing pastures for nature, keeping places for foxes, and deer, and coveys of quail to keep living and growing and making their place in the world."

Delores remembered the passion in her brother's voice, the way he named each creature with a quiet reverence, and how she knew he was envisioning each group of flora and fauna as he spoke. A heartfelt preacher proclaiming the love of Jesus had nothing on Calvin Mullinax; the wonders he saw on a daily basis were to him every bit as profound as the Father, Son, and Holy Ghost.

"We leave the honeysuckle and trumpet vines to keep the hummingbirds happy, and we've got trees that've been homes for the wildlife for hundreds of years, and will be for hundreds more," he had said. "When God looks at this place, He has to know we love and respect it, because we take care of it."

"I suppose He does," Mama had said, but Delores could hear the doubt, maybe even a smidgen of resentment from something or someone long before Cal. "But you need to be honest with yourself," she said. "How much of that taking care are you doing for the Lord, and how much is for you?"

Delores felt a sharp pain in her gut—guilt—though she couldn't be sure who or what she felt guilty for. Should she have said something back then, tried to intercede for the sharp and nasty tone her Mama had taken with Cal? But she'd been just a girl, she knew even less of what was really going on than Cal did. And Mama loved Cal; she was only telling him what she thought he needed to hear. Still, if Mama could've seen the future, seen all the pain he had coming down the road, would she still have said the same things?

An orange-striped cat darted out into the road; Delores screamed, then swerved to the right, veering off a steep shoulder and then jerking the wheel back onto the highway. She tasted bile as her heart beat in her throat, but smiled as she saw the fleet-footed mongrel already across the highway and halfway up a pecan tree, an empty bird feeder hanging from a lower limb. Her mind raced back to her mother's words.

"You do things for the land, you borrow money, and plant again. You need a new harrow when you're still paying off the tractor from two seasons ago. But you claim you're doing it all for the land," Mama had said, her eyes narrowing, her voice no longer sounding like the mama they knew. She set down her glass and used the rag to wipe down the countertops, rubbing harder with each new thought.

"December comes," she said. "Your children learn way too early there ain't no Santy Claus. So then there's no Santy Claus, there's no Lottie Moon offering, hell there ain't been no tithe for the Lord in five years, 'cept what you hide from the egg money or change from the grocery store you don't let on you have. You put out buckets to catch water from the leaks in the roof. You let your children wear hand-me-downs of other people's clothes." Delores remembered her confusion as to who "you" was supposed to be: she was talking as though to Calvin, but Cal had no children.

"You cash in your life insurance. You take a second mortgage, and a third, and you don't tell nobody." She spit out the last word with vengeance, her voice a raspy witch's cry, like an evil storybook character had taken over their mother's soul.

Delores had understood so little of it back then, yet now, years later, she could recall it almost word-for-word. She could see Cal's face, ghostly white, his eyes glistening with held-back tears, his mouth an open "o" silently begging Mama to stop telling this awful story that no one wanted to hear. Yet Mama kept on, speaking as though not to them, but to another presence in the room. A presence that until that night had been a sacred one—that of their father.

"But Mama," Cal had pleaded, gritting his teeth and staring into her eyes, "I don't know what you mean, Mama. We've had some hard times, but we're doing okay. Me and Sis are grown, too big for Santy Claus, and we're getting by just fine. There's lotsa folks that's got less'n we got, and when the next crop comes in, we'll be even better. We'll be caught up at the bank, and maybe we can even fix up the house some, like you've always talked about. We don't need much, we could be looking real good in just a couple of—"

"Son, we won't never be caught up. Maybe, if we got out of this place, maybe there'd be hope. We've tied every penny into this farm for the last thirty years, and it ain't much more ours than it was the day we took over. Maybe if we gave it up, then we could move into town and just break even. You're young. You could get you a job with a future, one with benefits and a retirement plan. Your sister could get out and meet people, see another way of life than this hand-to-mouth ya'll have grown up in." She seemed to be winding down; her manic, pointless tidying became less intense, and her voice sounded softer, kinder, more mellow. But the words she offered scared Calvin even more.

"Leave?" Cal cried. "How can you even think about it? This is our home, and more than that, it's Daddy's home. To sell it off and just leave, that'd be like selling off a piece of him, is that what you want?" That was when Calvin broke down. The dam burst, tears dripped down his reddened face and his muscled torso was racked with shameless sobs.

Mary Pearl laid down her rag and walked across the room to her son. As she anchored him in her arms, he first tried to push away from her, then let himself be folded into her bosom as she shook her head and ran her fingers through his hair.

"There, there, now," she murmured. "Ain't nobody gonna sell off nothing. Your daddy's blood, sweat, and tears are in every acre, and he was walking the fencerows with you, teaching you to love it the same as him from the first day we brought you from the hospital."

"He did?" Cal asked, sounding more like a child than the man-of-the-house he was trying to become. They had heard those stories countless times, but on that night Cal wanted to be told again; he needed the reassurance that he, like his father and grandfather before him, belonged with the Mullinax land.

Mary Pearl held out her hand, motioning for Delores to join them in an awkward embrace. Cal wiped his face, then cleared his throat in manly fashion, as though his recent breakdown was simply a seasonal bronchial attack. His mother followed, sniffling loudly and rubbing her red-lined eyes. Delores showed no sign of tears, but stared downward, pretending to examine her mother's worn canvas shoes. Delores seldom cried in front of others, but she could tell from the heated burning sensation of her nose that she was once again sporting her "Rudolph" look.

Crossing a rural creek bridge, Delores saw road signs communicating the mileage to Cussetta, Cuthbert, and Dawson. Deep in her own reverie, she'd driven more than halfway home without realizing it.

What had happened after the strange huddle ending their terror that night? Did they sit down at the table and have a snack before going to bed? Share old memories and funny stories? Pull out the Whitman's Sampler box of family snapshots, with a tiny Calvin driving the tractor from his father's lap and Mary Pearl braiding daisies into her daughter's hair? Did they pray?

Try as she might, Delores could never recall any other events about the night in question. They never spoke of it to one another, and never again did the two children hear the voice or the words of the mother they had seen that night.

Delores reached for the radio dial, finding an instrumental tune that fit the melancholy feeling she couldn't seem to shake. "Sleep-walk," she thought the song was called, an eerily beautiful melody set to a pensive, almost ominous accompaniment.

"Poor, sweet Cal," she whispered, pondering as though sleepwalking.

Whether awake or asleep, her brother's world was a nightmare that no one could stop.

"Sure, Imogene, I don't mind. You stay there and get those little 'uns squared away. I wasn't 'sposed to go in 'til second shift today anyway, so I'll just cover yours and you can come in whenever you can. I was just planning to stop by Cal's new place and check on things, but I can do that after work as easy as before. No problem, sweetie." Delores hung up the phone, almost glad to be going on to work instead of just sitting around until later.

She had settled into living alone, staying busy with her job at the panty factory and being on hand for any questions that came up about Cal's new house.

After eighteen months of stitching quarter inch elastic to thousands of thin nylon leg holes, Delores made her quota with little effort and often relieved the workload of other women. Bertha's nervous condition had caused her to jam the machines three times in one week, so Bertha had doubled up on the pills to try and relax. She'd calmed down considerably, causing friends to watch her even more closely; she'd fallen asleep in the break room last week, and in the bathroom stall just yesterday.

Aunt Mamie Fincher, the eighty-pound, eighty-year-old granny who crocheted slippers for all the ladies on her shift, was so knotted with arthritis she could no longer sit for more than a half-hour at a time.

Three small children prone to asthma and an abusive husband prone to hooch made clocking in late a regular occurrence for Imogene Etheridge, the company's youngest worker next to Delores, yet all of these women had an ally who kept their jobs, and therefore their families, safe.

Delores developed a routine and stuck with it, staying busy enough to seldom realize she was lonely. Cal had insisted she use his new truck as transportation, so she washed and waxed it every week, by hand. His bird dog had stayed on at Oakland with his friend, Will, but the butcher kept saving him soup bones, and Delores still delivered both bones and kibble to Will's door every Thursday.

The new house was fast becoming a reality, and Delores stopped by often, bringing sausage biscuits, thermoses of hot coffee, freshly baked cookies, and other treats to the workers. It seemed reasonable to her. These men were building a new life for her brother, and Cal would be helping them if he could. She should at least do something.

And despite Cal's intentions, she still brought in extra money by working at the Sundown on weekends.

While Mr. Foster, Cal's boss at Oakland and hers at the factory, now seemed to avoid all contact with her since Cal's accident, Horace Hall, the Sundown owner, had taken it upon himself to be a sort of surrogate brother in her own brother's absence.

"Don't worry about the Sundown," Mr. Hall had told her, calling to check on Cal back at the hospital in Atlanta. "I can get some gal to fill in or just serve from the bar myself. You stay there and take care of your brother. As long as you want a little weekend job, missy, you've got one with me. Always."

Delores hadn't known what to say, mumbling "thank you" as he began to talk again.

"Your daddy was a good man. I knew him for years, and your brother's cut from the same cloth. Hardworking men and proud of it. Good men," he said. "Not like these—" He didn't finish the sentence, and the sudden silence in her ear seemed loud and abrupt.

She wondered if she'd lost the connection, but then he spoke.

"You stay with your brother. You tell him the whole town's pulling for him. We are, but he probably won't much want to see anybody for a while. I imagine he's taking it pretty hard. You stay home and do what you can for him, he'll be more comfortable with family. He'll be all right, Cal will, he'll just get up and move on, cause that's who he is, God love him. It'll just take a while."

Again she was lost as to what might be the right thing to say, feeling relieved when it sounded like he didn't need an answer.

"Well, you take care, Delores," he said, a summary statement like he was about to finish.

"Yes, sir," she answered, hoping their awkward conversation was signaling to close. "Thank you for calling."

"And remember, you need anything, I mean anything, you call me, you hear?"

"Yes, sir," she said.

"Take care of your brother," he said again. "And if you get ready to come back to work, just come on. There's a place with your name on it, whenever you get ready."

"Yes, sir."

"Goodbye, now." He hung up.

It was months before she saw the inside of the Sundown again. Cal had thought that between his settlement money and the fact that he'd be able to work again soon, there was no need for his little sister to go back to being a barmaid. According to him, she'd even be able to quit her day job in the fall and finally enroll at the vocational school. Delores listened and smiled, wanting to go along with him but knowing that the best laid plans weren't always fail-safe. After Cal was released from the hospital, Delores spent her weekends at home, allowing time with her brother until he left for Warm Springs after Christmas.

Living alone for the first time in her life, the weekends seemed to last forever. The sounds of arguing or sex on the other side of an apartment wall made her feel uncomfortable, like she was purposely trying to fulfill her own lackluster life by spying and eavesdropping on a more interesting one. Television was all reruns, and the library closed before her workdays ended. There was nowhere to escape in the tiny apartment and nowhere to go for a change of scenery. Then she remembered her job at the Sundown.

Unlike the factory, working at the bar was like working independently. The owner might stop in for a few minutes or be there for the whole night, but more as a customer than a boss. She knew what to do and she did it, never feeling like she was being evaluated under scrutiny. The work varied from extremely busy nights, which flew by, and slow ones, which seemed to last longer but were like getting paid to stand around and do nothing. No two nights were exactly the same, an inspiration never afforded by factory work. Her hourly pay was a little over minimum wage, with tips beyond that. So on the Friday after Cal's departure, Delores drove to the Sundown immediately after work.

Mr. Hall was behind the bar, sitting on a crooked stool and playing a game of solitaire beside the cash register. Breaking into a grin when he saw her in the doorway, he came out from his perch and hugged her in a fatherly embrace, something he'd never done before.

"Long time, no see," he said. "I heard your brother's off to the government place, learning a trade. You doing okay by yourself?"

"About to climb the walls. You needing any weekend help?" she asked, her eyes scanning the room and its lone customer, parked in a corner with a dog-eared *Albany Herald*.

Mr. Hall let his gaze follow hers, then shook his head and laughed.

"Don't let it fool you, you know how deceiving Friday nights can be. Give 'em an hour or two to change clothes and grab a bite to eat. It'll be standing room only by eight." He picked up an empty beer bottle from his customer's table and headed back toward the bar.

"Don't be too sure," said the voice behind the newspaper, laying it on the table and revealing a pale, thin, middle-aged face with long, black sideburns and a receding hairline. "Bruce" was embroidered in red on the pocket of his khaki shirt.

Mr. Hall stopped and turned back. "You got inside information?"

Bruce smiled, revealing crooked yellow teeth. "All you can eat special at Big Jack's Catfish tonight. 'Til closing."

Mr. Hall considered, then said, "They'll eat and leave. Strongest drink Jack serves is iced tea." He tossed the bottle into the trash and took a fresh beer from the cooler. He winked at Delores, nodding toward Bruce. Delivering the fresh drink, Mr. Hall said, "Well, Big Bruce, how come *you're* not over at Big Jack's tonight?"

Bruce wrinkled his nose and shook his head. "I like to fish, but I don't much like to eat fish. And I won't never eat no catfish."

Mr. Hall dropped his jaw in mock amazement. "What kind of Southerner are you, Bruce? And what kind of Dumas County boy won't eat a good mess o' catfish?" He looked to Delores. "Miss Mullinax, have you ever heard of such a thing?"

"Don't guess I have, though Southerners' appetites can differ sometimes. My brother wouldn't ever eat chitterlings, and I'd rather starve than have to even smell turnip greens. But I love some good fried catfish," Delores said.

"What on earth would a fellow have against catfish, Bruce? I just can't imagine," Mr. Hall said.

Bruce picked up his newspaper, but didn't open it until he'd answered the question. "First of all," he said, "they're nasty. Those bony fins are sharp as knives, can go straight through your hand if you don't watch out. And they're ugly as sin—those ol' wiry whiskers—got a face like Castro, or that, what's his name? Ugly old guy—Ernest Borgnine."

Delores stifled a giggle.

"So they're ugly. So what?" asked Mr. Hall. "I've seen some cows and pigs and chickens, for that matter, that I wouldn't wanna marry, but they taste just fine looking at me from a plate. What's the real story, Bruce?"

Bruce opened his paper, straightened it with a firm snap of a shake, then pulled it downward, just below his eyes. "I don't eat no catfish," Bruce said in a more serious tone. "Because they're bottom feeders. And I don't eat shit."

With that he disappeared back behind his reading material, picking up his beer for a draw, obviously finished with his end of the conversation.

"Go home and grab a bite," Mr. Hall said to Delores. "Be back here by seven-thirty if you can. I'll stick around a while, let you get the feel of the place again. Think you could close up for me tomorrow night? I hadn't been out to Sam Erwin's poker game since before deer season."

"No problem," Delores answered. "My brother used to play poker at Sam Erwin's."

"Cal's taken more of Sam's shirts than the damned dry cleaners. Fine card player, Calvin was," he said, then correcting his error. "I mean—is," he added, not looking at her when he spoke. "Go home, take a load off a few minutes. Gonna be a busy night, I hope."

Delores left the bar missing her brother more than ever. *It's like they've already written him off,* she thought, *like he doesn't count anymore, like he's a non-person.* He was missing an arm, not a soul.

She hurried home to a tuna sandwich and a hot shower, then dressed in dark slacks and a pale sweater. Pulling her hair into a neat ponytail, she added a smile's worth of lipstick and grabbed her purse. Hopping into the shiny new truck, she started the engine and headed for her new-old job. *At least I'm going somewhere,* she thought, and for the first time in months, Delores smiled.

The Sundown was already picking up when she arrived a little after seven. It was fun seeing familiar faces. Smiling as she listened to their stories, Delores mixed drinks and drew beer almost non-stop for the first few hours, not realizing how she was hustling until the crowd thinned around ten-thirty. She grabbed a tray and gathered the empty glasses once they were down to a table of three and two regulars at the bar. Elbow-deep in a sink full of suds, Delores suddenly felt the distinct aura of being watched. Looking up, she saw young Phillip Foster, outlined by light from the jukebox and staring directly at her.

Delores's stomach knotted up in butterflies when she first saw Phil. That stupid, stupid night last summer, the night she behaved like the poster child for every small town redneck girl who got drunk with a rich pretty-boy and fell for his bullshit, *that* was always the first thing that came to her mind. But in the light of everything that had happened to Cal, her problems seemed pretty trivial, and she was glad no one knew about that night ever existing. Since Phil still acknowledged her but treated her no differently, she wondered what had really happened then. Did he remember? If he did, why did he pretend it never happened? That seemed a bit cold. But she couldn't write him off as heartless; he seemed to truly worry about Calvin. Always.

Before the accident, Cal had a strange relationship with the Foster family. On the rare nights that old Mr. Foster stayed at the lodge instead of his family home in Albany, Cal would have dinner with him, coming home late and smelling of cigars and whiskey. And although Cal was friendly with all the farm workers, he seemed to be the only one of them who really got along with Foster's son Phil.

"Boy's a spoiled brat," Delores heard one of them say to her brother. "Thinks he's too good for everybody but you, Cal. But that's all right, we got your number, buddy. Smart move, being friendly with the boss's son."

Yet Cal never agreed, trying to stick up for Phil without offending the others. "He's an okay guy," Cal would say. "He's a fish out of water, trying to walk on land. We wouldn't do much better in his world, if we got thrown in and were expected to swim."

They'd all shake their heads as in disbelief, but Delores believed he'd at least given them something to think about.

After the accident, Phil came by almost every day. Cal had gone over for dinner with him once, like he used to do with old Mr. Foster, but after that he started doing anything he could to avoid Phil. Phil still came over, started bringing things as an excuse—books, comics, magazines, cigars and liquor. If Calvin saw Phil first, there would be no answer to his knock at the door. If Phil managed to catch Cal off guard, he'd accept whatever Phil brought, but give some lame excuse and send him away. And if Dolores asked anything about Phil, her brother brushed her off completely. Said he was the boss's son, a decent guy but a rich boy who'd never know them outside the workplace. So she never dared take the subject of Phil Foster any further.

If Delores were there when Phil came, Calvin sent her to the door. Her first experience at turning Phil away had been horrifying; she had not seen him since the forbidden night at the river. However, nothing registered in Phil's face, not then or any of the other times he stood at her door. After a while, she decided she would forget it as well.

Phil seemed different in the light of day. She remembered how he was never comfortable talking until he'd had a few drinks, and standing on the small porch of their little house, he seemed awkward, even shy.

"Uh, uh, hi, uh—Delores," he'd say, not like he'd forgotten her name, more like he needed permission to say it. "I—uh—I wondered if Cal—uh, I mean I came by to see him—uh, if he's all right? I mean, I wanted to see about Cal, if he, uh—if he feels all right," he stammered, then added, "I brought some books he might like."

This was not the obnoxious guy in the fancy car, nor was he the playboy that talked about beautiful places she'd never been. This was a frightened boy, wanting to see his friend but ill-prepared to communicate with her in order to make it happen. Delores thought it almost cruel to send him away, though her first allegiance was to her brother.

"Cal's taking a nap, he hasn't slept well lately," she'd often say. "I try to leave him alone when he's resting peacefully. He wakes up every few hours at night." At least that was true. Cal's scream-filled nightmares affected her sleep as well.

"Let him sleep," he'd always answer. "I—I'll leave the books."

"I'll tell him you came by." She'd take the books, and Phil would wander away towards the lodge.

Delores bent down into the cooler and retrieved four long-necked Buds. Setting them on a tray, she saw Phil standing in the same spot. Still staring at her, he smiled as their eyes locked. *I wonder which guy he is tonight*, Delores thought, but she couldn't help smiling back.

At the bar, he ordered his usual Scotch and sat down, staring at the Clydesdale horses, Delores, and the ceiling, intermittently. With his second drink, he began to ask questions about Cal's recovery. By the third, he seemed genuinely concerned and was strangely planning the rest of Cal's life, like a father for his son.

"They teach basic skills to use with the hook, but this learning a trade theory is a crock. Cal's too smart for that, it's an insult to his intelligence," Phil said. "Once he learns how to function without embarrassing himself, he needs to go to college." He said it with no hesitation, like it was common knowledge everyone should already know.

Delores was shocked. "College?" she asked. "What kind of college? He always wanted to go to ABAC, the ag school in Tifton, but that was back when he thought he'd be farming the rest of his life—"

"ABAC's a good school, but it's only a two-year institution," Phil said. "He could start there, then go on to UGA, or UA, or Auburn. And he can farm, in a big way. He should; anybody that loves it like he does would be crazy doing anything else."

"But his arm—the hook—your dad and that lawyer said people with hooks shouldn't be—" Delores took her soapy rag and wiped down the space in front of her, using a dry rag to clean off the moisture. Boredom, frustration, worry, or even excitement sent Delores into an unconscious mode of manic cleaning.

"They're full of shit. I mean, pardon my French, he shouldn't be doing manual labor in places where he could be easily hurt, but Calvin's too smart to be used for that kind of stuff anyway." Phil took a sip of his drink. "There's plenty of guys that don't have a brain for much more than hauling or lifting. Then there's the ones like me, who can be almost smart with their hands, but couldn't follow directions from a book for love or money. Cal can do it all, and he sees and understands it all, the big picture. Cal needs to learn the serious parts, the stuff you gotta be smart to learn, the chemistry and biology and earth science. And financial stuff."

"To *farm*? Why would he need all that to farm?" Delores was confused, but interested. She liked to hear the thoughts of someone who really knew her brother, someone who'd say out loud he was much more than just another field hand. And where was this leading? Was he saying that there was still something out there for Calvin, something even better than all he'd ever dreamed?

"Calvin could use all that to do more than just farm. He could manage a farm, several farms, a plantation. He could steer the direction it took, make it not just a farm but a successful business. Learning economics, he could invest farm earnings. Learning financing, he could use one farm to subsidize another. He could use changes in the economy to work for him, not against him. Combine what Cal knows now with what he could learn in college, and he'd be an unstoppable entrepreneur."

Delores squeezed her rag as she took in what Phil was saying, elated that someone talked about her brother in the future and not just the past. Without his asking, she refilled his empty glass. "I don't know about all the big words, but I can just imagine how happy he would be," she said dreamily, rinsing a glass and setting it the drain basket.

Phil reached over the bar. He laid his hand over Delores's, still holding the wet rag. He looked directly into her face. "No one I know deserves it more," he said, his hand lingering for a minute, then giving a small squeeze and releasing.

"But college is expensive," Delores said. She thought for a moment. "He shouldn't be building that house," she said, her voice suddenly on the verge of tears. "We don't need that house, I knew he signed the papers too soon, why didn't he—" She stopped, wondering why she was blurting this to a stranger, why she was losing control. She looked the other way, moving random objects behind the bar, trying to look busy while she willed away the burning in her eyes.

"Delores," Phil said. "Hey—look at me, okay?"

She turned around slowly.

"I didn't mean to upset you, I mean—you shouldn't be upset. Everything will be okay," he promised. "The house is a good thing. Everybody's gotta have a place to live, right?"

She smiled. "But if he could go to college, he should've saved the money for that, not the house. He'll have to live somewhere if he goes to college, and he can't pay for both."

"He can get financial aid. There's probably all kinds for people with disabilities like his. And he's smart, he can apply for scholarships, too. And besides, he probably needs a year or two to get used to the prosthesis, get fully independent before he starts anything new. But once he's ready to roll, I'll bet there'll be no stopping him."

"Are you sure? How do you know all this stuff?"

"I don't know specifics, but I know it's possible. I know there are student loans, and other government programs. But before we plan Cal's life away, shouldn't we wait and let him make some of the decisions?"

Delores took a deep breath and felt her stomach unclench. "Yeah, I guess so," she said. She smiled and reached into the sink for more soapy glasses. He looked at her. She liked the fact that he looked at her, but she also felt the need to do something, hoping it would make it less obvious that she liked it.

"Well, tell me, what do you do for fun?" Phil asked.

"What do you mean?" She held up a glass and rubbed hard around the lipsticked rim.

"Fun, you know, things that make you feel good, for no reason. Every time I see you, you're working."

"You've seen me at home. I wasn't working then," she said, rinsing the glass, setting it in the drain, and reaching for another.

"Actually, you're working there, too. Answering the door, cooking, cleaning, taking care of your brother. Do you work everywhere you go?"

"No, silly. No one works all the time."

"Well, where else do you go?"

Delores thought. The answer did not come quickly. "I go to the grocery store, the post office. The bank," she said.

"Still work. What do you do for fun?"

"I go to the library when I can get there before it closes."

"The library. How old are you, eighty?" he laughed.

"No, and I like the library," she insisted.

"Okay, let's try something else. What do you like to do?"

"Read," she teased.

"Okay, fair. What else? Do you like to sing? Dance? Play an instrument?"

She shook her head. "Can't sing, don't play anything. I like to dance, I guess."

He nodded. "Now we're getting somewhere. Do you like to watch movies? Play tennis? Paint? Read palms? Attend Klan meetings? Play cards, gamble, bet on boxing and horse races?"

Delores shook head, trying not to giggle.

"Coon hunt? Handle snakes? Speak in tongues? Perform circus acts?" He was obviously pleased with his rant.

So was Delores. "I like to watch movies," she said. "I liked to play baseball as a kid, was better than most of the boys my age. I've only played cards with my family, and we played for peanuts or Tootsie rolls. I don't hunt, but I love to fish. And I like to cook and to sew. That's about it."

"Impressive," he said. "And here I had you pictured as only a workaholic. And how do you feel about eating?"

Delores looked puzzled, then made a silly face. "I guess I feel okay about it. I mean, it doesn't rule my life, I hope, but sure, I like to eat. Everybody has to eat, sometime."

"Indeed we do. Which brings me to my next question. Would you, Miss Mullinax, consider accompanying me tomorrow night, to perhaps dinner and a movie?"

Delores put down the glass she was washing, dumbfounded. She hadn't been asked on a real date since, she couldn't remember when. But did he mean it? It didn't matter, anyway. "I'm working tomorrow night," she said. "I just started back tonight, and can't ask off the next night."

"Okay," Phil said, considering his next move. "What hours do you work?"

"Five until closing on Saturdays."

"But you close at midnight, right?"

"Yeah, I get out around twelve-thirty or so."

"Perfect. Not such a conventional date, but who says we have to play by Emily Post? Let's say I come by again tomorrow night, and we can leave as soon as you lock up."

Delores was confused. "Where are we going? I mean, where would we be going, if I agree to this?"

"The Atlantic City of South Georgia," he said, miming the rolling of dice. Delores had no idea what he meant.

"You work in a bar, and you've never been to the Plantation Club on Saturday nights?"

"No. Isn't that the place on the left, going towards Albany, set off from the road? I thought it was just a place for gamblers and such."

Phil laughed. "I don't know what you mean by and such, but yes there is gambling. There are card tables in the back, but most of those guys are high rollers from out of town. In the front there's a bar, tables, a dance floor and a band that plays from ten or so until five in the morning. Sometimes the bands are pretty good."

"They play until five in the morning?" Delores stopped washing glasses.

"The people that work in bars and clubs from Albany, Americus, even a couple of hours away in Tallahassee and Dothan, they all close down at midnight and head for the Plantation, only open bar in Georgia against the Sunday liquor laws. So what do you think? You want to take a walk on the wild side? We don't have to stay until closing, but we can if you want to. Just play it by ear."

Delores considered. "I—I guess so," she said.

"And afterwards, I make a killer omelet, if you're so inclined."

Delores smiled, standing still and trying to decipher what she really thought about Phil Foster. She'd first seen him as a spoiled rich kid, stuck on himself and too good to even look into the eyes of anyone from Dumas County. Then there was the thing with his drinking. Unlike others she saw come and go through the Sundown, his poise and even his intelligence seem to increase after a few drinks. And there was his relationship with Cal. She knew there was something strange in the way Cal avoided him after the accident; and yet here in the bar, she could see in Phil a genuine concern for her brother, a concern Phil didn't voice for anyone else.

Of course, there was the thing at the river, last summer, but she was sure Phil remembered none of the bad part, and she really didn't think there was a bad part. They both went to sleep, and for that she was more than grateful. Grateful enough to give it a second chance.

"Not sure I trust you enough to try your cooking," Delores announced, "but it would be nice to get out and let someone serve me for a change. Do I have to wear anything special?"

"Come as you are, my dear," he grinned. "You could wear a croaker sack and still be the classiest broad there. I'll come by around eleven, hang out 'til you're finished. Even help out if I can." Phil drained the last of his drink and set it on the bar, rising and pulling on the jacket draped on his bar stool. "See you tomorrow," he said before turning to go. "Take care."

Delores watched as he swaggered past tables and out the door.

What the hell I am thinking? She turned back to wiping down the bar and straightening the wine and whiskey glasses hanging over her head. The three or four regulars still nursing their drinks looked up for a second, then back down.

Oblivious to it herself, Delores Mullinax was singing with the jukebox.

When Phil arrived the next night, Delores almost lost her nerve and considered telling him to go on without her. He wore a linen jacket, his farmer tan brilliant against a starched white dress shirt; and something about the way he smelled made her want to lay her face against his neck and breathe him in.

Though she'd spent hours deciding how to dress, the fact that she was wearing a white butcher's apron to protect her dress made her feel awkward and frumpy in his presence. Phil, however, seemed not to notice her clothing at all, a fact she had no idea how to take. Did he think she intended to wear the apron all night? Did he think she dressed so badly, anyway, that it didn't matter? Did he dress up on purpose, to call attention to the country bumpkin he'd be ridiculing to his friends? Why had he asked her out in the first place?

Phil sat at the bar, talking to a couple of Oakland guys and to Mr. Hall, who was manning the bar for the night. Phil ordered his usual Scotch, but then switched to seltzer water. At eleven- forty-five, Mr. Hall told Delores to take off her apron and get out, that he'd close up. "Go, kid—have some fun for a change. I've known grand-mothers that get out more than you do."

She felt herself blush beet-red, hating her lack of a social life being comic relief for the whole bar. She wasn't even sure how Mr. Hall knew about it, why he just happened to decide to work tonight, like the whole town was in on the joke. Delores set down her empty tray, grabbed her purse, and headed for the restroom.

Untying the apron in front of the mirror, she wondered why she'd thought her simple cotton dress was so special. Sure, it won first place as a 4-H project, but that was two years and two lifetimes ago. It had taken her days to get the fitted, angled shoulders perfectly darted and lying flat. The notched white collar was cut on the bias, flowing evenly against the neck seam of the navy voile print, dotted with fields of white flowers and the tiny, occasional red rose. She had covered the little round buttons and the wide, cinching belt in red fabric of the same shade. It had been the most complicated, most grown-up, most take-the-world-by-storm garment she had ever owned, and now it was just a dress.

Delores shook her hair from its ponytail and covered her lips with a matching red lipstick. *Might as well get it over with*, she thought, wadding the apron into a ball and heading out to meet her doom.

The Plantation Club was unlike any club Delores had imagined, though her experience in such matters was limited. She'd seen it from the road, every time she'd been to Albany, for as long as she could remember. The building was painted a dusty rose and trimmed in cream, baring a steep roof, no windows and art deco letters spelling *The PLANTATION* backlit across the front. A loan mimosa tree, reminiscent of Florida landscapes, stood in its front yard while all the trees in back of the building were tall Georgia pines. Its very presence in the center of Dumas County and twenty miles from any sign of civilization was a puzzling enigma to anyone who gave it much thought.

"Nice to see you again, Phil," said the man taking money and stamping hands at the front door. "And who is this classy young lady?" The man smiled at Delores.

"Delores Mullinax," Phil said, "meet Warren Irvin, owner, proprietor, and overseer of this fine establishment." Mr. Irvin offered his hand, which she shook quickly, not knowing what else to do.

"What a pleasure," Mr. Irvin said. "Let me know if Phillip gets out of hand. I've known his family long enough to take him over my knee, personally, if he doesn't behave." Phil laughed, took her shoulders and gently guided her through the entrance and to the left, where a large room of small tables covered three sides of a large dance floor, directly in front of a raised bandstand. He chose a table near the front and pulled out her chair to seat her first.

So far so good, Delores thought. The band played a slow Platters' tune, and the dance floor was close to full. "You've got the magic touch," crooned the lead singer, a thin, dark-haired boy looking no older than her.

He's really not bad, Delores thought, though the lack of harmony behind him made it a different song than the one she'd heard on the radio. He played rhythm guitar, and the other musicians included two more guitarists and a drummer. A saxophone and several percussion instruments sat on stands.

"I like these guys," Phil said, leaning forward to talk directly into her ear above the band. "They're really versatile. The other band they use is good on the up tempo stuff, but only so-so on the ballads."

He didn't seem to expect comment, and Delores was glad. As easy as talking to him had become, it was like starting over from scratch without the bar and her job separating them. A waitress came to take their order. When Phil asked what she'd like to drink, Delores went blank, raised her hands in a questioning motion, feeling like an idiot. Phil placed his hand over hers on the table, then turned back to the waitress.

"Two Bacardi and Cokes, light on the rum, with a slice of lime," he said. The waitress placed two paper napkins at their table and left.

"So," Phil said, "you know what everyone else drinks, but have no ideas for yourself. Interesting."

"I don't drink much," she replied. "I don't really know what I like. Is that stupid?"

"Not at all," he reassured. "Pretty much what I figured, which is why I chose. If you don't like it, you can try something else, or just

134 ← Elaine Drennon Little

go to straight Coke next time. I'm not trying to get you wasted and take advantage of you. Unless you want me to, that is."

The way he said it meant everything. He knew she was uncomfortable, and he only wanted to make her feel better, and he did. She smiled back at him, then turned her attention to the band. The slow song had ended, moving directly into to the easily recognizable intro to "Jailhouse Rock." A few couples left the floor while a hoard of dancers jumped up from their seats.

Phil spoke above the drums and the cheering crowd. "Wanna dance?"

"Sure," she said, on her feet.

Phil grabbed her hand and led her to the center of the floor. Delores hadn't danced in public since—maybe since her high school prom, but it had always come naturally for her. She and Cal had danced with the radio their whole lives, and with music like this, dancing was the only way she knew to express the way it made her feel.

The dance floor was packed with hardly room to move. A tall blonde girl with a pink sweater and a high pony tail was swinging her head from side to side, her hair actually slapping Phil's face. He grinned, shrugged his shoulders and moved closer to Delores. *He's a pretty good dancer*, she thought to herself. Delores hated dancers who showed off, dancing for the sake of calling attention to themselves more than celebrating the music.

Without a word, the two of them created a pattern and fell into it, breaking out into a little more creativity with each verse, but sticking to their original swing sequence with the chorus. By the final tag, the whole dance floor was clapping in time, singing along. As the chord sustained and the applause continued, the bass guitarist was already beginning the next song.

Delores and Phil fell into an easy rhythm, simple and then more complicated variations of the Carolina shag, as though they'd been dancing together for years. One of the guitarists picked up the sax, and during an extended instrumental, the dancers set up a Virginia-reel like pattern where each couple danced through a long line, then split up and became part of the line when they reached the end. Then, once again, the ending chord was still being held as other band members hammered out the beginning of their next crowd pleaser. The tables were nearly empty, the dance floor painfully pushed together.

Phil grabbed Delores in a quick hug. "Sheesh," he said, his mouth on her ear. "If I don't get something to drink, I may pass out on you. You mind sitting this one out?"

"Please," she said. "I love to dance, but it feels like it's a hundred degrees, at least." His hand on her shoulder, he used his other hand to part the waves of dancing couples and meander their way back to their table.

Delores swallowed half of her drink before sitting down. The ice had melted a little, and she could hardly taste the liquor at all, but the lime slice gave it a wonderful, clean taste. "Wow," she said. "This is good. I'll bet it was *really* good before the ice melted."

"Want another?"

"Please," she said. "I'm famished." She used the tiny straw to inhale the rest.

"I'll go to the bar and order, that should be faster. The same drink okay, or something different?"

"This is great. The same. Only—" she hesitated. "Make it regular strength. We're sweating too much to worry about the alcohol, don't you think?"

"My thoughts exactly! But I'm driving, I may get some water for myself. Be back in a minute."

"I'm off to the ladies' room to wash my face," she said.

"Sure. Just don't let any of these losers sweep you off your feet. I've got the best looking date here, and the best dancer. Let me enjoy it, okay?" He left for the bar.

Delores sucked her drink down to the bottom, then turned back the glass for the ice chips. Gazing at the dance floor, she noticed how none of the guys seemed as fluid as Phil. And though a few of the girls were perky and cheerleader-like or could move their hips to appear almost naked, none of them were that great either. She imagined the picture she and Phil had made, dancing, and she liked the image she superimposed between the gyrating bodies. They had looked good, she knew they had. *And the more we dance, we'll just get better.*

Delores headed for the line that must lead to the ladies' room. She felt a swoon of delight and confidence she hadn't felt in a long time. Inside the restroom, she realized she didn't need to use the facilities, but took the opportunity to wet a paper towel and cool off her face and neck. Other girls at the mirror were re-applying heavy coats of eyeliner and rouge, and she wondered why. In the humid nightclub, it all ended up beneath their eyes, giving them a ringed raccoon look. She looked at her homemade dress, comparing it to the trashy pencil skirts, the childish poodle skirts, and tight sweaters around her. Hers *was* a classy dress, as nice now as two years ago when she made it.

The head-swinging blonde was there, taking down the ponytail, then leaning over and brushing her hair upside down. Delores liked the way it looked and decided to do it, too. Taking her own brush from her purse, she leaned over, her head almost touching her knees, and vigorously brushed her hair. Then she stood up quickly, snapping her head so that her hair fell back and away from her face. The result was astounding—brushing her hair had removed any tangles and made it glossy and shiny, but the simple slinging of her head gave it a windblown and careless appearance. It was sexy, effortlessly sexy. Pulling the hair away from her face showed off her clear skin and sparkling eyes, free of the aging make-up seen on other faces. She took her single lipstick from the pocket of her purse and touched up her mouth, then smiled at her reflection. She wanted the night to last a long time.

When she returned to her seat, Phil was sipping seltzer water, with another Coke drink beside it, and two such drinks at her spot.

She took a long pull on her drink, then noticed that Phil was staring at her. Staring and smiling. It gave her a giddy feeling but also a sense of power. She took another pull, set down her glass but remained standing.

The drummer sang, beckoning them to come on over where there was shaking going on. "Wanna dance?" she asked.

Phil grinned, stood, grabbed her hand and pulled her to the floor.

They danced until the band broke, shagging and jitterbugging and inventing their own combinations to "All Shook Up" and "Great Balls of Fire" and "Shake, Rattle and Roll." They ran to the table and downed the rest of their drinks, making it back to clown through Fats Domino's "I'm Walkin'" then fall into each other's arms for "Only You." Her face against his white shirt, Delores felt the wet heat of his chest soaking through to her cheek, his breath cool against her neck as he lifted her hair and nuzzled there.

There were smells—smoke and liquor and all kinds of sprays, lotions, colognes and body odors—that made up the big picture, but the close-up and personal smells of just Phil and Delores stayed securely in their own little space, an invisible box that wrapped around them and put them in a tiny world of their own. Delores was drenched in sweat yet didn't feel dirty. She saw no one familiar yet didn't feel lonely. She was in a place of which her mama would *not* have approved, yet it was all right. She wasn't doing anything wrong, and she was a grown woman on a real date. It all felt different because it *was* different, like the next part of her life was finally starting to happen. And it had definitely been worth waiting for.

"I can hardly breathe in here," Phil said, covering his mouth as he cleared his throat. "Want to go outside and get some air before the band comes back?"

"Sounds wonderful," Delores admitted, waiting for him to stand and then following his lead. As the pushing crowd almost separated them, she brazenly put her hand on his shoulder, feeling the eyes of those watching as they maneuvered towards the front.

Reaching the entrance, Delores realized that Phil had brought his glass of ice water with him. He took a plastic cup from a stack at the door and poured his drink into it. She wished she had brought hers as well, but not bad enough to fight the crowd back to their table.

"I'll share," Phil said. Outside, leaning against the car, he held the cup to her lips. The unexpected bitterness startled her.

"Not fond of quinine?" he asked. "It's an acquired taste. Call me weird, but I love the taste of Alka-Seltzer, as well."

"No, thanks," said Delores, "Though the coldness of it almost makes the bitter part okay."

"Well, let's make the most of the part you like. Allow me," he said, taking a single ice cube and setting the drink on the hood of his car. Holding the cube between his thumb and forefinger, he traced Delores's lips once, twice. She felt a cool, thin line of water dribble to her chin. He followed the dripping line down her chin, down her neck.

She could not stifle her shiver as the melting cube continued down her neck toward the cleft between her breasts, but Phil smoothly diverted the line to her right shoulder, then her left, and her right again, drawing a cool and delicate necklace on her skin. When the water touched fabric, it seemed to dry completely before filtering through the cloth. Phil lifted her hair in the back, drug the quickly shrinking ice chip to complete the necklace, then drew a straight line between her shoulder blades as it disintegrated in a wet vapor.

His hand still holding her hair, he asked, "Still bitter?"

"No, perfect," she said, looking into the eyes of the man who had given her the first night of a new life. "Not bitter at all."

He pulled her forward and kissed the top of her head, much like she'd seen parents kiss a much-loved, beautiful child in classic movies. Part of her wanted more, but this was good, too, and she wanted to savor each new sensation. He let her hair down, grabbed her waist and gently turned her around, with her back against his front. He spoke softly, moving her hair so that his lips brushed her ear as he spoke.

"Thanks for coming with me," he said. "You deserve better than this. You out-class every girl here by a mile. For me, you make this run-of-the-mill place new all over again. I'm having a blast. Thanks for—for just being you."

The arms wrapped around her waist gave a gentle squeeze as he kissed the back of her neck, his throat making some kind of vibrating sound she could feel more than hear. She wanted to turn around and kiss him—really kiss him—but having him behind, so close and yet out of reach, was a strangely erotic tease as well. She stood still and simply let it all happen, enjoying every breath, until the sound of the band pulled them back inside.

They listened as the first song began, screaming "Elvis!" and running back to the club's entrance. The dance floor was full, but not as uncomfortable as the last set. Delores wondered if this meant they'd all be leaving soon, then banished the thought from her mind, thinking only of the music. It was a great set for dancing, with an extra long version of "Tequila" which ended featuring the two most spirited couples—an older man and woman who looked like professional ballroom dancers, and Delores and Phil. At the end of the song, Phil lifted her high above the crowd as she lay back over his shoulder in a final pose. The crowd, even the band members applauded. And then, the last slow song of the night, a Sam Cooke masterpiece.

But as all good things must come to an end, the band announced the final song of the night, and Delores was less than impressed. She and Phil looked at each other with puzzled faces, shook their heads, then burst out laughing.

"What the hell—" Phil said. "*Witch Doctor?* After they played such good stuff all night."

"What a joke," said Delores. "They actually expect people to dance to that?" But people were, in fact, dancing to it, frantically if not gracefully.

"I've never actually stayed 'til closing before," Phil said. "But I'm thinking this place will be a zoo in about four minutes. Wanna try to beat the stampede?"

"Sure," Delores said. She grabbed her purse as he took his jacket and they scurried out the door.

Pulling out of the parking lot, Delores noticed that the magical box that had insulated them all night was gone, replaced by an awkwardness not felt inside the building. Turning right onto the Albany highway, neither spoke for several miles, the open wind cooling their bodies and filling their lungs with the smell of longleaf pines. Just before the Nolan city limit sign, Phil broke the silence with an announcement.

"I know I said I'd cook you breakfast, but that just seems too ordinary, now. I mean, I've taken girls to the Plantation Club before. Afterwards, we'd go to the lodge and drink more, or party more, or whatever. Dolores, tonight was the most fun I've had in a long time. I want to take you home, kiss you goodnight, and take you out again—tomorrow. That is, if you'll still go out with me."

Delores reached across and kissed his cheek as an answer. She sat still, hearing the whooshing of air go past her ears like the orchestral score running through the climax of a movie. She wondered why she'd never before seen that the night sky was not black, but a brilliant blue, the twinkling stars like diamonds on a satin drape. And that power lines stretched between creosoted poles could look like long velvet ropes outlining the way home. As Phil slowed down for the stop sign by the Flint Bridge, Delores saw a possum dining on something at the edge of the road. Startled by the headlights, he looked up at them, then went back to the meal at hand.

"Have you ever noticed," Delores asked, "that right in the face, possums look a lot like little panda bears?"

Phil smiled and tousled her hair. "Not until tonight. But now that you say so—" He kissed her cheek and never finished his sentence.

He did exactly as promised—took her home, kissed her at the front door, and left her. Delores watched from the window as he sat in his car for a minute, then two, then three, and as his key turned in the ignition, she ran out the door.

"Don't go," she said, out of breath for fear of not catching him. "Let me cook *you* breakfast."

He shut off the car but didn't move. "Sweetheart," he said. "I have to be honest. I don't think I can eat. I can't eat, or sleep, or—I'm not even sure I can drive. I just want to look at you, to be in the same room with you, and I'm not sure I can trust myself to keep being a gentleman."

"I don't want you to be," she declared, surprising herself but knowing it was true. "Come inside. Don't let it be over, yet."

They walked inside, hand in hand, but when the door closed, she kissed him as the new woman of the new life she'd begun just hours ago. Carrying her to her bedroom, he reverently removed the 4-H dress designed years before in wait of that very night. They spoke little, giving full concentration to the sights, smells, tastes, and feelings new to that night and never to be completely foreign again.

Though neither was aware of the time, they would both later recall a particular kiss that coincided with the break of day. They would almost fall asleep, several times, but upon realizing this fact would start the whole procedure again, in a different order or a different room or simply repeating something wonderful from minutes before.

At some time past noon, Delores closed her eyes and fell into a dream. She awoke naked but wrapped in blanket on her bed, her dress from the night before folded neatly over a nearby chair.

Stumbling into the kitchen, she looked out at the driveway and knew she was alone. A sharp and empty pain seized the pit of her stomach, and that was when she saw the note left on the table, scribbled on a Nolan Pharmacy pad she kept on the counter for grocery lists.

Delores, You looked so peaceful, like Sleeping Beauty, I didn't have the heart to wake you. Going home, need to shower and shave, I smell awful. Come to my house—around 5? Will cook you a REAL dinner, fit for a princess. Can't wait to see you again. Love, Phil.

She slipped the note into the blanket against her naked breast, and went back to bed, which smelled of *him*, and not bad at all.

They spent Sunday night at the lodge, Delores rising in time to go home and shower before going to work. On Monday night, they had dinner and a movie in Albany, then retired to Delores' apartment. Tuesday night she cooked for him, her mother's pot roast and Cal's favorite blackberry pie. He promised venison steaks on Wednesday.

←

Imogene Etheridge was late to work on Wednesday, and for the first time, Delores was a few minutes late and not there to cover for her. Imogene arrived a few minutes after Delores, and the two hoped their little indiscretion would go unnoticed. It didn't.

Mr. Foster strode into the sewing room, seeming to follow Imogene as she rushed in to take her station. However, the object of his attention was Delores.

"Miss Mullinax," called Mr. Foster from the front of the room, "I see you're a bit late getting started this morning, as are some of the others. You girls should realize that this habit of laziness will not be tolerated." Although it was Imogene who was truly late, Mr. Foster spoke as if to admonish them all, continuing to stare at Delores as she hurriedly wound thread onto her machine bobbin. "Imogene, you start at Delores' station today, since she's at least gotten it ready to work. Miss Mullinax, I need a word with you, in my office. You can start up another machine when you return."

He walked out the door. The room remained silent until enough time lapsed for his safety from hearing distance. Then they all talked at once.

"Who put a bee in his bonnet this morning?" snickered Aunt Mamie, causing several of the girls to smile.

"I'm sorry, Delores," said Imogene. "I'm the one who's way behind the clock. I don't know why he's got it out for you today."

"Yeah, Delores is the one who covers all our butts when the going gets rough. Why is *she* the one in trouble?" questioned Bertha.

The room began to hum, the start up of sewing machines accompanied by varied explanations on why each lady thought the boss was after Delores. Delores said nothing, relinquishing her machine to Imogene and starting the long trek through the factory to Mr. Foster's executive suite.

The secretary motioned her through the reception area and back to Foster's office, where he sat behind a huge, ornate desk. "Have a seat, Miss Mullinax," he said, gesturing toward the navy leather wing chairs facing him. "But first, close the door there."

Delores swallowed hard and reluctantly took a seat in the closest of the tall, stately chairs obviously intended for someone more important than a sewing machine operator. *What is this about?* she thought, wondering both why she was singled out and why this was a seemingly private meeting. She had never seen the inside of this office, and she wasn't sure any of her peers had, either.

"It seems that, unless we're not up to snuff in our record keeping," he said, flipping pages in a manila file folder. "Today is the first time you've clocked in late since you've come to work here."

Delores said nothing, her head bobbing slightly in an almost-nod, her eyes shifting toward the floor.

"Answer me, Miss Mullinax. Was today's example of punctuality your usual performance, or an exception to the norm?" He sat still, awaiting her reply.

"I, I—have always been on time, sir. Today wasn't—was *not* the norm—at least not for me. I'm usually early, I guess 'cause I grew up on a farm—"

"So you admit that today you arrived later than you have in the past, in fact, later than you've clocked in throughout all your employment here," he said.

"Yes, I guess so, sir," she said.

"And do you have an explanation for this sudden change in your work ethic?"

Delores was silent, trying to gather her words in a way that might be the most pleasing to Mr. Foster. She didn't know what he wanted or why he was so interested in her employment record. Even though she was probably the most punctual employee on her shift, it seemed that her one-time indiscretion had become a matter of monstrous importance. She took a deep breath and let it out slowly, knowing she was buying time to find the right answer for a question she didn't understand.

"I'm really sorry, Mr. Foster. I value my job here, and appreciate how—how you didn't—you didn't punish me—I mean, I got to keep my job and all, after my brother's accident. I really want to be a good employee, and I always try to do my best and be on time and follow the rules and—"

"Were you following the rules when you arrived late today?" he asked.

"Well, no sir, it's just, I overslept—something I never do, and I swear it won't happen again—"

"Is there a reason you think that the rules have changed for you, Miss Mullinax? Is there a motive behind your thinking that for the first time in your employment of nearly two years that you suddenly believe you can clock in anytime you like?"

"No, sir, I—"

"Will you be clocking out in the same manner, leaving whenever you feel like it? Do you plan to work every day now, or just on days you particularly want to come in?"

Delores was speechless, embarrassed, and tears welled up behind her eyes, but she willed them to stay in place. She would not break down in front of Mr. Foster, no matter how much he harassed her. She made no reply to his questions, but he continued on as if she had.

"Tell me, Miss Mullinax, exactly what has transpired which caused your new attitude about your job requirements?" He looked back into the folder of papers. "It seems that just last week, when you clocked out on Friday, you were still an exemplary worker. Must've been an amazing weekend for you, to change your whole personality in less than four days. What happened, Miss Mullinax, do tell me." His voice was part mocking, part judgmental, and simply frightening. Delores had never been talked to in such a hurtful manner.

Looking up at Foster's cold and accusing stare, her face warmed. Surely he couldn't know about—

"You're blushing, Miss Mullinax. Certainly a young woman of your—" he paused, "questionable morals isn't blushing like a school-girl over activities you flaunted freely for the whole community to see. From what I understand, you seemed proud of your antics in that night club/honky-tonk, and you didn't appear to make any effort to conceal who slept in your bed afterwards, either. I'd say your attempt at being a delicate girl-next-door is a joke. Far too little, far too late."

Delores stood as she felt a tear trickle across her cheek. Wanting to run out the door, out of the building and never come back, she stood stiffly as though her feet were encased in cement. She bit her lip and swallowed hard, afraid if she opened her mouth she would vomit. She didn't know if she was being fired but almost hoped she was; she never wanted to be near this man, or even near the place where she'd been made to feel so vile and disgusting. More than anything she wanted to leave, but somehow she couldn't. She stood like a frozen zombie, feeling Foster's vehemence penetrate her every fiber, her heart and her esophagus burning like fire.

"Sit down, slut," he said through his teeth. Delores had never been called such a name, and the Delores she had been until just minutes ago knew this was reason enough to leave immediately; yet the new, damaged Delores sat down, as if submitting to the humiliation and punishment she must deserve.

"I'm not through with you, not by a long shot," he said, standing and walking over to the varnished oak credenza against the wall. He retrieved a glass tumbler from inside the cabinet, lifted the lid of a black leather ice bucket, and dropped ice cubes into his glass. From the three ornate bottles sitting beside the bucket, he chose the one with the clear liquid and poured it over the ice.

Delores had no idea what the liquid was, but since the other two were brown and amber in color, she assumed they were liquor, the clear one probably vodka. However, the rumbling in her belly and the fire in her throat made her long for a drink of water, and seeing the clear glass sweating with cold was mesmerizing. Delores stared at the glass, grateful for the hypnotic attraction that took her anywhere away from being who and where she was. If Mr. Foster noticed, he didn't show it, downing his drink, refilling it and returning to his desk.

"Delores," he said as he seated himself. "You like to dance?"

Delores said nothing, concentrating on the melting ice cubes tinkling against the tumbler.

"I asked you a question." His voice was harsh and percussive.

"I—uh—I guess so—" she stammered, never taking her eyes from the glass.

"Don't be shy, it's a little late for that," he said. "They say you were the featured attraction, barely left the floor all night. Made the girls jealous, and the men wanted to be—in my son's shoes, so to speak— at least when he took his shoes off that night, for sure." Mr. Foster sneered at his own joke. "Did you like that, Delores? Do you like to be looked at, noticed, desired?"

Delores made no attempt to answer.

"You're a decent looking girl," Foster said "But I have to admit, you surprised me. Quiet, you keep to yourself, and I've never seen you dress like a slut, either. 'Course, I've only seen you in the sewing room. Still, that's the way it is sometimes; it's gals that act like scared rabbits in the day that can rut like rabbits in the night. Does that pretty much sum you up, Delores?"

Delores said nothing, lost in her dream of the cool, clear water and ice on her tongue. She focused on the glass, almost tasting its biting cold against her teeth.

"Well, Delores," he said. "We need to get a few things straight. You may be a little spitfire in the bedroom, but here, you operate a sewing machine. Shift work. No special privileges—it's a privilege, not a right—for you to work here in the first place. Understand?"

Still staring at the glass, she nodded.

"Do you want to keep working here, Delores?"

She shifted her gaze from the glass to his face, looking just above the top of his head as not to make actual eye contact, but to appear that she was. She continued to nod.

"Until now you've been a good worker. I like to think I'm a fair man. I'd like to keep you here, but you'll have to abide by my rules. Are you listening, Delores? This is important, that is, if you want to keep your job."

"Yes, sir," Delores said, acknowledging his toupee with a small, forced smile.

"I'm not your father, Delores. You're legal age, you can do what you want to do outside this building. You can shake your little fanny for all southwest Georgia. You can drink like a sailor, party 'til the wee hours, put on a show like a striptease queen. You can bed down with a new fellow every night, or half a dozen at a time if that's what strikes your fancy. As long as you do your job with the credibility I've seen before this week, I have no right or intention to pass judgment on anything you do outside of work hours or this building."

Delores looked above his eyebrows now, wondering if she had misunderstood this whole conversation. Some of the things he said were mean, but—could he be joking? Maybe this was some kind of rich people humor that she didn't understand, since she'd never really known any rich people. His voice was beginning to sound lighter, and every time he said something hurtful, he seemed to counteract it with something nice, well, maybe not exactly nice, but at least not hurtful and almost nice. The lilt of his voice, especially when he said "I'm not your father," reminded her of her own father's voice: his diction and grammar were different, but the soothing timbre of a wise older man made her feel nurtured and cherished. Delores couldn't help herself: she looked directly into his steel gray eyes, hoping to see the missing link that would make her understand what he was saying.

"You're a big girl, Delores," he said, "and you're free to be whatever kind of woman that makes you happy."

Delores smiled; her daddy had said something like that, that he'd always wanted her to be happy.

"But," Mr. Foster said, "there is one thing that is within my rights to speak of, and it's something I will not allow. Not at any cost."

Delores was confused. Maybe he did want to step in for her daddy. Of course, he never could, but it was kind of sweet that he might want to.

"Whatever kind of woman you want to be—a church-going wife and mother, a good-time girl, or an outright whore—you will not be anything to my son. Not now, not ever."

Bile formed in her throat as her eyes began to sting, and she crossed her arm over her heaving stomach. She stared back at the glass of near-melted ice, willing herself not to retch. This time, she didn't think it would work. This time the water did not look soothing, or cool, or satisfactory in any way. Flashing before her eyes was Phil's glass of seltzer water at the Plantation Club, its unexpected bitter taste, then the sensuous, guilty pleasure she felt when he rubbed the ice cube around the back of her neck. She looked back at Mr. Foster, his hard eyes condemning everything she'd felt in those most intimate of moments, turning all she'd believed as magic into evil and filth. With a quick gasp, Delores held her convulsing midsection with one arm and covered her mouth with the other. Trying to stand, her awkwardness only reseated her, rocking the chair on one leg and almost toppling over.

"Good God," cried Mr. Foster, jumping out of his seat for the credenza. Lifting the ice bucket, he removed the pristine white hand towel beneath it and handed it to Delores. With a violent heave, she lowered her head, then vomited into the towel as quietly as possible. As she tried again to stand, Foster motioned that she remained seated.

"Don't need the whole plant knowing your business," he said, and for just a moment they actually agreed on something. Picking up the phone on his desk, he pressed a lighted button and then spoke.

"Carolyn, can you get me a 7-Up or ginger ale, a couple of clean hand towels, and—" he thought for a minute. "Some crackers or pretzels, if you can get your hands on any. Or some Pepto Bismol. Anything to help a queasy stomach." He listened for a second and then hung up.

Delores retched again, this time bringing up nothing, but choking on tears and starting a coughing fit. Mr. Foster sat quietly, leaving her alone and pretending to read something in the file of papers until he arose to answer the soft knock at the door.

"Thank you, Carolyn," he said to his secretary. "And hold all my calls for the next—until further notice."

"Yes, sir," Delores heard her say as he closed the door.

Mr. Foster handed Delores a cold, green bottle of 7-Up, an unopened roll of Tums, and a handful of white paper napkins. The bottle was well-chilled and sweating against its outside.

"Thank you," she mumbled as she took his offerings.

"Drink slow," he said, "probably the best way to keep it down." Delores looked up at him, confused.

"My wife had a sensitive stomach," he said. "The least little thing that would upset her, she'd be running for the bathroom. I should own stock in a ginger ale manufacturer." For just a moment he looked thoughtful, almost kind, and Delores allowed herself to imagine her boss in a different setting, being someone else altogether. It sounded like he really cared for his wife—were there other children besides Phil? What did they do together, as a family? Did he dress differently, less formal, the way his voice had softened and become less rigid when mentioning his wife's stomach troubles? In the short time she'd known Phil, he'd never mentioned his family.

Delores took another sip of the ice-cold drink; she could feel its medicinal fizziness as it traveled down her throat and into her belly, which made a grateful but embarrassing growl upon reaching there. She looked up, but Mr. Foster showed no sign of hearing it, and she semi-smiled at his merciful gesture. She gently peeled back the foil on the roll of antacids, popping two into her mouth and carefully folding the foil over the remaining tablets. Biting down into their chalkiness, she followed them with another swallow of 7-Up. After belching silently into a napkin, she drank again. The awful feeling of minutes before was beginning to retreat.

"Feeling better?" he asked, looking up from his work. "Take your time, I'll wait. We need to have a serious discussion, and I need your full attention. Finish your drink if you need to." He shuffled through some other things on his desk, and Delores sipped the 7-Up, dreading whatever message awaited, but anxious to get it over with.

"Being such a smart girl," Foster began, "You may have noticed that my son is not the sharpest tool in the shed."

Delores knew the expression well, but it didn't seem like one her boss was likely to use. Especially about his own son. She sat expressionless, waiting for more.

"It took special schools and tutors to get him through grade school, and his college career, already bought and paid for, was cut short by his own thoughtless behavior. But Phillip is my son, and he will have his own place in the family business, however less-than-white-collar that place may turn out to be. Phillip is a Foster, and he will behave as a Foster, despite his occasional backsliding adventures. Are you following me, Delores?"

"I think so, sir," she said, while in truth, she was not.

"Phil is a good looking kid, and I suppose he's had his share of free and easy lady friends. Are you with me?" He looked Delores in the eye, like a one-on-one, over-zealous schoolteacher. She nodded.

"He's never had a serious girlfriend, but when he does, it will be with a young lady who meets the family's approval."

Delores's stomach tightened again, and she tried to unwrap another tablet without calling attention to the fact she was doing so.

"Tell me, Delores, are you aware of how much Oakland has done for your brother and, subsequently, for you, after his unfortunate accident?"

Delores nodded nervously. "Yes, I mean yes sir, and we really appreciate it. Cal couldn't have been in better hands when he got hurt, and your getting him into the special rehab place is something I'd don't think we could've managed—"

"That's right," Foster interrupted. "Neither you nor your brother would have had any idea where or how to get him the rehabilitation he needs. And you may not know this, but there's a right-to-work law in Georgia, and farm laborers sign on at their own risk. As long as your brother had been involved in farm work, he surely knew better than to get as careless as he did when he caused his misfortune."

"But it was an accident," Delores said, never imagining that someone could refer to Cal's getting hurt as an act of carelessness. She turned up her drink bottle and swallowed; the quick motion caused her to swallow the wrong way, bringing on an embarrassing fit of choking. Mr. Foster looked back at his notes as her eyes watered and she regained control of her breathing. When the coughing ended, he began again.

"I try to take care of my workers in the best way possible, and I never stopped to lay any blame on why Calvin's injury occurred, however, I could have. I could have refused any help whatsoever, since Calvin was a seasoned farmer and knew the risks. We've been harvesting peanuts for twenty years, and no such accident had happened before. As a matter of fact, his is the only injury of such in the farming history of Dumas County, as far as we could tell. Still, I've always been fond of Calvin, and I know you two young folks have had a pretty rough deal in life. I wrote off his medical bills as an extra farm expense. Didn't make much profit for the season, but it was the right thing to do. Now setting him up at Warm Springs cost a pretty penny as well, but I sincerely hope he can learn himself a trade, since farming is out of the question for him now. But to sum it up, Miss Mullinax, Oakland and I have gone far beyond the call of duty for your brother. Far beyond."

Delores knew this was leading somewhere, but she was still confused at what Mr. Foster wanted. He had done wonderful things for

Calvin, and they were forever indebted to him. But now it sounded like it was Calvin's fault, and that they—she and Cal—had somehow been ungrateful for Foster's help. Or was it something else? She didn't know.

"Thank you, Mr. Foster," she said, her voice quivering. "We can't thank you enough, and Calvin will always—"

"I'm not asking for your thanks, I don't need it." Mr. Foster sound insulted at her words, but continued his own confusing speech. "Your brother's medical bills were paid. He was given a very generous cash settlement, along with the rehab he's receiving now. I'd say that's beyond enough for one man to take as profit from his own mistakes, wouldn't you?"

"But it was an accident, he didn't—"

"That's right. We wrote it off as an accident. Oakland settled with your brother, without ever bringing up what legal experts felt should be explored; his mental state, unnecessary hurrying, careless procedures. He was known to invent dangerous contests with other workers in order to flaunt his physical superiority, thought of himself as the top of the heap despite being one of the youngest men working. We went without mentioning damages to equipment, valuable harvesting hours lost that day for all the men, and what it did to morale for the rest of the season. We called it an accident, and that's what it will remain."

Delores sat dumbfounded, hearing her brother described as someone she didn't know. She couldn't imagine anyone thinking of Cal this way, but obviously they had.

"Unless," Foster said, intentionally slowing down, "your family wants to pull out of the settlement and take this to court. Unless you want to give up what you've already taken, and let a judge decide where to put the blame."

Delores froze as she processed his words. Cal's settlement— the check had been cashed and a good chunk of it already spent. He'd bought the truck, the land for his new home, and paid the contractors who were putting the house together for his return. Could Mr. Foster take the money *back*? What about the medical bills? Would he suddenly owe for them, too? Delores felt a cold chill run through her body, imagining her brother suddenly destitute and owing amounts he would never pay off in a lifetime. Where would they go? How could they even live? And Cal, in the fragile state he'd been in since losing his arm, would he even want to live under such circumstances?

"Miss Mullinax," Foster said, "I don't know or care about your intentions concerning my son. I realize it is possible that you looked on your dalliance just as he did, a one night/one weekend stand. Or perhaps you fancied yourself as beginning a new relationship, one that would continue to grow into something more permanent? Whatever your thoughts on the subject, here is what you need to understand. You will not be seen with my son, alone or in public, ever again."

Delores sat stone-still, refusing to give in to the tears she held back.

"You are my employee. Your brother is an ex-employee, righteously settled with after a work-related accident. We, the Foster family, owe you and your family nothing whatsoever," said Mr. Foster. "This is a small, nosy community. My son is living here while learning a skill to work him into the family business, but he is not now nor ever will be a part of the community, in a social context. Do you understand me, Miss Mullinax?"

Delores nodded and stared at the wall.

"My son is not your boyfriend, not your partying buddy, not anything to you. Any friendship he assumed with your brother ceased when they no longer worked together. You have no business at the lodge, and my son will not be seen in your home. Do you follow me here?"

Delores continued to nod, wringing the wadded paper napkin in her lap.

"If you can abide by these rules, I see no problem with your continued employment here. It would also mean that your brother's settlement would not be questioned. You love your brother, and you certainly wouldn't want to do anything that could jeopardize his happiness, would you?"

"No, sir," Delores said, a single tear sliding down her cheek.

"Now, do you think we can come to an agreement here, Delores?" He was smiling now, a tight, sneer that showed he was totally in control of the situation at hand.

"Yes, yes, sir. I would never do anything to—"

"And do you think this little conversation is enough? Can we keep this between us, and not involve anyone else? I think that would be the best for everyone, don't you Delores?" His smile grew bigger, and scarier.

"Yes, sir. Really. I mean, yes, sir," she said. Tears trickled down both cheeks, and she smeared them off with the withered napkin.

"I think I'll step out of the office for a few minutes," Mr. Foster said as he stood. Delores stood as well, but he motioned for her to sit back down. "It would probably be best for you to stay and get yourself together," he said. "Why not use my restroom to fix your face. You know the girls will have questions. Any idea what you'll tell them?"

Delores swallowed hard, looked at the floor, then back up to her boss. "I'll tell them you got onto me for being late, and that we need to watch the clocking in, from now on. That's all."

"Very good, Delores. You *are* a smart one. And are we perfectly clear on—the other matter?"

"Yes, sir," she said, "perfectly clear."

"Good," he said, walking out of the room, quietly closing the door and leaving her to ready herself for the sewing room.

When the ladies returned from lunch, Delores was already there. She looked pale and red-eyed; though she'd washed her face, it was obvious that she had been crying. Imogene, who sat next to her, spent an hour trying to attract her attention, but Delores stared straight ahead and refused to make eye contact. Aunt Mamie rose from her machine and walked over behind Delores.

"You doin' alright, baby? I declare, you're looking a little peaked. Anything I can do for you?" Delores kept sewing, looking straight ahead, as though Aunt Mamie were nowhere in the room. Getting no response from Delores and the evil eye from Imogene, the older woman went back to her post.

"Delores Mullinax," proclaimed the nasal voice of Mr. Foster's secretary through the square wooden box at the front of the sewing room. The voice was loud enough to penetrate through all the clanging machinery, but with chirping, static-y accompaniment as well. "Delores Mullinax, please report to the main office for a telephone message. Delores Mullinax, please report to the main office now." The intercom switched off with a static blast and a loud click.

Delores switched off her machine and left the room, ignoring the stares and puzzled looks of her friends. When afternoon break was called, they all headed for the smoking tree, but Delores did not join them.

On her way to get her brother from the Institute, Delores stopped at the lodge and left a note for Phil.

> *Going to Warm Springs to get Cal. Cannot see you for a while.*
> *Will explain later. Do NOT come to my house. Do NOT say anything to anybody about the time we spent together. Please don't come over, and you can NOT tell my brother anything about us. I will explain when I can, but it may be a while. Please respect my wishes on this. My brother is all the family I have, and I have to protect him. I'm sorry if I have hurt you. Please believe me—Really.*
> *Love, Delores*

Chapter 11
January 1959

Warm Springs, Georgia

Calvin

CAL AMBLED OUT, TAKING IN HIS NEW SURROUNDINGS. Cracked sidewalks led to a dull brick building. The paint was peeling on the old wooden wheelchair ramp. He walked up the stairs to the faded green double doors. Pulling them open, he walked into the front hallway. The smell of Pinesol and urine assaulted him.

A woman in a wheelchair sat diagonally in front of the desk; a thin guy in coveralls, who looked like he might be her son, signed paperwork. She stared at the floor, drooling. A large girl about Cal's age shuffled through the lobby. She touched every object as she moved through the room. When she reached Cal, she grabbed him in a strong bear-hold. His face was in her greasy hair.

You're purty," she said. He could feel her breasts smashed against him. "Will you be my boyfriend?" She smelled of onions.

Cal tried to pry himself away. A middle-aged man with Down's syndrome rushed in, looking about frantically until he saw Cal's new friend.

"Tina," he screamed. "I'll save you!" He ran head-on into Calvin, knocking Cal, Cal's suitcase, Tina, and himself to the floor.

"Stahhhpit, Hahvey," Tina cried. "He's my new boyfriend. I don't love you no more." She lay across Cal's abdomen, talking to the floor, her girth pinning Cal to the linoleum.

Harvey rolled about like a ball-bottomed doll, finally stretching onto all fours and then painstakingly rising. It was at that moment that both he and Tina noticed Calvin's hook.

"He's a bad man," cried Harvey, pointing. "He's a—a—a bad—boat man!"

Cal could hardly breathe. He'd hit his hip on his suitcase when he fell, and it throbbed. "That's a pirate, you dumbass," Tina said. "And he ain't a pirate. Pirates have eye patches and earrings." She pondered the thought for a moment, then added, "I like pirates, though."

"You're bad, too, Tina. You're a whore," said Harvey, dragging out the word like "hoe-er," putting his hands on his hips and staring down at them.

"Am not." Tina tried to look over her shoulder at him. "You just call me a whore cause I won't sleep with you." She stuck out her tongue like a five-year-old. Cal cleared his throat.

"But you did, Tina, you did," Harvey said. "You slept with me in my room 'til Mrs. Thomas came in and found us. You was asleep, Tina, you was with me, in my room, 'til she came in and—"

"You're a idjut. I fell asleep in your room. But I didn't *do it* with you. You don't even know how. You didn't even try—"

A large coffee-colored man in white scrubs came through the doors. "Okay, Tina, Harvey," he said. "This is no way to treat a new friend." He pulled Tina to her feet, then offered his hand to Calvin. Calvin braced himself with his good hand and got up on his own.

"This is my new boyfriend. He's got a hook," Tina said.

"He try to hurt Tina with it, he was gonna tear her up before I jumped on him and—"

"I'm sure he was not trying to hurt Tina." The man winked at Calvin. "And it's never good to attack someone when you don't know the circumstances," he said to Harvey.

Harvey began to cry. He had a white doughy face and hair the consistency of corn silk. "But I didn't mean to tack him, I thought I was doing good. He shouldn't have that hook thing out like that. They won't let me hold a real knife cause I might hurt somebody, by mistake. They shouldn't let him have that hook. It ain't fair." Harvey burst into sobs, snot mixing with tears.

"It's okay, Harvey," the kind man said. "Now why don't you go wash your face. It's almost time for crafts."

"Crafts—oh boy! I make good crafts," Harvey said, suddenly happy again. "I make you a present?" he asked Tina.

"I'm staying with *him*," Tina said. She grabbed Cal's hook and yanked possessively. Cal winced.

"Now, Tina," the orderly said. "Remember how we've talked about keeping our hands to ourselves, especially with people we don't know?" He gently removed Cal from Tina's grasp as Harvey left for crafts.

"But I know him. I love him. He's my boyfriend!"

"Tina," he said sternly, "what's his name?"

Tina pursed her lips. "I forgot."

"Tina," he said in a deeper tone.

"What's your name?" she asked Cal, putting her hand on her hip and batting her pale eyelashes.

"Tina," the man said again, "go back to the rec room. Dr. Lamb will talk with you about this later."

"Not Dr. Lamb," she whined. "You ain't gonna tell Dr. Lamb. Please?"

"Go back to the rec room, Tina," he said firmly. "We'll talk later." Tina put her mouth in a pout. She turned and stomped back the way she'd come.

"Travis Ford," the man said, offering his hand to Cal. This time Cal accepted it.

"I guess you're new; try not to let that little scene color your outlook on the place. Tina and Harvey are two of our more interesting characters. How long you been here?"

"I just got here a few minutes ago. There was a man at the desk, so I waited, then the—Tina—she came out and—"

"Enough said." The man laughed. He was about six foot two and had friendly eyes. "Tina's a handful, though basically harmless. Haven't checked in yet?"

"Uhh, no," Cal said.

"Let me help you. What's your name?"

"Cal. Calvin Mullinax."

"Where're you from, Cal?"

"Nolan, Dumas County. A farming accident," Cal said, looking at the shining steel where his arm used to be.

"Tough break, man. Still, you seem to be doing okay. You can learn some coping skills and go back to a normal life. Some of the folks here'll never see that option." Travis walked to the desk. "Edna, this is Calvin Mullinax. You got his name in that book of yours?"

Edna, the dour, middle-aged woman with a blue-gray bun, sat up straighter, squinted and ran her finger down an appointment book. "Mullinax. Yeah, you see Dr. Lamb first, at eleven. Through the red door and down the hall to your right," she said without looking up. "You can leave your suitcase here. Someone'll bring it to your dorm room."

"I'll show him to Dr. Lamb, Edna," Travis said. He motioned Cal ahead. "Onward, to ecstasy!"

Dr. Lamb was an overweight, middle-aged man who liked to show off his vocabulary. After a few basic questions about Calvin's disability and previous education, he explained that the next few days would consist of an evaluation, a battery of tests. The word "test" made Cal stare questioningly at his hook, which the doctor understood immediately.

"Don't worry," he said. "They're oral tests."

For the next two hours, Cal interpreted ink blots, identified pictures, did simple math calculations and answered general information questions any fourth grader would have known. At the end of his session, Dr. Lamb said, "I'll see you tomorrow at the same time. You're assigned to room seventy-two, with no roommate at present, but don't expect it to last. With just a hundred twenty beds, we stay at maximum capacity most of the time."

Cal found his room with no problem, his suitcase already unpacked and placed in the particleboard drawers. His meds, however, were nowhere to be found.

He went back out to the front desk. "Excuse me," he said to Edna. "Do you know where the people who unpacked my things would've put my medication?"

Edna was writing something in her notebook and did not look up. "Clients are not allowed to self-medicate," she said like a robot. "Medications prescribed by our medical staff are dispensed individually at specified times."

"But these are prescription medications." Cal stared down at her tight, unnatural-colored hairdo. "I've been on them since my accident and surgery. They gave me a three month supply when I left for here."

"If our doctors think you need drugs, they will prescribe them." She put her finger to her tongue and turned the page. "This is not a flophouse or an opium den. Go back to your room, Mr. Mullinax."

"But some of it is—" he fought for the right word, "—mandatory. I'm not supposed to stop taking it 'til my doctor tells me. It's for making my—" Cal hated the words associated with his new body. "Making my stump fully close up, without matted tissue, and to cut down the risk of infection."

"You can talk to Dr. Lamb at your appointment tomorrow." She had a sing-songy way of talking that made him want to scratch her face. "Go to your room now, before I have to call security."

"Fine, then," he snarled, pushing the swinging door with unnecessary force.

Dr. Lamb finally prescribed an anti-anxiety drug for what he called Cal's "issues with his new condition," but claimed the other medications were unnecessary. Also, the question seemed moot: staff members unpacking Cal's things said no medications were in his suitcase, so he must have left them at home. Cal knew there must be some happy health workers tonight at his expense, but what could he do? He figured he'd tough it out for a while and see what happened.

Cal was tested, observed, retested, analyzed, psychoanalyzed and taken apart piece by piece, only to find that he was "of above average intelligence" and "mechanically inclined." He learned that less than ten per cent of the more than one hundred residents at the Institute were physically handicapped, and for half of those, their physical problems were considered secondary. In the area of job training, career guidance taught two skills that, if mastered, could land clients in a job at a local factory: lining bobby pins onto a cardboard sleeve and fastening safety pins to a metal circle. As the testing continued, Dr. Lamb promised "skills therapy" when "a satisfactory evaluation was made," but Cal had his doubts.

Five days after the testing began, Calvin was called by intercom to report to Room #17 for "occupational therapy." *At last*, he thought. *Finally something that might matter.*

A young, attractive blonde wearing a yellow sweater and smelling of lemony cologne introduced herself as Julie, his therapist. "We'll work together three times a week," she said, "working on both gross and fine motor skills and coordination. Ready to get started?" She smiled, evoking an air of sunflowers and cool breezes.

His first task seemed to be a game of sorts. He was seated at a table bearing a wooden roulette wheel. In a box on the table were numerous wooden pegs in a variety of sizes. Julie spun the wheel, and Cal's task was to insert as many of the pegs as possible into the holes on the side of the wheel. He caught on fast, realizing it was easier to grab up pegs of one size with his hook and use his good hand to insert into the appropriate holes, then repeat the process with the next size. To his astonishment, the speed of the spin increased as his skill got better. Still, Cal rose to the challenge, and the box was empty before the wheel reached maximum speed.

"No fair," Julie laughed. "You seemed to have had previous sorting experience. But your use of the hook will get better faster if you stop cheating with your other hand." Cal laughed, too, then realized she was serious in what she said.

"But don't I need to be using both, since I have both, and will ultimately work with them at the same time?" he asked. Julie rolled her eyes like he made no sense, and made no comment.

"Don't I need to learn to use it all, a new way, to get back to doing real work? I mean, isn't that what this therapy is really for? To figure out how to compensate for my lost arm, and still do my job?" Cal asked.

Surely if he showed her he understood his weaknesses, showed her how much he wanted to get better, then she'd know he was ready to get down to serious business. And she'd help him. She'd use her crazy Las Vegas games to make him better. She could teach him things; he was someone she could help enough to get out of this place. She might be as excited about this as he was, Cal figured.

"There are a variety of skills feasible for the handicapped, given proper training from experienced professionals and a willing attitude in the client," Julie said, her cheerfulness fading into a stiff, all-business demeanor. "Perhaps you should spend some time thinking realistically about your job limitations. You will not return to the same life you had before, but you can have a successful life of a different nature."

She opened the door, a nod of her head ushering Cal out. She made no eye contact, inspecting her cuticles as she spoke.

"What do you mean, 'of a different nature'?" Cal said.

"You won't become a surgeon or a concert violinist, but you can be part of the work force, and you aren't disabled to the point of being a drain on society. You can have a productive life, if you face reality and keep a good attitude."

Cal waited for more, but Julie's silent stare indicated that she was through talking.

"Yeah, right," Cal mumbled. He walked out the door.

That night seemed the longest in quite a while. Cal missed the painkillers, which he'd progressed to using only at night. More than the painkillers he missed the alcohol he'd used to set them in motion, and there was no alcohol in Warm Springs. The skin around the end of his stump had turned pink and swollen, and he noticed a slight unfamiliar odor around it.

Cal sat up in his sweat-drenched bed and walked over to the sink for a cool washcloth to bathe his face, then what was left of his arm. He went back to bed, dreamed with eyes open, and repeated the washcloth procedure until sunlight signaled a new day.

The next day there was no roulette wheel in sight. Julie sat at the table with a red plastic box, hollow and covered in holes of various geometric shapes, obviously a child's toy.

"Sit down, Cal," Julie said with a nod.

"For me?" he said, gesturing at the toy as he seated himself.

"As a matter of fact, it is," said Julie. "Today will be devoted to fine motor coordination." She opened the box's top and emptied its contents onto the table; three dimensional circles, squares, rectangles, diamonds, and stars in primary colors.

"It's Tinker Toy day?" Cal asked, wondering what cat and mouse game she had planned.

"Children's educational manipulatives aren't just for kids anymore." Julie allowed herself a smile. "I've found this particular one to be quite helpful for improving fine motor skills. Shall we begin?"

"Sure," said Cal. He grabbed a handful of objects with his good hand, then plucked out a blue star with his hook, dropping it gingerly into the star-shaped hole. He repeated with a yellow circle, then a green square. *No problem, piece of cake*, Cal thought. Feeling smug, he relaxed and let his mind wander, taking in Julie's small, pert breasts under her sky blue sweater. Today she smelled more floral than citrus. He wondered if she had a different theme for each day of the week, like the panty sets his sister had yearned for in the Sears catalog.

The next star, a red one, caught on his hook, causing Cal to jam the shape sideways, half-in and half-out of the box. Embarrassed, he shoved harder, hooking the entire box onto his metal prosthesis. Expertly wiggling his shoulder, he clamped and unclamped the hook, then tried to shake the box off the hook, to no avail. Plastic against metal made a noisy rattling sound.

Cal wanted to slam the damned thing on the table, busting it wide open, sending baby toys flying across the room. He reached to his forehead with his good arm, using his sleeve to wipe away the layer of cold sweat that was a part of his person these days. Who was this self-righteous bitch, forcing him to do silly shit he'd never have the need to do with-or-without his arm, making him feel like a useless idiot, not offering him any skills or training that a real man in the real world could possibly use? He wanted to break the box, the table, the toys, and if any exploding debris caught her pretty face, that would be fine, too.

He wanted to hurt something or somebody or both, but he didn't want to be accused of a temper tantrum while playing with toys. So Cal sat quietly, continuing to try and gently pry or shake or mentally project the flimsy red box from his metal appendage.

"The object here," Julie said, "is not only to place the right shapes through the corresponding holes, but also to do so with agility, grace, and precision. You're a big boy and of course you're insulted at playing a child's game, but this can help you more than you realize."

Her scent of roses seemed to stifle the air with its artificial sweetness. Cal noticed a small, black mole peeking out of her neckline. He said nothing, still attempting to remove the box, but with less agitation, stilling it quietly on the table and working to remove it from the hook with his good hand.

"Speed isn't everything, you see," Julie said. "If you take extra care in small spaces, you won't run into problems like you're experiencing now." She gestured to the box on the table. "Practice precision, and speed will come later."

She sounds so smug, Cal thought, *with her two hands and two legs and everything perfect and where it's supposed to be.* Why would a woman who looked like her choose this kind of profession? She probably went to college, somebody paying top dollar, for her to sit here, in her perfect little skirt and sweater, treating grown men like retarded kids. Cal pictured her going home, to some little brick house with a picket fence, telling her husband or boyfriend or even her parents and some frilly little dog about the pitiful losers she worked with. They'd look at her with glowing smiles, thinking how wonderful she was, out making the world a better place, one pathetic loser at a time. She even believed it herself. Then Cal thought of Delores, alone in that sad little apartment, giving up her dreams of business school for a shift job at the panty factory.

Smug bitch, he thought. *If you only knew.*

Cal wanted to leave, before he blew up and told Julie what he really thought of her therapy. But as useless as the place was, it was probably expensive, everything medical was expensive these days. And Mr. Foster had already paid for his stay here, as part of the settlement agreement he'd signed before coming. If leaving was breaking the agreement, could Foster turn around and take back the money? Surely not. He already had the money, had paid for his land and paid the contractors building his house. The rest was in the bank. He'd cashed the check. It was a done deal.

"But I don't teach kindergarten, or whatever the job is where this skill is so damned important," Cal said through his teeth. "And I'm willing to do whatever it takes to compensate for my arm, but this is ridiculous. I need to learn how to lift and pull, use leverage for moving heavy weights, shift gears on a tractor. Mr. Foster didn't pay you guys primo dollars to have me playing with baby toys."

Julie slammed her manicured hand on the tabletop, a gesture that looked stern but made hardly a sound. "Mr. Foster," she said calmly, "didn't pay a dime for your rehabilitation here. This is a government subsidized program. Your thanks should go to gainfully employed taxpayers. Like me." She sucked in and clenched her perfect teeth.

Cal's mouth dropped open. "But Mr. Foster said—"

"I don't know who this Mr. Foster is or what he told you, but this is not a private institution. People come here when they don't have insurance, can't pay for medical care, and need to find some way of supporting their existence on the planet. Some are retarded and basically useless beyond the simplest rote tasks. Some have physical handicaps that render them excused from manual labor. Virtually none of them have any education to speak of, and our teaching them to sort forks and spoons or fold towels is the closest they've had to schooling in decades. We do the best we can for the poor creatures, and at best they can find menial jobs that somewhat subsidize their care. Then there are the ones like you, Mr. Mullinax."

"Like me?" Cal said. "You mean you don't count me with the useless and retarded?"

"No, Mr. Mullinax, you are worse than the poor mental defectives we serve," she said. "Most of them were born that way, of people just like them, with no hope of doing any better. Our country has a legacy of caring for such people, though surely we'll one day see the error of our ways. But the ones like you, who have earned a good day's wage and are capable of taking care of themselves, you are just here for the free ride. A paid vacation, if you time it right, maybe for the rest of your life. Probably got hurt on purpose with this in mind. A little pain, some good drugs for a while, then a free ride on the government train for as long as possible."

Calvin saw the last three months in a high-speed movie in front of his face. He was on the tractor, whole, sweating profusely and counting the rows left to harvest. He was grabbing the pitchfork, hoisting it over the side of the picker and watching the clouds. He felt the white-hot tearing pain, saw the field around him flicker and fade and go black. He smelled alcohol, then saw the hospital, its needles and tubes looming larger than the faceless white-clad drones who carried them. He saw himself in his little house, learning to light cigarettes, feed himself, wipe his ass. He saw the friends who now avoided him, the boss who bought him off, and the sister who put him in this godforsaken place, believing it was for the best.

"Yeah, I got myself hurt on purpose," he said finally. "Who wouldn't give his right arm for a chance at all this?" Cal used his good hand to sweep across the room, then stood and walked out. The plastic box still dangled from the hook.

"I take it that you're through for the day, Mr. Mullinax?" Julie said, remaining seated.

"I'm through with this damned place forever," he said as he headed down the hall, never looking back.

Cal kicked open the door to his dorm room, too riled up to stay there. Going down the hallway, he stopped at the empty nurses' station. When he reached for the doorknob, it was miraculously unlocked. A black rotary phone sat centered on the desk, the friendliest face Cal had seen since his incarceration there. He grabbed the receiver and dialed the operator.

"Nolan, Georgia," he said. "Nolan Manufacturing." A few seconds later, a slow southern soprano answered.

"Could I get a message to Delores Mullinax?" he asked.

"We can't call her off the line, but we could have her call you on her break, if it ain't long distance. Or I guess I could take a message, if you like."

Cal saw a bovine-like nurse at the end of the hall.

"Tell her that her brother called," he said quickly, "and tell her to come and get him, right now." He hung up the phone before the nurse stepped inside.

"Why are you in here? Are you looking for drugs? There are no drugs in here, and patients are not allowed behind the desk. I'm calling security," she said, grabbing for the phone.

"No need," Cal said. "I was gonna ask—what time it was, but then I saw the clock. Sorry to bother you, ma'am." He kept walking.

"Don't come in here again," she called to him.

"Don't worry," he said. "You folks are safe from me, most definitely."

Closing the door to his room, Cal realized he was still wearing the silly plastic box of shapes like a queer fashion accessory. Releasing the lever on the hook, the box came away with a simple nudge.

Maybe I'll keep it as a souvenir, he thought. *Something concrete, something to remind me what a waste of time this place was. To make sure I'm not exaggerating, making up the whole bad dream.*

Calvin dropped the child's toy in his suitcase.

The house on stilts was well in progress when Delores delivered her brother back to Nolan. Driving by, she stopped so that he could investigate.

The outside walls were up. Calvin climbed the newly finished stairs and walked through the empty doorframe of his new home. The bittersweet smell of fresh cut pine opened his sinuses and seemed to quell the narcotic-craving nausea he'd been battling the past few days. Inside he saw the skeletal frame, waiting for sheetrock, paint, and paper. He leaned against the 2x4's, checking their sturdiness. He smiled at the rectangle cut in the wall, where the hub of his wiring would rest. Slowly crossing the dusty plywood floor, he stopped at the great room's center, two tall windows with a box-like seat underneath. He sat down, reverently, looking out across the slow-moving, brown-blue Flint River. This place was his.

Breaking away from his long awaited moment of joy, Cal saw Delores still in the doorway, staring absently at nothing, seeming deep in thought.

Like she seemed the whole way home, Cal pondered. He turned back to the river. Something about Delores was different. She'd been so excited before he left, talking about color schemes and appliances and such. Now it was like she was in the building but still far, far away.

Surely she didn't think his leaving Warm Springs, which turned out to be pretty much a government nuthouse, was gonna cause any problems down the line. Cal could see now that he should have left the place the first day. If Harvey and Tina hadn't given him a clue, the medication issue should've been a full-scale alarm. They couldn't do anything there to help him, he'd have to help himself, which he intended on doing. But Delores was a woman, and like their mama, she worried about the damnedest things.

He'd talk to his sister about how the Warm Springs Institute really was. They'd laugh about it, forget about it, then get on with their new and up-graded lives. This house was gonna be great. He could work on his own motor coordination skills, and he'd be back helping on some farm, somewhere, by the fall. Delores could quit the factory, quit the bar, and go back to school then, too. They were a little off schedule, but not doing bad, either. Yeah, he'd talk to Delores about whatever was bothering her.

But not today, he thought. Today was for being happy. Things were better now. He'd call the doc tomorrow, have him check out his stump, put him back on whatever meds he might need. Cal smiled, looking back out at the bright sky and the lazy river. Happy—for the first time in way too long.

Chapter 12
February 1959

Delores

A FORTY-EIGHT HOUR STOMACH BUG WENT THROUGH the girls at the plant. Gradually, they all contracted it, but only Delores seemed to keep it far beyond its two-day course. She blamed her friends, saying every time she'd start to feel better, another one of them would re-infect her. It was a shallow story, but the only one she had; and the girls were too kind to say what she suspected they really thought, which was the truth.

Her tummy troubles had started in the awful one-on-one with Mr. Foster, which she could easily chalk up to nerves. Then there was the excitement of Cal coming home, the agony of avoiding Phil, and the stress of worrying what Mr. Foster could do to her brother. The horror of just imagining the outcome if Cal found out about Phil, if Phil found out about his dad, if Mr. Foster found out she had any communication at all with his son. Or if the man simply changed his mind, and decided to turn the Mullinax purgatory into literal hell, just because he could. These were Delores's thoughts of every waking moment, plaguing even her dreams. It was no wonder she'd given up on the simple acts of sleep and digestion, leaving her thin, red-eyed and disoriented like the effects of a serious illness. But when days turned to weeks, there was nothing to do but seek the truth she already knew.

She took Cal's truck, claiming to have planned a girl's day out with Imogene, telling him they'd be going to Albany for shopping after work. An hour later, Delores sat on the Naugahyde examining table in the office of a doctor she'd never seen, in a small clinic thirty miles away. On the mimeographed form attached to a clipboard, she'd given her name as Mrs. Martha Smith and claimed to be twenty-four, a housewife with no insurance. She used her mother's birthday and printed that she was born in Bibb County, which she hoped was Macon, though she wasn't sure. She said her husband was Johnny Smith, employed by Pet Milk Corporation, and she gave him Cal's birthday. She didn't know his social security number and left that space blank. A pale, brunette nurse with bouffant hair and a no-nonsense demeanor had asked further questions, like if she smoked cigarettes or drank liquor, and when was the date of her last period, which she didn't remember. The nurse checked off something on the clipboard, cut her eyes quickly to Delores' left hand, then exhaled with a snort and left the room.

Stupid, stupid, stupid, Delores thought to herself, grinding her teeth and clinching her stomach. *I go to the trouble to invent jobs and birthdays, and I don't bother to fake a wedding ring. She's probably writing me up as a prostitute while I sit here.*

Another nurse, this one blonde and chubby, came back with a plastic cup and two faded cloths folded with military precision. "All right, Mrs.—*Smith,*" she said, "First we'll need you to empty your bladder into this cup. The restroom's just down the hall to the left, and I'll be waiting outside. After that, you will take off all of your clothes, including your brassiere and panties, and put on the gown on top." She nodded to the stacked cloths. "It ties in the back. Since the back is open, you can use the second cloth to wrap around you until the doctor comes in. Understand?"

Delores nodded, though in truth she understood nothing. In nineteen years of doctor's visits, she'd never been asked to remove all her clothing, a level of humiliation she didn't know possible.

"But first we need the urine sample," the nurse said, as she handed the cloths to Delores. "Go ahead, I'll be waiting right outside the door. Skit skat." Delores took the cup and walked out the door to the restroom. Closing the door behind her, she felt dismissed like an errant stray cat. She did as told, awkwardly returning with the plastic cup of warm urine, her face flushed with embarrassment.

"Good girl," the nurse said. "All right, let's get undressed. Don't keep the doctor waiting." She took the cup and disappeared down the hallway.

Back in the examining room, Delores's stomach was a mass of knotted muscle, her mouth tasting of acid and her head aching of held back tears. The gown was soft and antiseptic-smelling, but thinner than a worn bed sheet. The two ties at the back left her entire backside exposed, and she wrapped the second cloth around her, then sat on the edge of the table, awaiting whatever indignity came next.

She indeed did not keep the doctor waiting, in fact, Delores waited for what seemed like a half hour, staring at the pale green walls and wondering what instruments of torture waited behind the metal cabinets. The room was unusually cold, and she kept her arms crossed over her breasts to cover her nipples, painfully pointing out through the thin cloth. Startled by the sound of the door opening, she jumped involuntarily, dropping the cloth and then grabbing it quickly, trying to cover what she could.

"Didn't mean to scare you, there," a soft-spoken, gray haired man said. She assumed he was the doctor, followed by the bouffant brunette from before.

"No need to wrap up, though, that top cloth has to come off anyway. I'm Doctor Jenkins," he nodded as he went about his business.

The nurse reached over and started to remove the cloth, but could not because Delores was sitting on it.

"Stand up so I can get this off," she said, sounding put out by Delores's lack of cooperation. Delores stood quickly as the nurse snatched the thin but shielding cover away. Delores sat back down quickly, the paper-covered surface sticking to her buttocks with a crackly sound.

"Go ahead and lie down on your back," the doctor said. He pulled a small stool with wheels and a brightly lit metal lamp to the end of the table.

"Put your feet in the stirrups," he said, the nurse grabbing her feet and stuffing them into something cold and metal.

The doctor was sitting now, inches away from the end of the table. Her legs were apart, where she was wearing *nothing*. "You'll have to slide down some, way down," he said.

"Slide your bottom down," the nurse said, still sounding mad. "Your bottom should be at the very end. Come on, more. More, more."

Delores raised her knees, pushing her feet against the cold metal and careful to keep her feet planted in the right place. It was like she was throwing her privates into the doctor's face, the most embarrassing and disgusting act she'd been a part of. She wanted to jump up and run out, killing herself would be better than being here, but there was no way to run out with any dignity, either. Virtually naked in the back, with her breasts and private parts visible through the front's thin covering, the whole world would know she wore nothing underneath. There was no way to escape and nowhere to go without exposing herself to countless others, not just this doctor and nurse combo. Delores shut her eyes tight and continued to push downward toward the edge of the table.

"There you go, that's good," the doctor said, just as she felt her buttocks hanging off the edge. *Surely this is the worst*, she thought.

It wasn't.

The nurse pushed over a rolling cart, it's top covered with a white towel. She removed the towel, then helped the doctor put on tight, plastic gloves. Lying flat, Delores could not see what the cart contained, but could hear the clink of plastic and metal, the rubber band–like sound of the stretchy gloves, then a wet, squirting sound like squeezing a half-empty plastic bottle.

"I assume you've had a gynecological exam before?" the doctor asked.

"No, sir," Delores answered softly, staring into the ceiling tiles.

"You'd think a married woman of twenty-four—" the nurse said, but was stopped by the doctor.

"Now, Norma, she's young," he said. "It's time, for sure, but sometimes when there's nothing broke, we don't rush out to have it fixed."

He's at least trying to be kind, Delores thought.

"All right, ma'am," he said. "This is gonna be a little cold, and then a little uncomfortable, but it shouldn't cause you any real pain. And I can't stress to you enough, the more you let yourself relax, the less uncomfortable you'll be. I've done this for going on forty years, and I swear to you it's the truth."

She felt his gloved hand spread something ice-cold and jelly-like on the opening of her vagina. When she looked down, she only saw the top of his balding head illuminated by the light shining between her legs. The sound of the wet goo being spread with the rubbery glove made her cringe with disgust, even more so as she felt the gloved fingers probing inside her.

"Speculum, please," he said, and the nurse handed him an object.

Delores felt something hard and cold being pushed inside her, and she covered her mouth with her hand for fear of vomiting.

"Now's when you really need to relax," the doctor said. He seemed to have stopped pushing, and Delores caught her breath. Then the object inside her expanded, painfully stretching her as though ripping her apart.

"Don't fight it, honey," he said. "The more you tighten the harder it is against the vaginal walls. Just relax, and you'll stretch naturally, without pain, and we can have this over in just a minute."

Delores shuddered and let out a cry, biting her lip to hold it in the best she could. She felt the hard thing grow wider and wider, while both the doctor and the nurse concentrated on staring at her down there. The doctor made adjustments on the instrument, turning some sort of wheels that made a noise. She felt an involuntary gag as she remembered her daddy teaching her "right-y tight-y and left-y loose-y" for adjusting the water faucet. Delores could feel both the heat from the lamp and the doctor's actual breath on her most private openings, and she wasn't sure how much longer she could stand it. Tears streamed down the sides of her face, landing in her ears and causing her to toss her head from side to side.

"If you want it over with, you need to be still," said the nurse.

"Try and relax, honey," the doctor said. "Breathe through your mouth, slow. In and out. In and out, I'm almost done here. In and out—" On the last *out* she felt the hard thing retract, still feeling sharp but not tearing, and then she felt a gentle pull as it was removed completely. She closed her stinging eyes and sighed.

"You can sit up now," the nurse said.

Delores felt her skin stick to the paper as sat upward, smearing the sticky goo with her woman parts. The white sheet was nowhere to be seen, but she smoothed the gown over her front and tried to pull enough fabric behind her to cover her butt, with little success. She saw the doctor removing his gloves and throwing them into the trash.

"I'll see you in my office after you dress, missy," he said as he walked to the door.

The nurse remained, giving Delores a handful of tissues. "You'll want to wipe yourself off before you put on your underwear. You could see a smear of blood, it happens a lot on the first visit. The doctor's office is at the end of the hall," she said as she left. The sound of the nurse's voice told Delores that *she* didn't expect to see any blood, not from girls like her.

There was nasty, sticky stuff on the white paper, with bright smears of blood as well when she wiped between her legs. She dressed quickly, and as a last grasp at saving her dignity, Delores tore off the soiled white paper from the table, balled it up and placed it in the trashcan. Folding the gown to its original square, she left it on the now-naked table, its metal stirrups shining brightly, beckoning their next victim.

The doctor sat behind a desk, framed diplomas and awards on the wall behind him. He looked up at her and smiled. "Come in," he said. "You can close the door behind you."

Delores was grateful it was only him for the rest of the visit, feeling sure the hateful nurse was off somewhere passing judgment on her private parts and private life.

"Sit down," he said, motioning to the chairs in front of him, upholstered in a brown brocade fabric and shaped somewhat like the chairs in Mr. Foster's office. Just the thought of her last meeting in such a place brought a bitter taste to her mouth.

"Feeling better now?" he asked with a smile.

Delores wanted to like the man, but it was hard to like anything about this visit, considering the reason she was here. "Yes, sir, I guess," she said. "I'm sorry I was—" She had no words to finish her sentence. *Sorry I acted like a baby? Sorry I lied? Sorry I've brought shame on myself and my whole family?* There were too many choices, and none of them really worked.

"You have nothing to apologize for," he said. "A lady's first visit to the gynecologist is always a little frightening, and I have the feeling no one really prepared you for it, either. You didn't talk to your mother, a sister, a friend before coming?"

"No, sir. My mother died, I don't have a sister, and—my friends don't really talk about—"

"I see. Well, considering that, I think you did really well for your first time in the stirrups. It's never as hard as the first time, they tell me."

Delores tried to look into his eyes, but they were too kind, too grandfatherly. If their eyes locked, she might burst into tears. She concentrated on the words behind his head—Bachelor of Science in Biology. Master of Science in Chemistry. Doctor of Medicine, General Practice. Georgia Southwestern College. University of Georgia. Medical College of Georgia. Magna Cum Laude. Barney Thomas Jenkins.

"Well, Miss—" He looked down at the papers on his desk. "Mrs. Smith, I guess the main question you want to know is the obvious one. You want to know if you're having a baby. Right?"

"Yes, sir," she said to the diplomas.

"Is there anything else you want to tell me, before we talk about your situation?"

Delores looked down at her hands, then back towards the wall, but his eyes found hers before she could look away. Just as she expected, the floodgates opened. He handed over a box of tissues from the side of his desk.

"It's okay, honey," he said. "You're not the first to be in your shoes, nor will you be the last."

Delores blew her nose, wiped her face, and took a deep breath before she spoke. "I'm not married. I'm nineteen, not twenty-four. And I don't live here."

"I figured as much," the doctor said. "Good thinking on your part; small towns are all notorious for spreading the news before it is news. You mind me asking where you live?"

"Nolan," she said through clogged nasal passages.

"Your parents?"

"I wasn't lying about that. Both my parents are dead. I live with my older brother. I work in a factory, but I was saving up to go to vocational school in the fall."

"The father of the child?"

Delores sucked in air, then burst into sobs. "There is a child? Why couldn't you just tell me?" Suddenly freezing, she wrapped her arms around her torso, her chest heaving.

"Actually, I can't be one hundred per cent sure until later today, but from my experience, I would say yes. Around five to six weeks, I'd calculate. But, you've heard of the rabbit test, haven't you?" Delores nodded. "I can't tell you for sure until the rabbit test is complete."

"So there's a chance?" Delores pleaded.

"There's always a chance, but I think you need to start facing facts and looking at your options. The baby, if indeed there is a baby, what about the father?"

"No," Delores said. "He can't know. Ever."

"Now, honey, is that really fair? It takes two to tango, and he has a responsibility to—"

"No," Delores said again, then, "It's complicated. His father warned me, he could take away my brother's house. My brother lost his arm and doesn't have a job, and if he finds out—" Delores gasped, then covered her mouth with a wad of tissue and began to retch, tears mixing with vomit. The doctor picked up his phone and punched a button.

"Norma, we've gotta a little upchucking situation. Can you bring us some necessaries? Thanks, honey."

Dr. Jenkins reached under his desk and pulled out a second, unopened box of tissues. "There, now. Everything's okay. Use all you need. I've got ice coming, and crackers, and—"

The nurse knocked while entering, rushing to Delores with a silver bowl, wet and dry towels, a paper cup of ice, a can of ginger ale, and a sleeve of saltines. She pulled Delores's hair away from her face, and handed her the bowl. Wiping her face with the wet towel, she laid the rest on the doctor's desk and left.

"Call if you need anything else," she told the doctor.

"Thank you, Norma."

After a moment, Dr. Jenkins spoke again. "Listen, honey, just stay in here a while. I need to see another patient or two, but there's no reason you can't sit here 'til we get those results. Try to relax. And I've got a few things you can look at while you wait. Just try and calm down."

Delores nodded, wiping her face and wishing he would just leave. She needed to be alone, at least for a few minutes. Reaching on a shelf behind his desk, the doctor pulled out several brochures and a thin blue booklet. He laid them face down beside the crackers, then patted her on the shoulders.

"Relax, now, we'll talk in a bit," he said, heading out the door.

When she heard it shut, Delores opened the ginger ale and poured it over the ice. Its cool, stinging bite cleaned the vile taste from her mouth and rapidly began to settle her stomach. She set down the bowl, then reached over to see what kind of information the doctor had left.

The blue booklet was straightforward and to the point: *Preparing for Childbirth: A Young Mother's Guide*. It had diagrams, old-fashioned cartoons, and looked to be produced by the same people who made *What Every Girl Should Know*, the pink booklet they'd received in seventh grade health class when the girls were separated from the boys for the menstrual cycle lecture. The gray, tri-folded pamphlet was more or less just a commercial for Similac Infant formula and other products by the same company. The third brochure was the most colorful and on stiffer paper, making Delores curious to examine its contents.

The cover boasted the title "The Florence Crittenton Home," written in fancy Old English lettering which wrapped around a stately crest of some sort. The words were superimposed over a glossy color photo of an antebellum-type mansion, sitting at the top of a tree-lined hill. Delores had never heard of Florence Crittenton, but she sure liked the look of her home. It reminded her of civil-war era romance novels she and her mother had loved to read. She opened the brochure to see what it was all about.

The contents listed a letter from their president, an article on fall fundraising events, lots of pictures from their recent 60th Anniversary celebration, and two full pages of testimonials. As Delores read on, she learned that Florence Crittenton established homes for unwed mothers all over the country, and this particular booklet was dedicated to the Charleston, South Carolina branch.

Charleston, she thought, almost smiling as she remembered her first lengthy conversation with Phil, when he talked of Savannah, and Atlanta, and Charleston—all those beautiful cities he knew and she could only imagine. But what a fool she had been, listening to his pretty talk, thinking despite their backgrounds, they were basically the same. Yeah. And look where she was now.

Delores shook her head as if to shake the memories away. She examined the pictures, reading the captions of the more interesting ones. *"Family living skills and rewarding craft projects are all a part of the Crittenton design."* Several young women were seated at sewing machines. Two thin teenagers, pregnancies not showing yet, were standing at easels and holding long paintbrushes. A girl in her last weeks was knitting a tiny bootie, almost finished, while two others were winding a skein of thread into a ball. They all bore zombie-like smiles, eyes on their work, not the camera.

"Girls remain on track for classes with high quality academic instruction." This picture showed a standard classroom, a teacher at the blackboard explaining an equation while a roomful of female students wrote in notebooks. Seated at tables, the various stages of growing bellies were camouflaged.

"Girls have regular doctor's visits, and a nursing staff is present on site at all times." Girls stood single file, waiting their turn as cheerful nurses recorded each girl's weight.

"Happy social activities enhance self-esteem and physical well-being." This was a large caption with several photos below, showing what looked like a Halloween party, then a Christmas tree with gifts, and lastly, the same vacant smiles wandering about a barnyard with some farm animals. *Weird*, Delores thought.

She licked her finger to flip the page, which was stuck to the previous one. Pulling the two apart tore a little of the page's edge, but the double spread which followed was a dozen variations of the same scene, the overhead caption reading *"Our Fairy Tale Endings."* The final two pages were filled with photos of handsome, rich-looking couples, standing and smiling while holding ridiculously over-dressed infants.

"We knew the moment we saw our little Elizabeth," said Mrs. Chauncy Tolbert IV, "that this is a union of Divine Inspiration. God bless the Florence Crittenton home and the wonderful work they do."

"Our son, Horace," explained Dr. Williams H. Warren, "will have every opportunity a young man could imagine—a quality home environment, travel experiences, the best in education. The Florence Crittenton Home provides impoverished children with little hope a chance for all the best things in life."

Delores looked at little Horace, dressed in velvet knickers with a vest and bow tie, looking awkward, uncomfortable and much like a tiny old man. His father, also wearing a bow tie, held Horace out towards the camera, a foot away from his chest, as though afraid the infant might soil him. The mother wore a severe suit with a peplum, spectator pumps, white gloves and a pillbox hat. The whole family seemed more like department store mannequins than real people.

"Opal Anne is the light of our lives," claimed Mrs. Opal Leggett of Montgomery. "John and I were not blessed with children of our own, but through the Florence Crittenton Home, we are able to experience the next best thing. We're proud to give Opal Anne a life outside of poverty, two loving and responsible parents, and a fine, Christian home. I shudder to think how she might have ended up without the Crittenton Home, and us." Mr. and Mrs. Leggett looked like Superman's parents—two or three decades too old to be raising an infant.

Delores's stomach heaved again. She swallowed the bitter liquid, wiped off her mouth, and finished the last of her ginger ale. Delores Mullinax, nineteen and single-with-no-hope-of-a-husband, was pregnant. Hanging around for the rabbit's final verdict was useless; she needed to get out of the stifling environment and head back to Dumas County.

Then she'd decide what to do with the rest of her life.

"C'mon, Sis, it's Saturday night," her brother said, looking out the window in their rented apartment. "You're outta the Sundown at twelve, when the night's still young. Come on out to the house; that pig we been cookin' oughta be peakin' about then." It was three in the afternoon, and Cal was finishing off a six-pack. "Bring some of your girlfriends if you want, specially if they're purty as you; we'll be livin' the good life, partyin' all night!"

"Grow up, Cal, there's more to life than partyin' all night," she said. "Besides, Sunday's the only day I can sleep in: I'm comin' straight home when the Sundown closes. You can find your *own* girlfriends." Delores stood in the bathroom with the door open, getting ready for work. She ran a wide-tooth comb through her hair before pulling it back into its customary ponytail.

"Have it your way, Party Pooper, but I wish you'd come, just the same. It's our house, our new life we're celebratin', and it don't seem quite right with you missin' out on it." They locked eyes and she almost smiled, then looked away.

"You've been celebratin' for two months straight. You're gonna have that fancy tree house a damned pigsty before you get plumbing or electricity."

"We've got plumbing, we've even got electricity. We're just waitin' on the drywall guys, who're sposed to start Monday, and when they're done, it'll only take a few days to do the paint and linoleum. We could be moving in come another week or two," Cal said.

"So you're not partying at the river as you call it, you're having brawls and card games and all night orgies, right there in that new house that ain't even finished yet. I bet it's filthy as—"

"We are too down at the river. The weather's been so mild, build a little cookout fire and it's damned cozy. We have electricity, but there ain't no furniture or nothing, so we stay outside."

"You're telling me you don't take people inside? Come off it, Cal."

"I show folks around, if they ain't seen it yet, but we don't party in there, and the only folks that's been inside without me were a couple a gals that had to go to the bathroom. Guys just as soon go outside—"

"Cal," she said, "I know how boys like to go outside. And it's *your* house, and I don't really think you're gonna let it get totally trashed.

Mama taught you better. But I don't have any intention of joining your little celebration, not tonight or anytime soon. I'm coming back here and going to bed after work."

"But couldn't you come for just a little while?" Cal begged. "We're barbecuing a pig. You love good roasted pork."

"Love it a bit too much, I'm afraid. I've put on a few pounds, and I'm currently on a strict diet before I bust out of all my clothes. The subject is over. No roast piggy for me," Delores said.

Delores wondered if Cal had seen the slight thickening of her waist, but then again he had always said she was too skinny. Maybe he didn't notice at all. He was her brother, maybe he was too used to her to see the changes.

"You sure you're goin home, alone, to sleep?" Cal teased. "You ain't bringing over that mystery man you was slippin' out with a while back?" Delores rolled her eyes. "I'm coming home, alone, to sleep by myself. I've yet to meet a man that's worth the trouble of anything else."

"Fine, babe," Cal said. "You come back to Mrs. Short's apartments, get some shut-eye while you can. If there's any pork left by morning, I will bring some home, and ten-to-one you will eat some, silly diet or not. And remember, don't get too attached to this place. We'll be moving soon, by the end of the month at the latest." Cal leaned forward and embraced his sister in a quick hug, awkwardly holding the prosthetic metal arm at his backside.

Delores returned his gesture with a girlish squeeze, sealing it with a breakaway nudge to his jaw, turning her own face away in disgust.

"Good God, Cal," she said. "You smell like the Pabst Blue Ribbon assembly line. No wonder you use your sister for scoring a date."

"Bullshit, missy, I only let you think so to make you feel useful," he proclaimed, adding, "you—who work as a barmaid."

"That's *Miss* Barmaid to you, Plowboy," she said, busying herself with checking her purse, her keys and a quiet getaway.

"Good luck tonight," Cal said as she reached for the front door.

"Y—you, too," she stuttered. "See you tomorrow?"

"If not before," said Cal. "And remember, there's always time to change your mind."

"Sure," she said, waving as she hurried out the door.

Though Delores was sure the girls at work were beginning to talk, Cal had no suspicions whatsoever. All those last weeks before the new house was ready, she expected every day to come home to a Cal-on-fire, raising hell for bringing shame on the family, and even more hell when she refused to tell him who else was involved; but it didn't happen. Cal's naiveté about his sister's predicament bought her the precious time she needed—time to think, and reflect, and make decisions.

Delores had heard tales of a backstreet doctor, just north of Albany, who could take care of such problems for a fee, but this was an option she never considered. Though she'd run out of her first doctor's visit empty-handed, after several sleepless nights Delores turned to the public library for more information on the Florence Crittenton Home. She also read about the Baptist Children's Home and the Vashti Methodist Home for Girls. But in the end, she could not sever herself from this tiny new leaf of her family tree, this unexpected chance at regaining the all-important sense of family she lost with the death of her parents. She simply could not let go, and once she realized this, the rest became clear.

Delores could never let her brother know the father of her child, and it was imperative that the Foster family be kept in the dark as well.

I've gotta do right by Cal, she thought to herself, knowing that with the blink of an eye, Mr. Foster could take away what little happiness her brother now found in the world. If Delores kept the child, no one, absolutely no one, could know the origin of his or her birth. And so her plan began.

Soon after that first doctor visit, Delores spent weeknights much the same as always, but became more mysterious about her weekend activity. She claimed to have "blind dates," or "nights with the girls," even "don't ask, don't tell" nights, for the first few weekends Calvin was at home. Since parties, poker games, and all-nighters were a staple in Cal's lifestyle, Delores often came home long before her brother; but just to make sure, she budgeted her money enough to spend several nights alone in Albany motels, careful not to be seen by anyone. She hinted that there might be a "special guy," but gave no further clues.

After a month of such activity she went back to her usual solitary living. Convinced of his sister's innocence yet relieved that she seemed to have at least some kind of social life, Calvin asked questions but didn't worry. Delores knew what he was thinking; he often teased her about being obsessed with what other people thought. In his eyes, she was way too socially conscious to ever let herself be caught in a compromising position.

With any luck, Delores hoped to keep her news a secret from Cal until time to move into his new house. Though she knew it would break her brother's heart, she assured herself that a clean break was the best course for all of them. She continued working at the factory, saving her money and planning for the new family she and her baby would become.

Delores cried often, but only at night, when she was alone. She cried for her mother, her lost dreams, the child who would never know a father. She cried for Cal, who pretended life was one big party, drinking to fill the void. Delores knew her brother was lost, afraid, and without direction. She had always believed she could help her brother through the horrible patch of bad luck he'd been dealt, but right now she just couldn't. She had problems enough of her own.

If she moved in with her brother, he'd never find himself again. Cal's present living conditions wouldn't do for raising a baby, but if he straightened up just to take care of her, Delores knew he'd become an old man overnight. Cal needed to work and find a good woman and get on with his future.

By the time she was showing, Delores had made peace with herself, actually looking forward to the little one who would share her home. *The Lord never puts on you more than you can bear,* her Mama'd always said. Delores didn't have a lot, but she had much more than some folks. She could feed and clothe and love this baby, and they'd get on just fine.

Hopefully, Cal would find a bright spot to hold onto as well.

Her plans were made, she found a place to live, made a budget she could get by on, and sketched out the next year or two of her new routine. *It ain't perfect by any means,* she thought, *but at least I'm moving forward.*

It was a typical Friday night; the usual Nolan regulars quietly celebrating a weekly paycheck with their presence at the Sundown. A few decent tippers early in the night gave Delores a faint glow of happiness as she calculated the nest egg she was trying to accumulate. Mr. Hall had left her to close again, and though the place was nearly deserted by midnight, it had been a decent night altogether.

A queer feeling nudged the pit of her stomach as she pulled her mama's old Chevy into a parking space outside their apartment, right next to Cal's truck. A single lamp shined through their window, and she couldn't see much else through the half-closed Venetian blinds.

Cal's home this early on a weekend, she thought, *and alone? Maybe he's feeling under the weather, or else—maybe he just left his truck here.* She was constantly after him about securing a designated driver for his weekend party nights; perhaps he was finally listening. Still, she couldn't shake her queasiness as she climbed the front steps and opened the door.

Cal sat rigidly behind a half-empty gallon of Jim Beam. He looked at her with eyes that cut her to the core, then he drained the remaining liquid in his mason jar and set it beside the bottle.

"Good night at the Sundown?" he asked, his eyes reddened and his face glistening with perspiration. "Or did you even go there tonight? Seems I don't know much about where you're hanging out these days, or what you're doing either." He reached for the bottle, opened it, half-filled the glass, and drank it down in one gulp. He slammed the glass down so loudly Delores jumped.

"Slow down, Cal," she said. "It's not going anywhere, and besides, you're still on meds that may not mix too well with straight liquor."

"I don't need advice from my baby sister, especially when she can't seem to use good judgment in her own life, let alone for anybody else's."

Delores remained standing in her wintry jacket, holding her purse. She knew the time of truth had come, but stayed caught in a moment where time stood still.

"Why didn't you tell me, Sis?" he said, tears in his eyes. "Were you ever gonna tell me, or were you just waiting 'til everybody in town knew, or 'til I could see it for myself?" He wiped his hand at his face, averting the path of his tears under the loose pretense of pushing hair from his eyes or wiping away sweat.

"Cal, I never meant to—"

"We're family, Sis," he cried. "I'm the only family you got now. Did you think I wouldn't help you, wouldn't be there to—"

"It wasn't like that, Cal." Now she was crying, too, her voice racked with sobs as she subconsciously clutched at her abdomen. "I wanted to tell you, I needed you so bad, but I was so ashamed, and—"

"Who is it? Where is the sonofabitch, and what is he planning on doing here?" Her brother sounded more wounded than hellfire-like mad.

Maybe I can calm him down, she thought, *get him focused on having more family and not so much on where the baby came from.* "I let them down, Cal," she said, sniffling loudly to pull back the head full of wet mucus that threatened to escape her nose and flood the room. "Mama and Daddy; they taught me right from wrong, and I've been a good girl, always, and then suddenly, I wasn't. It just happened. It didn't *feel* like it was wrong, and it happened so fast, I–I—"

"Accidents happen, Sis, and nobody'd believe you were anything but a good girl with unlucky timing. A helluva lot of good marriages

188 ← Elaine Drennon Little

start out the same way. But why are you waiting so long? When are you planning on—"

Okay, Delores thought. *This is definitely going the wrong way, and going there fast. I've gotta stop him before*—"No, Calvin, it's not like that." Delores raised her hand like a traffic cop, stopping her brother in mid-sentence. A moment of dead silence filled the room with the severity of an oncoming train.

"Well, little sister," Cal finally said. "If it's not like that, then pray tell, what exactly is it like?"

Delores chose her words carefully. She set down her purse and unbuttoned her jacket.

"I'm waiting," Cal said through clenched teeth. Never taking his eyes from his sister, he reached for the bottle, refilled the mason jar, then replaced the lid onto the bottle. He picked up his glass and took a long draw. When he set it back down, Delores spoke.

"I won't be getting married, at least not now. It wasn't that kind of relationship." She removed her coat and hung it on the hook beside the door. Her gaunt face was now void of color, but her words were delivered evenly, if with a slight quiver.

"Well, well," said Cal. "Then what kind of relationship was it?"

Delores could hear his teeth grinding from across the room. She continued to look downward, saying nothing.

"Speak up, Sis," he said. "Cat gotcha tongue? Surely a young woman of such mature relationships can shed a little light on the subject. Tell me all about this *relationship.*" With sarcasm, he used his one good hand in an exaggerated gesture of quotation marks.

Delores remained silent, still looking at the apartment floor.

"I guess it'd be too old-fashioned to call him your boyfriend, right? Besides, I haven't seen any I.D. bracelet or class ring or anything."

Delores said nothing.

"I don't know about you, but I'm almost glad Mama's gone. I'd rather remember her in that silver casket than imagine her finding out her own damn daughter's nothing more than what she'd call a Jezebel. And what Daddy'd call a streetwalking whore."

Delores ran to the bedroom, slamming and locking the door. She fell to the bed, using her pillow to stifle her own sobs, but her brother was just getting wound up, screaming outside her door.

"Did he leave you money, or were you too cheap for even that? He was at least white, wasn't he?"

Though his voice had risen to a fevered pitch, it cracked in obvious pain on the last word. That's when Delores heard the sound of his knees hitting the floor and then his body crumpling against the hollow door. He snuffled, attempted to clear his throat of bubbling mucous, and let out a slow, nasal whine.

It was a sound unlike any she'd heard before—more pleading than the baby goats just separated from their mothers, more painful than the young bulls who'd been reduced to steers by way of a sharp knife. It was the sound of the one person she loved more than anyone else on earth reduced to a helpless, whimpering child, because of what she had done.

Delores sobbed along with him, quietly, wrapping her arms around herself and rocking silently on her childhood bed. Finally, she stood and walked to the door, opening it slowly lest her brother might fall, then lowering herself to the floor.

She wrapped her arms about his shoulders as he did the same to hers. They held on, rocked, and cried some more, never noticing the mixture of tears, sweat, slobber, and snot they shared against their necks, their faces, their hair. With closed eyes she wondered if they silently watched a snapshot montage, one of the same and different moments that had made them a family. For minutes or hours or perhaps half the night Delores embraced that family—those already gone, leaving, and yet to come.

She knew the harsh words were not finished and that unanswered questions would continue to bring pain, but she could at least relish the gift of this temporary cease-fire. And she could continue to remind herself; that any moment to love and feel love in return was indeed a treasure.

Chapter 13
March 1959

Calvin

BY MOVING DAY, THINGS HAD CHANGED CONSIDER-ably. Cal took the last of his boxed items away from the apartment, leaving Delores, who had finally gotten it across to Calvin that she would not be moving to the house on stilts. She claimed to be happy, and she was determined to make her own way. Calvin agreed to table the argument, for the time being.

"Like Mama always said," Delores had explained, "I've made my bed, now I got to lie in it." She turned the corners of her mouth in a smirk, but Cal saw her quick shiver. The Mullinax family was poor but proud, and as far as they knew, there'd been no babies born out of wedlock before now.

"You do what you gotta do, Sis, nothing wrong with that. But can't you lie in your bed in our new house just as good as you can anywhere else? It's your house, too, Delores, and the little critter's, if you'll just let it be."

"You know I appreciate it all, but I did this to myself, and I've got to stand on my own two feet. There's a project house going vacant next month, where I can walk to the factory in ten minutes and to The Sundown in less. Imogene Etheridge's mama keeps kids in a house two doors away. I can make this work, and I have to. I have to make it right."

She seemed to have thought things through and it was Cal's last intention to upset her, but something just didn't set right. Her ideas were all out of whack, it was like she was sentencing herself to purgatory for a crime she didn't commit. And he couldn't simply stand by and watch.

"Yeah, but you sure as hell didn't do it to yourself, either, like you claim. Where's his part in all this? Is he gonna be there for you? Is this a ploy to give ya'll the time to work things out, get things together for a more permanent situation? Is this—"

"Cal, I don't—"

"Is he at least helpin' you out, tiding you over," Cal's speech became louder and faster, "while he gets his sorry ass in gear? Does he even have a damned plan? Where the hell *is* he?"

Delores stared at her shoes.

"Well?" Calvin asked.

Finally, Delores took a deep breath and said, "He's not around, he's not helping out, he doesn't know about it. I wouldn't tell him if I could, it was a one night mistake, and I won't make things worse by adding him into an already messed up equation."

"What do you mean, 'you wouldn't tell him if you could'?"

Delores swallowed hard, pushed a loose strand of hair away from her face, and cocked a hand on her hip. "I never even knew his damned name."

Cal sniffled, feeling his nose run and wiping it on his sleeve. "Damned cold," he muttered. "I don't believe you, but I know when you get this pig-headed about anything, you won't let go 'til lightning strikes, so I'll let up on you for now. But it just ain't right—"

"Calvin—" she said, sounding like their Mama coming back from the grave.

"Okay, Sis, I'll let it be for now. But don't think I won't stay on you 'bout moving in with me. This is my family, too. We're all we got left, and your little critter is gonna know his Uncle Cal, hell or high water."

"What makes you so sure it's a boy?"

"Boy or girl, I don't care. Your kid is my family, no matter who the no-account, sorry-ass, good-for-nothing—"

"You *said* you were letting up on me. Could you leave it at that?"

Cal sighed. "I guess so, but I'll be back. I'll keep comin' back til I talk some sense into your pony-tailed head." He hugged his sister with his good arm, sliding the metal hook through the elastic band that held back her hair.

"Gottcha!" he said, sporting a blue and gold circle around the tip of his mechanical claw.

Cal kept trying, but Delores never gave in, and Calvin's home remained a bachelor's quarters. Delores stayed at Mrs. Short's another month, then Cal helped take her few belongings to the project house.

"Are you sure you're sposed to be moving in today? There's still some stuff left here," Cal called from the back bedroom. "Looks brand new."

Following the sound of his voice, Delores stood in the doorway with her mouth hanging open. A crib sat in front of the window, a light shade of oak and outfitted in yellow ruffles and blankets. A brown teddy bear sporting a green bow tie sat in the middle. In the corner was a rocker—their mother's rocker that Cal had previously taken to his own place.

"The folks at the store said yellow worked for girls and boys. And that little chest," Cal pointed beside the crib, "was in the back room at the home place. I think Mama used it to keep her sewing things."

"She did," Delores said, walking over and rubbing her hand over its top. "The first drawer had the button tin and cigar boxes of bobbins and thread."

"Mosta the thread looked rotten, and I'm afraid there was evidence of a mouse or two camping out there. The dress patterns were pretty nasty. I burned most of it, you can't be too careful about germs around a baby, you know."

Delores smiled at her brother.

"I scoured it out good, fixed the bad bottom in the third drawer, then stained it near's I could to the color of the crib. Hardware's new, too. I wanted to fill it up with little clothes, but I figured I'd need your help in that department. Found a used high chair, too, gonna fix it up for you, any color you want, maybe paint his—or her—name on it, but I guess you won't need the chair at first."

He reached into the middle drawer and pulled out a shiny fruit-cake tin, rusted in places, but clean as a whistle. Calvin shook it for effect, making a full, clanking sound. "A blast from the past," he said.

Delores wrapped her arms around him, squeezing tight as she cried into his shoulder. "I love you, Cal," she said.

Cal jerked back and looked at her. "This is supposed to be a happy day, what's this crying for?"

"I *am* happy, Cal," she said, "happier than I ever thought I could be, under the circumstances. I'm happy I got this place, and that I don't have to be a leech and live off you. I'm happy I've got a crazy brother that knows more than I ever dreamed about babies and stuff like that. I'm ever so happy you found Mama's button tin. And I'm happy that you still love me, and that we've got each other, no matter what. Maybe things *can* get better, maybe we might do all right yet!"

It was the first time she'd let on to Cal how much she worried about where her life was taking her. "Things'll get better, Baby Sister, you can bet your sweet little ass it will," he said. "Mama'd be damned proud of you, girl, you're a woman who can take care of herself." Cal put his calloused hand on her cheek. "She'd be damned proud," he repeated. "But if you ever change your mind and want me to find the sorry, low-life—"

"Not now, Cal. Today can it just be us?" She placed her own thin hand over the hand on her face.

"Sure, Sis, sure," he said. "Today, in my baby sister's first home of her own, there's just the three of us."

The house on stilts was everything Cal had hoped it would be, and being out-of-work gave him plenty of time to add the finishing touches and do them right. The pale oak floors were nice, but a little too pristine; sanding and adding a dark stain gave the whole place a richer, more masculine feel. He used an even darker stain on the outside stairs, covering it with several coats of creosote and then polyurethane. Deciding he didn't like the too-shiny metallic finish of the gold knobs and hinges on his cabinets, he carefully took them off and repainted them with flat paint, then rubbed them with black to simulate an antique patina.

He chose furniture with care, traveling to Albany, Tallahassee, and Dothan where he checked out the stores, then left to compare prices and mull over what he wanted. After weeks of deliberation, he ended up with a few well-chosen pieces that seemed made for the place. His house had become a home; in the kitchen he hung his mother's iron skillets, in the living room, his father's guns, and over the bed, his parent's wedding picture. He bought a second dog and acquired a cat. After scouring miles of woodland along the riverbanks, he filled his little yard with native plants and river rock.

There was nothing else to do but find a job, and Calvin was ready.

Oakland was still the county's largest employer of farm labor, but Cal had cut his ties there and had no desire to go back. Ichauway Plantation, in the far south of the county and owned by "the Coca-Cola Woodruffs," was the largest farm in acreage, though nearly half of it was kept as a game preserve and not farmed at all. Pine Bloom and Tarver Plantations bordered Oakland; actually more industrial farms than plantations in the literal sense.

After talking with his friend Mr. Danner, the county extension agent, Cal prepared a simple resume of his farming experience and hand-delivered copies to the larger farms in the county. Mr. Danner also took a folder of copies and kept them in his truck, sharing them with any of the smaller farming operations who might be interested, and promised to keep an eye out for any job possibilities in the area.

Always outgoing and personable, Cal took his job hunt seriously, looking his "farming best" and taking the time to talk to every prospective employer he could find, even those not currently looking to hire. Remembering the things he admired about Mr. Danner, he spoke clearly, complimented each man's current operations, and tried to use casual conversation to show his extensive farming knowledge without seeming a know-it-all. Because many of the older farmers still believed in practices he and Mr. Danner found comical, Cal nodded, smiled and let them assume he was also schooled in following the almanac and planting with the phases of the moon. Cal knew that those who owned their own land, no matter how small their acreage or allotments, had the upper hand. He could be obedient and comply with those in charge, and who knows, maybe he'd find a way to educate *them*, and they could all profit from working together. It had worked for Mr. Danner, maybe it would work for him, too.

But as time moved on, it seemed that nothing worked; it was as if Cal had somehow been cursed or blackballed before he set foot on any farm, big or small.

"A very nice resume, Mr. Mullinax," the Ichuaway overseer had said, standing outside and extending his hand to Cal's good one, awkwardly. He glanced quickly over the paper, almost as a formality, as if he knew everything on it before Cal showed up. "We're not hiring anyone at this time, I'm afraid, but will certainly keep this on file. You never know when things'll change. Good luck with your job hunting."

As if dismissing Cal, he turned and walked away, heading into a small building labeled "office."

You'd think a farm big enough to have an office would do its interviewing in one, Cal thought as he plodded back to his truck.

Trying to hide his disappointment, he stopped himself from spinning off in the loose gravel of the parking area. Though he'd only been on the plantation a few times, Cal had always admired its massive entrance gates, acres of green fields surrounded by humongous oaks, and bright red barns worthy of calendar prints. A boy in grade school had told him there was a cemetery for bird dogs, with real marble headstones bearing pictures of the deceased canines. The boy had also said that cats were not allowed there, since Ichuaway was a "bird sanctuary," whatever that meant. Cal wondered if these ideas were truth or legend.

"Guess I'll never know," Cal said aloud, turning on Highway 91 and heading back towards Nolan.

At Nilo, Pine Bloom, and Tarver, Cal was received the same way, only less formally. The overseers were usually working and had to be hunted up or waited for, had no use for the conversational banter he'd prepared, and took his typed white paper with dirt-crusted hands, barely glancing before laying it aside. No one was hiring, and they all said they'd get back to him later, none of them sounding as though they would.

In less than two weeks, Cal had been to every farm in the county and was following the few outside leads Mr. Danner had suggested. Everyone was cordial, and no one was hiring. They made it sound final, like there were no plans to hire in the future, either. Like the farming community would forever remain the same as it was, that day in 1959.

A few of the smaller farmers ventured to ask a few questions about his injury and the hook he now wore.

"You kin drive a tractor with that thang?" asked Enoch Tabb, the seventy-year-old corn and barley farmer who still kept a team of mules, "just in case."

"Yes, sir," Cal said. "Took me a while to get re-adjusted, but I spent some time out at Mr. Danner's, and we got it figured out. Can drive a combine, change implements, do pretty much what I did before, just look a little funnier doing it. And it actually helps me with moving cows—some of 'em think it's a cattle prod, and pick up the pace a little when they see me coming."

Mr. Tabb did not seem amused. "Well, ain't it dangerous? If that thang got hung on something, it'd have to pull your whole shoulder off now, wouldn't it?"

"First of all, sir, I'm pretty careful about how I use the hook, and I don't see much of a chance of that sort of thing happening. But the truth is, if the hook got caught on something, I would simply release it from its holster, and I'd still be here, unattached. In that way, I guess you could say it's safer than a real arm."

Mr. Tabb shook his head and spat into the dry ground below. "Still," he said, "you got hurt, got hurt bad, when you was working at Oakland. I feel for you, I do. Shouldn't a happened to no man, bless your heart." He scratched at the dirt with his foot, looking downward, away from Cal. "But I hear tell they paid you a pretty penny for your troubles. You get hurt here, I couldn't afford to help you out the way they did. This little ninety acres is all I got. I was looking to maybe take on another'n to help out here, but I'm sorry, son." He looked up. "I just can't afford the risk. I've gotten along this long without no help, I reckon I'll keep going. But I wish you the best. Have you thought about trying in town? Maybe at the gin or the peanut mill? It's only seasonal, but it's probably as much as you need, not having a family or nothing. And a lot safer, I'd think. You don't want hurt yourself, there."

Mr. Tabb turned and walked under his pole shed, puttering with an old plow, leaving Cal standing alone in the bright sunlight.

Cal thought about following him, pleading further, but it was no use. Cal knew men like Enoch Tabb: once their mind was set, there was no sense in arguing with them. He headed back to his truck, forgoing the next two farmers on his list, and heading home. He knew the only open arms he'd find today were those of Old Crow.

Cal continued to look for work, but less often, with less vigor, and some days not at all. Evenings, he collected a menagerie of fair weather friends whose sole purpose in life was to get more wasted than the night before. Yet this was not Cal's life, he could stop when he wanted, and often did. It was only after long spells of hopelessness that he engaged in such reckless behavior, and besides, who cared?

When there seemed to be no need for farm labor in Dumas, Mitchell, Early, Calhoun, or Miller counties, Cal decided to take matters into his own hands. In his treks through the countryside, he had seen several small acreages going fallow, and decided to investigate.

The Cecil Medders farm, still owned by the family but not worked since Cecil's death two years ago, sat still and unattended on Clear Lake Road. At the courthouse, Cal learned that the farm was nearly sixty acres, but also contained three family homes where Cecil's children still resided. Jack Hudson's farm was also owned by descendants, each of them living somewhere else and hoping to sell the 200 acres to any bidder they could find. The Hammontree place, fifty-two acres with a nice cotton allotment, had skirted foreclosure for nearly a decade, living from harvest to harvest with second and third mortgages, yet the family swore the land would remain theirs. This part Calvin understood completely.

On a warm spring Monday, Cal dressed in his best khakis, a dress shirt, and the only tie he owned, heading out for the appointment he'd set up with the loan officer at the Dumas County Bank. He took with him the deeds to his house and land, his truck title, and his checking and savings records from the same bank.

All the tellers greeted him with smiles—his former high school typing teacher, the wife of the Oakland overseer, the white haired Miss Overby who'd worked there as long as he could remember and probably before. A thin man with slicked back hair, wearing a blue jacket with a gold tag branding him "R. Hugh Harlon, Loan Officer" ushered him into a small room in the back.

The meeting was short; Mr. Harlon stepped out to make copies of Cal's papers, then returned with a handful of carbon-backed forms for him to take home, fill out, and return. Cal had prepared, even practiced, what he'd wanted to explain about his situation, but the loan officer seemed uninterested in anything he had to say; handing Cal a plastic folder for his sheath of documents, he extended his hand and dismissed him.

"We'll look over your assets and let you know if anything can be worked out," Mr. Harlon said, ushering Cal out the door. The smiling women were all engaged in their work, not one of them looking up as Cal walked through the lobby office and out into the street.

Chapter 14
May 1959

Phil

PHIL HAD ADJUSTED TO LIFE AS A WORKING MAN, YET no one particularly noticed. Strangely, the driving from town to town, which both he and his father had assumed would be his preference in duties, grew monotonous, whereas work on the farm was more pleasant as time went on.

Despite Phil's deficiencies with the written word, he flourished in hands-on activities, and his memory for day-to-day agricultural life was like a sponge; he never forgot anything and easily linked prior knowledge like a seasoned farmer. Sometimes, as he watched the long rows ahead of him from the seat of the tractor, Phil imagined talking with his father, discussing long-range plans for the farm, and witnessing Dad's shock to realize his son was not incapable of complex thought.

He cut down on his drinking, made healthier eating choices, and went to bed at a decent hour. At night, he dreamed of the forthcoming father-son bond as he fell asleep in the study with a single glass of wine for company. For the first time in many years, his confidence was growing again. He would talk to his father. The day would come that he'd no longer be seen as the family fool; he just needed time for it all to unfold.

Phil planned to ask about working at the farm full time. He could make his father proud. He would gain his father's trust, build a better relationship, and make it work, as soon as the time was right. It was his one long-term goal that never changed.

It was a gorgeous April afternoon; the slight breeze and the smell of rich, freshly turned earth made early pre-plant harrowing a job every farmer loved. While daydreaming of nothing in particular, Phil noticed a large, unfamiliar vehicle parked at the end of field, just inside the gate. Pulling closer, he recognized the bow-tied, silver-haired gentleman he'd come to know as his father's attorney step out of the car, walking to the end of the row Phil was harrowing. The man brushed off his seersucker suit, then removed his hat, which he held in his hands in front of him. Phil stopped several feet before the end of the row, turned off his tractor, and climbed down to meet him.

"Mr. Moorhead," Phil said, extending his hand to the older man. "What brings you out today?" Phil had seen Robert Moorhead in various settings with his father for most of his life, but he couldn't imagine why he drove his shiny Chrysler into an unplanted field, alone.

"Call me Robert, son. You're not a little boy anymore," he said as his trembling hand grasped Phil's warm, soil-dusted one. "I'm afraid I'm the bearer of sad news." There were red lines in his eyes and dark circles beneath. His bottom lip quivered as he slowly spoke.

The smell that had been fragrant just minutes ago soured, turning Phil's stomach queasy and his mouth dry.

"You know your father left for Little Rock today," he said. Phil nodded as if he knew this, though if he'd been told, he didn't remember it. His father rarely kept him abreast of his travels.

"He boarded his flight in Albany at seven-twenty this morning, and caught another flight in Atlanta that would have him there late this afternoon."

Stop, Phil thought. *Just stop. I may be slow but I'm not stupid. Why else would Mr. Moorhead be here?*

"Unfortunately," the older man continued, "your father never made it to Little Rock. Son, today's Pan Am flight to Little Rock went down in flames on the outskirts of Tunica, Mississippi. There were no survivors."

Phil looked up at the Easter egg sky, the cottony clouds, the too-bright sun. How could a day so picturesque bring such horror? How could he be here, waxing philosophical on the cosmic beauty of nature while his father burned to death in the same sky? He had been imagining some great homecoming when Daddy would be proud of him, while Phillip Foster III drew his last breath.

Phil did not scream, or cry, or bow his head, as a good son would do. As the overpowering smell of nature mixed with the stabbing pain in his gut, Phil fell to his knees in the fresh-plowed soil, replenishing the earth with the contents of his stomach.

Not knowing what to do, Mr. Moorhead looked in the other direction. When it seemed that Phil had no more bile to spew forth, he stepped closer and patted the young man on his shoulder, inducing an outburst of sobs as Phil slowly stood.

"I'm sorry, sir," Phil jabbered, choking on his on mucous.

"No offense taken, son. We all deal in our own ways."

"But my dad would've—" Phil's voice broke again, a rush of tears and snot flooding his face. This time he stepped aside, wiping his nose on his sleeve.

"I talked to your sisters on the phone," Mr. Moorhead said. "They'll be planning the arrangements tonight, at your father's house in Albany. My office will look over the businesses for the next few days, I told your sisters not to worry over any of that. We'll meet later next week. You'll need some family time together, first."

Phil heard the man talking but didn't really process the words. Time had stopped, the world had stopped, and it was hard to see anything beyond the painfully colorful day, here in the field.

"Let me take you back to the lodge, where you can get ready to go and see your family," the man said.

See my sisters? Phil thought. For some reason, the idea of his sisters as family seemed foreign to him. Suddenly, it was brilliantly clear that *the farm* was his closest relative, the closest link to his father he would ever have. The idea, though strange, was comforting, and more so than the idea of meeting with his sisters.

"But I need to put up my tractor," Phil said.

"Surely one of those farm hands can do that," said Mr. Moorhead. "Your place is with your family. Let the help take care of the tractor."

Phil stood straighter, seeing for the first time his family position among the workers. "Actually," he said, clearing his throat, "I'll need to meet with all the men before I go. They need to know about Dad, and they should hear it from me. One of them will give me a lift back to the lodge, after I've talked with them. But thanks for the offer. Besides, I'm a bit aromatic to ride in your car. Thanks for coming to tell me, personally." Phil put out his hand, and the two shook.

"I'll see you later, at your father's house," Mr. Moorhead said. He nodded, walked back to his car, and left.

Phil stood, a silent tear slipping down his cheek. When the bright sun seemed to dry out his wet, salty face, he climbed back on the tractor and drove to the next field, where he stopped his friends and told them the news. Clifford drove him to the next field, and the next, and finally the pole barn, until all the workers knew.

In all the pain of that long afternoon, Phil did learn one new and astounding fact: Strong, earth-loving, sweat-smelling men are never afraid to hug. Or to cry.

Days passed. There were funeral home hours, where friends of the family stood around awkwardly, and left. There were home visits involving mountains of food they barely touched. There was the funeral, a church they rarely visited filled with a few friends and hundreds Phil didn't know all "paying their respects." There was the reading of the will, which was either in legal language neither Phil nor his sisters could understand or so dumbed down they were embarrassed. Everything was in trusts; none of the children were expected to actually run anything, and the Foster estate would continually make money for partners, stockholders, and subsequently, the Foster family in coming generations.

Despite the fact that Phil had, just weeks ago, dreamed of becoming an integral part of the farm, the death of his father crumbled his confidence to ashes in the wind. He never had a chance to tell his father how he felt about farming, though he'd often imagined just what he would say. He never asked him about the guns, a part of his family history he wanted to share. He never found out why his father had told all those stories to Calvin and not to him. He would never talk to his father about any of those things, and he would never have the chance to make him proud. It now seemed like a child's dream, and Phil felt humiliated to even think back on it; so he didn't.

The sudden shock of tragedy changed Phil to a near-recluse. Though his worker-friends stood by him in the beginning, they backed away after the urgency subsided. They found it easy to bond in the hard times, but afterwards, in the day-to-day matters, they didn't know how to react, so they stayed away. Some expressed concerns, and they all liked Phil, yet they were anxious as well. Since he'd had no real relationships with family members, his sisters had no idea of the changes in Phil. And they scarcely came around to see.

Phil worked sporadically but drank on a daily basis. Unlike the frat boy binge drinking of his college days, he was drinking alone. He ate little and consumed alcohol until he passed out. Often suffering from nightmares, he would awaken two and three times a night, needing more and more alcohol to get back to sleep. Even the friends who suspected his problem were afraid to confront him or offer help. He often stayed inside for days into weeks without being seen.

Phil stayed on in the lodge until the wine cellar was nearly gone. By then he had a trust fund to spend. He tried to reach his sisters, but they never returned his phone calls. Leaving town with no itinerary for returning, he wrote his farewell:

Girls—

Checking out—Gonna see the world and have some fun. No plans for the future. Might as well live up to the old man's expectations.

Chapter 15

Calvin

THE BABY CAME, A PERFECT BABY GIRL DOLORES CALLED Mary Jane. Dolores seemed happy to see Cal when he'd show up at her door, but he was always clearly a visitor and nothing else. He'd offered to stay, sleep on the couch, let her get some sleep for a few nights, but she dismissed him before he'd finished the offer. He'd wanted to babysit, or take them to doctor appointments, or just *be* with them for more than a couple of hours at a time, but Delores was totally independent—she needed *nobody* and seemed proud of it.

He'd been making plans for them, all in his head, but special ones he was saving for the day she came to her senses and realized they were still a family. His second bedroom—the one where he kept his tools, fishing tackle, and a few furniture odds and ends along with mystery boxes from the home place—was the smaller of the two, but plenty big enough for him. Delores and the baby could take his room, fix it up any way she wanted; there'd be room for both bed and crib, then maybe twin beds when the child was older.

He'd already started thinking about later on, when little Mary Jane needed space of her own. For himself, Cal could build four walls around the corner stilts; start with one big, simple room, same size as the whole house upstairs, with maybe a bathroom. He could partition up his sleeping quarters, then maybe set up a woodworking shop or something, to fill in some of the empty space. They'd all share the living area upstairs, but this way, the girls could have their own place, and he'd have his. Cal's little bedroom would become

Mary Jane's, and she could paint it any color she wanted, no matter what her fussy mama said, he'd see to it she had something of her own. Cal liked planning for the years ahead with their family, in the home that would grow along with them.

Just months ago, he would have thought, too, about his own children, the ones he'd have with the wife he had yet to meet, but the possibility of such a wife seemed less likely than ever. Though he'd adjusted to all kinds of physical changes with his new appendage, using the shiny metal hook with the opposite sex was as awkward now as the first day he had it. Somehow, the very idea of the cold metal interacting with the soft skin and delicate structure of a woman made Calvin feel more like a machine than a man. Sure, he could lift and raise, hoist and pull, manipulate objects for the same effect he could with a real arm, but this was day-to-day *doing*, interacting with other objects to achieve a goal. And even though he could still touch, stroke, caress a hand or cheek or brow with his "good" hand, just having the cold, tool-like facsimile in the same room with the kind of girl he'd want to impress felt vulgar—he couldn't explain why, but the feeling was always there; the hideous, glaring taboo that everyone saw but no one could mention.

So Calvin kept his distance from pretty girls—actually, from girls in general, after what he referred to, in his head, as "the thing with Claudette."

On the weekends she didn't have her kids, Claudette showed up wherever Cal and his friends chose to drink. A two-hundred-pound, thirty-five-year-old mother of three, Claudette worked as a desk clerk, payroll clerk, bookkeeper, and jack-of-all-trades at Walter Perry Tractor Supply. The store's only female employee, she knew every machine in the place, as well as thousands of parts that accompanied them. She knew what-went-where, what-could-be-replaced-with-what, and which repairs were faster or more economical. She could also lift the front end of a tractor, take apart any motor, and recognize any part by its size and serial number. On another note, she made the best chili, pot roast, and German chocolate cake in three counties.

Claudette became "one of the guys" as she tagged along with John and Mike, the two diesel mechanics who were Cal's best drinking buddies. In actuality, she could drink any of her male friends under the table, but seldom did, going out for more of a social than alcohol-driven need. To Calvin, the two men seemed viciously rude to her, constantly labeling her with hurtful monikers to her face.

"Claudette, you big ol' bull dyke," John had said to her, the first night Cal saw her with them. "Sit your fat ass down. Hey, Mike, we can tie one on tonight," he called. "We got us a designated driver— that is, if we can fit in the car with her!"

Claudette just laughed along with them.

Cal looked at his friends in disgust, then back at Claudette. He thought he saw a flicker of hurt or embarrassment as his eyes met hers, but she quickly took Mike's beer, finishing it in one gulp and burping out loud.

"You'll make yourself fit if you expect me to take you home," she said, "and that's if I'm of a mind to do you a favor. Can't say that I owe either one of you homos a damned thing." Mike reached over and hugged her, then punched her on the shoulder as hard as he could. She didn't even flinch. "Anyone sitting there?" She eyed the empty chair next to Calvin.

Calvin stood and pulled out the seat, the way he would for any woman. Claudette sat down without reservation. Cal wasn't sure how a woman of Claudette's demeanor would react to his glaring metal arm, but she said nothing.

"Damn, Cal," John said. "Don't go all 'southern gentleman' on us. It's just Claudette, ain't like it's a real woman or nothing."

"Damn yourself, John," Claudette answered. "Why didn't you tell me you had a friend you didn't meet on the chain gang. Bet he can read and write, too." Then she turned to face Cal, holding out her hand, like a man, for a handshake. "Guess I should know better than to expect these fools to introduce me," she said. "I'm Claudette. And you're—"

"Cal," he answered, awkwardly offering his left hand. "Calvin Mullinax." He held her fingers but for a few seconds. It was a large hand—as big as his own—with a strong grip, but her skin was surprisingly soft and supple.

"Mullinax," she said, still looking into his eyes. "You're their buddy that got hurt at Oakland last fall?"

Cal froze. He knew he'd been talked about—an accident like his would have been the biggest news around back when it happened—but the reality of imagining such a conversation, perhaps at this very table, made him feel embarrassed and exposed.

But Claudette kept talking. "Tough break," she said, looking at his hook, then back into his eyes. "You've been to hell and back, haven't you? Damn, I can't imagine going through what you have. You must be tough as damn nails, with a spirit to boot. What you doing hanging out with the likes of these assholes?"

"Cut the crap, Claudette," someone said. "Just cause he's missing an arm don't mean he's hard up enough to go home with you." The men snickered, and Calvin thought he saw a blush as she reached into her purse.

"I'm going to the bar to order," she said. "Can't blame the waitress that skips over *this* table." She stood, then looked at Cal while pretending to address the others. "Ya'll need anything else?"

"Just tell her to send another pitcher," Mike said. But Claudette had already gone.

She returned with her own mug of draft, and a waitress soon brought two more pitchers. At first, Cal held back from his usual drinking pace, unsure of this large but not-so-uninteresting woman at their table. Yet soon he was comfortable, the two of them exchanging light conversation as she continued the caustic, sarcastic banter with the others. Someone ordered a round of schnapps to accompany the beer, then another, and another. At some point later, when standing to go to the john, Cal's right arm, always heavy and clumsy when he drank a lot, knocked over a half-full pitcher onto Claudette's bosom, which caused him to stumble and fall forward into her lap.

Seething with anger and humiliation, he reached and pushed against the table with his good arm, trying to raise himself up and escape from the embarrassing scene he'd caused. But his arm angled more downward than he realized, tipping the table and causing all the mugs, in various stages of fullness, to come sliding downward.

Then, as if the world suddenly went into slow motion, the mugs all stopped, only a little from the fullest one sloshing over its side.

Claudette caught five beer mugs and an empty pitcher in her right hand, setting the table upright at the same time. Her left arm was wrapped around Cal's shoulder, her hand resting calmly over the silver hook. With a singular move, she jostled him into a sitting position, then lightly kissed the top of his head.

"You are one rowdy fellow," she said. "I never had to shower myself in beer just to get a man to put his head on my shoulder, but I believe maybe for you, I might just do it all over again." She rubbed her hand over the hook, as natural as any caress. "But I probably need to go to the ladies' room to wipe off the excess. You mind walking with me? I may be a little woozy when I stand up, you think you could help me?"

As she helped him to his feet, Cal stood taller than he had since back when he'd had two arms. He put his good arm around her shoulders, wondering how he could help her walk when he could barely move himself, but they made it to their respective restrooms. When he came out, she was waiting. Back at the table, they all were too drunk to care what was going on; a couple of guys had left, others had scattered. Cal remembered that Claudette would be driving them home, and he was more than grateful. He didn't notice who rode in the car, and didn't remember much of the ride home. It was just one of those nights.

The next day, Cal awoke alone with a monumental headache. Downing two pain pills, he slept another hour, then ambled into the kitchen. The coffee pot was filled and ready to turn on—strange, he didn't remember getting it ready the night before, but what the hell—maybe he was more organized when totally wasted.

When he opened the refrigerator, there was some sort of unbaked pie there, with a note on top. *Breakfast—Bake at 350 for 40 minutes.*

Had Delores been by? When, and why? He'd never had pie for breakfast, but followed the directions, deciding to take a shower while he waited.

Going back into his room, things there looked different, as well. The covers were straightened, folded back, showing an imprint of where he'd lay between them but otherwise perfectly intact. The clothes he'd worn the night before were folded and hung over the chair. His shoes were in the closet, his wallet, keys, and a folded napkin lying across the dresser in a perfect line.

Cal took off his prosthesis, which he hadn't removed before bed, and addressed another strange question about the night before. He turned on the shower, making the water as hot as he could stand, and stood beneath it until the room was total fog.

Toweling off and stepping out of the bathroom, the house was filled with a smell so wonderful Cal sucked hard to breathe it in. The coffee was ready, but another fragrance took precedence.

Peeking into the oven, Cal groaned at the scent of sausage, covered in layers of eggs and bubbling cheese. Who put such things in a pie?

Smells like breakfast in heaven, Cal thought. The piecrust edges were turning brown, and glancing at the clock, he wondered if his stomach would allow him to wait the ten minutes more the mysterious note had instructed. He cheated and took it out in five.

After eating nearly half the pie at one sitting, Cal washed out his plate and coffee cup, leaving them in the dish drain. Cal continued to flirt with the idea that his sister had been there. He didn't really believe it, but it was a great idea for the start of a new day. Then the truth came out, like it or not.

Cal drove into town that afternoon, put gas in his truck, bought laundry detergent and dog food.

"Cal, my boy," said Ronnie, who worked the afternoon shift at Bill Tom's Gas & Go. "Have a good time last night?"

"Yeah, I guess," Cal said. "Same old, same old."

"So it's a regular thing, eh?" Ronnie asked, acting as if this were major news.

"I guess, but don't we all? I mean, we drink a lot, but hell—we live in Nolan. What else is there to do?"

"I guess. But we don't *all* do it. Some of us would rather do nothing at all. But I say 'to each his own.' Whatever floats your boat, like they say."

Cal shook his head. "See you around," he said to Ronnie, climbing back into his pickup to go.

There were knowing smiles and whispers at the grocery store and the barbershop. Seeing Walter Perry at the post office was the worst.

"How's it going, son?" old Walter asked. "You ever find any permanent farm job around here?"

"No, sir, no one seems to be hiring these days," Cal said.

"It's a shame, but at least you got your house and all, and no family to worry about." The old man grinned. "At least not of your own," he added. "Drop on by the store sometime, why don't you?" Mr. Perry said. "I'm sure there's folks that'd *love* to see you, if you know what I mean."

"Sure thing," Cal muttered, hurrying as quickly as he could for the safety of his truck.

It didn't take a rocket scientist to put the pieces together; in fact, Cal had known since he opened the folded napkin on his dresser. No note, nothing sappy, simply a name and a phone number: Claudette, 734-5215. A Nolan exchange.

Claudette lived in a yellow wooden house, just a stone's throw from the project where Cal's sister lived. There was a live oak bearing a tire swing in front, and the yard was filled with bikes and trikes and anything with wheels. Claudette's ex had left her with three tow-headed boys like stair-steps in height. Cal had seen them out playing in the patchy grass-and-dirt yard, a rusty, kudzu-enhanced chain-link keeping both the boys and a few mixed-breed dogs from the residential street. He'd heard Delores mention how they always looked dirty and unkempt, but he'd thought to himself that they always looked to be having fun, just boys being boys. Funny, he'd thought about the kids often as he passed by their home, but he'd never once given a thought to the woman inside. And now he didn't *want* to think of her. Cal succumbed to a wave of guilt he couldn't quite explain and didn't want to ponder.

Cal didn't call Claudette, as the phone number suggested, but was surprised at his joy in seeing her at the pool hall a few nights later. Only nodding at her across the room at first, after several beers he accepted her challenge in a game of eight ball. He thanked her for taking him home before, then bragged on the wonderful meal she'd left in the refrigerator.

"I love to cook," she said, her voice sounding softer, girlier than he'd noticed before. "I figured you feel pretty rotten the next day, so I just kinda threw together something easy with what you had in the frig. Nothing fancy, just home cooking."

"It was pretty fancy to me," Cal said. "I can scramble an egg and heat things from a can. Grill things. That's about it. I'd say yours was the fanciest meal cooked in my house so far!"

"You should let me *really* cook for you sometime," she said. "Tell me your favorite foods, and I'll see what I can do. I love a challenge, with three boys under eight, I get so damned tired of making sloppy joes and chili dogs I could scream."

"But I love sloppy joes and chili dogs," Cal said. "And when I was their age, I wanted to eat nothing else. My mama did get me hooked on a few other favorites, though. Do you make shepherd's pie?"

"Sure do."

"Brunswick stew?"

"The best."

"Stuffed pork chops?"

"Now you're talking up *my* alley. How 'bout stuffed pork chops, with a side of Brunswick stew, some fried okra, mashed potatoes, and—what do you like for dessert?" She was teasing him, but it was sweet, kind of like the way his mama had teased him, though he'd never really noticed it until she was no longer around to do it.

"I love pies of all kinds, but my mama made this special cake for my birthdays. It was chocolate layers, with chocolate icing that had coconut and pecans—"

"German chocolate!" Claudette shouted. "That's my favorite, too. I won a blue ribbon at the fair in Albany, back when I was in high school. Two of my three boys always want it for their birthdays, too."

"What does the other one like?" Cal asked, enjoying the talk of little boys and their likes and dislikes.

"Banana pudding is his favorite. Once I found a banana cake recipe, with chocolate icing and vanilla wafers on top, that's the only cake for him. He'd still rather just have the pudding, but the cake's easier to candle-up and cut."

"Can't blame him on that, though I might like to try the cake, just to be sure," Cal said.

They played a few more games. Claudette bought a pitcher and kept filling his mug, and when the owner dimmed the lights and started stacking chairs, Cal realized that once again, he was in no shape to drive home.

"I hope you don't think I did this on purpose, to take advantage of your—" Cal knew his words were sloppy and slurred, but she didn't seem to mind, placing a "shushing" finger over his lips with a smile.

"Shhhh," she whispered. "Don't worry about it. Just let me take care of you. Every boy needs a good mama now and then."

Again, Cal remembered nothing of the ride home or what happened when he arrived, but awoke again to a clean house and a pre-prepared breakfast. The bedcovers were a little mussed on *both* sides this time, which concerned him, but not really.

Claudette's just a drinking buddy, he thought. *Well, a buddy and a mom, kind of both. She's like one of the guys. I can't imagine her even wanting to have sex*—Then he remembered her three sons, which meant she must have at some time or other. But he knew he didn't have sex with Claudette. No way.

She began to invite him over for dinner with her kids. He tried to turn her down at least one of each three times, since he didn't want her to infer the wrong idea. The kids were a trip, good little boys who loved to play but knew to mind their mama. And she could cook like nobody's business. But they weren't dating, he wasn't interested in her that way, they were just friends.

When the guys began to tease him about her, he and Claudette made a mutual decision to meet more on the sly, she had her ex to worry about, too. It really worked better that way, he could drink with his friends on weeknights, then, when her ex-old man had the kids, he'd go out drinking with Claudette.

As time progressed, Cal decided he enjoyed his drinking with her more than with his other friends. "The thing with Claudette" stretched from weeks to months to a couple of years, not much of a traditional relationship, but one that seemed to work. A couple of nights a week, Cal had supper with Claudette and the boys, always going home around dark. Cal became quite fond of the kids, fixing their broken toys, telling them stories, even taking them out on the river to fish.

On weekends, when the boys were at their dad's, Cal concentrated on getting as knee-walking, shit-faced, tow-up inebriated as possible, Claudette driving as he made the rounds to all his usual haunts. If towards the end of the night he slurred or stumbled, she could talk for him, steer him in the right direction, or, on a few isolated occurrences, simply pick him up and take him home. After a while, she'd done it so often that sometimes folks called her, often on weeknights, to come and retrieve Cal from the Sundown, or the pool hall, or some late night card game, just come and peel him off the table or the booth or the floor, so that no one had to call the sheriff.

He called her his best friend, but they never kissed or even held hands. He never bought her a gift, but remembered her boys on birthdays, Christmas, and sometimes no special occasion but that they "needed" new ball gloves, a pup tent, or winter coats. On her weekends at the house on stilts, she made sure the cupboards were full and the laundry kept up. She bought lotions for massaging his stump, ice cream for uplifting his spirits, *Readers' Digest* and *Field & Stream* for redirecting his restless thoughts.

Cal was drinking more than ever, but he believed life was good, at least as good as he could expect. Yet in those moments, on those blurry, hazy, not-of-this-world-nights, Cal was as lost as Claudette in sharing his broken-but-still-kicking body with another human being. When she lifted him from wherever his stupor had left him and laid him down in his private bedroom, Cal had two strong arms and a healed soul.

And because it was she who healed him, if only for that moment, her face, and hands, and body belonged to no less than an angel. If only he could have remembered these things on the days after, when he was sober.

It was not Cal, or his friends, or even Claudette that put an end to their strange relationship. It was Delores.

Cal had stopped by on his way to supper at Claudette's, bringing by a few trinkets for the baby—a cloth book about animals, a squeaky rubber-like whale, and, as a last minute idea, the plastic box of shapes he'd brought home from his last day at Warm Springs rehab, so long ago. Little Mary Jane would be two years old soon, and Cal was still often unsure about appropriate gifts for babies, especially girls.

Delores folded clothes—sheets and towels—on the kitchen table. Mary Jane ran to the screen door as he pulled into her driveway.

"UnkCal! UnkCal!" she cried, showing her mouthful of baby teeth and the Mullinax dimple they all wore in their right cheeks.

The room smelled of simmering chicken and dumplings, and Cal almost wished he weren't committed to Claudette and the boys that night. He knew Claudette's meal would be equally as good and with plenty to spare, but his sister's kitchen smelled like home: just drawing in the familiar fragrance made his parents feel just around the corner.

Delores jumped up to unlatch the screen, and Cal grabbed his niece in a single swooping gesture.

"How's my little Mojo girl?" He ruffled her golden curls with his good hand, and she laid her face against the familiar hook that held her.

"Mojo *love* UnkCal!" She switched her head to his shoulder, reaching out to embrace Cal's mechanical arm in a bear hug. "Unk-Cal play! UnkCal play Mojo, now!" She jumped down and ran back to her room, returning holding a love-worn bear, a naked doll, and pulling by a string a dog with a slinky-toy middle.

"Of course, baby girl," he said. "And I brought you some new play things, too." Calvin open the crinkled brown bag he'd secured under his good arm.

"Book," the little girl said, turning a page, placing her face against its inside, then turning again. "UnkCal bring book—am-mah-mah book," she enunciated, proud of conquering the big word.

"That's right," Cal said. "It's an animal book. And what kind of animal is this?" he asked, pulling from the bag the whale, squeezing it and making it shriek.

"Fish," she said. "UnkCal bring fish!" She reached for the toy and squeezed it again. She screamed along with its harsh squeal, Calvin hugging her in return.

"More toys? You're gonna have her downright spoiled," Delores said, smirking while shaking her head.

"It ain't much, and besides, she's gotta know her 'Unka Cal' is the next best thing to Santy Claus." Cal grabbed the little girl again, swinging her in a big circle as she hugged to her chest the new book and toy.

"What dare, what dare, UnkCal?" she asked, bumping against the last bulky object in the bag he still tried to conceal. Cal set her down on the floor, reached under his arm, and withdrew the last item.

"Aw, pitty, pitty," she exclaimed. Mary Jane had not mastered the "pr" sound. She grabbed the box, shaking it and giggling at the colorful objects.

"Wait, look here," Cal said, carefully taking the box from her tiny hands, lifting the box top, then shaking out the many shapes inside onto the sparkling clean floor of his sister's kitchen.

"See here," he said as he closed it back. "These go inside the box, can you put them in?" Cal picked up a yellow moon, then a blue star, slipping them through the corresponding holes. The baby grabbed a handful, mimicking her uncle without a clue on how to accomplish the task.

"This may be a little beyond her comprehension level," Delores said, watching her daughter attempt this new and daunting adventure.

"Yeah," Cal said, "but look at her trying—it's a sight to behold." He stretched his arm around his sister's shoulder, the two exchanging looks as the determined little girl scooped handfuls of shapes onto the box top, watching them fall aside, then scooping them up again.

"Have a seat," Delores motioned to a kitchen chair. "She'll be working on this one a while, I guess." She sat in a chair facing her brother where they could both watch Mary Jane, Delores still folding towels.

"Funny you happened by tonight," she said. "I was just thinking of you. Made Mama's chicken and dumplings—you just can't make it for less than a crowd. I was thinking about calling you, then there you were, pulling up to the door."

"I'm just on my way to supper, wish I could stay, but I already promised. I've been meaning to stop by, had these things for the baby—"

"Supper plans?" Delores said. "You mean, like, a dinner date? Who is she, Cal? Why didn't I know? And—" Delores looked him up and down, taking in his frayed dungarees, shabby plaid shirt, worn brogans. "—Why aren't you dressed for the occasion?"

"It's not really a date, Sis," Cal said. "Just supper with a friend. We do it once a week or so, nothing like you're thinking. Just a buddy of mine—wait, do you know ol' Claudette, that works up at Perry's tractor place? You remember, she lives on the corner, right as you turn out of the projects and back up towards the water tower."

"Claudette Fair, that—that—," Delores's eyes tightened. "That *she-man*, slut, alcoholic, streetwalking, welfare mom that's slept with half of Dumas County, with her kids in the next room?" She man-handled a towel into submission, jerking it with a snap, then smoothing it and stacking it onto another. She grabbed a handful more and continued with the same vigor.

"Aww, Sis, be nice. She's what mama called a 'right full-figured kinda gal,'" Cal said. "But you know as well as I do that you can't judge a book by its cover. Claudette's a hard worker, ask Mr. Perry, or anybody up at the tractor place. She's a good cook, a good mother to those boys, despite the fact that sorry Rodney Fair don't do right by 'em at all. She does the best she can. She's my good friend, and she ain't no slut, either." Calvin's voice grew deeper, gritting his teeth as he spoke.

"Oh, she ain't, you say? And how would you know, Cal, about the personal life of the ex-Mrs. Fair? Just how good a friends are the two of you?" The pitch of Delores's voice went higher as the color in her cheeks flamed a rosy pink.

"Just good friends, that's all," Cal said. "Not that it's any damned business of yours. Claudette's my drinking buddy, and I spend a little time with her boys now and then, that's all. She helps out with the woman-chores at my house, and I help her in return. That's all."

"What kind of woman-chores, Cal? Dear God, you're not sleeping with her, are you? You realize you could end up with god-knows-what-kind-of diseases, don't you? And besides, what kind of help could she need from you? Rodney Fair lives just down the road, at Clear Lake. I can't imagine anything she or those boys might need around the house that he wouldn't be willing to take care of. Unless she's needing—" Delores hesitated.

"Just *shut up*, Delores," Cal said through his teeth. Little Mary Jane began to fret, and Cal picked her up, bouncing her on his knee.

"Good baby," he whispered against her ear, nuzzling her curls as he murmured softly. "Good girl, Mojo," he said as she lay her tiny head against his chest.

"That ain't her damned name," Delores said with a tightened jaw, reaching across the table to caress her daughter's leg. The baby clung to her uncle, patting his shoulder as he hummed wordless sounds against her neck.

"Sweet Mary Jane," Cal murmured, as he corrected the name. "Sweet baby girl." He kissed the top of her head as she continued patting him with her chubby, baby-hand.

"I know she's your buddy, like one of the guys, Cal, and I know it ain't none of my business," Delores said, "but I just worry about you. You don't need to get mixed up with her is all. You can do so much better." She looked away, not wanting to continue eye contact.

"What are you saying, Delores?" He raised his voice, but barely, not wanting to upset the child. "It ain't like you to think you're better than anyone else, and to be honest, it ain't real becoming to you. Just what's your beef with Claudette?"

"I ain't got any beef with her, personally, I reckon," she said. "I just don't think it's good for you to be spending time with her. There's things they say about her, you know. She ain't a real good person, and I can tell you she ain't much of a mother, just from riding by the house every day."

"What kind of things do 'they' say, Delores? And who the hell are 'they'? And how in God's name can you tell what kind of mother she is from riding by her house? Can she tell the same about you?" Little Mary Jane was becoming restless, and climbed back down to her new toys on the kitchen floor.

"They say she sleeps around, Cal, with anybody who'll lay down with her. Don't care if they're old or young, married or single, she'll lay down with a man in the afternoon and then speak to him and his wife, on the street, the next day, and not think a thing about it. She's a slut, Cal, she'll do anything wearing pants, that's why Rodney left her."

"That's not what happened at all," Cal said. "And just where do you get your information? You're not cozying up with Mr. Rodney these days, are you? God, Sis, that guy's pure trash—"

"I'm not 'cozying up' with *anybody*," she screamed, biting her bottom lip and sucking in the tears that filled her eyes, a single droplet streaking her cheek.

Hearing her mother's duress, the baby began to cry. Delores kneeled down and scooped up her daughter, then stood and walked to the kitchen window. Her brother rose and followed.

"I'm sorry, Sis," he said, standing behind her and placing his good hand on her shoulder. Mary Jane reached up and placed her hand over his.

"It's not just seeing her from the road, Cal. Sure the kids look dirty and they're out with the yard dogs all day, but they look happy and well-fed, I guess. And they're not in the street. But Imogene's mama, who lives next door—" Delores faltered.

"Delores."

"Let me finish, Cal," she said. "Imogene's mom says sometimes she leaves, in the middle of the night. Like the lights are out and they've all been in bed for hours, and then a light comes on and she's out the door, gone for an hour, two, even three before she gets back."

"Sis, you know that's being nosy. Ain't nobody's business if she gets up in the middle of the night, and you know that."

Delores turned around to face her brother.

"It's not the getting up, Cal. It's not that anyone cares where she goes or what she does, it's just that she *leaves*." The baby began to squirm, and Delores let her back down, where she ambled back to her toys.

"Claudette leaves, Cal. She gets in her car, and drives away, leaving those three little boys alone, for hours. It ain't right. What kind of a mother would do something like that, and why?"

Cal was silent, staring at his niece, who had once again began to stack the colorful shapes onto the top of the hollow box. Mary Jane had but one parent, but there was no doubt she would never go unwatched for a single minute. He could see his sister's concern, yet his heart went out to another woman, the one who would take such precious chances—for him.

"Imogene's mother don't know everything," he said. "I'll bet if she goes, there's somebody else in the house. I'm sure there is," he said, though without much conviction.

"You know Imogene's mother, Cal. She's got eyes like a hawk and a mind like a steel trap. If there was any chance of those boys being watched over, she wouldn't say anything. She even kinda likes Claudette, but she's worried for those boys. She's been thinking 'bout saying something to Rodney."

"Why that nosey old bat," Cal said. "If she says one word to Rodney, the Fair clan'll have the whole courthouse turned against her. Rodney don't want or need those boys, but he'd love to take 'em away from Claudette, just for pure meanness. You can't let her say anything!"

"It ain't like I can do anything about it, Cal. Mrs. Sanderson does what she thinks is right, and can't no one—" Delores dropped to the floor and grabbed the baby, who was coughing and making gutteral sounds. "Spit it out, baby, spit it out to Mama," she said, reaching her fingers into Mary Jane's mouth and extracting a red star and a green circle. The child screamed as Delores further probed her mouth and throat.

"I'm sorry, baby, but Mama's gotta make sure you didn't swallow anything," she said, the baby shrieking louder as Delores gagged, pried open her little mouth with both her hands, then turned her upside down, shaking her as screamed, her cherub face turning beet red.

"No harm done," Delores said as she uprighted the child. "The pieces really are too big to swallow, but not too big for this little bugger to try. We might need to put this up for a few more months."

Cal was already on his knees, gathering the shapes and placing them back into the box. "Damn, Delores, guess I really screwed up this time," he said, standing up and holding the box with his hook.

Delores reached up and hugged him, Mary Jane stepping between them and hugging both their knees. Cal leaned down and gathered her to his shoulder with his good arm, leaning forward to hand her over to her mother. "Go see your mama, now, baby girl," he said. "Unka Cal's gotta be going now."

"Calvin," Delores said. "But you just got here."

"Got some things to take care of. I'll come by and see ya'll later in the week," he promised. "And I'll take this back to my place, 'til she's a little older." He motioned to the plastic box hanging on his hook. He reached over and gave them both a peck on the cheek, then headed out the door.

He never made it to Claudette's for supper.

And so it ended. Calvin never went back to Claudette's house. He didn't return her calls, and he tried to dodge any place he might run into her. When she finally tracked him down, on a Friday night at home, he delivered the lie he'd planned for the inevitable occasion.

"Look, Claudette," he said, glancing about the room and never meeting her eyes. "You've got the wrong idea. I ain't in love with you, and I ain't never gonna be. You got some good little boys, but they've got their own daddy, and I ain't lookin' to be one. You and me are just buddies, it's all we've ever been, but you got the wrong idea and just took it too far. So it's probably for the best we just don't hang out anymore for a while."

Her rough, tanned face turned a ghostly pale, her eyes misty. "But, Cal," she said, "we're been the same for going on two years. My boys love you, and I thought we got along just fine."

"Well, they don't *need* to love me, they've got their own daddy, just a mile away. And it ain't fair to him to have them boys thinking I'm—"

"Did Rodney say something to you? Is that what this is about?" Claudette went from awkwardly frightened to downright mad, which was a little easier to deal with. Cal had always hated to see a woman cry, no matter what the reason.

"Rodney ain't never said a thing to me, but I wouldn't blame him if he did. They're his boys, Claudette, and it ain't fair to 'em for you to go confusing 'em, making me out to be more than I am to 'em, with their real daddy right up the road."

"Cal, you've been more of a daddy to my boys, taking them fishing, taking care of things they needed, than Rodney ever—"

"Well then I was wrong, too, but it's over. I'm not confusing those pore younguns anymore, Claudette. I ain't their daddy, and they don't need to think I am."

"But you're so good with them, and they love you, and who knows, maybe one day—"

Cal hated to do it, but figured it was better to go on and get it over with instead of stretching it out. Like pulling a tooth. Jerk it hard and get it on out.

"One day, my ass, Claudette. Listen to yourself! I ain't never said the first thing to you about moving in, or getting married, or for God's sake, making myself them boys' daddy. I've never said anything of the kind, ever, but obviously you had your own plans for me, without letting me in on 'em, right, Claudette?"

Claudette's strong, man-like posture wilted like a wet dishrag, tears streaking her face as she nibbled her chapped lips. Trembling, she reached out to touch Cal's shoulder, but he slung her arm back at her, pulling away from her touch as though disgusted.

"Keep your hands off me, you nympho. Haven't you even noticed how I can't stand that shit?"

"But, Cal," she sniffled, "I know you don't like to be all touchy-feely in public, but you've never—"

"I've never what? I never told you I liked being felt up and slobbered on, have I, Claudette? But have you stopped to think about it? No, not as long as you're getting what you want."

"But Calvin, we've been together, alone, we've been making love for—"

"Look, Claudette, get real. We don't 'make love.' Has it ever crossed your mind that I've never been able tolerate your taking off you clothes unless I've been totally shitfaced?"

The room went still. Suddenly Calvin was aware of the clock ticking on the wall, the full moon glistening on the river through his picture window, the baby-powdery smell of the lotion Claudette favored.

And the hefty, strong woman who could lift an engine block was now reduced to a damaged moth dried onto a headlight.

But not without a swansong.

Blinking back tears, Claudette sucked in once, then, trembling, made a fist, drew it back, and punched Calvin's left eye with all her might. Then she turned and left.

Calvin saw stars, but still watched through the window as she threw herself into her car and drove away. She would never know that on that night, it was Calvin who couldn't stop his own tears.

Chapter 16
September 1974

Mojo

WHEN THE NEXT FLOOD CAME, I WAS IN HIGH SCHOOL, an old soul pretending to love Three Dog Night, love beads, and hip-hugger jeans, but still listening to my uncle's Hank Williams albums and wearing cast off clothes from girls at the local Baptist church. When this flood came, Mama packed up *everything*, even the yard sale appliances that didn't work, and we took it all to Uncle Calvin's.

Uncle Cal didn't work during that flood; in fact, by that time, he seldom left his house at all. It was then that we found out just how bad off he was, almost a hermit. The moody guy who would laugh and joke, then yell and slam doors was gone, replaced with a sickly old man I hardly recognized. His skin was pasty and yellow, and the hair he had left had turned white. He seemed partly asleep even when he was awake. It made me want to cry that Mama's long ago prediction had come true. God knows she never *wished* it to happen. It just did. It was hard to believe he was not even forty—he looked twice as old.

A colored boy from my school brought his staple goods once a week: Jim Beam, Coke, Lucky Strikes, VanCamp's pork and beans, Premium Saltines. And this had been going on for months. I'd never really noticed Roosevelt Hawkins except to hear his name called in a class or two; he never said much out loud, that I'd heard. But here, he seemed more like a grown man than a kid my age.

Every day he brought Uncle Cal his few necessities and helped him bathe, if Uncle Cal felt like it. Then he sat in the chair beside the bed and explained everything he could think of about the goings on in Nolan that week. Sometimes it was farm stuff—lots about the weather and whose crops were looking the worst. Uncle Cal asked a lot of questions about Oakland Plantation. He smiled when he heard they might be doing poorly, but he never stayed smiling long. Talk about Oakland always ended with Uncle Cal getting mad, ugly mad.

That's when Roosevelt would change the subject, which he was pretty good at doing. Sometimes it was politics, what the folks were saying about running the sheriff out of town, or moving the town square further uphill in case of floods, or closing the high school and shipping us off somewhere else. Sometimes it was pure out gossip. Mama'd try to make me leave the room when it got too bad, but it didn't matter. I could hear good enough from anywhere in the house. They'd talk about whose wife caught him cheating, who stayed out all night drunk, whose wives stayed gone a lot or spent too much money. Some days I'd wonder where a boy like Roosevelt could find out all these things, but not bad enough to ask him. He was like a drug Uncle Cal needed just to keep drawing breath. Rosie, as he called him, stayed until Uncle Cal was asleep, then silently nodded his head at me and Mama and left.

At first Mama said she was gonna let Roosevelt go, that she could take care of Uncle Cal. But after she watched just one night of their ritual, she changed her mind. He needed Rosie's stories like we needed a place to stay.

We never moved from the house on stilts after that. Mama did her best to make Cal eat better and help him cut down on the booze, but she must've known it was too late.

It was Sloppy Joe day in the lunchroom, not my favorite, but by far not the worst. Standing in the cafeteria line with a plastic tray, I touched my milk carton to my sweating face. The two goons in front of me talked about football, and Melissa Moorhead, our resident beauty queen wearing a pantsuit seen in *Seventeen* and too much Love's Baby Soft perfume, left a space the size of an invisible person behind me. I was used to it. She had to be careful: being poor could be contagious—I sure *wished* it was. Beyond the serving room, the intercom boomed a warbled message.

"Mary Mullinax. Mary. Jane. Mullinax. Please report to the attendance office."

I walked out and headed for the attendance office. I knew something was wrong when I saw Mama on the bench outside the door. I could tell she'd been crying.

"Get your things, your books or whatever," she said. "You won't be back for a few days."

"Why?" I asked, not really wanting to hear the answer.

"Just get what you need, I got Cal's—" she gasped, then breathed out, "I got the truck out at the front of the building. I'll meet you there." She took off without waiting for an answer.

There in the cab she took both my hands in hers, looked directly into my eyes, and whispered, "Baby, your Uncle Cal passed away this morning. It's just me and you now."

Tears fell down her face as she pulled me to her. We stayed just like that for a while, my thoughts going willy-nilly all over the place. I guess I'd known for a while that my uncle's days were numbered and that I'd never see the old Uncle Cal again, but I fought facing it head on and fell into just watching my mama, holding her thin, strong body and just imagining the pain inside her. Sure, it hurt me, but I still had *her*, though she was crying her eyes out, I knew she'd bounce back in a heartbeat if needed to, if it was for me. I had her to lean on—but all she had was me, and what good could I do? I held her tighter, it was all I could do; then she drew away.

Her gray-blue eyes were streaked with red, and her cheekbones looked painfully sharp under her pale skin. As always, her long ash-blonde hair was drawn back in an old elastic band, and for maybe the first time in my life, I saw what a beautiful woman she still was, even crying.

"Now Cal had friends ever where, and I imagine they'll come as soon as they hear the news. We need to clean up the house good, and they're expectin' us at the funeral home tonight. The next few days is gone be hard, but we'll do it cause it's what we have to do." Mama handed me a handful of Kleenex, then she wiped her face with her own. "Cal was a pistol, but he had a heart of gold. This is the last thing we can do for him, so we've gotta do it right."

She cranked the truck and we headed home.

I cried like a baby over Uncle Cal. It seemed like every inch of the house triggered some memory of him—funny stories, old songs, day-to-day stuff that wouldn't be much to tell about, but was precious all the same. Mama cried too, but she never broke down in front of anyone but me, at least that I knew about. At home, there was a navy blue skirt and two blouses hanging in my closet, and a pair of cheap flats to match. They looked new.

"Wear the white one to the funeral home," Mama said. "Go ahead and get you a shower and wash your hair now. Cal set a sight in you, and you want to look good for his last get-togethers. Wear the one with the flowers to the funeral Saturday." She walked out of the room. I did as I was told.

She was right about my uncle's friends. The phone started ringing around three, and the first casserole arrived at four thirty. People we barely knew, and didn't think Cal knew either, brought more food than that house had ever seen at once. Pans of fried chicken, pitchers of tea, hams, vegetables, desserts of all kinds. I wasn't hungry at all, but Mama made me eat. She drank a glass of tea and then disappeared into the bathroom, running the water for a long time. Mama never could eat when she was upset, but she sure thought that I could. Guess I did, back when I had her around to make me.

We arrived at the funeral home early, to talk with the preacher about the service on Saturday. It seemed weird, talking to a preacher about Uncle Cal, who never went to church. It was the Methodist preacher, who I'd never met, since the Baptists had the biggest "outreach" programs for Bible school and such, but I was glad we got this preacher instead. He talked in a whispery voice about "Mr. Mul-linax," and for a minute I didn't realize that Mr. Mullinax was Uncle Cal. He said he'd been talking to several of my uncle's friends, and that he was certainly loved by a lot of people. I liked that, and Mama did, too. He said he'd like to use "the Lord is my shepherd" as the scripture verse, and Mama was okay with that. Then he asked if her brother had any favorite hymns. Mama's eyes opened twice as wide, then she just kind of sighed.

"Cal was crazy about Hank Williams," she said, "but I'm afraid I can't tell you about his favorite hymns. It's just something we never talked about." Mama looked like a frightened child, younger than me, as she explained herself.

The preacher smiled, a smile so kind it made me think of Uncle Cal himself. "I'm a big fan of Mr. Williams as well," he said. "I'm sure I can find something appropriate to say, and those are really all the questions I have for you. Do you have any for me?"

We didn't. He led us into the viewing room, where Uncle Cal was resting on a white pillow in a shiny brown box. He wore a blue shirt with a collar, dressy-like, but it wasn't buttoned at the top and he wore no tie, thank goodness. He had on clean blue jeans and a belt with a tractor on the buckle, one I hadn't seen him wear in years. The room was kind of cold and smelled like flowers in a refrigerator. My uncle's face was pale, but the lines around his eyes and mouth had simply disappeared. His thin hair and thick beard were shiny and combed, the white strands glowing like silver. He looked like he was sleeping—a good, peaceful sleep with happy dreams.

Mama leaned over and kissed him. She looked back to me, but I shook my head. She was okay with it. I knew he would be cold and clean-smelling, like the room. I wanted to remember the real Uncle Cal, the one who made pirate jokes about his missing arm, treated his pets like people, and quoted Hank Williams like some folks quote scripture. The familiar mannequin in the wooden box looked nice enough, but he was not my uncle.

We walked about the room and into the outside area, talking with the people who came. A lot of them were Uncle Cal's friends, but there were women from the factory who came to see Mama, as well. Mr. Danner, from the 4-H club at school was there. I figured he might be a friend of my uncle's but he talked to Mama for a long time, and then to me, too. They talked about the time Uncle Cal raised a pig for 4-H, how he was the Grand Champion and won a hundred dollars, but then Uncle Cal wouldn't eat bacon or pork chops for the next six months, afraid that he might be eating "Wiggly." He said Calvin was one of the hardest workers he'd ever known, and that he was proud to have known him. That meant more to me than anything else I heard the rest of the week.

Mr. Danner was a Baptist, I'd seen him leading the singing at revivals I'd been to. He always dressed nice and drove a nice car, and talked more like a teacher than a farmer, always putting the words together just right. But he wasn't too fancy to know a good man when he saw one, and he went out of his way to let us know how he felt.

The funeral was a graveside service at the Nolan Cemetery. A dark green tent shielded the casket, a few plants, and twenty folding chairs covered in velvet and sitting on a carpet that was supposed to look like grass. Beside my grandma's grave, Uncle Cal's wooden box was covered in lapping branches of the blossoming cotton plants, long brown grains of wheat, and tasseling corn. It took my breath away: Mama hadn't prepared me for it, but the moment I saw it I knew it was just what he'd have wanted. We looked at each other and smiled.

"From Mr. Danner," she whispered. "Cal loved to watch crops grow, they used to talk about it." I nodded. "But I'm glad there ain't any peanuts," she added.

That was a given. The way I saw it, picking peanuts took a big chunk of my uncle away, years before he was finally laid to rest.

My uncle's friends seemed uncomfortable and out of place under the tent, so most of them stood around it, shifting from one foot to the other and staring at the dry grass. The preacher welcomed them and they gathered a little closer, but not much.

The preacher read from the Bible and then prayed. Then he talked about living and dying and saying goodbye. "Cal was a man who loved nature, and beauty, and life," he said. He was calling him Cal, like he knew him, I thought. I was hoping he really did.

I gazed at my mama, pale as a ghost. She was staring at the group of Uncle Cal's friends and looking like she'd seen one herself. There, in the middle of the clump of obvious farmers, wearing overalls, or khakis, or Dickies' coveralls, was an out-of-place fellow in a sport coat, a tie, and grey trousers. He was a bit haggard, but handsome nonetheless. All the men knew him, though he seemed nothing like them.

And Mama—Mama stared straight at him, and him at her. I watched from the corner of my eye, wondering who he was and how this unknown man could take her concentration away from her only brother. In one way, I wanted to thank him; it was like she stopped hurting for a minute or so, but I wanted to hit him, too. Who the hell was he to come between Mama and Uncle Cal?

Then the weirdest thing happened; just as I watched, while trying to seem like I wasn't watching, they saw each other. Their eyes locked. Finally, Mama smiled the tiniest smile, then nodded in such a way that you had to be staring to notice it at all. The man smiled— he had a warm, beautiful smile—and nodded, bigger than Mama. Then they both turned away.

And they never looked back at each other again.

The preacher was deep into his message. "He lived simply and kept a good attitude. Despite a number of hardships, he had never lost his faith in his Creator or in seeing his mother again, in their new home in the sky."

Mama's tears were like a faucet then, but she never made a sound.

Then the preacher started talking about light. He said that Jesus was the light of the world. He said that people with near-death experiences often remember only a great light, and spoke of the joy of stepping into the light. I didn't really understand what he was getting at, but I kept listening.

One of the men outside the tent stepped closer, taking an object out of his pocket. He held something shiny and put it to his mouth. Quietly at first, then louder, the sound of a harmonica filled the air. He was playing a melody I'd heard before, but I couldn't remember what it was.

The preacher wasn't preaching anymore, he was talking in a sing-song sort of way. Like men-English teachers who read poetry out loud, 'cept this preacher sounded more like he meant it, not like he was showing off, the way *they* do. He and the harmonica weren't together, like the words of a song go with the music, but they fit together like they were carrying on a conversation. Sometimes one would talk, sometimes the other. Sometimes they'd talk at the same time, but you could always tell they were listening to one another all the while. Sometimes the harmonica would hold one long note and then move just a little toward another one, back and forth, over and over, where you never could tell where one ended and the other begun. It was like nothing I'd ever heard before, and I wanted it to go on forever.

Before long I recognized the words, practically knew them by heart, but didn't sing along in my head, the way I usually would have. They made it a different song, one that had never been sung before, and probably never would be again. It was for Uncle Cal. He could hear them, and it was something as beautiful as he deserved.

The song went on as we all listened, those awkward fellows looking up now, looking at each other, at the sky, at the preacher, at the harmonica player, at me and Mama, even at the casket. And though some of them were crying as well, they were smiling, too. Sad to see him go but glad they were alive to be here with this song and this moment.

"Now I'm so happy," the preacher said. "No sorrow's in sight." His eyes were closed and he seemed to have finished, and the harmonica was winding down, when all of a sudden he stopped—not faded, stopped, as if to signal some important statement that would change the rest of the world.

The preacher opened his eyes and smiled. He looked at us, then at the casket, then back at all of us again. He raised both his hands and looked upward, saying

"Praise the Lord—I saw the light."

There was silence, then the harmonica played a long, sad chord.

"Amen," the preacher said, and he stepped across to us, shaking our hands.

The crowd of mourners followed.

Monday morning came. Mama was dressed for work, yelling at me to get up and get moving before I missed the bus for school. When I tried to argue, she shut me up quick.

"There's a time for mourning and a time to get back to living. Your Uncle Cal woulda said the same. And if we aim to go on eatin', after all this funeral food goes bad or runs out, whichever comes first, I gotta keep working."

"But Mama," I said. "Everybody at your work knows. And Uncle Cal just died Thursday."

"I'm aware of when your uncle died, Mary Jane. I'm also aware the future's lookin' you dead in the eye, and you have gotta stay in school and keep your grades up, that is, if you wanna be able to leave the great city of Nolan one day."

Well, that was that.

We went back to our regular routine, a little sadder but still keeping a stiff upper lip around each other. We gave the house on stilts a good cleaning, even washing the dogs and getting some cheap nylon collars with little tags that were supposed to kill fleas and ticks. Mama threw out the sheets and blankets that smelled like what I came to know as the last months of Uncle Cal, but she did it when

I was at school so I didn't notice 'til a week later. She bought a calendar printed with brightly colored English gardens and some little plastic air fresheners at the dollar store, but the look of the place remained the same.

Mama dusted the gun rack with a gentler touch, like it was something precious and valuable. Sometimes I would find myself staring at the picture over the couch, and I swear those dogs playing cards would look back at me.

We were doing the best we could, through the fall and winter, then spring came.

Then Mama got sick.

At first she called it a bad cold and went back to work anyway, hacking and coughing with every breath. When she passed out at her sewing machine, an ambulance took her to the twenty-bed hospital in Baxter. Imogene, her best friend at work, came by that day, after I was in from school. She told me what had happened, and what Mama wanted me to do.

"She says she won't be there more than a day or two," Imogene said, "and that you could take care of things on your own, but to make sure you knew she could come home anytime she wanted to, so not to put off doing the dishes or changing the sheets "til you felt like it."

Imogene was around Mama's age, but she'd "lived hard and been put up wet," as Uncle Cal woulda said. She had the body of a show-girl with the face of an aging alligator.

"I'm thinking she'll at least be there another three or four days," she said. "My ex-husband gets the kids on Wednesdays. I'll go see her then. You wanna come with me?" she asked.

I said nothing, so I guess the eyes looking up at her said it all. She embraced me, hard, folding me into the forty-inch bosom that towered over her girlish waist. It gave and fell downward as I nestled in her arms. She smelled faintly of sweat and talcum powder, the way my mama smelled after work. Her hands hugged down my shoulders and waist, then she pulled away.

"Chile, you ain't big as a washin' a soap," she declared, pretending to sound like the mammy we'd only seen in ancient movies, "with little ol' legs like chicken wings."

Uncle Cal had taught me well. "My legs reach the ground, and they'll carry me wherever I go," I said.

She hugged me again.

"Take me to the hospital with you, please," I said. "I need to see her. Take me with you, if you can."

"I'll come by Wednesday, after work. If you ain't here, I'll wait. Sound okay?"

"Sounds great," I said.

"Okay, then," she said, standing up straight, looking towards the door. "You got everything you need? Food, lunch money—report cards, permission slips, $1 for a year of the Weekly Reader?" Imogene still had a kid in primary school.

"We shop for the whole week on Saturday," I told her. "I'm fine, for everything except a way to see my mama. Thanks, Imogene."

"No thanks needed," she said. "Your mama's done a world of favors for me and a lotta other folks, and as long as I've known her she's never asked for a thing for herself. Helpin' you kinda makes me feel better, like I'm not takin' advantage." Her voice faltered. "And besides, now I can take advantage of her again, if I need to, and I got me like a free pass, you know?"

A week later Mama came home, still coughing up blood, but with enough drugs to knock her out between times. Imogene stayed for the first few days, then school was out. She went home to her kids, and I was there to stay beside Mama both day and night.

At first I slept in a chair, never leaving her side, but as time went on, I worked up the nerve to sleep in on my own bed across the hall. We settled into a kind of routine, not an easy one, but we were adjusting and beginning to feel more comfortable. Then one morning, just before sunrise, she called my name. I woke up excitedly, thinking she was finally getting better.

When I walked in, the room was pale yellow in the first morning light and Mama was sitting up in bed, her faded cotton nightdress open at her neck, which was pale and corded with thick, blue veins.

"You want your breakfast, Mama?" I asked.

"No, Mojo, I don't want anything to eat, and no more damn medicine, not right now, anyway," she said. Her voice was barely audible but stern just the same. "I want you to sit up," she patted the bed. "And listen to me, now, while you can."

I went over to the bed and sat next to her. I knew what she meant: This was important. I sat up. I listened.

"I won't be here when you graduate, I'm afraid, but I'll see you, just the same." Her voice was thin and raspy and the words came out with great spaces in between. "Considering you're almost eighteen, DFACS will probably look the other way. You ain't never been in no trouble, so folks'll probably just let you be, rather than have to take you on like a charity case. This house we're living in, it's already paid for, and it already belongs to you."

"Whattaya mean?" I asked. It was all I could say.

She paused, the broken shade flapped in the morning breeze and mama's face lit up briefly before the shade flapped back down again.

"Your Uncle Cal left you this house, that and the land around it, and everything else he owned. We talked about it, and decided it was the best thing to do." She stopped and swallowed, and her lips quivered. I could hear the rasp of her breath. After several seconds she kept on. "He knew he was dying, and I knew I was sick, but we figured by the grace of God we could make this thing work out. God willin', it did." She tilted her head at me and I saw her eyelids twitch like they did sometimes before she cried.

I said nothing.

"Damn, Mojo," Mama said in a surprising burst of energy. "Think about it." Her words came out in a rush. "You own the place already, though you didn't know it 'til this minute, with me as a trustee or some legal name like that, and if you can lay low and keep your nose clean 'til you're eighteen, no one on God's earth can change that."

"But, Mama," I said, sucking back the overflow and trying not to cry. I followed her story, but didn't want to live in the moment. Not then, not ever.

Mama sagged down again like a wilted flower, but she kept on. "I've got lung cancer, baby. It ain't gettin' no better for me. You keep your grades up. Get you a little job after school. Folks'll think they're doing you a favor, but they'll be getting' a good worker for less'n they'd pay a grown person, so don't think you owe 'em nothing."

She took a deep breath in and closed her eyes as though for strength. Her lids looked delicate as the shells of tiny bird's eggs. "There's some life insurance money Cal took out on me—don't you spend it on nothing but school, ya hear?" She opened her eyes and looked at me fiercely. "You gotta place to live, free. Your job'll pay the 'lectric bill, other little bills. You eat for free at school, and if there's ever a one-time month you can't cover it all, you're a smart girl, you'll know who to go to for help." Her voice weakened with each phrase. She sank back down on her pillow.

"Mary Jane—I want you to know I love you," she said. In the silence that followed, I heard a bobwhite call outside, but mostly all I heard was the in and out of Mama's thin breath. "I always did," she said. "You've been the one thing in my crazy life that's been worth it all. And some of the ugliest, and silliest fights I ever had with your Uncle Cal was 'cause a you. For some reason, it always seemed like he could show you how he felt, and you'd believe him, and I was always just the hard-ass bitch that was your mama."

I felt a knife stick in me that coulda cut through the state of Georgia.

Mama swallowed. Reaching over she patted my hand with hers. It was dry and light as paper. "But you're a good girl, Mary Jane, and you're smart. I've always been so proud of you, you're everything any mother, rich or poor or whatever, coulda wanted. And I've always felt that way, Mojo." Her voiced cracked on the last word.

I couldn't help it, I leaned over and tried to hug her, I wanted a chokehold of life that would connect us 'til Armageddon, but she pushed me away and shook her head: She hadn't finished.

"This ain't the best life you coulda got, girl, but they're folks out there got it a lot worse than you, baby. You're a Mullinax—if we ain't nothin' else, we're strong. You be strong, too, baby," she said. "Be strong for Uncle Cal." She closed her eyes.

"And for you," I added, smiling like the village idiot. The lump in my throat was like a grapefruit, but I stayed strong.

I was a Mullinax.

Mama died at home on the Fourth of July. While illegal fireworks resonated on the river, I washed her off, changed her gown, brushed out her hair 'til it fell like gold silk over her shoulders, and then I called the funeral home. Having just lost Uncle Cal, I was a seasoned pro: I did what I had to do, and I did it well. I should've thanked Uncle Cal for giving me a trial run.

I stayed on in the only completely un-mortgaged-and-paid-for home my family had ever known. The dogs playing cards smiled in approval, and I smiled back. This was our house, and they were my guardian angels.

Oh yeah, they moved the town. No joke. The county commissioners voted, and they figured out a way for some kind of government grant. The whole town: post office, courthouse, grocery store, drugstore, and health department all abandoned their buildings and built new ones on a hill overlooking the Flint River Bridge.

I had me a job at Treadway's Grocery, deep frying chicken, catfish, and quartered potatoes in the all-new deli section. It paid the light bill. With a discount on groceries, they let me eat in the deli for free.

My senior year was the pits. The year I was supposed to graduate, the county voted to consolidate Nolan High with a neighboring county high school, making it Baxter-Nolan High School, a stupid name if I ever heard one. We had a new, two-story building I lost my way in nearly every day. The Baxter kids treated us, the "Dumb-Ass Doom-Us" county kids, like pure shit.

Now *that* was different. At Nolan High, I was white trash. And I'd been in the same class with the same kids for eleven years. And although I was never student council material, being there that long gave me what they call a street cred, at least. Like, the cool kids would be nice to me when it was time for an election or something. And I was used to that. But now the kids who used to be *cool* were the white trash, so that made the ones like me—less than shit? The Nolan kids, the previously popular ones, were so distraught at not being *anybody* that their entire focus was on making someone else feel worse than them—and that someone would be any kid like me.

In the summer, I had worked every day. It was understood that I'd go to work on afternoons and weekends when school started, but that was before Mr. Treadway realized the deli would be the biggest hit in Nolan history: Durham's Café had closed and there was no fast food. Everyone has to eat.

By the end of September, he realized he'd have to hire a fulltime day worker for the deli.

"You know I'd love to keep you on, Mojo, but I'll be paying that person already. I can't afford to keep you on just for after school and weekends," he explained.

It was enough for me. I quit school and went to work at the deli fulltime.

My house on stilts was just a quarter mile from the Flint River Bridge: At night I listened as eighteen-wheelers passed by, going north to Columbus, Macon, Atlanta. Going south to Florida.

Always going *somewhere.*

It was a cold day in hell when anything stopped here.

Chapter 17
1982

Mojo

I PAID HIM NO NEVER MIND, NOT AT FIRST, I DIDN'T, AND I meant not to at *all*, but after I talked to him, well, things changed. People aren't always as bad as you think they're gonna be, you have to at least give them a chance, before you make a decision about them. My mama didn't trust nobody, 'specially men, though she must've trusted one at least once or I wouldn't be here. Anyways, I guess my ways came from her. When I was in school, I was never much interested with the boys, they seemed to like girls that acted all silly and wore nice clothes every day, so I ignored them, and they did the same with me. Didn't bother me. I was fine, just me and Mama, long as she was alive. Course, then when she died, I was pretty much in a trance: I didn't do a thing she wouldn't have approved of, other than quitting school, for a least a good year or two.

No, I wasn't what you'd call "celibate," I think the word is, but I was still a virgin when I turned eighteen. Then there was Marty, he worked at the Sing Station by Treadway's Market. We kinda had a little thing there for a while, but I guess it wasn't meant to be. We're still friends, though he avoids me more than I'd have him to. Love him like a brother, I do, but I could never fancy myself being "in love" with him, and it seemed wrong to keep on like we was if I knew I wouldn't never feel the same as he did. But Marty's a good guy, he is, and I wish him the best. Honestly.

I worked at Treadway's more than five years, and I still fill in when they're hard up and need a favor. But they paid me minimum wage and not a cent more 'til I left 'em. I guarantee you the gals that replaced me make more than that. When I fill in there now, it's time and a half, sometimes more, but I don't say nothing. Like my mama said, it's all water under the bridge. But I learned early on that a waitress making minimum plus tips is a hell of a lot better job than a cook or a cashier that never gets more than a smile extra. And waitresses in the bars make a lot more than the ones at Shoney's, so it was just common sense that I learned the ins and outs of the nightlife.

I've worked a lot of bars around Albany, starting at the Jolly Fox— it seated eight hundred, had road bands and cash-prize dance contests, and all the waitresses were eighteen to twenty-four, naturally or diet-pill thin. Worked my ass off there on weekends, but picked up more in the smaller places during the week. Got to see the clientele as the same types, only different faces, everywhere I went. Learned a few things, a waitress friend and me made up a list I kept on the fridge for a while:

Unwritten Rules of Night Club Life

1. *The younger the guy, the less likely he is to have any money.*
2. *All truck drivers lie, though they'll probably be up and gone before you have time to prove it. Salesmen sell shit you don't need on a daily basis: Think about it.*
3. *Men who want to be all romantic and touchy-feely in public are always married—to someone other than who they're all touchy-feely with.*
4. *Always bring change in quarters and small bills. Alcohol makes for sloppy arithmetic.*
5. *Stay away from the guys in the band.*

Yeah, I know, that's the one that should've reminded me. But like I said, you can't keep living thinking everybody's gonna be just like you thought they would. And I did stay away, in the beginning. Didn't listen to a word he said, just smiled and played dummy like I do with all those musician guys, he wasn't the first. Yeah, his singing, when he was singing for the sound of the song and not for the response of the crowd, his singing could take you places. But when the song was over, he was just another guy in the band, he didn't fool me. And I more or less told him so that first night at the Plantation.

The Plantation Club was no club at all, and the weekend partiers who walked through its doors showed little in common with Old South aristocracy. Open only on Friday and Saturday nights, it existed for those involved in the club scene of neighboring towns, real nightclubs that obeyed state laws and local ordinances. Dumas County seemed to operate by a government all its own.

The common "Blue Law" outlawing the sale of liquor on Sunday had been going on in Georgia since the repeal of prohibition. In college towns, kids paid ten bucks apiece before midnight, then stayed and drank until the kegs were dry. In Atlanta, Macon, and Columbus, last call at eleven-thirty allowed patrons to buy as many drinks as they wanted at once, and the bands played non-stop until one a.m.

But bar-hoppers in south Georgia partied longer and harder than elsewhere in the state, courtesy of the Plantation Club. Twenty miles outside of Albany on a flat stretch of open road, a cinderblock building with pool tables, a dance floor, two full bars and a live band left no holds barred from 10 p.m. to 5 a.m. on Saturday nights. Since the bars closed down in every small town in a fifty-mile radius, the Plantation Club was the place to be for folks who wanted to rock the night away.

Danny's band, Devil's Whiskey, had played there for two weekends a few months back, and they were back for a three-month stint this time. That Danny was a piece of work, the kind that thought he was put here as a gift from God just for women to look at. He sat on a rickety stool on the stage, tuning his guitars and messing with his amps. He had at least a half dozen pedals and boxes at his feet, more doodads than any of the rest of the band. Come to think of it, he had more stuff than any musician I'd seen in south Georgia. Like he should have been in Foreigner, or Queen, or the Rolling Stones; not some weekend musician playing in the middle of nowhere. As he looked down, his shiny, shoulder-length black hair fell forward into his face, like he was staring at the floor, but I knew his kind. Danny Hatcher might have acted bored, but guys like him were always scoping out the scene, looking to score free drugs or women or anything else that might amuse him for a night.

I fixed up my tables for the night, lighting the candles and setting out cocktail napkins. Listening to conversations close to the stage, an older guy was talking to Devil's Whiskey about last week's band.

"Thank God they're gone," he said. "Sure, the Saturday Night Fever crowd likes them, I mean, they play Bee Gees, but they're too candy ass for us. Glad to have ya'll," he told the band.

"Yeah! Had a damned girl playing keyboards," a bearded guy in a Miller Lite cap said. "Played okay, but singing that disco shit. If you're gonna have a three-piece band, you need a guitar." He pronounced it git-tar. "You can't play no real music without a guitar."

That Danny smiled and nodded, acting like he actually gave a damn about their musical opinions. Then again, he probably thought the damned Beatles couldn't compete with *him*.

"Well, I liked 'em," said the over-tanned blonde with the stiff Farrah Fawcett cut. "Anyhow, they probably won't be back. Their drummer got busted in the parking lot Friday night." She turned toward the stage and smiled, unaware of the gooey gloss on her front teeth. Danny took a rag from his amp, wiped off the strings of his glittery Stratocaster and set it on the guitar stand. Walking to the bar, he pretended he nodded at the folks already at tables but didn't really look anyone in the eye.

"Bud in a bottle," he said to Gracie, the bartender who was close to my mama's age, but my buddy just the same.

"You gotta tab?" she asked, knowing full well he'd run a tab the night before. I loved Gracie.

"Yeah," he said. "I'm with the band. Danny."

Gracie nodded, handed him a long-necked bottle and marked it in spiral notebook, never looking up.

"Thanks," he muttered, taking a seat at the bar. He gulped a long swig and surveyed the area, which was half-assed busy for an early Saturday. In just a couple of hours, the place would be uncomfortable, standing-room-only.

Two other waitresses stood at the end of the bar, waiting for their drinks. They smiled at Danny, those knowing smiles that give all waitresses a reputation for being easy. He acknowledged them with a brief nod, then reached in his pocket for a cigarette. Flicking his lighter and taking a long drag, he glanced to my side of the room at crazy Linda, another waitress who must've worked every bar in town at one time or another. We stood together, holding our trays. Linda looked back at him, pouted her lips in his direction, then looked back at me, calling him an asshole under her breath. She laughed, then took her drinks and moved on to her tables. Danny continued to stare, now at just me.

He shook his head back, letting his hair fall toward his face, again pretending he saw nothing, but I saw him checking me out through a section of his rock star hair. I'm not stupid: I know I'm not model material, but I have my mama's eyes and a thin frame that looks decent in the right clothes. My hair is my best feature; golden brown, thick, and wavy. That night it was tied in a loose ponytail on one side of my face, draping over my shoulder to below the breast. I was dressed for comfort as well as for tips: I wore a sleeveless denim shirt, tied in a hard knot at the waist, and tight white jeans.

"Another Bud, please ma'am," Danny said to the bartender. He twisted off the top and walked toward the stage, trying his damnedest to catch my eye as he walked by.

I walked past him, on towards my tables. I could feel the heat of his stare, as warm as the embarrassing blush I felt rising in my cheeks. Guys like that made me feel dirty, like they could see me naked when

I was totally covered up. I guess it made some girls wanna get naked as well, but not me. I had enough crosses to bear without taking up with the likes of that Danny. Or so I thought.

By eleven thirty most tables were full, and the dance floor was comfortably appreciative. The band was doing forty-minute sets, three fast songs to every slow one, with long instrumental rides whenever possible, saving themselves for the after-midnight crowd. I'd just as soon have 'em play more slow ones; it was a lot easier to service my tables when folks were moving slow and close together than when they were shaking it off the floor and in the aisles. It was right dangerous some nights. The band wrapped up the set with a sure thing, one that never failed to fill the dance floor.

Danny sang about being superstitious and believing things he couldn't understand. *Fool,* I thought to myself. That boy didn't believe in anything beyond his own conceit or his next conquest. The dancers broke out in wild applause on the last echoing chord.

"Thank you," Danny said, adding a "hell, yeah! Thank you, folks. We're Devil's Whiskey," he grabbed his beer for a quick swallow, "and we're taking a short break. Be back in twenty minutes for an hour-long set of your dance favorites. If you have a request, write it down and give it to a waitress." He paused. "And please, folks, don't forget to tip your waitresses. They're working their pretty little asses off for you." He smiled and shared a quick glance at *me,* starting by looking dead in my eyes, then glancing down quickly to my behind, eyes lingering there, and then looking back at me, grinning. Then he leaned back to bring in the band on the downbeat for an ending tag.

"When you believe in things that you don't understand, then you suffer—" Five eighth notes kept the dancers suspended in midair, drunkenly waiting for the song to continue, standing clueless until all the band members had left the stage.

I took advantage of the break to take orders from my customers; the band was so much louder than the old jukebox, and it was nice to talk without screaming for a change. A couple of guys made smart remarks about my "pretty little ass," thanks to Mr. Hatcher they now *all* seemed to think my behind was fair game to talk about. Who the hell was he to do that to me? I joked back with obnoxious customers, took their orders, and headed back to the bar. Didn't he tell them to *tip* my little ass? Hope they listened that far.

That Danny worked the room the way he did most weekends: letting loud, drunken older guys buy him drinks, showing off their fat wallets to girls they hoped to impress. There were hugs and kisses from girls he acted like he barely knew, but may have slept with after one gig or another. He smiled and smooched and acted like they were all best buddies. A leggy redhead drug him to the dance floor for a dry hump to the jukebox, but only for half a song, and long enough to squeeze her ass cheeks in front of everybody, while she rubbed everything God gave her against his front side. Honestly, when did all the normal-looking girls become weekend street walkers? I tried not to watch, but it was hard not to. The bar scene had gotten a lot more brazen in the past few years.

I emptied my trash and took my orders to the bar. Danny grabbed two more beers and meandered back to the stage, accepting hugs and pats on the back. I stood waiting, wishing the room had better air conditioning or that there was a way to outlaw cologne and require anti-perspirant.

To start this set, Danny strapped on the flashy white and chrome guitar, the "Travis Bean" he'd be paying for another two years. He counted off the first song, and I watched the dance floor fill.

Danny sang, his voice as near a match to David Bowie's as his grinding lead guitar to the original. The crowd went wild. Rednecks who'd never let a Bowie look-alike cross their own county line were dancing, clapping, and lifting their hands toward heaven. The song ended but the drummer's bass pedal never stopped, continuing straight into the intro for Stevie Wonder's "Living for the City." Not one couple left, and tables began to push against the walls, making for an outer edge of dancers around their assigned space.

It was kind of fun to watch the change in those girls' dancing in the next set, and I was kind of sorry for the poor guys they were partnered with. The girls would dance at the guys in the band, mainly Danny, doing stripper-like moves with their clothes left on and looking directly into his eyes. If one girl noticed another trying the same antics, the floorshow became a slut-off right there for the world to see.

Danny sang—this time about a girl who was black and "sho-nuff pretty." There was not a black face in the redneck crowd, but a half dozen female faces seemed to think he was singing to them, smiling and preening and bobbing their heads. He sang about her short skirt and sturdy legs, and girls in high-heeled sandals and shiny dresses lifted up their skirts, revealing even more leg and thigh, reveling in themselves as Danny sang on.

The dance floor was full, my tables empty and pushed together as I tried to figure out which drink went where. I sat down my tray and waited. As I stood listening, I realized that my knees were bending to the back beat, and my arms were involuntarily flexing as well. I could feel the pulsing of the bass guitar in my chest, and for no explicable reason, I wanted to be dancing, too—to be swaying, singing along, participating in the music. What the hell?

I watched the dance floor. With every verse, the rifle-rack-bearing, Dixie-flag-wearing, sons of Lynard Skynard danced to their heart's content, oblivious to the fact that their roots might be just a generation beyond the KKK. They sang from the dance floor, badly, but they sang. *"Living, just enough, living for the city, just enough!"*

Before the applause could start, Danny began the intro for "Long Train Running," and they all screamed with pleasure. They stretched the song to almost ten minutes, with two guitar solos and a harmonica solo, then sailed straight into Pink Floyd's "Money," then Ray Charles's "Money," then stopped and took stock of the energy level.

"Do we keep rockin' out," Danny screamed at the dancers, "or do we need a slow song or two?"

"FREEEBIRRRD," some guy yelled from the back of the room.

Danny grimaced, but then smiled. "How 'bout one for the ladies?" he said. "A nice slow song, find yourself a pretty lady and hold her close, then we'll finish out the set with another good dance tune."

"FREEEBIRRRD," the guy yelled again.

"A song from Elvin Bishop," Danny said, and a few guys in the crowd applauded. "For the ladies, guys, get the ladies up and dance."

As Danny began the smooth, lyrical opening of the song, I watched the dance floor change shape like a slow-moving kaleidoscope: Some couples left the floor, others left tables in the far corners of the room to be a part of the center. Some remained but moved closer or farther away from the stage. The mass of frantic individual movements disappeared while groups of two became one, and the groups of one made a new vision altogether. The music was slower, so the people moved slower. Their shapes became a pattern of soft colors rippling as if in wind. I stood there, mesmerized, not even thinking about my tables or the drinks or collecting any money. I just stood there and listened.

The words were corny, but sweet. He'd had a million girls (and *Danny* probably had) but none of them meant anything until, suddenly, with one girl, it happened. Yeah right, I didn't particularly believe it, for him, but he delivered the song well, made me believe it for *somebody*.

Danny sang and I thought about my nonexistent love life. I'd never been in love, nor really wanted to be. But maybe I could. Listening to the band, right then, I thought maybe I could be normal, like other girls. Have those relationships other people had. Maybe.

"Fooled around and fell in love," he sang, and that was the rest of the song. Over and over, the same thing. There were some nice vocal "aaaah's" and then a beautiful guitar ride. Then it went back to the same words, monotonously, over and over. Was that what love was? Just endless mumbo jumbo, useless words that made you redundant and stupid? Who the hell needed that?

I grabbed my tray and straightened out the drinks for those that were seated, collecting their money and taking their next orders. I looked out into the crowd. The colors I thought were waving in the breeze were really just standing still, rubbing body parts against one another and rocking from one leg to the other to keep from falling down. So much for the sweet mystery of love.

Danny counted off the next song, which re-filled the dance floor. "Here's one from Tin Lizzy," he told the crowd. "Last song of the set. Come on up and dance!"

I grabbed my tray and headed back to the bar.

"Hey, Mojo," said Gracie, behind the bar with her purse strapped across her shoulder. "Could you fill in for me a few minutes?" I gladly ducked under the end and took her place. I needed a change of scenery.

Within minutes he stood at the bar, right in front of me. It was like I couldn't escape. A big woman wearing a too-small shirt advertising Daytona Beach gave up her seat for him.

"Thanks," he said, grabbing a bar napkin and wiping the sweat from his brow.

"Could y'all play "Sweet Home Alabama" for me?" she asked. "I's born in Alabama and that's my favorite song."

"Sure," he agreed without making eye contact. "No problem."

Then he raised his hand, trying to get my attention like some innocent schoolboy. Like I'd fall for that garbage. "Budweiser?" he asked,

"Sure," I said. I opened it for him and wrapped a napkin around its base. "You're in the band, right?" I asked, remembering the look on his face when Gracie showed the same kind of attitude.

"Yeah. Danny," he said.

"You guys are good," I said, adding, "I really like your singing." Why the hell did I say that? It's like the words just fell out of my mouth, without asking me first. I looked at the floor, turned quickly and waited on another customer.

Danny finished his beer in a couple of swallows. I brought him another. "Thanks," he said. "You're new, aren't you? What's your name?"

"Mojo," I said.

"Mojo?" He raised his eyebrows. "Unusual name for a girl. Can't say that it really fits you, but it's interesting."

"It's not my real name," I told him, "just what I've been called all my life."

"Oh. What's your real name?" he asked. "If you don't mind me asking."

"Mary Jane," I said. "It doesn't really fit me, either."

"Maybe it does," he said. "A pretty name for a pretty girl."

"Whatever," I said. "Need some more beer?" I asked. Had anyone noticed that this guy drank like a fish?

"Not this second," he said, standing. "But can I get a couple for next set when I come back from the restroom?"

"Sure," I said. "I'm going back on the floor when Gracie's off break. I could bring 'em to you." *What? Where did this dumb blonde voice keep coming from?*

"That would be great," he said, and headed off to the john.

They started back with Clapton's "I Shot the Sheriff," and before the song was over, I was bringing three Buds and setting them on Danny's amp. They covered Foghat, Steely Dan, Hendrix, Grand Funk Railroad, more Doobie Brothers, and of course, "Sweet Home Alabama." As the dance floor filled for "Knocking on Heaven's Door," I caught myself singing as I carried a tray of drinks to a table near the stage. I was definitely under the influence of something.

On the band's next break, he caught me beside the waitress station. "Hey," he said. "You doing anything after we close down?"

I shook my head. "Are you crazy? When they turn on the lights and start running people out, it'll be 5 a.m. When we clean up all the tables and turn in our bank, it'll be closer to six. I don't plan on doing anything but going home and going to bed."

Danny placed his hand under my chin, turning my face towards his. "Would you like some company?" he asked.

I took a deep breath, then used my own hand to remove his from my face. "I may be young and green, but I'm not ignorant," I said. "There's plenty here that'd be happy to oblige you, Rock Star." I swept my hand across the room. "Go talk to them. I brought you beers because I'm a waitress. That's my job." I turned and walked away, not knowing if I was about to laugh or cry. Danny followed me.

"Mary Jane," he called. I could feel him watching me in the crowd.

"Mojo suits me fine," I answered, flipping my hair over my shoulder like a cheerleader with attitude. "Now please, leave me alone. I'm working here."

"Mary Jane," he said again, catching up to me. "I'm sorry. I was really just kidding, I—"

"You were really just kidding now that you know I won't. But if I'd said yes, you wouldn't have been kidding at all." The room was loud, and I was glad he couldn't hear the shaking in my voice.

"I–I—you're right." He stopped, speechless, then seemed to gain his composure. "And I was being an ass. Working nowhere but night-clubs for five years has left me a little jaded about women in general. But being turned down by you was—the nicest thing that's happened to me in a long time. Let's start over. Can we?" I kept walking ahead, emptying tables, dumping ashtrays.

"I've gotta go back to work now," Danny said, "but this conversation is not over. Understand?"

I said nothing.

"Damn, Mojo, can't you at least answer me?"

"I don't even know you. Why do I have to keep talking to you, or understand anything? Go back to work. Go sing your songs. Go on and leave me alone."

"Can I play something for you? What would you like to hear?"

"The sound of your footsteps leaving in the opposite direction," I said.

"Okay, Miss Smart Ass, point taken," he said. "But it's last set, maybe even just two or three songs more. Isn't there anything you'd like to hear?"

I thought for a moment. "Something slow, but not corny. Something *you* like, something you think you do well. Something you don't usually play."

The drummer and bass player were already on stage, starting "Some Kinda Wonderful," probably the only song they could start without him.

"You've got it, Mary Jane," he said, saluting me as he walked away.

The crowd thinned out and the dancers were fewer. Though the song was of shuffling tempo, two of the couples were simply embraced and swaying, as if hearing a ballad all their own. After just a verse and chorus of the song, Danny cued the others to the ending. During the mild applause, he turned back to the band. "Just follow me," he told them.

Danny switched guitars. "Last slow song of the night," he announced. "Everybody get close." He struck a mellow, ringing chord, and the drummer answered with a rain-like tinkling on the cymbals. Both faded out. Then Danny established a bluesy rhythm of two chords. The others joined in, adding little fills then laying back in no hurry for the melody to begin. "From George Benson," Danny said.

Danny sang in a different voice than he'd used all night, a genre-less, color-less voice that imitated no one, but was simply a new instrument used as the medium for a melody. They sounded so different—it was almost as if someone had found a way to play the jukebox through the sound system. I heard it, that different sound that made me want to forget my customers, my tips, *everything* and just go stand by the stage and listen; so I tried with all my might to put it out of my head. My mama had warned of such voodoo in the music of a man's voice, and until that moment I'd always believed I could abstain from any such foolishness.

The song was beautiful, but it was late at night and people were drinking. It was one of those songs that could mean a thousand things, have a different meaning for each person who listened. It could be beautiful and touching to some, or downright torture to others, yet they'd all take away something from it.

But then Danny began to scat, and this was beauty on a new level.

From the first note onward, this new sound in the universe was exquisite. He scatted through a verse, a chorus, another of each. And although the bands there always ended with an up-tempo tune, suddenly the lights came on with Danny still scatting, ending on a slow, bluesy tag: *"We're lost—in a mas-querade."*

No one complained. Danny wiped off his strings, put away his box of pedals, packed up his guitars and headed out. He stopped at the bar, where by then I was sitting, counting my tips.

"Forgive me?" he asked, standing a good two feet away, like he was giving me some space.

I thought for a minute, then answered, "Sure." I had that naked feeling again, so I looked away, but then added one last remark. "Nice song, by the way, but I'm still going home alone." I felt the blush coming, but I smiled anyway. Danny smiled back.

"Would it be okay if I called you sometime?" he asked.

"I guess so," I said.

"How? I mean, can I get your number?"

"I live in Nolan," I said. "M. J. Mullinax. I'm in the book."

We saw a movie the next week, *A Star is Born*, my request. Danny liked Kristofferson but thought the movie was totally sappy. He took me home, kissed me at the front door, hung out for a while, but made no effort to stay. He was back at the Plantation for the week-end, where he still worked the crowd but was pretty friendly with me. I invited him to go fishing on Sunday, and he accepted.

We spent the day on the river. Having never been inside a house on stilts, he asked a lot of questions at first, which ended up making the rest of the conversation come pretty easy.

"Wow," he said as I met him at the door. "This is unreal. What's the rent on a place like this?" I ushered him in, where he acted magnetically drawn to the picture window and its view of the river. "To wake up to this every day," he said, "might almost make it worth living in the sticks."

I wasn't sure if this was a compliment or an insult.

"There's no rent, it's mine," I said. When Danny looked confused, I explained, "My uncle built the place. He left it to me when he passed away."

"Oh," Danny said, "I'm sorry." There was awkward silence.

"It's okay, it's been several years now," I said. "You ready to do some angling?"

From the look on Danny's face, I was pretty sure he didn't know that angling was a word for fishing, not juggling iron or sword swallowing, but I didn't say anything. It was kind fun seeing him as the one at a loss for words.

"I grabbed some bait over at Kelley's yesterday," I said. "But all they had was mealworms. Guess that'll have to do. I'll get 'em out of the fridge."

He tried to be cool, but I could read him like a book. *She keeps worms in her refrigerator,* he was thinking, never hearing of such before. He'd told me he'd been fishing as a kid with an alcoholic uncle, but I'm guessing his uncle must not've used live bait.

"Poles are out back," I said, returning with a small cardboard carton. "Let's do it!"

Danny followed me down the steep staircase and into the back yard. I'd tried on half the clothes I owned before he came, deciding on a soft blue halter with cut-off jean shorts, plastic flip flops punctuating rhythm with every step. Once again, I could feel him watching me from behind, but this time I didn't feel naked at all, just—special, though I wasn't quite sure why. When we reached the bottom of the steps, I grabbed the two cane poles with red and white plastic bobbers and kept walking, now at a lively pace. Danny followed.

"Where are we going?" he asked, sounding none too confident about this adventure.

"Just a quarter mile or so, my own private treasure trove," I said, pushing a lock of hair behind my ear. People had told me that in bright sunlight, my brown hair was a hundred shades, glistening from chestnut to amber to strawberry blonde. At that moment I was really hoping that Danny noticed it.

The bare, muddy banks folded into a clump of trees—huge live oaks, tall pines, and a scattering of dogwoods in full bloom, treetops touching and filtering out the sun. Just as the trees thinned out and the light began to seep in, I veered closer to the water, stopping at the single, misplaced palm tree that's always been my favorite.

"What the hell?" laughed Danny. "This is Georgia, and we're nowhere near the coast. How did this get here?"

"Isn't it great?" I asked. "It's been here as long as I can remember. My uncle use to bring us here, me and my mom, we'd have picnics sometimes, or just fish. When I was little, I used to pretend I was on an island, my own island, like Robinson Crusoe. Or Gilligan's Island. Or some exotic place only rich people knew about. Silly, but I loved it. And I've never seen anyone here but my family."

"Damn," Danny said. "That is weird. But you have seen more than just your family here."

"How do you know?"

"I'm here. Does that make me family?"

I rolled my eyes at him, like a flirty teenager, and then pushed him gently. "Probably not. Depends on how good you can fish." I used my foot to smooth out the moist dirt and twigs underneath the tree, then sat down. Danny did the same. I opened the carton, pulled out a fat, wriggling worm and hooked him to a line, then handed the baited pole to Danny.

"Don't expect this next time, but I guess you *are* my guest and all," I said. Danny took the pole and cast into the water, looking relieved when it went in without a hitch. I baited my own and did the same.

Danny breathed easier when he felt a bite, then pulled in the first fish, a rainbow trout, small but not too small. I would've hated to admit it, but I was having a good time watching him out of his element. I liked him better when he wasn't so cocky and sure of himself. Within the hour, I'd landed two medium catfish and a small bream.

"You're pretty darn good at this," he told me. "You and your mom still fish together?" I smiled, thinking of how Mama woulda said Danny was now fishing for more than his dinner.

"My mama died when I was in high school. I'm a family of one, as they say. But I still fish, alone out here. Kinda makes me feel closer to 'em, her and Uncle Cal, both." I stopped. "I guess that sounds crazy to you."

"No, it makes sense. Doing things you did together would have to make you feel closer to them, and out here has kind of a magical feeling, anyway. I mean, I can see how you'd pretend it was your own little island. It really does seem isolated from the rest of the world. This place is great—special."

I placed my hand on his arm, looking into his eyes. "Thanks," I said, "for not laughing at me. I know I can sound like Ellie Mae, but it's nice when someone seems to get what I mean. Thanks."

Danny laid his hand on my knee. "No thanks necessary," he said. "And I love Ellie Mae—she's totally hot. Do you have any critters?"

"I have three cats, and maybe five or six more that stop by occasionally for food," I said.

"No raccoons or possums?"

"I had two dogs," I said. I pulled my hand away and looked out at the water. "Uncle Cal's dogs, Hank and Jerry Lee."

"For Hank Williams and Jerry Lee Lewis?"

"Yeah. I know, crazy—"

"Not crazy. Cool," said Danny. "My cat's name is Clapton."

"Clapton? That's ridiculous," I said.

"Okay. You said you *had* two dogs?"

"Yeah. I guess they came with the house. Hank died from a snakebite, the summer after Mama died. I thought I had to be the unluckiest person in the whole world. First Uncle Cal, then Mama, then Hank. Got to where I wouldn't let Jerry Lee outta my sight, left him inside when I wasn't at home, watched him like a hawk, treated him like a damned baby. But I was so scared I was gonna lose him, too."

Danny listened as he pulled in another fish, this one a large mouth bass.

"That's one a beauty!" I told him.

Danny grinned. "Yeah, he is, but damn if it ain't weird hearing a girl say it. Anyway, finish telling me, what happened to Jerry Lee?"

"He died in his sleep."

"How sad," he said, spearing another worm onto his hook.

"We all gotta go sometime," I said. "He died this year, on Valentine's Day. He was sixteen years old; that's ninety-six in dog years."

"I guess he did have a pretty good life," Danny agreed.

We laughed and joked, told stories about our pasts, though Danny asked most of the questions and I filled in the blanks. When we'd caught more fish than we could possibly eat, we gathered them up and headed back to the house.

Together we cleaned the fish. Grabbing a guitar from his car, Danny played Beatles' songs while I cooked. After dinner and several beers, I broke down and asked him to stay that night.

That was the best part—he said no. Not mean-like, no like he didn't wanna take advantage. "Not until you're sure." That's what he said. Then he kissed me and was gone, whistling "If I Fell" as he walked down the steps and out of sight.

That did it for me. This was the real thing, and I knew it. He still went slow, and I went along with it, but I knew this was who I wanted to wake up next to, forever.

A month later, I was doing exactly that.

Chapter 18
1985

Phil

CONTRARY TO HIS BELIEF, PHIL FOSTER'S TRUST FUND didn't last forever, and in his last weeks of easy money he was found stabbed but still alive in a New Orleans alley. Waking up in an indigent hospital, the first face he saw was a young priest, reading his last rites.

"Brother Ron?" Phil asked, thinking he was a boy at King's Academy again, and that this was the kind pastor who'd given him such hope.

"No sir, I'm Father Jeremy, the new assistant chaplain. Father Don will be in on Monday," he said.

Phil closed his eyes. He wasn't a kid anymore, and no one could come in and fix things. He hurt all over, had no one to call, and hoped he could simply will himself to die before anything worse happened.

"You gave us a real scare," the man said. "You're in God's hands, and He brought you to a place where you can get better. Don't be afraid, the Lord's been with you every step of the way."

Phil tried not to listen, he had no use for their godly mumbo jumbo, but then he had a flash of memory. Horrible memory, too painful to endure.

Two girls—were they girls? They smelled like patchouli and coconut. Two people at least dressed as girls, offering him—sex? Drugs? He couldn't remember, he only knew for sure that they offered something and he wanted it. They laughed, drinking from a plastic flask and snorting cheap grade coke from a vial around someone's neck.

258 ⟵ Elaine Drennon Little

Then he was on the ground, face down. They kicked him, stepped on him with their spiked heels, making holes in his skin through his clothes. They took his wallet, his lighter and his stash, then—

God, the pain. Straight through his back and into his belly. Pain like he didn't know was possible. He groaned just remembering. "Stop," he screamed. "Make it stop—"

"It's okay. Just breathe. God is with you. You're safe now, no one can hurt you," the priest said. He sounded—nervous? As though he was grasping for the words as he said them. "Remember, He brought you here. You're safe." Phil listened as the kind voice continued.

"Remember the twenty-third psalm," he said. "The Lord is my shepherd, I shall not want. He maketh me to lie down in green pastures. He restoreth my soul..."

The horrid visions disappeared. He saw green fields, and livestock, and bright blue skies with cottony clouds. He could see tall oaks move in the wind, Spanish moss billowing beneath their branches. Phil cried real tears as the priest held his hand and continued to recite.

"He leadeth me beside the still waters..."

A nurse came in and added a vial of something to the bag dripping into Phil's arm. He began to smell freshly turned earth, stacked bales of hay, sweet green corn about to tassel. The priest gained confidence and momentum as he continued his recitation.

"Yea, though I walk through the valley of the shadow of death..."

Phil had been there, he knew. The valley of the shadow of death. A real place, though he had to see it to believe it. And yet he was here, in this still, quiet place, with this man holding his hand and reciting these beautiful, soothing words to comfort him. He didn't deserve this. If the God of all things had sent him here, for this wonderful second chance at life, surely *his* life was worth something.

"Surely goodness and mercy shall follow me all the days of my life," the priest said. Sure, he'd seen a few days without much goodness or mercy, but how much had he given to expect any back? He knew the Bible said nothing about karma, but Phil believed in it, just the same. And if this wasn't some damned amazing goodness and mercy, what the hell was?

"...and I will dwell in the house of the Lord forever..."

Phil wasn't seeing a church, but he was connecting with the place he knew he was meant to return. Phil had misinterpreted the story of the prodigal son as a child, confusing his disability with something he had purposely done wrong. He dreamed of making his father love him again, but it didn't work. Once he realized his mechanical abilities at the farm, he'd again imagined proving himself to his father, another parallel with the parable. This dream didn't work either. Phillip had opted for the charmed existence of fun and good times to make up for the pain and loneliness in his life, but good times could not buy real happiness.

The valley of the shadow of death, Phil thought. He'd had to go there to know what he really needed. What he'd had all along.

Though diagnosed with anemia, a necrotic liver, and declared HIV positive, Phil made what seemed a rapid recovery from his near death experience. Connecting with Father Jeremy, he meditated, prayed, and was ready for release in less than two weeks. Phil headed back to his first love—Oakland Plantation—his farm.

Chapter 19
1985

Mojo

TIME MOVES FAST WHEN THERE'S A LOT GOING ON, AND those first months with Danny were the best times I'd known. Well, most of the time they were.

It was awkward at first, but I guess all relationships are. I'd never really lived with anyone outside Mama and Uncle Cal, and it was altogether different with someone else's things in my space. It was hard not to say anything when he set glasses and cans on the furniture with no coaster underneath, but I learned to keep my mouth shut after the second hole in the wall. After a month or so, I don't think he ever took a dish to the sink, threw a paper in the trash, or picked up his clothes or towels off the bathroom floor, but the other bedroom, which he turned into his studio, looked like a music store showroom. And dear Jesus, the beautiful sounds that came out of that room— I could never be tired of hearing those wonderful sounds.

Maybe it was because we were never there at the same time too much: I worked every night and three mornings a week. Danny practiced weeknights and was gone every weekend. Occasionally we'd end up at the same weekend bar, but those times were more pain than pleasure—I loved to hear him play, but hated pretending to be just a friend, the way we had to for the sake of the crowd.

"Rock bands that want a following can't have married men," Danny said, with me all the while saying we weren't married, so what did it matter.

"When the women see you're taken, it's like cutting off your balls. Might as well go back to the Elks' Club gigs. No one's filling a local house to see Donny and Marie," he said.

"Donny and Marie are brother and sister," I told him. "And they're not a rock band, playing local jobs. You don't make any sense."

"I make plenty of sense," he'd say. "If women know you're with me, they'll put out the word, and you'll get no tips. Then they'll leave and the guys will follow. Then the management will blame the band, and we'll be looking for another gig. Simple as that."

"A few pissed-off women can't take away my tips, or take all the men from the club. You exaggerate," I said.

"Well maybe that's not all," he'd say, raising his left eyebrow, grinning, and looking me up and down that way that always made me weak in the knees. "Maybe there're things I wanna keep under wraps." That's when his hand would caress my butt, or his finger find a nipple, or he'd simply pull me against him, hard and throbbing. And I'd forget about whatever point I was trying to make. Always.

Filling in at Treadway's finally paid off. Only twenty-four and they offered me the manager's job. The beat-up Pinto I'd been driving for three years was on its last leg, so I figured having a permanent job, with benefits, was like the Great Almighty saying it was okay go down to the bank and go get in debt like the rest of the world. I was finally growing up.

When I told Danny, he grabbed me in a bear hug, then cradled me in his arms like a baby and carried me to the bedroom, where we kissed and necked and made love like horny teenagers. Afterwards, he told me to dress up, he'd be back in an hour and we were going out. We never went out together, and Tuesday nights weren't much for the partying scene, but I didn't care, I was on cloud nine.

We went to Floyd's Steak & Seafood, a really nice restaurant despite the generic-sounding name. We sat just in front of the huge rock waterfall in the center of the room, and the sound of the water made me think I had to pee every few minutes, but it was still real nice. We ate steak and lobster from each other's plates, laughing at Big Barney, the three hundred pound crooner behind the cocktail drums, and grooving the sounds of Gary Carter on bass and Steve Hughes on the grand piano, rock and rollers in the highest sense who had obviously sold out. Danny had played with Big Barney, "back in the day," he said. Big Barney acknowledged Danny but didn't look too happy to see him.

I wore ankle strap heels and a black satin halter dress I'd bought on sale and been saving forever, and Danny was his usual rock star handsome in a black tee, stonewashed jeans and a tweed blazer.

Stuffed beyond belief, we said no to any dessert, then Teresa, a girl I'd worked with at the Cubbyhole across town, brought over what looked like an old-fashioned soda fountain milkshake, garnished with two pink straws and a cherry on top.

"Compliments of Floyd's," she said, "and that fellow at the end table." She nodded toward a thin, balding fellow with huge ears and black horn-rimmed glasses. His loud patterned plaid coat and exaggerated features made him look like a retired circus clown.

"That's Milton Garrett," she said, "the county commissioner." Her eyes lit up to signify this was someone of real importance, so we tried to look impressed. Neither of us had ever heard of him.

"We make this after dinner drink only for him, he brought in the recipe and we keep it for when he shows up. A family recipe, or whatever. He calls it Mother's Milk. It has five liqueurs, vodka, brandy and a half-gallon of vanilla ice cream. We always make too much, on purpose, so all the folks working can get a taste, for free. Just thought I'd share the wealth tonight." We laughed, Danny pulling his chair in closer and putting his arm around my shoulders.

"I ain't seen you in ages, and you look great. Special occasion?" Teresa asked.

I'm sure I blushed, but before I could say a word, Danny jumped in.

"Absolutely," he said. "This beautiful lady and I are celebrating a new life together." I looked at him and wondered what the hell he meant.

"You're getting married?" Teresa squealed. I was sure they could hear her at the back of the room. I wanted to dig a hole and crawl in, but Danny fixed it—he was ready for her.

"Not right now, but it's in the plans," he said, kissing me like he'd never done in a public place.

"Oh my God," Teresa cried. "It's always the quiet ones that break down the big studs. Congratulations, honey." She hugged me, telling Danny, "You've got you a damned fine girl."

"Don't I know it!" He kissed me again. I don't remember Teresa leaving, the band playing, or anything but continuous kisses interrupted by quick sips of the most amazing drink I ever tasted. I wondered if even heaven could be this good.

We talked about my new job, how great it would be to have a steady income and give up weeknights in bars. We decided it would be crazy for me to give up weekends, the money was too easy, and maybe I could put the weekend money in savings, for later.

"For things that may show up on down the road," he said, raising his eyebrow again. Oh God, I wanted to start those things, right then, right there at that very table, though my Mama did raise me better. But if he'd of asked, I'm afraid I'd've got butt naked in the middle of that restaurant, just for him, and loved every damned minute of it. Ain't it just crazy, the things you do for love, in the heat of the moment?

On the way home, we talked about his band; they were signing with an agent, about to start a tour beginning in Tampa and working their way back up the east coast, big clubs with big-name groups, and with a little luck, there could be a recording contract within the year. It killed me to think about being separated that long, but Danny said he'd come back whenever he could, and with my new job I'd be able to take a few days off and go see him sometimes.

"Like little vacations," he said. "Sunbathe by day, see the band at night, sleep in hotels with room service. All the best for the love of my life."

It was crazy. Danny only mumbled "I love you" when he was drunk and damned near asleep, and now I was the love of his life. But God, it was wonderful.

Danny was asleep when his head hit the pillow. Sure, I was disappointed, but still so high on life that I didn't care. I got naked anyway, wrapped myself around his warmth, his hairy chest, the smell/feel/taste of him and drifted away. Heaven.

The next morning we made love, dressed, and headed for the bank. My first bank loan covered a used Les Paul, a Mesa Boogie amp, and a two-year-old customized van for Danny and the band. An investment for our future. I felt like a million bucks.

I never made it to Florida—getting off work was too risky, and the Pinto couldn't be trusted that far. I did catch the band at Bananas in Macon. Rumor had it that Gregg Allman was coming by and might sit in. I played avid fan in the crowd again, Danny stopping by my table and speaking only once.

I didn't mind. I had work the next morning anyway, and I'd started cleaning a few houses on the side, for the extra cash.

You do what you have to do, dreaming all the while of the better days ahead.

I just wished to hell the better days would get there soon.

Danny was back in less than two years and mad as hell about being back, but I knew he was more hurt than mad. The mood swings and violent temper were just his manly way of covering up the bawling little boy who'd lost his dream. My heart broke watching him, but he was way too much the "macho man" to admit his pain to me or anyone else, so I helped him out the best I could and waited for better days. Funny, the whole time he was on the road, the "better days"

I'd dreamed of were simply the days when he'd be home, but I guess my dreams are a lot simpler than the way things work out in real life.

For the first year, they'd played a circuit: Crown Liquor Lounges and Master Hosts Inns, with a few independent clubs, all within a hundred mile stretch between Tampa and Clearwater. Not exactly the Ritz, since the best he could brag to me was that most of the paying customers were old retired people who came south to die, but they kept the clubs full and making money, and clubs full of rich old men attract girls who want free drinks. Unfortunately for Danny the girls brought the cocaine. Coke seemed to be everyone's drug of choice then, and Danny's new vice fell easily into place.

Before the road band, pot was the only drug Danny'd seen on a regular basis. Alcohol was a staple and Georgia marijuana was everywhere, but those were the only crutches he used back then. The popular Quualudes had only made him sleepy, and he'd shied away from needles and the people who used them, but when Devil's Whiskey signed with an agent to work the Florida coast, he soon found his drug, and it claimed his heart and soul.

Danny claimed that once cocaine entered his life, he bought what he could afford, but used it stingily and seldom shared. Knowing I'd love him anyway and try my best to understand, he explained to me how he learned to spot the girls most likely to be carrying, and those were the ones he'd let accompany him to his room at night. He'd talk to people all over the club—customers, bouncers, managers, waitresses, bartenders, male and female. From the stage he'd talk to the dance floor, joking with the guys, dedicating songs, making eye contact with girls who enjoyed it. If necessary, he'd hit another club after work, but Danny could usually score before midnight on a weeknight, and always on weekends.

He didn't share his coke, but he always had liquor—the good stuff—Crown Royal, Smirnoff, Tanqueray, Jose Quervo. Seldom drank it himself, but poured freely for the ladies with the drugs. He followed a game plan. At the girl's house, he'd:

(1) Do their coke, plying them with as much liquor as possible.

(2) Go back to hotel, work on music 'til the sun came up, or longer.

Of course, that's the version he told me, but hell, I wasn't born yesterday. I'd say much more than likely there was always a middle step between those two, which'd be simply "do *them*," meaning the girls with the coke. Danny was a ladies' man before he knew me, and I have enough common sense to know when the cat's away, the mouse will play. If the night's activity happened in his room, never leaving the hotel, it ain't rocket science figuring out how that went.

The original Devil's Whiskey didn't last more than three months on the road. Glynn, the drummer Danny'd known since junior high school, had always been their weakest link, but it never mattered in the southern R&R venues they'd played in south Georgia. He was cool and he was loud—what else mattered? Yet Glynn's bass foot became noticeably slower when playing six nights a week, particularly with the more complicated dinner set tunes they'd added. After several offensive remarks from their agent and a group of waitresses nicknaming him "Leisure Boy" because his leather jacket was cut from a leisure suit pattern, Glynn took a bus home to Albany on a Saturday night. The club's bartender, who'd heard their repertoire continuously for three weeks, quit his job and started as drummer at their new gig on Monday.

Jimmy left the band before the first year was over. He missed his family and was tired of living out of a suitcase. Their agent quickly found a replacement: A thirty-nine-year-old New Jersey native who had played the Florida coast for fourteen years, this being his sixth band in that time span. His wife and two children lived in Tarpon Springs with her family, and he went home several times a week and could only practice on Tuesdays and Thursdays between eleven and three.

This was the real beginning of the end, Danny complained. The band rarely rehearsed for rehearsal sake, they only got together to learn new tunes now and then, to keep the club owners from complaining. Danny practiced at least two hours daily and usually more.

His practice habits were the most popular nightly joke between songs. By the end of their second year, their new drummer had married a widow and "retired," and the bass player had found a house job nearer his family. Danny and Tommy, his keyboard player and best friend since high school, took two weeks off and restructured.

Together they bought a state of the art rhythm box, a cocktail drum set, and a keyboard bass. They worked up a repertoire of sixty songs, hoping to have enough variety to play small dance venues as well as better paying, elitist supper clubs. They celebrated their first booking by purchasing an 8-ball of fine grade cocaine.

On Saturday night, the police raided Sandy's by the Sea, finding two illegal immigrants in the kitchen, an underage waitress, two rolled joints in a purse behind the bar, and two ounces of cocaine wedged behind Tommy Fowler's Leslie speaker. Tommy was taken into custody.

Danny loved me, and he knew it was time to come home. He made no claim to the drug charges, packed up the equipment and left for my house on stilts in Dumas County. My man was home at last.

After a few months in exile, bemoaning the loss of his dream, Danny found a weeknight gig, playing with a band of eighteen-year-olds in an East Albany dive. When his van was in the shop for a new alternator, I dropped him off one night, did some shopping and came back for his last two sets.

Danny played circles around the others, but with his leadership they weren't that bad. The thing I couldn't get past was the way he acted; I'd never seen him look so unhappy while playing. Usually, Danny was the type who might be half dead from pain and fever, yet not notice if the music was cooking, especially on his solos. That night was different: he never cracked a smile, and the looks he gave the other musicians made me feel sorry for them. He didn't talk between songs, and at times he shook his head, directing the others as though beating the notes into them with his guitar. I saw him chug four beers while on stage, during a set.

When the band took a break, there was no announcement, they simply stopped. He came to my table, grabbed a chair, and began to yell at me.

"What are doing back so soon?" he asked. "I thought you were going shopping or something. Jesus, you know we've got another set, don't you?"

"Of course I do, Danny," I said. "I just haven't heard you in a while. Ya'll sound pretty good, ya know. The way you talk, I was expecting a lot worse."

"We sound like shit," he said through his teeth. "If you think any different, you're obviously fucking tone deaf. This is embarrassing. I can't believe you're gonna be here for a whole set more."

"That's silly. I've heard you for years, and I love to hear you no matter who you're with. And this band—they're not Devil's Whiskey, but if they're just out of high school, it's probably a great experience for them, playing with you."

"They don't know jack shit," Danny spat, "and they're the most arrogant little mother fuckers ever. They don't deserve to play anywhere, even here." He slammed his fist on the table, spilling what was left in his beer mug and the glass of club soda I was drinking. I jumped up and ran to the bar for a handful of napkins.

I ran back and began wiping up the spill.

"Damn, Mojo," he cried. "You go all the way to the bar and don't bring me back a beer?"

"I'm sorry," I said, standing up to go back to the bar. He pushed me roughly back down into my chair.

"Never fucking mind," he said. "I'll get it myself after I go piss." He was halfway to the restroom as he finished the sentence.

Their last set consisted of five songs all stretched into ten minutes or more. I was pretty surprised to hear such over-played tunes— "Can't You See" and "That Smell" were bad enough, but "Free Bird"?

Danny had always refused to play that one; no wonder he was in such a horrible mood.

The ride home was awful. No matter how I changed the subject to try to take him to a happier place, Danny remained in his deep blue funk. I drove while he punched at the radio dial, finding nothing there to please him. Two a.m., and the rough Georgia highway back to Nolan was flat, straight, and uneventful, a light still on in two or three farmhouses at best on the thirty mile drive. Japanese beetles and lightening bugs bounced off the windshield while the scenery stayed the same. I rolled down his window and breathed in the night air, smelling freshly burned-off fields mixed with the heavy scent of pine tar.

"Goddam redneck AM shit," Danny mumbled, finding only static-y versions of pop-country, whiny country, three chord tunes considered rock in the fifties, and the Good Time Gospel Hour. "I'll be in the fucking graveyard before a decent FM station comes round here." He settled for the only FM station audible in Dumas County, still country but at least a decent signal. *All my exes live in Texas,* some guy sang.

"How shitty can you get?" Danny said, then turned up the volume and actually listened to the end. "Damn," he said. "Decent sounding country fuckers! Not my style, but clean. With fiddle, and pedal steel, and two, no, *three* guitars, all trading licks with no one stepping on toes. Nice and clean."

He listened to a bit of the next song, looking out at the little scenery offered. The mood didn't last long. "Goddamned rednecks," he said through clenched teeth. He was looking at the most lit up structure on the highway so far: a single-wide trailer on concrete blocks, sporting two late-model sports cars and a variety of toddler toys in the yard.

"What a fucking fiasco in priorities," he said. He shook his head. "Looks okay to you, don't it, sweet thang?" he said. I didn't know what he meant, so I just watched the road and said nothing.

"My quiet, caring, hard-working, dumb-as-dirt little Mojo," he said. "You got a soft spot for any rednecks down on their luck that can still aim for that hillbilly American dream, don't ya, gal? You got some whiny excuse for all of 'em, bless your heart."

He smiled at me like I was retarded or something. I bit my lip, determined not to cry. I knew he was drunk, probably high as well, and in an awful mood because of the band, but still, it hurt. It felt like I was a dirty, stray dog he enjoyed kicking for the hell of it. I told myself I wouldn't cry. I knew once I let go of the first tear I wouldn't be able to stop, and then we'd fight for the rest of the night.

I won't cry, I thought. *Hell, no, I will not cry.*

He fiddled some more with the radio. Oldies station—Dr. Hook was singing about being on the cover of *Rolling Stone.*

"God, when did this song come out?" Danny asked. "Oh yeah, we played it in my first or second band, back in high school."

"Really?" I asked, hoping I could get him into a happier conversation.

"Yeah. Back when we played school dances, then Moose and Elks Club jobs for a hundred bucks a night. Happy as hell to be playing at all, for real money, but dreaming of better clubs, with bigger pay-checks and a younger clientele. We had big dreams."

"Yeah, but you actually lived those dreams, later on," I said. *Please God, let this be the right thing to say. Let him think about something happy.*

"Yeah. We couldn't wait for week-long jobs with free bar tabs, free women, and a new place to go every week. Publicity photos in news-papers, ads that announced your arrival, your name in lights on the marquis."

"Cool," I said, nervous but hoping for the best.

"And then the big dreams," he said. "The ones you didn't dare voice out loud, but you couldn't stop thinking, all the time. Dreams of being a *real* band—on the radio."

"Of course," I agreed.

Danny began to hum along with the song, sounding happy. He

slipped his arm around my shoulder, then moved it to caress my hair, my breast. I watched the road, but suddenly wanted to hurry the hell home. He always had that effect on me.

"I miss the old band," he said. "I miss playing for the thrill of playing."

His fingers found a nipple, teasing me while he talked and I drove.

"A good night with a good crowd that's really into what you do. Maybe a joint on break; mellows my senses, really helps me work on my tone." He slipped his hand under my blouse, then under my bra, feeling me get pointy and hard.

"Mellows me," he said. "I can focus on a single note, bend it, shape it, listen to all the overtones hanging in midair…" His hand left that breast and moved to the other, making the other nipple burn and ache the same way. He gently pinched it, then moved back to the first.

"You can almost see the tiny particles of sound as they drift … Drifting … and falling … blending." His words slowed. "Blending and melt—" He grew silent.

His hand went limp and fell to the side, still inside my top.

I looked over at the man I loved.

He was sound asleep.

Maybe he'd feel better tomorrow…

As time went on, he told me more about life on the road. His cocaine days—by the time he stopped, he was in pretty deep. Danny said after that first line, he was sure this was the only drug he'd ever want again. There was an excited, deep-breath feeling, like the anticipation of Christmas morning, or waiting for a big surprise, or getting ready to perform something you knew you'd do really, really well. There was none of the slurring or stumbling or awkwardness that could slip up with alcohol, and none of the silly giggles, the drifting off or crazed munchies that could come from pot. He felt clear-headed, and alive, and happy to be alive. He could've talked to Beethoven, or Hitler, or a bum off the street, or Einstein, and enjoyed every minute of it. He could have washed windows, peeled potatoes, or watched paint dry and learned from it. Reading the phonebook would be inspirational. With a supply of this drug, Danny was convinced he could go back to Algebra II and not only pass, but find it pleasurable. The possibilities were endless.

"In road bands," he told me, "there's always an endless supply of so-called friends, people to pass the time with tonight and not remember next week." I could see where Danny would get tired of such, he wasn't that much of a social animal, and when he didn't have his self-required number of hours to practice, he could turn into a real jerk.

"The rest of the band got off on it," he said, "but it was the one thing I hated about road life. I didn't want to hang out, I wanted to work on my music. But you can't do that with a bunch of guys, or with couples, or groups or whatever. You're stuck with them. You had to hang out at their houses, or sit up all night drinking with them, or watch their stupid movies or listen to stories about their kids or their dogs or worse than that, have to tell them stories about *you*, knowing you'd never see those damned people again, so why the fuck should they care?" Danny would tense up just thinking about it, so I could imagine how crazy it would make him on the road.

"Yeah," he said, "and nobody understood. The guys in the band would get mad about it, say I was a prick and a bastard and I only cared about myself, that I didn't care about the band. How the hell could they say that? Because, to me, *they* were the ones that didn't care about the band."

He'd known them, well, most of them, damn near his whole life, but once they had the road band, they were different. It was like they had a real band, with an agent who booked them like they had a steady job, so now they didn't have to get any better. Like it was over—all they had to do was learn a few new songs now and then, and they were set for life.

"The band was different," he said, "it was like we had nothing in common anymore. They were just happier than pigs in shit—they could play those same damned thirty-five songs every night, go have a few beers with whatever local yokel asshole was kissing up to them that night, then eat at the Waffle House, go to bed, get up and do it again the next day. And it sucked."

It was the times when he talked like this, when he really talked about how he felt, that I knew we belonged together. Even if he drank 'til we fought and he passed out, I knew things would work out for us. He trusted me, he confided in me. Together we could make it work, I *knew* we could.

"Before the road, back when we only dreamed about being a band full-time, we worked at getting better," he told me. "We practiced—alone—not just learning new songs. Worked on speed and technique. Listened to music—all kinds of music, not just songs we wanted or thought we needed to play. We talked to each other about all kinds of stuff we'd never play, but to me, the talking seemed to make us understand one another better, and make us better musicians, too." He smiled that sweet, little boy smile that melted my heart.

Danny'd changed since going on the road, but it was nothing I didn't think we couldn't fix. He was pretty much drying out from drugs the hard way, I suspected, since cocaine was expensive and not easily found in south Georgia. I'd of loved to see him drink less, but I guessed it was better to wean him off one vice at a time. I made sure he had plenty to eat, and he had plenty of time to practice his music now, which always made him happier. There were days he seemed so restless I thought he'd go crazy, but at least it wasn't every day. After a while, he started making contacts with old buddies, and he pulled together a second band, one I figured he'd enjoy more, so he could quit the eighteen-year-olds as soon as the new band acquired some bookings. It was touch and go for us personally, but I tried to take it in stride—it was up to me to get Danny back to his old self.

He'd come home to me. I'd make it all better. I knew I could.

Chapter 20
1989

Phil

PHIL RETURNED TO THE FARM WITH A WEAKENED BODY but a happier soul. Knowing his days were limited, he looked at the world with kinder, gentler eyes, appreciating the simple life and leaving the pain and anger behind.

Within a few years, he and the ancient field hand Will restored the former Oakland Plantation to a smaller but profit-bearing farm. Renting out the cotton and peanut allotments, they maintained fifty beef cattle, pasture for grazing, and summer corn to be stored for winter's feed. Phillip lived in the hunting lodge, and he moved Will into the largest tenant house, where he kept two old barn cats and a few chickens. When Will died in his sleep on the first day of spring, the animals became Phil's.

Phil was at Treadway's Market buying cat food when he first saw the cardboard sign taped to the front door. "Housecleaning— Inquire Inside." He had thought about getting a housekeeper, the once-a-week kind, he guessed, if such a person existed in rural Dumas County.

Phil grabbed a Coke from the cooler near the counter and set the cat food down. "Hot enough for you?" he asked the girl at the cash register. Mojo, people called her, though he didn't know why.

"Sure," she told him. He watched her slender fingers move over the numbers. He wondered if she were the housekeeper, or if some-one else had just come in and posted the sign. "Three fifty-five," she said. He handed over a ten.

"S'posed to rain overnight," he said. "Cool things down." The girl took his money and nodded as if she was afraid to speak. She was Calvin's niece, Calvin Mullinax, the friend who used to work for his Dad, back in Oakland's heyday. Pretty little thing, though she didn't look to weigh a hundred pounds. She gave him his change without looking at him. Petite, soft-spoken, with those sad, beautiful eyes like her mother before her. A perfect target for a wife-beater: The kind that wouldn't fight back.

"Thank you kindly," Philip said, raising the cold Coke and grabbing the cat food bag.

"Come back now," she said. But she still didn't look at him. She pressed her hair over one side of her face like Phil had seen her do many times. Long sleeves in the summer, hair arranged to cover the latest "accident." As usual.

"Is that you hiring out for housecleaning?" He pointed to the sign with his Coke. She looked over at it with those dreamy, half-haunted eyes.

"Yes sir," she said. He looked at the sign one last time, and then he walked out, trying to memorize the numbers in his head. He didn't know what made him not ask her right there and then.

Sitting in his truck, drinking the Coke, he could see her through the glass, sitting on a stool, flipping through a magazine. She was married to Danny, local big shot musician, walking around like he was God's gift. Phil had heard Danny's band at the Plantation Club, the few times he'd ventured out on weekends. Danny had left town for a year or two, supposed to be playing big concerts, signing a recording contract, gonna be the next Elvis Presley the way people carried on. Then all of a sudden he was back home and those two were married.

She works so hard, Phil thought. *Keeping Danny in fine amps and guitars and a van to haul his gear in, while she's still driving that old Pinto that's more Bondo than car.* She was managing Treadway's and working the Plantation Club on weekends, still it was no secret as to what had been going on when she wore her hair down, covering up one side of her face or the other. Danny was playing one-nighters for fifty dollars and his bar tab. And now the girl was cleaning houses, too, along with her other jobs.

A week or two later, Phil ran into her at the dollar store, looking gloriously happy and grinning from ear-to-ear.

She was alone, walking through the section with all the things for little babies and small kids. She picked up a fuzzy blanket and held it to her face. Then she took a little dress, tiny and covered in ruffles, and fluffed it out in a full circle. The miniature Nike shoes were more than she could stand: She put two fingers of each hand in a shoe, then made them run over the rack of tiny clothes.

Phil turned away, pretending to examine cans of motor oil, but angling himself to keep watching. She moved on to the most mundane of baby things—bottles, cups, bibs, disposable diapers, big jars of Vaseline—seeming equally excited with each new item.

Little Mojo must be having a baby, Phillip thought. *Sure hope the child fairs better than its mother does.*

About that time she saw him, waved, and walked forward.

"Hi, Mr. Foster, how are you today?" She smiled.

Phillip was surprised she knew his name. She'd never called him by it before.

"I'm fine," he said. "And don't you look happy?"

"Oh, just happy to be here," she said. "Beautiful day, ain't it?"

"Indeed," Phil said as she walked past him. "Uh—Mojo?"

She turned back. "Yes, Mr. Foster?"

"Do you know anybody that does housecleaning? Like once a week or so?" Phil grimaced, knowing she'd already answered the question.

"Yes, Mr. Foster, I do housecleaning. Is that why you asked?"

"Well," Phil stammered, "...yes."

"Do you need someone to clean your house?"

"Yes, I do."

"You live at that lodge place, over at Oakland?"

"Yes."

"You be there Saturday morning? I could come by, see what you want done, and figure out a good time for me to come each week."

"You'd do that for me?" Phil asked, smiling.

"Yes sir, sounds good. I'm gonna be needin' some more work, got some bills comin' in."

She smiled a million dollar smile never associated with bills.

"Okay then, I guess I'll see you on Saturday," Phil said.

"Sure thing, see you then." She turned and walked out—gliding on air.

Chapter 21
1989

Mojo

I T WAS THE FIRST WEEK OF DECEMBER, AND THINGS WERE going so good it didn't seem real.

Danny was doing a lot of Christmas parties, solo stuff, where he made good money and didn't have to deal with anyone else, and that always made him happy. He'd been practicing a lot, learning actual *Christmas* songs, fancy, jazzy arrangements like you'd hear in the background at Christmas parties on TV. I worked every weekend for the whole month at the Plantation Club, maybe a little more, if I didn't start showing.

I had three regular housecleaning jobs, two older ladies and Mr. Foster, who didn't really need that much work done and paid me way too much. I worried about Mr. Foster. He was getting thinner all the time, and took a lot of medicines I didn't think he wanted me to know about. I guess that's the reason I kept going back, though there was the guilt about taking his money for not doing much work. He seemed to want the company, and I really believed he needed to be checked on now and then. Living so far out, all alone, who would be there if something bad happened? We formed a strange and awkward friendship, kind of becoming stand-in relatives.

I knew Danny didn't want kids; he was too much of a child himself to be any kind of a father. Thirty years old, still playing gigs at pool halls, strip clubs, and dives. Other than the road band that sent him home broke, strung out, and so depressed I was afraid he'd hurt himself, he hadn't had a real job since he was sixteen, pumping gas.

I worked a lot, but I was pretty good with my money. And as long as Danny had enough to eat, had clean clothes to wear, had plenty of time for his music and could pretty much do whatever else he wanted, he didn't really notice if I was there or not or how many hours I worked. I'd never told him how much folks paid me for the cleaning jobs.

I knew I could make this work, I knew I could. I'd just been to Albany for my first ever ob-gyn appointment, and I was so excited I could hardly stand it. But that wasn't all.

I'd figured it all out. After my appointment, I went to a bank, one in Albany, and started me another bank account. I put some baby furniture and things on layaway, too. And whether Danny was ready or not, I would be.

I lifted up the mattress one more time, just to sneak another peek at my special things. A wooly yellow blanket, good for a girl or a boy. A picture of the crib, and chest, and high chair I'd bring home soon.

I thought of the crib set up in the east window, where I could open it and let the baby listen to the crickets, and katydids, and the ol' Flint River running by our little house on stilts. On the chest I'd set the little cube filled with colorful shapes, the one I knew was part of my history, though I never had the chance to find out how. And over it, I'd hang the picture of Mama and Uncle Cal, young and smiling, so that they'd be there with us, too.

I lifted up my little bank book—five hundred dollars in savings and more to come. I looked at it all one last time, then tucked the bedspread and grabbed my purse. It was time to be at the club; a good tipping night could be a wind-up swing or a car seat.

It was a good night, a Friday, and we were packed 'til after four in the morning. I felt higher than a kite, just thinking about the life I was about to live. I was tired-but-wired as I drove home. I pulled in the driveway, surprised to see Danny's van at the back. He usually came in later than me.

I hurried up the stairs to see if he was awake. Opening the door, I caught the sickly sweet smell of reefer. The house was wrecked; clothes, books, dishes, everything thrown about like some police search in a crime drama.

"Danny?" I called. "Danny, honey, are you up? What happened in here, babe? You guys musta been partying hearty—" I tried to laugh. *Please, God*, I thought, *don't let him be mad. Drunk or stoned or passed out—Even—even if he's with a woman, I can handle it, God. Just don't let him be—*

"MotherfuckingwhoreBITCH!" he screamed as he staggered out from the bedroom. He wore my favorite shirt—the soft, gray denim with the black velvet collar—the one I bought for his birthday. It was untucked and open, held by a single button, his chest hair glistening and his lucky Saint Christopher showing through. He was sweating, his usually-perfect black hair loose, but moist at the temples and hanging in matted clumps. "And just wherethehellavyoubeen, whore?" His words were barely intelligible.

"I've been at work, Danny, at the Plantation, you know that, baby," I tried to explain.

"And how do I know that, bitch? How the hell do I know what you've been doing, you lying—" He lunged forward and grabbed me by the neck.

I knew the position well: If I relaxed against the chokehold, I could breathe. If I didn't fight, he'd simply shove me away in a few minutes. And as wasted as he was, the shove forward might put him on the floor, and out for the night. I could handle it, I just had to think it out and not do anything stupid.

"Just howfuckindumbd'you think I am, bitch? You think you's gonna pulloneoveron me, slut? Huh? Huh?" His bourbon saliva sprayed across my face.

"I don't know what you mean, Danny. Honest, I haven't done

anything wrong. Really. And I'm just glad you're home and we can be together—" I stammered, trying to sound sweet, and normal. Sometimes that worked, too. I could get through this, I knew I could. I concentrated, watching how the breeze through the open window moved the sheer curtains, just barely, but made no difference in the stagnant air filling the room.

I smelled Danny—liquor, and sweat, and hint of spray starch, and something else—the smell of *him*. The way he tasted, the squeaky feel of his skin, the way the sheets smelled after we made love: the smell I chose to never wash away 'til he came home, back when he was on the road. Crazy, how he was one squeeze away from choking me to death, and I could think about that. But I could, I had to hold back from actually trying to kiss him or something, but—I couldn't. Not this time, I had more to consider than just me.

"Like fucking hellyousay," he said, "howthefuck you 'splain this?"

At that point, I saw it: He let go with one hand and drew from the table behind him the blanket, the pictures, the bankbook—the very objects I'd tucked beneath the mattress just hours ago.

"Huh, bitch, yougonefuckingsplain this?" He coughed up a mouthful of liquor-laced mucus, then spat directly into the yellow blanket, leaving a vile, rusty canker on its quilted down surface. "And whatthehellis *this*?" he asked, producing a receipt from the doctor, reminding me of my next appointment.

"But Danny, baby, I was gonna tell you, I was, I swear, I was waiting for—"

"Shut up!" He threw the receipt on the floor and slapped my face with his free hand. "You wasted $150 on this shit, and you was planning on going back?" He slapped me again.

"I was waitin' for Christmas, Danny," I cried, tasting blood. "I was gonna tell you for Christmas."

I tried to see Christmas, in later years, with a child and homemade ornaments, a letter to Santa Claus, and a new, improved Danny, singing Rudolph and Jingle Bell Rock, in a perfect world I knew would

never happen. That's when it registered that no music was playing—
not from his studio, or the radio, not on TV, not anywhere in the
world that I could tell. And realizing that silence was like sharp pains
in my ears: I was almost relieved when Danny yelled at me again.

"The hell you were. I won't have it! I told you I don't want no
damned kids, you knew better. Hell, you're never here—How the
hell I know it's mine, you fucking whore?"

I saw his knee coming for my stomach, and I jerked away just in
time. The silence was still there, but I filled it with nursery rhymes,
in the back of my head.

Ride a cockhorse to Banbury Cross...

"No, Danny, no—you know it's yours. I've never—"

"I don't either know it. Fucking kid's a bastard just like you are. I
shoulda known trash breeds trash."

Now he was after my stomach with his fist. I crouched down to
the floor, covering my womb with my head and hands.

To see a fine lady upon a white horse...

"No, Danny, please. Please don't hit me there! Please," I screamed.

"Got it all planned out, doncha? Saving up money, lots of it, hide
it in a bank I don't know about. Plannin' on buyin' all this exthspesiff
shit—"

Focusing on the nap of the brown shag rug, I felt a spray of spittle
hit my hair, but I didn't—I couldn't—look up.

"Thisfuckinshit for that bastard kid," he said, "and you think I'm
gonna sitaround and take it? Huh?"

He kicked at my stomach this time, but I offered my head in its
place. It hurt like hell, but it knocked him off balance. Now we were
both semi-sitting on the floor.

He pushed me down, half straddled me and raised his knee.

"Please don't, Danny," I begged. "Hit my face, please, Danny, hit
my face."

He obliged. He slapped me, again and again, calling curses with
each slap.

Rings on her fingers and bells on her toes...

Later it turned to punches with his fist, showing surprising energy for a drunk. At some point I felt my jaw go, then my nose, when a great burst of fresh blood showered him.

He swore and tried to wipe the blood from his eyes. He fell backward and passed out.

She shall have music wherever she goes...

I stayed put for what seemed like an hour, just to make sure he was out.

Chapter 22

Phil

IT WAS SUNDAY MORNING, EARLY, BARELY DAYBREAK when Phil heard a car pulling up in the driveway. Not fully awake, for just a minute he thought it was Will, then remembered that his old friend was gone. More curious than frightened, he jumped out of bed and grabbed a flashlight, the closest thing to a weapon he saw handy. An arsenal of weapons downstairs, he kept not so much as a slingshot around to defend himself.

His father would have labeled him a fool.

Looking out the front window, he recognized Mojo's sad, abused Pinto, lights still on but the motor turned off. He heard the car door open yet never close. No one exited the car. Accompanied by Will's old tomcat, Phil stepped out into the yard to see if she needed help.

Phil had never seen anyone as badly beaten up, not ever. Her nose was obviously broken, and he'd wager there were more broken bones as well. Blood caked from her nostrils to her chin; he wondered about her teeth. Other cuts and scratches covered her face and arms, some still seeping blood. One eye was ringed in black and swollen shut, the other completely red, her neck covered in swelling bruises. There was no way she could've driven there, yet she had.

She was trying to get out of the car, raising herself up, only to continuously slump back down into the driver's seat, babbling incoherently.

"But I need to work, I gotta work," she said, tears leaking from her closed eye, the other staring into the early dawn. She seemed oblivious to Phil's presence when she suddenly gasped and fell over against the steering wheel.

Despite the illness that now left him frail and weak, adrenaline kicked in, and Phil easily lifted her tiny body from her car to his truck. She never opened her eyes or made a sound. By the time he reached the emergency room, he believed she was dead.

Chapter 23

Sheriff Wally Purvis

IT WAS LIKE NOTHING WE'D EVER SEEN IN DUMAS COUNTY, and I hope to God I never have to see such again.

That Foster boy never was worth a damn, a disgrace to his family, a lot of folks thought. Don't believe he ever had a job in his damned life, just kept busy spending his daddy's money, 'til the last few years when he piddled around on what was left of his daddy's farm.

It was a tragedy 'bout ol' Mr. Foster, he was a good man. His family opened the panty factory that brought jobs for all the women folk. Took care of his farm workers, too—Mojo's uncle, that Calvin Mullinax, lost his arm working on the Foster farm—probably his own fault, not paying attention like young boys'll do, but ol' man Foster did right by him—sent Calvin to some fancy rehab hospital the President went to, mind you—and gave him money besides that. But like happens to a lotta folks, that Calvin got him a little money, then he got to feelin' sorry for hisself, expectin' something for nothing, and he never worked again. Slap drank himself to death. Died in that crazy house where Mojo lives now. Yeah he did . . .

But old Mr. Foster, he was a good man. We was all right happy when that boy o' his left here, just a month or so after his daddy passed. We was thinkin' he was gone for good, figured we'd never see him again.

Then like a bad penny, he just showed up, few years ago. Some folks said it was when his money ran out. Some of 'em said he came home to die. Some said he had cancer, but it turned out to be a lot worse than anybody imagined, hell, cancer woulda been better. He's the only person I've a-known of to have that AIDS mess, God help us. He did keep to himself though, didn't bother nobody, well—nobody that didn't need to be bothered, I reckon.

Now little Mojo was a good girl, never had much, but she was a hard worker. Heard some talk, long time ago, bout maybe that hoodlum Phil Foster boy bein' Mojo's daddy, but Delores never would admit to it. Strange how they all ended up, though.

That Danny Hatcher was a sorry one for sure, and Mojo's a lot better off without him. Still, I hope I never see another scene like that one, not never.

You see, Mojo just showed up at the hospital, somebody left her there. We didn't know about her for two or three days, when she first woke up, she didn't know where she was or how she'd a-got there. And by the time we knew where she was, well, it just wasn't the right time to put her through all that.

A call came in from that Phil Foster, oh, about two in the afternoon. He didn't say who he was, but we pieced it all together afterwards. Said to send a police car and a ambulance to the house on stilts. He said to go there first, then he said there was some trouble at the lodge at Oakland, but it could wait. He hung up.

I didn't know what to think, but I called the ambulance and took off to Mojo's. Sent a deputy out to Oakland, but he didn't see nothing so he joined back up with me.

That house was tore apart, trashed, beer cans and liquor bottles all over the place, a little white powder with a cut-off straw and a razor blade there on the kitchen table.

And there on the floor was ol' Danny, what was left of him. Half of his face was splattered to the wall.

'Course the coroner said Danny never felt a thing, he was passed out drunk and stoned and God knows what all when it happened. But then he said whoever killed Danny kicked him, too, forty or fifty times, *after* he was dead.

I'd done called the coroner and was a'waitin' on him and my deputy to get there, when I thought to stroll through the rest of the place, in case there was anymore evidence they'd need to take in with 'em.

The back bedroom didn't even have a bed, though we did find one stood up in the closet.

It was clean and neat, posters of rock bands and black and whites of old guitars framed and hanging on the walls, everything in its own place. The room had a couple of chairs, a rug, and enough wires and music equipment to fill the front end of a music store. Can't say most folks woulda saw a need for it, but did look nice.

The little bathroom was nice—one wrinkled teeshirt on the back of the commode really stood out against the neatness of matching curtains and towels and the like. It was all yeller and green—made you feel clean just to stand there.

But then I went in the real bedroom, and it was a sadder sight, if that's possible, than the one I saw coming in.

The room was wrecked—every drawer pulled almost out with contents hanging on the sides, closet wide open with hanging clothes thrown to the floor, Mojo's family pictures hanging crooked like something'd done shook the house.

With covers stripped from the bed and the mattress hanging off, a pale, bruised Phil Foster lay on the bare box springs. Facing the door with his hands by his head, I could imagine him just taking a breather while he waited for something or someone. His position made sense, but with his cold-eyed stare, there was no doubt: Foster was dead.

I went back to the lodge after they took away the bodies. That lodge is a right nice place. Got some huntin' trophies, mounted bucks, some fine fish, and the place is clean as a whistle. I called out, looked around, saw nothing. Last place I looked was like an office— I'd heard tell about Ol' Man Foster's gun room, but it was more like a museum in my book. Every gun shinin' like it was brand new, each one labeled. It's a pity.

Together we decided Foster'd gone down to the river and killed Danny, planning on coming home and surrendering peacefully when we came to get him. Guess the thing he didn't count on was that his frail heart and body just wouldn't hold out for that much excitement. Doctors say he died of natural causes, related to his prior condition.

Foster didn't have much, but he left the lodge and all the guns to some "historical society." To some folks, that makes him a hero. Hell, some folks'd say what he did to Danny made him a hero.

Not to me. I believe in doing things by the book.

Still, I gotta admit, at least Foster's way, we can be sure he won't be serenading any other trusting gals to his sorry way of life. Still, it's a pity...

Chapter 24/Epilogue
Pansy, AL
1995

Ms. Mary Jane Mullinax

SOMETIMES IT'S JUST TIME TO MOVE ON. UNCLE CAL talked about getting out, Mama talked about it, but I guess I'm the one that finally did it.

I sold the house on stilts to a nice Mexican family, looked like three or four families, but their money's just as good as anybody's, I say. Folks in Nolan are still talking about it, but they can just keep talking. That's one place I *won't* be visiting anymore.

I realize now that Uncle Cal was right: We should've left Nolan a long time ago. I still can't believe the things I see here every day that I bet won't happen in Dumas County for another hundred years. To me, Nolan seems trapped in time, owned by some unknown god calling all the shots, and anyone choosing to stay there is a pawn. If that kinda life is okay with you, I guess Nolan's an okay place to live. But finding out that there are places where I can be just as good as anybody—I never had a clue my life could be this "normal," and respectable, and—good!

Here in Pansy, there's single parents who still finish school, get real jobs outside of bars and factories. And their children get invited to birthday parties, Bible school, and Vacation Reading Club. We got us a Neighborhood Watch, and it's neighbors looking out for each other, not spying and gossiping about each other. People of all colors go to the same church, and public schools are good schools for *all* children.

Strange thing—the same Flint River that flowed by my little house on stilts followed us out of Georgia stopping just next to the state line. I felt a little sad thinking that the muddy water I'd considered almost a family member wouldn't be going with me, watching over me as we started a new life, but maybe that was a good thing. It was time for greener pastures, cleaner water, and a place where our little family could grow.

I guess what I'm trying to say is, in real towns, a person really *can* start over.

I still think about Nolan, our house on stilts, Mama and Uncle Cal. But my family is with me wherever I am, and I like to think we *all* have us a fresh start. Like Mama said, the past is all just water under the bridge. I think I finally know what she meant.

I still think about Mr. Foster, sometimes. Poor Mr. Foster. There was a time, back when I worked for him, that I kinda pretended like Mr. Foster was my real daddy. Ain't that crazy? I mean, once I spent a little time with him I realized it was just a kid's dream made from bits and pieces of small town talk, the kind where everyone guesses and nobody knows.

But in a way I wish he had've been, since what he did for me gave me the greatest gift I'll ever receive. My treasure, and the joy of my life.

I finally went back and finished school. I work in an office and have health insurance, dental insurance, and a pension plan. I own a home, pay bills, pay taxes, go to church, and live like respectable folks, the way Mama always wanted but never quite got to. And here in Alabama, not a soul knows or cares what happened in Nolan.

Gotta go now, my boy'll be getting off the bus any minute. Oh yeah, my baby lived, and he's in second grade, goes to Cub Scouts and made the Honor Roll at Pansy Elementary.

I named him after the two best men I ever knew: Calvin Phillip Mullinax. He looks like my Mama, with a little of me, a little of

Uncle Cal, and—well, he got the best parts of everybody.

He can sing like an angel, plays the piano, and wants to learn the violin! His piano teacher says he's a natural talent, and he practices everyday, without being told—he loves it.

I so wish my Mama could see him, her and my Uncle Cal, but I like to believe they can. And little Calvin's Daddy—God rest his soul—maybe he's found peace, wherever he is, and can enjoy seeing that the best part of him lives on, too.

The folks in my family had some hard times, there's no doubt about it, but they did the best they could with what the Lord gave them. That's all any of us can do, I reckon.

My Calvin, he loves to hear stories about the kinfolks he's never met. He likes the ones about the home place, his beautiful granny, and his daddy, the rock star. He even likes to hear about the floods, riding boats down main street and such. But when he's tired, or scared, or holding out for his favorite, there's only one story that'll do.

"Tell about Calvin," he'll say. "The *other* Calvin—with his cat, and his dogs, and his pirate hook—in his house on stilts..."

My boy. The sum of all the people I've loved. Every now and then, things *can* work out right.

Acknowledgements

A WRITER CAN PUBLISH ONLY ONE BOOK AS A *FIRST*, and a part of me believes I should thank everyone who has influenced me to the good, bad, or in-between in my quest to earn being called an "author." Since I don't think this idea is actually doable, I will start with the most obvious: The whole of Baker County, Georgia, where I lived my first twenty years.

From the ever-present farmer's voice that lives in my head (otherwise known as "Daddy") to Virginia Jones, the favorite high school teacher who suggested I "should write a book," the voices of Newton, not Nolan, nurtured me, taught me, and gave me the words to relive it all again. Thank you, Baker County, for the real slice of Americana I envision when I want to see the world as inviting, interesting, and inherently good. Special thanks to the farmers who explained huge concepts to my narrow realm of understanding—Clifford Allen, Vann Irvin, and the late L.T. Simmons.

I'm forever grateful to Suzanne Kingsbury, fiction author and book doctor extraordinaire, who shared both technical and personal support in this journey. Many thanks to the faculty and administration at Spalding University, where I enjoyed the single-most exciting experience of my second half-century. Mentors Roy Hoffman, Rachel Harper, and Silas House not only agreed that I *could* write a novel but cheered me on and held my hand while I did so, as did fellow writers and new best friends Michael Morris and Angela-Jackson Brown.

Thank you, Rhonda Cooper, for not only explaining first-hand the mechanism in a prosthetic arm, but for sharing your pains, embarrassments, and triumphs in facing physical handicaps in a small town. Several years ago, a kind and helpful group of gun-intelligent members of the Zoetrope Writers Community helped me craft an imaginary gun collection, a perfect list for this book. And without the Atlanta Writers Group, I might still be writing letters to would-be agents who send back the same, tired rejections.

It is with highest appreciation that I thank my agent, Amanda Wells of Sullivan-Maxx Literary Agency and ALL my new friends at WiDō Publishing, acquisitions editor Allie Maldanado, editor Summer Ross, and managing editor Karen Gowen. You have made a dream come true and opened the door for "the rest of my life," I hope.

On the strictly personal side, I most of all thank my family. Amber, my beautiful vigilante, you are an excellent proofreader, idea-bouncer, re-reader, and friend. You know me better than anyone. Meredith, my red-haired brainchild, you play a mother's best devil's advocate, and you're the biggest reason I strive to do my best. I want to one day make you feel just a fraction of the pride I feel for you. Joe—these Baker County stories are as much yours as mine, in fact, I can't really remember where my tales end and yours begin—they're too deeply entwined to separate. Thank you for your words, your wisdom, and for just being such a special part of my life.

To all my friends and loved ones—Thank you for giving me the life I live. This story is a small token gift back to you...

Author's Bio

ELAINE DRENNON LITTLE spent thirty-odd years as a piano teacher, lounge musician, and public school music educator before retiring to the life of a writer. Her previous print publications are all in journals and magazines for music education. Claiming her 2010 MFA from Spalding University as her "middle-age gift to herself," she currently lives in North Georgia with hundreds of books and her three-legged cat, Ahab. *A Southern Place* is her first published novel.

elainedrennonlittle.com

CPSIA information can be obtained at www.ICGtesting.com
Printed in the USA
LVOW132133070713

341740LV00009B/1310/P